PAIN AND INK AND PASSION

"I want to see your tattoo now," Bobby said, "All of it."

Ashleigh sipped from her drink, holding it with both hands, looking at him over the rim of the glass. "All right," she said. She put the glass on the coffee table and slowly unbuttoned the leather blouse, keeping her eyes on his, meeting his challenge with her own.

When her breasts spilled free, the tattoo of the black widow spider seemed to jump out at him. "It's beautiful," he said. "*You're* beautiful."

Ashleigh smiled and arched her back slightly.

"It almost looks alive."

"It is," Ashleigh said.

"Will it bite me?"

"Touch me and find out."

His hand was soft and gentle as he traced the pattern of the web and stroked the spider's slender, deadly body.

Ashleigh leaned back on the couch. . . .

TATTOO

tattoo

dale banks

PINNACLE BOOKS
KENSINGTON PUBLISHING CORP.

PINNACLE BOOKS are published by

Kensington Publishing Corp.
850 Third Avenue
New York, NY 10022

Pinnacle and the P logo Reg. U.S. Pat. & TM Off.

First Printing: August, 1995

Printed in the United States of America

For Pat LoBrutto:
a fine editor,
and a better friend

Prologue

Twice during her descent from the Hollywood hills, his face mocked her from billboards, and again his cruel smile that millions of women found so attractive burned into her back from the billboard across the street as she stood outside the tattoo parlor.

The studio was closed, blinds tightly drawn against the world. Around her, the gaudy neon lights of the street began their nightly penetration of the enshrouding dusk as the Chamber of Commerce people fled the street, only to be replaced by those who lived in the night, the scavengers and the bottom feeders now slowly emerging from a thousand dens and lairs, blinking in the harsh glare of the flickering lights. She knew that ageless prelude well.

Inside the studio, she knew that Burke waited, reading one of his endless parade of books, surrounded by his tattoos.

Ashleigh Thomas had stood there before, ten years ago, when her California's driver's license had said she was twenty-one, though she was only sixteen. That long-ago afternoon, the tattoo parlor had been open, although empty of customers. Burke had been there, reading. He had glanced up from his book and caught her eye. Frightened and alone, Ashleigh had fled. She had been both prey and predator then.

Now, however, she rapped lightly on the windowpane. Burke opened the door almost immediately. "Hello, Ash."

"It's good to see you, Burke."

They embraced briefly. Their lips touched chastely.

He locked the door and turned to find her looking at the designs and patterns on the walls—delicate butterflies spreading decorated wings, bleeding roses and flowering vines, angry serpents rearing from the sea, eagles with poised talons, daggers piercing hearts, fabled creatures from mythology, dragons, unicorns, helpless maidens impaled by omnipotent gods. She pointed to a cobra rising from its coils, hood spread ominously, tongue flicking. "This is new. For a biker?"

Burke shook his head. "A woman. A legal secretary."

"On her back?"

"It starts on her belly and goes up between her breasts. Making love to her now will be like making love to the snake. Her nipples were pierced. She wore rings in them."

Ashleigh shuddered and touched her own breasts. Her nipples were always so sensitive. "I can't imagine that," she said.

"Her name was Janice. Such a plain little woman." Burke shrugged. "You can never tell what secrets are hidden beneath the veneer."

"Were her tits as nice as mine?"

"No."

Ashleigh smiled and turned to the centerpiece of the shop, a nearly life-sized portrait of a bare-breasted warrior goddess. She stood tall and statuesque, golden hair framing her beautiful face and falling to firm, heavy breasts.

Ashleigh had been the model.

"You're still as beautiful," Burke said. "More."

It was Burke's masterpiece. It graced perhaps a dozen bodies in varying sizes. Burke would put the tattoo only on those he deemed worthy.

"Thank you," Ashleigh replied. "You look good."

"Older."

It was true. His hair was thinner; his beard had more gray.

"Would you like a drink?" Burke asked. "I have champagne for you."

"A glass of champagne would be nice. You're always so thoughtful, Burke."

She turned to his book, his place carefully marked with the leather bookmark she had given him. He was reading

Proust—again. He had introduced her to Proust and Balzac, Dostoyevsky and Tolstoy, Dickens and Conrad and James and Lawrence and Joyce. And so many others.

Ashleigh smiled as he handed her the champagne flute. "Thank you." She sipped at the wine. "Take your shirt off, Burke, I want to see it."

He removed his shirt and tossed it aside, turning his back to her.

"I could do so much better now," Ashleigh said, looking at her likeness that she had tattooed on his back. It was one of the first professional tattoos she had ever done, a self-portrait. She put her arms around him and pressed her breasts against his back. "You should let me do another one, Burke."

"Perhaps. How is your work coming?"

"Sometimes . . . sometimes I think I'm getting better, but then . . . Her voice trailed off. She didn't want to tell Burke yet, not until she could show him her masterpiece. Restlessly, she went to the blinds and peered through a crack. He was still there, smiling down at her—the bastard. He would have been her masterpiece. She turned back and said, "We should get started, Burke."

"Which one?"

Ashleigh smiled. "The left, of course. Over my heart."

He nodded. "You can go in the back and change. I'll get ready."

"No," Ashleigh said. "I want you to do it."

He nodded again, that same eternal sadness filling his eyes as he watched her pull the blouse from her skirt. They had been lovers once, briefly. Then Burke had wanted to marry her; perhaps he still did; but he wasn't like Chance or the ones who would follow now. Ashleigh loved him too much for marriage. She didn't want to destroy him. And so now Burke took solace from his books and his work. He was a tattoo artist. He could have been one of the very best.

Ashleigh moistened her lips, her tongue flicking like the cobra on the wall. Her fingers went to the buttons of her blouse. Slowly she unfastened them, lingering over each, until the blouse slipped from her shoulders and fell to the floor.

The familiar rite had begun.

Ashleigh stood naked to the waist, like the goddess of Burke's portrait, breathing heavily, feeling the warmth swell in her loins and deep within her belly. She placed long, delicate fingers beneath her left breast and lifted it, offering it to Burke. Ashleigh cried out, throwing her head back as he bent and kissed her nipple, but she continued to hold her breast for him until finally he drew away, only to kiss her lips.

"Ah, Burke," she said, when he'd released her finally.

"You can still change your mind," he said.

"No." Ashleigh knew they weren't referring to the same thing. She kicked off her heels and unfastened the belt of her skirt, letting it fall, stepping gracefully away from its folds. Exquisite slave bracelets decorated her ankles. Burke had tattooed them for her. Ashleigh turned and went to the table.

The leather was cold on her back.

"In my purse, Burke," she whispered. "I brought them for you."

"What else did you bring, Ash?"

"Anything you want, Burke."

He went to the purse she had left on the counter. When he returned, she stretched her arms above her head, sighing as he handcuffed her wrists to a strut of the table. Now captive on her sacrificial altar, Ashleigh closed her eyes and waited.

Ashleigh moaned with renewed pleasure and the warm and soapy water ran down her belly as Burke washed her left breast with gentle hands, the first step in preparing the flesh for its decoration.

It was not necessary to shave her breast. The sparse, tiny golden hairs would not impede the needle, but Ashleigh wanted him to do it, just as he had shaved the back of her neck before tattooing the sunburst there, just as he had once shaved her legs when they were lovers.

Ashleigh again moaned softly as he caressed her breast with the brush, spreading the warm foam. He took her nipple, squeezing and pulling it, holding her breast taut for the razor. His grasp was painful, but she did not protest. Ashleigh knew she deserved it, but she fought the panic and bit her lip as the sharp blade stroked the swell of her breast. She held her breath and trusted Burke.

Finished, he rinsed the remaining flecks of foam away with warm water. Ashleigh opened her eyes and smiled up at him. He sprayed her breast with the alcohol then. It stung pleasantly on her newly anointed flesh. Ashleigh sighed. The opening ceremony was complete. Now, she was ready.

Burke drew on the blue surgical gloves. He was ready to trace the pattern on her breast, beginning with the nipple, still throbbing with desire and the aching memory of his grasp. The familiar hum of the needle filled the studio, reminding Ashleigh of an electric razor. His electric razor. That bastard.

She held her breath, waiting. No. I'm not ready. She pulled against the handcuffs that held her captive, but she could not escape. Not now, not ever. Her fingers waved helplessly as the needle descended toward the chosen breast. The glove on Burke's hand was clammy on her flesh as he kneaded her breast, plumping and positioning it so, just so. He was her artist and she was his canvas.

Ashleigh bit her lip as the needle roared, filling her ears with the thunder of a thousand waterfalls.

Now.

Ashleigh cried out when the needle penetrated her nipple, like a knife slashing her flesh. The initial pain always surprised her. How much the pain of creation hurt. Poor nipple. It was so hard and big and expecting gentle kisses. Instead . . . Ashleigh bit her lip. Ah, Christ, it hurt.

Burke used paper towels to dab at the droplets of blood as he worked. Ashleigh wished he would kiss the blood away. It would soothe the pain. She closed her eyes and imagined she was giving birth and the pain was only a sacrifice for the new life growing on her breast.

"Will it be beautiful?" Ashleigh asked, gasping as the needle moved over her nipple, piercing it a hundred times during the space of her question.

"Yes, as beautiful as the woman who wears it."

The pain lessened as Burke moved the needle away from the aureole of her nipple and began working on the pale skin of her breast. She thought of the mocking face on the billboard and the man who had betrayed her. That agony was still greater than any that Burke could inflict with his needles. Ashleigh smiled, reveling now in the pinpricks that so relentlessly pierced her skin and the ink that flowed into her, replacing her blood with a new life worthy of her work, her art.

The needle was a cruel lover, tormenting her with its heartless, unyielding caresses, filling her body with the sweet pain. *Oh, Chance, I loved you so much. Why did you do it? Why did you leave me?*

Did she whisper his name?

If Burke heard, he gave no sign. He poured the bright red ink into a small paper cup, dipped the needle like a quill pen, and began to add color to the tattoo.

Ashleigh endured the pain and a thousand memories and then he was done, spreading the thick ointment over the tattoo, carefully placing the bandage on her breast, trying not to hurt her anymore.

Ashleigh smiled up at him. "I'm sorry. We should have made love before. Now you have only one breast to play with."

"One big, beautiful tit to kiss. It's enough."

"Kiss me first, Burke."

Ashleigh clung to his lips greedily, thrusting her tongue deep into his mouth. She fought the handcuffs, wanting to pull him to her, to have the weight of his body heavy upon her as he fucked her.

But Burke pulled away, prolonging her agony.

Ashleigh closed her eyes, wanting each caress, each kiss, to come as a surprise, never knowing where the next sensation would appear—her lips, the swollen nipple, the swell of her breast, her belly, her thighs, the soles of her feet. Ashleigh waited, twisting her wrists against the handcuffs, growing impatient for his touch, wanting to put her arms around his back, hold him, feel the flesh where she had put her tattoo.

She heard him go to the refrigerator. Her tattooed breast seemed swollen and it throbbed painfully. *Please, Burke, hurry. Make me forget. Now, Burke, now. Please.*

He surprised her, as always, pressing a strawberry to her lips. She took it eagerly, bit into it, feeling its juice trickle from the corners of her mouth.

Oh, God, why can't I love you more?

Together, they ate the strawberry, crushing it as they pressed their lips together, juice and saliva and tongues becoming one.

He held her head while she sipped from the champagne flute. She drank awkwardly. The wine trickled from the corner of her mouth and Burke kissed it away. Then he poured champagne into her navel. Ashleigh cringed as the cold wine flowed down her belly into the pale hairs curling from between her legs.

Burke's tongue followed the rivulet of champagne, through the pale, moist hairs of her loins, tasting gently of her body and her desire.

The sweat on her tortured breast burned the fresh wounds, but she didn't care. "Oh, Jesus, I'm coming," she cried as his tongue thrust deep inside her. "Help me, Burke."

Afterward, Burke brought a blanket from the back room, where Ashleigh had once lived. He released her and they lay together beneath the blanket. Cradled in his arms, she was warm and vulnerable, satiated for the moment, happy and sad for the moment, as only Burke could make her feel. The others only fucked her. Burke was allowed to love her.

"Hold my breast, Burke."

His hand closed over her right breast.

"No, the other one. It won't hurt. I want you to feel the life growing on it."

Despite the gentleness of his touch, it did hurt, but Ashleigh didn't care. It was there, beneath the bandage, beneath Burke's hands, living, growing, pulsating with energy—and venom.

"I love you, Ash."

"And you know I love you." Still, she put a finger to his lips.

"Shh, baby, shh. I'll get you some champagne. It's your turn now."

She walked naked and proud across the room, the handcuffs still dangling from her right wrist. When she returned, Burke was sitting on the edge of the table.

"I want to suck your cock," Ashleigh said, handing him the flute. "Would you like that, Burke?"

In answer, he drew her arms behind her back and snapped the handcuffs shut again, imprisoning her wrists once more.

"Am I more beautiful this way?" Ashleigh asked, kneeling before him. Her breast throbbed.

"I'd keep you in chains always."

"Someday, Burke, someday. Give me some champagne, please."

He held the flute to her mouth. Ashleigh sipped the cold wine, letting it chill her lips and tongue, before she leaned over and teased him, using her tongue for those first gentle caresses.

She pulled away when he groaned, wanting to prolong his pleasure, as he had done for her. "Poor Burke," she said, "I only come to you when I'm in pain."

"It's enough," he whispered.

"Is it?"

Her mouth closed around him and she listened to his cries with sadness. She drank of his warm seed, swallowing it eagerly, extracting more, delighted that she pleased him. It was all she could give him. It was all she had.

"Oh, God, I love you so much," he cried.

Sadly, he watched her dress and then take a brush from her purse. She smiled at him over her shoulder. "I don't want to be alone tonight," she said. "Will you come home with me?"

"Of course."

Ashleigh lost the glare of his headlights in the rearview mirror when he was caught at a traffic light. She followed the twisting narrow roads that curved higher and higher into the hills until she reached the very top and parked in her driveway.

She stood at the edge of the cliff, waiting for Burke, looking down at the sparkling lights. They glittered in the dark night as though the heavens had been reversed and all its stars lay beneath her. Once, she had been down there. Now . . .

Burke pulled in and parked behind her car.

Ashleigh took his hand when he joined her. "Isn't it beautiful, darling?" she said.

"So long as you don't know what's hidden beneath the lights."

"Yes."

They made love again, together this time, and slowly, savoring each sweet kiss, each simple caress, climbing higher and higher to that explosive peak.

In the morning, he was gone.

Even before she removed the bandage, Ashleigh knew the tattoo would be beautiful. She felt it beneath the fragile covering, throbbing with ecstasy, living, growing, a creation feeding on Ashleigh's flesh for nourishment, waiting to emerge from its womb.

Standing nude before the mirror, the morning sunlight warming her body, Ashleigh licked her lips nervously, prolonging and savoring the moments before she removed the dropcloth that shielded a masterpiece from the connoisseur's view, remembering its birth when she moaned beneath the painful caress of the needle, fingers fluttering helplessly against the handcuffs, eyes closed, her breast exposed to Burke and his needle.

Ashleigh brushed aside her long blond hair and caressed the unadorned breast as her other hand went between parted legs to sift through the pale, already moistened tendrils of hair decorating her loins, gasping at the sensation. She watched as the woman in the mirror moaned, releasing her breast, and reluctantly withdrew her fingers from between her legs. It was too soon. Languidly she licked her fingers.

Again she touched the bandage, covering it with her hand, feeling the life of the tattoo beneath. Slowly, slowly, she lifted a corner of the bandage, watching the beautiful, agitated woman in the mirror. Swallowing nervously, she ripped the bandage free.

The black widow spider clung to its web.

Oh, God, it was beautiful, so beautiful.

The intricate web decorated her breast. At the center, its eight delicate legs spread across the pale swell of her breast. The belly pulsated with the rise and fall of Ashleigh's breath. Poised, the huntress waited with ready fangs for the hapless male to play its dangerous game of penetration—and death. The hourglass was a scarlet slash on its back. That was artistic license, of course, because in nature the distinctive marking was found on the underside of the spider's abdomen. Like Ashleigh, the spider on her breast was a beautiful and deadly mutant of nature.

Ashleigh laughed, the eternal female of the species knowing that the male was hers for the taking. If she wished, she could plunge her fangs deep into his flesh, paralyze him, devour him at her leisure.

The Spider

Chapter One

Bobby Cole was examining his body in the dressing room mirror—the tanning session that afternoon had touched up his skin and muscles just right—when Dan returned from his dance.

"She's out there, man, just like before."

"What's she wearing tonight?" Bobby asked.

"Man, you're not going to believe that dress. Black leather, and her tits sticking out. Jesus, you can practically see her nipples. But that spider, man, that's weird."

"It's beautiful," Bobby said. He thought it was the most erotic thing he had ever seen. He thought the mystery woman was the most beautiful woman he had ever seen. She had been there twice before. He had been dreaming of her since, and taken to coming to the club early, parking surreptitiously across the street to examine the groups of women lining up for admittance, hoping to see her, talk to her. But he had never seen her outside the club. She just appeared suddenly. Like tonight.

"You know what spiders do, man?" Danny said. "They eat their lovers."

"And now, here he is, ladies, the king of exotic male dancers, Bobby Cole." She always dragged his name out, like a basketball announcer. *Bobbyyyyyyy Cole!*

He slowly emerged from behind the curtain, teasing the room filled with women. The lights played over his body.

The squeals were deafening. Stupid bitches.

Oh, Christ, there she was, just like Dan said, sitting alone at the end of the runway, wearing black leather, in stark contrast to her blond hair and pale skin.

Slowly he danced toward her, tossing his long brown hair, collecting the dollar bills that women thrust at him, slipping them beneath the elastic of his red briefs.

Dancing above her, Bobby saw the web that decorated her left breast and the black widow spider that clung to it just above the leather. Oh, Jesus, it's beautiful.

He lowered himself before her, dancing now for her alone, twisting and gyrating slowly, sweat popping out on his body, glistening in the glare of the multicolored lights.

She had a bill on the table in front of her. Writing on it. Folding it slowly in half.

He danced closer, to the very edge of the runway, waiting.

Meeting his eyes and smiling, she reached up and pulled at his briefs, tucking the bill in, giving him a soft pat.

The place went wild with screaming women.

The music built to a crescendo as he danced back along the runway. When he turned, she was gone.

Impatiently, hurriedly now, he did another turn around the stage before slipping through the curtains.

The screams of the women followed him. The twins were backstage, waiting to go on.

He found the twenty and unfolded it. There was a phone number written on it in red ink. Nothing else.

Back in the shabby dressing room, he quickly dialed the number and was answered by the beep of an answering machine. No message. Damn, he wanted to hear her voice, know her name. "I have another show. I'll call then. Wait for me." He replaced the phone and grabbed the tattered telephone directory. The three-numeral prefix was a Hollywood number. Oh, Christ, please be there when I call.

"Man, she's stalking you," Dan said, "Gonna cut your dick

off with a butcher knife and hang it up on a wall like some trophy."

"I don't care," Bobby said. "I want her."

Ashleigh Thomas drove slowly through the gaudy streets of West Los Angeles. The piano melodies from the tape deck were soothing after the raucous cries of lonely women forgetting empty lives in forced gaiety as young men paraded sleek and oiled bodies for them.

She turned on Sepulveda Boulevard and wondered if he padded his jock strap. It didn't matter. If he turned out to be a good lover that was a bonus, but she wanted that smooth, tanned, wonderful body for her canvas. Ashleigh smiled in the darkness of her car. She had chosen well this time. Bobby Cole was perfect for her creation. This would be the seventh tattoo. Lucky seven. The masterpiece.

The streets were still crowded. It was only ten—early yet for the Friday night pleasure seekers moving relentlessly toward late shows, a thousand nightclubs and bars, or steamy embraces and frantic hurried coupling. Ashleigh skirted the congestion of Westwood, where long lines of people stood placidly awaiting admittance to the illusions of film. She drove north on Sepulveda, past the National Cemetery, and turned right on Sunset Boulevard, following the curving road past the university, carefully avoiding any glance toward the Westwood lights, where audiences waited to watch him make love to that bitch.

The tabloids slobbered over the perfect Hollywood couple, the fairy-tale love story of Heather and Chance. Lies. All lies. She had seen the sultry and erotic movie that made them famous, sitting in the darkness, watching as they made love, but it was wrong, not at all what Chance liked.

Ashleigh hated them now—the man she had loved and the woman who had taken him. The spider was restless with a predatory throbbing, as though it felt her loathing for the celebrated couple. Ashleigh slipped her hand beneath the leather, touching it, feeling it swell and grow menacingly, fueling her bitterness, her hatred. As she stroked her breast, Ashleigh knew the spider was agitated. "Soon," Ashleigh whispered, "soon now," and thought again of owning a small art gallery where her creations could be displayed.

One woman and six or eight, perhaps a dozen—no more— men on exhibition, gracefully arranged on pedestals of varying heights, perfectly lighted to enhance each of her masterpieces, while the patrons sipped champagne and whispered of beauty—and the artist's revenge.

Ashleigh had hurt and been hurt. Hurting was better. She delighted in the thought of their public humiliation. They would be displayed, of course, letting the world see the evidence of their betrayal. Heather would be the centerpiece, a work in progress with the garland of thorns Ashleigh had so carefully created on her breast only the beginning. A delicate chain of silver—"I can't wear gold," she told Ashleigh— would link her pierced nipples. And Chance. Dear, sweet, treacherous Chance would be banished to a far corner, forced to watch as Ashleigh streaked Heather's smooth body with new and hideous designs, destroying her beauty for all time with body graffiti. And then, it would be Chance's turn . . .

Let the tabloids croon of love then.

A horn blared, intruding on her thoughts of vengeance. Ashleigh sped through the intersection, wanting to be home now, but traffic was thick on Sunset Strip, and she was forced to slow down, creeping past one trendy club after another and the crowds that waited to gain admittance. At the next light, a young and grotesquely painted male prostitute groped his genitals and pursed his lips invitingly. Ashleigh ignored him and when the light changed, hurried to catch up with the flow of traffic and leave memories behind.

Finally, she turned left off the boulevard and climbed into the Hollywood hills, leaving the city behind, twisting higher and higher through dark, narrow streets, until she reached the cul de sac at the very top of the world.

Burke had found the house and helped her move from the back room of his studio. There hadn't been much then—the teddy bear, of course, her clothes and books, the single bed, a lamp, a chair. Most of the clothes, grim reminders of a different life, she had burned. The rest she'd kept and added to as whimsy struck her.

Until Chance.

Ashleigh stood outside and looked up at the moon. She loved the full moon. It was the only memory she cherished from the desolate, windswept wastes of New Mexico. The moon had been full the night she left, sneaking away to the truck stop where he waited for her. "I didn't think you'd come," he said.

"But here I am," she said, climbing into the cab. The roar in her ears as he moved the big truck smoothly through the gears was lyrical, exhilarating. She drank her first beer that night and complied when he motioned for her to move closer, to sit beside him. She received her first real kiss and gave her first blow job, relishing his cries and the power she exerted, as they thundered through the moonlit night at sixty-five miles an hour, listening to George Strait sing of love.

Two hundred miles later, the moon hung low over the western horizon as he pulled into a rest stop where she gave up her virginity in the sleeping compartment of the big cab. It was painful and unsatisfactory, not at all what she'd expected, but a small price to pay for freedom. Two rest stops later, it was better, much better.

There might have been arguments and protestations of love, but he paled when she smiled a little sadly and said, "I'm only sixteen Billy. You've been fucking a little girl."

"Jesus Christ, Jamie Lee, I thought you was twenty-three, like you said."

"I know, Billy." She kissed him lightly on the lips before jumping out of the cab. "Think of me sometimes," she said smiling up at him. "I'll remember you."

Ashleigh went into the house then, wondering if Billy still thought of Jamie Lee when he saw the full moon.

The answering machine had two messages. "Please, Ashleigh, call me. I can't live without you. Please . . ."

Ashleigh waited for the second message.

"I have another show. I'll call then. Wait for me."

Ashleigh smiled and erased the messages.

She chose *David Copperfield* to read while she waited. Burke had given her the Oxford edition of Charles Dickens for her last birthday and she was slowly reading through his gift of love, interspersing the Dickens with his recommendations of modern novels and others of her own choosing. It was appropriate to start a new novel tonight, just as she was beginning what might be her masterpiece.

She struck a match and held it to the paper and kindling in the fireplace. When it was burning brightly and fiercely, she sat on the couch, legs curled gracefully beneath her, and opened the novel.

"Whether I shall turn out to be the hero of my own life, or whether that station will be held by anyone else, these pages must show. To begin my life with the beginning of my life, I record that I was born (as I have been informed and believe) on a Friday, at twelve o'clock at night. It was remarked that the clock began to strike, and I began to cry, simultaneously."

Ashleigh read for a while, but like the spider, she was restless tonight and kept returning to the first paragraph. "To begin my life with the beginning of my life . . ." Her life had not begun with birth, not even on the night she'd left New Mexico. No, her life had begun the night she'd stood outside Burke's studio for the first time and the tattoos had burned visions into her mind. To begin my life with the beginning of my life, I realized I was an artist, a tattoo artist.

The telephone rang. Knowing it was not Bobby, Ashleigh let the answering machine pick up on the fifth ring. She stared into the fire and listened.

"God damn it, Ashleigh, I know you're there. Why won't you talk to me? I love you. I need you. Please, Ashleigh, please."

She went to the machine and erased his voice as easily as she had erased the first sixteen years of her life. Poor Jonathan.

He was the sixth tattoo. A failure. Another failure. Bobby Cole would be different. She knew it, felt it inside. The masterpiece was there, waiting to burst, through the fog that blurred and impeded creativity, into glorious reality. This time . . . this time the vision that she saw so clearly in her mind would appear on the canvas. It had to.

He would be dancing now, displaying her canvas for women who were strangers, but she knew he thought of her. Surrounded by women who wanted him, his dance was for her alone—and the spider that had enticed him.

Ashleigh put another log on the fire and waited.

When the telephone finally rang again, Ashleigh picked up on the fourth ring. "Hello, Bobby," she said.

"I don't even know your name," Bobby Cole said.

"Ashleigh Thomas."

"It's a lovely name. I was afraid it would be something insipid like Judi with an i."

"It's Ashleigh with an l-e-i-g-h."

"Better yet. And your voice. I've been wondering what your voice sounded like. It's better than I imagined."

Ashleigh laughed. "Is that all you've been thinking about, Bobby?"

"Is the tattoo real," he asked, "or one of those paste-on things?"

Ashleigh laughed again. "You'll have to come over and find out, won't you?"

When he arrived forty-five minutes later, Ashleigh opened the door—knowing it was him—and waited, a striking silhouette against the light that flooded into the yard. The lights of the city flickered in the distance.

"I feel like a Black Russian," Ashleigh said, when he stood before her, not speaking. His hair was still damp from a shower, and he smelled of cologne. "Would you like a Black Russian, Bobby?"

"I'd love a Black Russian."

"I won't be long," Ashleigh said. "Look around. There's music. Select something you like."

Ashleigh lingered in the kitchen, waiting to hear his choice. When the music started, it was Sinatra—another gift of love from Burke—singing of the lonely. Ashleigh carried the drinks to the living room.

Bobby Cole was on the couch before the fire, leaning back, eyes closed, listening. He wore faded jeans and a black shirt. His loafers were polished. He opened his eyes and smiled up at her. "Thank you," he said, taking the glass as she joined him on the couch. "What shall we drink to?"

"To Sinatra," Ashleigh said. Their glasses touched briefly.

"I would have guessed you'd choose hard rock," Bobby said. "Sinatra surprised me."

"He surprised *me.*"

"What are these?" Bobby asked, drawing one of two heavy photo albums to him.

"My portfolio," Ashleigh said. "I'm a tattoo artist." The albums contained the record of her successes and her failures.

"May I?"

"If you like."

He leafed through the collection of photographs. Arranged in chronological order, the series of tattoos steadily grew more elaborate, more accomplished. He stopped when he came to the warrior queen. "That's you," he said.

"That really shouldn't be in there. A friend did the original, but I put it on his back. I consider it my coming of age as an artist."

"It's beautiful. You're beautiful."

"Thank you."

Bobby stopped again when he came to the shot of Chance smiling for her camera, flexing his biceps and the soaring eagle on his arm. "Jesus Christ," Bobby exclaimed. "You know him? You did the tattoo?"

Ashleigh nodded and waited for him to turn the page to Heather John's breast and the garland of thorns.

"That eagle made him, you know? He was nothing before the eagle."

"I know."

He turned the page then. "I don't believe it." He looked up at Ashleigh. "She hides it on film."

"Makeup."

Bobby shook his head in disbelief. "This is great, but she shouldn't hide it. It's very erotic. Like yours. I want to see it."

"Perhaps later," Ashleigh said. "Tell me about yourself first."

"Is this an interview?"

"Kind of."

"I'm twenty-five years old. I graduated from Northwestern three years ago, School of Dramatic Arts. Since then, I've been out here, knocking on doors for auditions. My agent thinks I'm very talented, but all I've done so far is perform in some little theater and take more classes. My teacher thinks I'm talented, too. I don't have AIDS, and you know how I make my living."

"Do you have a girlfriend?"

"Not at the moment."

"You do like women?"

"Oh, yes."

"What's the last book you read?"

He laughed. "This is just too funny, Ashleigh."

"Why?"

"Here I am, drinking Black Russians with the most beautiful woman I've ever seen, and she wants to know the last book I read."

"Why is that funny, Bobby?"

"Because it was *War and Peace.*"

"Really?" Now Ashleigh laughed.

"Yes, really. It took me three months, but I read it. Every goddamned word."

"I'm impressed."

"You should be. Now I'm reading *Anna Karenina.*"

"Poor Anna. It was so sad."

"You've read it?"

"Of course. And *War and Peace.*"

"I see I'm not going to win a game of Can You Top This."

"Probably not," Ashleigh said, smiling.

"All right. Now it's your turn," Bobby said. "I want to know all about you, too."

"I'm a tattoo artist," Ashleigh said.

The silence built while he waited for her to continue. Finally, he said, "That's it?"

"I don't like my past, so I don't talk about it. As for the present, I am a tattoo artist. In my future, I'm going to be the greatest tattoo artist of all time."

"I want to see your tattoo now," Bobby said. "All of it."

Ashleigh sipped from her drink, holding it with both hands, looking at him over the rim of the glass. "All right," she said. She put the glass on the coffee table and slowly unbuttoned the leather blouse, keeping her eyes on his, meeting his challenge with her own.

"Oh, Jesus," he said, when her breasts spilled free. "It's beautiful. You're beautiful."

Ashleigh smiled and arched her back slightly.

"It almost looks alive."

"It is," Ashleigh said.

"Will it bite me?"

"Touch it and find out."

His hand was soft and gentle as he traced the pattern of the web and stroked the spider's slender, deadly body. Her nipple rose to the touch of his lips.

Ashleigh leaned back on the couch, closing her eyes, and stroked the back of his neck as he suckled. When he kissed her lips, Ashleigh put her arms around him, drawing him down to her. He fumbled with the buttons of his shirt.

"Yes," she whispered, helping him discard the shirt. "Skin. I want to feel your skin on mine." She pulled him close as she stroked the smooth, strong flesh of his back. Yes, oh, yes. It was the perfect canvas.

But when his hand went to her thighs, Ashleigh pushed him away and sat up. "No," she said. "Not yet. Not tonight."

"When?"

"Soon."

She stood and took their empty glasses into the kitchen.

Bobby followed and leaned against the counter, watching as she measured the vodka over ice and then filled the glasses with Kahlua. Ashleigh handed him his drink and asked, "When were you born?"

"July first."

"Cancer."

"Yes. What's your birthday?"

Ashleigh hesitated for only a moment before giving her real birthdate. The stars could not be deceived. "I'm Capricorn. January fifteenth. We're opposites."

"Opposites attract."

"Sometimes."

"Do you believe in the stars?"

"Yes. I have a friend who's an astrologer."

He embraced her from behind, pressing against her, lifting her breasts as though weighing them.

She felt his erection grow harder and said, "I'm glad you don't pad yourself for those women."

"I'm glad your living room isn't strewn with male trophies. Dan said you were stalking me."

"But I was. Aren't you glad that I did?"

"Why me, and not one of the others?"

Ashleigh took his hand and led him back to the living room. She stroked his back and traced the shadows that danced over his muscles. "Because the others are just showing off. You like dancing. You're not doing it just for the women, you're dancing for yourself as well."

"I didn't think you'd be a dance critic."

"There's another reason, too. I want to give you a tattoo. I want to create a masterpiece on your back."

"Like you did with Chance?"

Ashleigh shook her head. "A work of art."

"I don't want to be just a canvas. I want you to like me."

"I do, Bobby. I want you to take me to dinner. We'll go to movies. Walk on the beach together. We'll see what happens."

"But . . ."

"Yes," Ashleigh said. "I want to tattoo you. You are going to be my canvas."

* * *

They sat before the fire and talked. He told her about auditions and acting classes and growing up in the Midwest. Ashleigh told him of her long apprenticeship with Burke, of occasional modeling assignments, of taking extension classes at UCLA, in literature, history, and art—always art. When conversation lagged, he put his arm around her and they sat staring into the flames. She nestled in his embrace, smelling his cologne, liking it, liking him. Content for the moment, the spider rested.

"I want a picture of you," he whispered, caressing her breasts, "with the spider."

"But then you'll have my soul."

"Yes."

"Come with me."

Bobby followed her into the small second bedroom she had converted into a studio. More framed photographs and patterned tattoos decorated the walls. Her equipment was neatly arranged. The small vials of brightly colored inks lined a cabinet. A leather case contained her machine. A high-intensity lamp hung over the low leather-covered table.

"Is this where you'll do it?"

"If you agree, yes."

"And if I don't . . . ?"

Ashleigh shrugged, turning away to open a file cabinet and pull an eight-by-ten black-and-white photograph from a folder. "Then, you'll always have this," she said.

"Jesus, Ashleigh," he said taking the photograph. "You're so beautiful. Who took it?"

"A friend."

"He's very good."

Even though he had seen her house and yard only at night, Bobby recognized the scene. Ashleigh was standing in front of her living room window, white curtains behind her right shoulder. Light reflected off the leaves of a tree in the background. His eyes were drawn to her face, her eyes, and her sensuous lips, slightly parted in not quite a smile.

Golden hair framed her face, cascading over her shoulders. Although the picture had been taken indoors, the window might have been open and a soft breeze ruffling her hair. Her eyes were wide, soft, vulnerable, and tinged with sadness as she looked into a distance upon something that only she could see.

Bobby wanted to take her in his arms and kiss the sadness away. "Thank you," he said.

"You're welcome," Ashleigh said, kissing his cheek lightly.

Sometime before the dawn, Ashleigh stood in the darkened living room, still naked to the waist, facing away from him. Her pale figure was outlined against the curtains that held back the night. She stood there for a long time, as in the photograph, lost in some thought or memory. Bobby wondered what she was thinking. It was the image of Ashleigh Thomas that would haunt him for years and always fill him with regret for what might have been.

She turned to him then, opening her arms, and they danced slowly in the darkened living room. He held her tightly, crushing her breasts against his chest. "You have a cruel streak," she whispered in his ear. "Sometimes I like that in a man."

"I'll remember that."

"I can be cruel also. Remember that, too."

Dawn lit the eastern sky as Ashleigh walked him to the car, holding hands. Below, the city lights were muted by the coming light. He kissed her and stroked her back beneath the jacket she had slipped into.

"Come tonight," she said.

"I have to work, but I'll call in sick."

"No, come after your last show. I'll make dinner. I'm a good cook. It's one of the ways I seduce people. We'll have a midnight feast."

"You know I'll do it."

"Yes." There was no need for him to say he had agreed to the tattoo. "It will be beautiful."

"*Je t'aime,*" he whispered.

Ashleigh murmured a response. She might have said, "*Je t'aime, aussi,*" but he couldn't be sure.

Chapter Two

The reading did not go well.

Kathleen, both a psychic and an astrologer, also used the tarot cards to assist in her readings. She had followed the solemn rites, taking the tarot cards from their silken wrapping, caressing them as she would a lover, selecting the Queen of Wands as the court card representing Ashleigh, the blond, blue-eyed woman, before dealing slowly, lovingly, following the ancient ritual, until ten cards shaped the Celtic cross.

The second card after the Queen of Wands was the Eight of Swords, in which a young woman was bound, blindfolded, and standing in a watery waste before the eight swords. Reversed, the card signified freedom and the possibility of new beginnings.

It was not reversed.

Instead, the card was symbolic of bondage and restriction, indecision and fear. Other cards indicated that Ashleigh's immediate journey would be filled with pain, conflict, and a struggle for understanding. Happiness would be long in coming.

The Lovers indicated choice, temptation, attraction, and a struggle between sacred love and profane love.

Kathleen had been troubled. Ashleigh had seen it in her face, but the older woman had pleaded ignorance, saying only, "I can be wrong. I do not see everything. I do not understand everything I see. The cards are only a guide to what you must work on."

"It is a struggle for artistic success," Ashleigh said.

"Yes," Kathleen agreed. "And more."

"What?"

Again, Kathleen pleaded ignorance. "There are barriers now. It will become clear in time."

Still, Kathleen insisted that Ashleigh had much to anticipate—serenity, joy, success. When Kathleen came to The Lovers—representative of the struggle for love, beauty, and harmony—she knew about the man who had been born under the sign of Cancer. "He will be good for you," she said, "but he is not the one you are waiting for."

Ashleigh left the reading feeling uneasy, not because she believed the cards were a grim foreboding, but rather because she knew that the frustrating struggle was within her as she sought artistic freedom and the ability to translate the beautiful visions she saw in her mind to her canvas, to the flesh. That was her travail, her burden to be overcome.

Since Heather Johns had seduced Chance away from her, Ashleigh had turned to her art, working day and night over the months, feigning patience as she waited for the visions to burst through, taking six young men as her canvases, her lovers. Six times she had attempted to create her masterpiece. Six times she had failed, discarding the men each time as she would a sketch pad of idle scratchings.

Bobby Cole would be her success, her breakthrough.

Ashleigh was glad Burke was alone in the studio. She had not seen him since her quest had begun, not since he had tattooed the spider for her so many months ago. He smiled when he looked up from his book, marking his place, as always, standing and going to her, kissing her cheek.

"Can you stay for a while?" he asked.

Ashleigh nodded. "If you're not busy . . . "

He shook his head and locked the door, drew the blinds closed, and hung a placard in the window that said, "Back at five o'clock."

"How have you been, Burke?"

He shrugged. "The same. It's always the same. And you?"

"I'm fine."

"You look good. I like you better this way."

"You always have." Ashleigh was dressed simply, wearing jeans, loafers, and a coat over a bulky sweater that hid her breasts. Her hair was in a ponytail and she wore the glasses that she didn't need, but that disguised her beauty. "What are you reading?"

"Updike's *Brazil.*"

"Is it good?"

"It's different . . . strange. You'd like it."

"I'll get a copy. You're never wrong."

"I know you."

"Yes, you do. Better than anyone."

"Would you like some coffee? I don't have any champagne. I should keep it on hand."

"Coffee's fine. The tattoo is beautiful. Would you like to see it?"

"Of course," he said, smiling in the sad fashion that Ashleigh always found so captivating.

"Get the coffee."

When Burke was in the back room, Ashleigh draped her coat on a chair and lifted the sweater over her head. She was not wearing a bra.

Burke stopped, nearly spilling the coffee, when he emerged from the back. "My God, it's better than I could have expected."

"You're so good, Burke, you should do more."

"Your hair . . . "

Ashleigh nodded. Burke had once told her the exact moment he had fallen in love with her. She had been sitting, eyes closed, frowning in concentration as she loosened her hair. Now, Ashleigh tugged at the rubber band that held her ponytail. She shook her head and swept her hair free to cascade over her shoulders and breasts. She threw her head back and brushed her fingers through it.

Burke kissed her neck. Ashleigh held him close. "I can't,

Burke," she whispered, "I have a new canvas coming to-night."

He nodded and released her. There was no hurt in his eyes, only the sadness.

"You need a good woman, Burke, someone who can love you all the time."

"I lied," Burke said. "Things aren't the same. I'm seeing someone." He handed her the coffee.

"Burke, that's wonderful. Who is she? Tell me about her."

"She's a stockbroker and financial consultant. She owns her own firm."

"My God!" Ashleigh exclaimed, clapping her hands with delight. "Burke and a stockbroker!"

"Well, it's a small firm. Her name's Danielle. I call her Danny."

"With an i?" Ashleigh asked, remembering Bobby.

"D-a-n-n-y," Burke spelled.

"That's good. How did you meet her?"

Burke shrugged. "She came here wanting a tattoo. She was very shy, but very determined. I told her about you, said she might be more comfortable with a woman artist, but she wanted me to do it."

"Good for her. What's she like?"

"Like you. Tall, blond hair—but older—forty-five, very pretty. She likes sitting in her office, all dressed up in business suits, knowing that she's different from the people sitting across from her. She likes to wonder what her clients would think if they knew her tits were tattooed." Burke smiled. "She likes to talk dirty."

"Let me guess. Both tits?"

Burke nodded.

"She wouldn't be the snake or mythological type. Something delicate, I think. If she's like me, she might like a spider, but somehow I doubt it. A flower?"

"Yes."

"And a butterfly?"

"Yes again."

"I knew it."

"She let me choose the second one."

"I'll bet they're beautiful. I wish I could see them."

Burke smiled and again went to the back of the studio.

Ashleigh sipped her coffee, jealous of a woman named Danny, but happy for Burke. She smiled and wondered what Danny would think if she saw them together now, drinking coffee, chatting easily and comfortably like old friends—except that one of the friends was half-naked.

"What are you laughing about?" Burke asked, when he returned.

"Oh, I was just wondering what Danny would think if she saw me now."

"She'd be jealous. Angry."

"I'm jealous of her," Ashleigh said, taking one of the framed photographs Burke offered. In the photograph, Burke wore a dark suit. Ashleigh had never seen him in a suit before. Beside him, smiling into the camera, was an elegant and sophisticated woman wearing a gray business suit and a white blouse with a red scarf tied in a bow around her neck. Her calves were slender and shapely. She had swelling hips, and the suit jacket disguised the hint of a full bosom. "She's beautiful, Burke. I'm so happy for you."

He gave her the second photograph. In it, Danny's delicate hands with long fingernails painted a bright red lifted her large breasts in an offering to Burke. A red rose in full bloom decorated one breast, its long, thorned stem curved gracefully over the swell of the breast. On the other was Burke's butterfly, wings spread in adoration of the rose. "The tattoos are beautiful," Ashleigh said, "among your best."

"Thank you."

"I have an appointment with Simone Devereaux next week. She wants a scorpion." Devereaux was the latest smoldering soap opera beauty. "I'll do it at her place in Malibu."

"Always the artist to the stars."

Ashleigh nodded, still feeling jealousy as she looked at Danny's breasts and the erect nipples rising from big and dark aureoles like her own. Danny's full lips were parted sensuously and her eyes glinted with desire. "Do you love her? Does she love you?"

"Yes, we love each other, but I love you, too."

"You can love two women."

"So long as you're one of them."

"I'll always be one of them. I wish I could be the only one. Have you given her *The Story of O* yet?"

"I read it to her."

"Was she shocked?"

"After the first chapter, she asked me to tie her while I read and to read very slowly."

"She sounds like some stockbroker."

"She's a very dominant and forceful woman by day, and successful, a member of the Rotary Club and the Chamber of Commerce. At night, she finds it relaxing to give up control, to be dominated and told what to do. It's her secret that gets her through the day."

"Had she ever been tied before?"

"Only in her fantasies."

"Secrets and fantasies," Ashleigh said, looking off into a distance that belonged to her alone, "fantasies and secrets."

"We all have them, Ashleigh, even you."

"Yes, but they go unfulfilled until it's too late. Will you whip Danny, like O?"

"Only if she wants me to, but I'd rather not. For me, the ropes and handcuffs and chains are decorations only, like exotic jewelry enhancing a woman's beauty."

"Like tattoos?"

"Exactly like tattoos. You were beautiful before the first tattoo. You're even more beautiful now."

"I'm glad," Ashleigh said. "You're too kind and gentle to hurt anyone. That's why I love you."

Burke looked away.

Ashleigh thought he was perhaps embarrassed at her endearment, now that he loved another as well. I hope not, she thought. I don't know what I would do without Burke.

Turning back to Ashleigh, Burke said, "She took me to a

Rotary Club meeting as her guest, introducing me as an artist."

"But you *are* an artist," Ashleigh said. "The very best. I've
always known that, Burke."

"I've started painting again."

"Burke, that's wonderful."

"Danny's helping me to arrange a showing at a small art
gallery."

"Will you invite me?"

"Of course."

Before Ashleigh left, Burke photographed the Black
Widow.

"Could you tell them apart, Burke?" Ashleigh asked, as she
posed for his camera. "If it weren't for the tattoos, could you
tell Danny's tits from mine?"

"Always."

Ashleigh went into the night glitter of Hollywood Boulevard
then, still happy for Burke and hoping that Danny would be as
good to him as he would be to her, as he had always been for
herself.

If Danny found bondage relaxing, food shopping, while not
nearly so erotic, provided a similar release for Ashleigh, par-
ticularly when she was going to cook for a new man in her life.
She enjoyed planning meals, leisurely pushing a cart through
the aisles, contemplating each selection carefully. She used
food as a means of seduction, something special and apart
from her body and her beauty. Men would line up—and
had—to fuck her. But the man who enjoyed her cooking could
be someone special. Too few realized that. Burke, of course,
and Chance had always appreciated her meals, until . . .

Ashleigh chose two bottles of an expensive cabernet sauvignon to complement the spinach pasta with Italian sausage that
was one of her specialties, and a chardonnay to accompany
the salad.

Carrying the bags to her car, Ashleigh was followed by a dirty man with unkempt hair and beard. He carried a rag that had once been white and a spray bottle. "Wash your windshield?" he demanded harshly.

"No, thank you."

"Come on, lady, you got all those groceries. I got nothing. I'm just trying to work for a little food."

Ashleigh threw the plastic bags into the passenger seat and quickly locked the doors.

The vagrant smeared her windshield, grinning at her through the glass. Ashleigh backed out. He hovered beside the car. "Fuck you, cunt," he cried.

There were three messages on the answering machine. The first was from Bobby. "I'll be thinking of you tonight as I dance. I love you."

The second and the third were from the sixth tattoo. Again. "I must talk to you, Ashleigh, please call me." And then, a long and drawn-out wail. "Ashleigh . . . please . . . " The message ended with an anguished sob.

She pressed the erase button and went into the kitchen.

Ashleigh went into the bedroom and set the alarm for ten P.M. before stretching out on the bed, clutching Bear, the big white teddy bear that had been purchased with so much pain.

Sometimes, when memories haunted her nights, she could still taste the man's sperm flooding her mouth, overflowing and running down her chin as she choked, nearly gagging as the anonymous john cried out, twisting her ears, forcing her to continue in the darkness of his car long after he was spent. But he had not hurt her nor tried to cheat her of the money, even thanking her before driving away to whatever wife and children awaited him.

After cleaning herself in a dark alleyway, Ashleigh had gone directly to the novelty store, tears still glistening in her eyes, as she'd grimly purchased Bear. Ashleigh smiled in the dark security of her own bedroom now as she remembered standing in front of Burke's studio for the first time, shivering in the cold night and clutching Bear under one arm, staring with wide-eyed wonderment at the tattoos. That was the night Ashleigh had realized she'd be a tattoo artist. Still, she'd fled when Burke had beckoned for her to enter, only to return night after night before finally entering the studio.

Ashleigh fell asleep, only to be plagued by dreams in which the homeless pursued her through empty streets armed with spray bottles filled with caustic acids. Streams of acid sought her face, falling short to burn away the sidewalks, revealing moldering graves and skeletal fingers clutching at her legs.

She was sweating when the alarm went off, the sheets wet with her perspiration. Before showering, Ashleigh replaced the cotton sheets and pillow cases with black satin. She would have done so even without the frightening dreams, knowing what a portrait the whiteness of her body would make against the cold black sheets if she decided to take Bobby as a lover tonight. Perhaps she would wait . . .

For Bobby, Ashleigh chose a black dress suitable for a midnight dinner. Its off-the-shoulder design and low neckline allowed her to display a part of the web and the black widow. She decided against a necklace, not wanting to divert attention from Burke's lovely creation, but she slipped gold earrings on and brushed her hair back. She stood and smoothed the dress over her hips and twirled before the mirror, smiling seductively at herself. She dabbed perfume behind her ears and between her breasts.

In the living room, she touched a match to the fire she had laid early and watched as the logs caught. Then she checked the dining room table a third time. She could find no fault, although she straightened a knife at her place setting and a salad fork at his. Everything was ready.

The telephone rang.

Ashleigh froze.

His voice, angry and harsh, this time filled the room. "God damn you, Ashleigh. I know you're there. Talk to me, you fucking bitch . . ."

Ashleigh turned the sound down and then the bell on the telephone itself. If he called again, she would never know. Turning her back on the telephone abruptly, Ashleigh went to the kitchen and poured a glass of champagne, taking a tiny sip before lifting the cover from the simmering sauce. She stirred and tasted it and then lowered the heat even more. Its rich aroma followed her to the living room, where she settled on the couch in front of the fire to wait and listen for Bobby's car.

The flames hypnotized her and *David Copperfield* lay unopened next to her. Perhaps she would ask Bobby to read to her. He had the excellent voice of an actor, deep and strong, like Burke's. And she wondered what Burke and Danny were doing tonight. Had he tied Danny? And how? When Ashleigh and Burke had been lovers, he had never tied her, but only used the handcuffs to fasten her wrists behind her. Ashleigh would not have minded, no matter what Burke did, trusting him as no other man, not even Chance. Perhaps Burke thought she would have protested, refused him, or worse, laughed. But Ashleigh would not have scoffed at him, not Burke, not after he had saved her, given her so much. She could refuse him nothing, except giving herself to him in complete and total love. She wondered if she would ever be able to do that again after Chance . . .

Ashleigh decided that she would allow Bobby Cole to sleep with her that night when he appeared at the door wearing a suit—a business suit, not the jeans, open shirt, and casual sport jacket affected by so many young actors around town. He carried a bouquet of roses. There was no longer any thought of making him wait.

"Good evening," he said. "Are you the lady of the house?"

"I am."

"I'm working my way through college by selling magazine subscriptions. I have several that might interest you."

Ashleigh laughed. "Come in and tell me about them."

"Thank you."

"Would you care for a glass of champagne while we discuss them?"

"That would be very kind. You're the nicest lady of the house I've happened on tonight. The rest were screamers."

"I can just imagine."

"That was the problem. I shouldn't have told you I'd think about you during my performances. I got this giant erection on stage. The place went wild."

"Poor Bobby," Ashleigh said, laughing again. "Do you still have it?"

"Not at the moment, but something's stirring down there."

"Tell it to go away," Ashleigh said, taking the bouquet, "but not too far. The flowers are lovely. Thank you." She kissed his cheek.

"Not nearly so lovely as you."

"Thank you again. Why don't you pour while I get a vase?"

"Christ, it's good to see you. I was afraid you were in my imagination and that I'd never see you again."

"But here I am."

"Yes, you certainly are."

The candles flickered as Bobby raised his glass in a toast. "To us," he said. A log in the fireplace snapped and popped, Sinatra's voice filled the room as it had the night before.

Ashleigh smiled. "To us," Ashleigh said, "and to a beautiful work of art."

"And a beautiful work of art."

"You haven't changed your mind about the tattoo."

"I'm enchanted. You've cast a witch's spell on me. I can deny you nothing."

"And will you have me burned at the stake?"

"Only if you betray me."

"I might, but not tonight."

"Why, then, my lady the witch is reprieved."

"Reprieved, but not pardoned?"

"The executioner always awaits, brooding offstage."

Ashleigh shuddered and sipped at her wine, remembering her dream. "Let's talk about something else."

"I'm sorry," Bobby said. "I've frightened you."

Ashleigh shook her head, smiling across the table. "It's not you. I had a bad dream. It's gone now. Let's enjoy the evening."

"Evening is long past."

"We'll enjoy the night, then."

Bobby praised the sauce and the pasta lavishly, pleasing Ashleigh.

After dinner, Ashleigh poured cognac and then took Bobby's hand and led him up the stairs, her heels clicking lightly on the hard wood, to the loft overlooking the living room. "This is my favorite place," Ashleigh said. "I come here to think and look out at the city lights." She slipped her heels off and settled on the loveseat, patting the cushion next to her.

Bobby relaxed and sat next to her. "It's a terrific view."

The night was clear, and lights sparkled all the way to the ocean to the south. Below, Sinatra still crooned softly.

"It's beautiful on rainy days," Ashleigh said, warming the cognac with her hands. "Everything is gray and the rain streaks the windows and I'm here all alone. The rest of the world doesn't exist then." She turned to him and kissed his lips lightly.

She liked it when he didn't take her kiss as an invitation to paw and grope at her breasts. He had a sense of the dramatic. He would know when she was ready. She settled back again, relaxing, content to smell his cologne and allow her passion to build slowly.

"But isn't it nice to have someone with you?"

Ashleigh turned to him and tasted the cognac on his lips. "Sometimes. Tonight, it's very nice."

Bobby put his arm around her shoulders. She snuggled against his chest, feeling his breath ruffle her hair.

"What will my tattoo be?"

"I don't know yet," Ashleigh replied. "Something so special

takes a lot of thought. There's no hurry. We have lots of time."

She placed his hand over her breast, holding it there, feeling her nipple swell immediately and the pulsation of her breath through the spider. Ashleigh closed her eyes and waited, ready now, wanting him. Bobby groaned when she touched his erection. "Is this what the ladies saw tonight?" she whispered.

"Oh, God, you're going to make me come."

"We don't want that," Ashleigh said, sitting up abruptly, "not yet." She reached behind and slowly drew the zipper down.

Bobby slipped the dress from her shoulders, baring her breasts. "Oh, yes," Ashleigh murmured, leaning back against the loveseat as he kissed her nipples gently. "Oh, yes, darling, harder, bite me."

His hand was beneath her dress, stroking her thighs. She parted her legs and kissed him harder, caressing his tongue with her own.

"Let's go to bed," Ashleigh whispered hoarsely, smiling in the darkness, pressing his hand to the spider's sting, "it'll be more comfortable."

Bobby groaned softly when she squeezed his balls and again, louder, when she unrolled the condom along the length of his swollen penis. "Wouldn't those ladies be jealous," Ashleigh said, falling back against the sheets, "if they could see you now."

Ashleigh moaned and bit her lip as she guided Bobby into her. "Oh, God, you're so big inside me, fuck me, darling, fuck me fuck me fuck me." His weight pressed against her, smothering her. Ashleigh wanted to stroke the smooth, hard flesh of his back, feel the canvas where the tattoo would grow into a living art, but he pinned her wrists to the bed as he kissed her and began the slow, rhythmic movements that would carry them both to ecstasy.

Chapter Three

The idea came to her sometime during the night, when Bobby turned over and, still asleep, searched for her breast with his hand. He protested incoherently when she moved away, and made the brief note on the nightstand pad.

The Lovers.

When she nestled back, his hand covered her breast again and she lay against him, the vision taking shape in her mind before she drifted away and joined him in sleep.

In the morning, Bobby discovered the sunburst on the back of her neck when Ashleigh returned from the kitchen with coffee, her hair parted and falling over her shoulders to her breasts. When she sat beside him on the bed, Bobby leaned over and kissed it, asking, "why do you hide it?

"At work, I always wear my hair up," Ashleigh replied. "People like to know their artist has tattoos as well." She smiled at him.

"I want to see where you work."

"All right."

"This morning."

"It's almost afternoon."

"And then we'll have brunch."

"Good. I'm hungry, and after, we'll walk along the beach."

"And then we'll come home and make love again."

"What a wonderful day, darling."

"I love you, Ashleigh."

She stroked his back where the tattoo would be, glancing at the notepad. The vision was still in her mind, growing in clarity. It was almost complete.

The studio was not quite in Beverly Hills and not quite in West Hollywood. Sometimes, Ashleigh thought the studio should be named Not Quite Tattoos. It described her work, too—not quite a masterpiece. Bobby would be different. She sensed it again as they walked the half-block from the car to the studio. Her arm was around his waist as they strolled down the sidewalk with other couples and beneath his cotton pull-over Ashleigh felt the lean, smooth flesh awaiting the caress of her needles.

Dean was alone in the studio when they entered. He preferred working weekends, taking Mondays and Tuesdays off, leaving Ashleigh alone in the studio on those days. It was convenient for both of them.

After the introductions, Dean said, "There's fresh coffee."

"No thanks, Dean, we're going out for breakfast."

"Breakfast? At this hour?" He arched an eyebrow wickedly. "I guess we know what you've been doing. He's adorable, Ashleigh, dear."

"He's adorable, and he's mine," Ashleigh said.

"How very heterosexual of you."

"Pay no attention, darling. He's harmless, really. Dean is quite happy in a long-term relationship."

Dean smiled. "I like to keep in practice, though. Just in case. Is Ashleigh going to create one of her masterpieces on you?"

Bobby nodded.

"And what is it to be?"

"I don't know," Bobby replied. "She hasn't told me."

"Ashleigh, dear?"

"Not yet," Ashleigh said. "It's just taking shape. You know I don't like to talk about my work until I have it completely in mind."

"It doesn't matter, Bobby," Dean said. "She's very good. Much better than she thinks she is."

Bobby nodded again. He was staring across the partition that divided the studio from a comfortable waiting area with chairs, a couch, and a coffee table with neatly piled magazines.

Dean knew what he was staring at without looking. It was the life-sized portrait of Ashleigh as the warrior goddess that hung on the wall behind her work space. "She's lovely, isn't she?" Dean said. "But of course, you know that already."

"Who did it?" Bobby asked. It was so much better than the photograph in the album.

"Burke," Ashleigh said. "Burke is my friend, my mentor."

"Have you met Burke yet?" Dean asked.

"No," Bobby said. "I'm jealous."

"Don't be," Ashleigh said, touching his arm lightly. "It was a long time ago."

"I want one."

"All right. I'll ask Burke."

"Yes," Dean said. "Ashleigh is enough to make even me go straight."

Bobby strolled around the waiting room, looking at the multitudes of tattoos hanging on the walls, and then browsed through the thick notebooks that contained additional patterns and possibilities. "These are all of the standard things," Ashleigh explained, knowing that his eyes kept returning to the warrior goddess, "but I prefer custom work, freehand. It allows greater expression. The rest is just tracing."

"That's how you'll do mine? Freehand?"

"Yes."

"What if you make a mistake?"

"Then it's a failure . . . but I won't," Ashleigh said. Not this time, she thought. I can't. This time it will be perfect.

"Do people just drop in?"

"Sometimes. We mostly work by appointments. People call and ask for custom work. Next week, I'm going out to Malibu. Simone Devereaux wants a scorpion."

"Ashleigh is our tattooist to the stars," Dean said.

"Is she as bitchy as the character she plays?"

"She seems very nice," Ashleigh said.

"She's a beautiful woman," Bobby said.

"Now I'm jealous."

"But not as beautiful as you."

"That's better."

Bobby stood in front of Ashleigh's portrait again. As he looked at her image, Ashleigh stared at his back, the stark, beautiful lines of his tattoo suddenly clear, burning through his shirt, clean and complete in every detail. And then, just as suddenly as the tattoo had appeared to Ashleigh's eyes, it faded, leaving her with only a vague impression. Ashleigh closed her eyes and tried to recapture the likeness, but it was gone. When she opened her eyes again, Bobby was smiling. "I want one of the portraits," he repeated. She nodded, and together they resumed the tour of the studio.

Her work area was clean, neatly arranged, everything within reach—an adjustable high-intensity lamp, the tiny vials of ink, a box of blue surgical gloves, new needles. Ashleigh showed him how she mixed the various colors, pouring drops of ink into small paper cups for dipping her needle as she worked.

"I want a tattoo," Bobby said. "Now."

"No," Ashleigh replied sharply. "Not yet, I'm not ready." She softened her response with a smile and a soft caress of his arm.

"Please," Bobby said. "A sunburst, like yours."

"Soon, darling."

"Now," he insisted. "It can be anywhere you like. Someplace that doesn't show. It won't interfere with the other tattoo."

"All right," Ashleigh said. "Anyplace?"

He nodded.

"On your balls?"

"Oh, Jesus, if that's what you want."

Ashleigh laughed. "I was just teasing, darling. Someday, perhaps, but not today. I don't want anything that would interfere with making love to me tonight."

"Breeders," Dean hissed with mock disgust. "I'm going for a walk."

"Drop your trousers, darling," Ashleigh said when they were alone, "and get on the table."

"Shouldn't we close the blinds or something?"

Ashleigh laughed. "You show practically everything you have at the club and with me you're modest . . ." Ashleigh paused. "You know when I've finished your tattoo, the big one, I will display you at the convention. There'll be hundreds, perhaps thousands, of people there to see you."

"I don't care."

"I just wanted you to know it's part of the bargain."

"This isn't a business deal, Ashleigh. I'm doing it for you."

"It has to be for you, too."

"It is."

Ashleigh nodded. The smile returned to her face. "Get on the table, darling."

Bobby stretched out on the leather-covered table. Ashleigh tugged his jeans lower and traced a pattern on the smooth flesh of his left buttock.

"I'm getting a hard-on," Bobby said. "I didn't know a tattoo would be so erotic."

"You won't think it's so erotic when I start working on you."

"What are you going to do?"

"A custom," Ashleigh said, "something special just for you, darling." She worked quickly and efficiently, assembling the materials and equipment, arranging the necessary inks and tissues for blotting the blood, adjusting the lamp, drawing on the surgical gloves, cleansing his flesh.

"That's cold," he said.

"It's zero hour, darling," she said, switching on the machine, speaking over its buzz. "Don't jump when I make the first line. It'll feel like you've been cut and it will hurt, but it won't be unbearable."

Ashleigh frowned in concentration as she lowered the machine to his skin. She turned and looked into the full-length mirror on the opposite wall, memorizing her features. When she turned back, she was ready to begin.

"Damn," he exclaimed, as she drew the first line of her face, and then he was quiet.

From the first stroke, Ashleigh entered another world, feeling the exultation of creation, and she knew the tattoo would be good.

The outline quickly took shape. She gave herself full and sensuous lips, slightly parted, thinking, as she worked, we'll call it "Invitation to a Kiss." Her eyes were partially closed, but enticing, like her lips. When her face was done, she switched off the machine and sat back for a moment, smiling at the sight of her own denuded face etched in dark ink. Although she wasn't usually attracted to women, she found her baldness strangely erotic.

"Are you done?" Bobby asked.

"Oh, no," Ashleigh said, blotting the blood from her likeness. "That was just the center of the sun."

Again the machine whirred and power flowed through her fingers to the machine, forcing it to make wide and bold strokes as she outlined the sun's flames around the face, giving it a wild and tempting appearance. When she began to fill in the yellow of the dancing flames, the tattoo took on its own life, provocative and sensual. Ashleigh wanted to cry out with pleasure. It was more than good.

Dean returned and stood behind Ashleigh as she filled in the colors. "Very nice," he said.

"The tattoo, or the butt?" Ashleigh asked.

"Both, of course." He went and sat at his desk. "You'll be very pleased, Bobby," Dean said over his shoulder.

Ashleigh sat back and looked at her work. "Now," she said, "you're one of us, darling. Take a look in the mirror."

Bobby stood at the mirror. "It's wonderful. Thank you."

"It'll be much better when it heals." She applied the ointment and then put the bandage on. "You have to keep it moist so the colors will set properly."

Bobby leaned over and kissed her forehead. "Will you do it for me?"

"Every day," Ashleigh said. "Maybe even three or four times a day."

Worlds converged on the boardwalk. Like Hollywood at night, Venice by day was a curious melange of the staid and respectable with the outrageous and bizarre. Tribal cultures merged—outlaw bikers, gangbangers, gays and lesbians, fitness freaks, beach bums, surfers, fishermen, the homeless, the deranged, self-styled preachers, college students, punks—all came together in an uneasy alliance, attracted by the lure of the sunwashed beach and the jutting pier.

The beach recognized no color or national origin—white, black, Asian, Hispanic—all gathered to worship at this strange shrine.

Middle-aged couples—and older—longtime residents who remembered and longed for better days, joined the Sunday afternoon parade nonetheless, strolling hand in hand between the beachside tables where hustlers hawked their cheap wares and the old and established restaurants and shops of the boardwalk.

Exhibitionists abounded and provided free entertainment for anyone who cared to watch. For the rental price of skates or roller blades, anyone could perform on the stages of Venice.

Beneath the veneer, however, violence seethed and bubbled, always threatening to overflow its confines. Gunshots were not uncommon. Gangs sometimes clashed. Bikers drank and fought. Petty thieves roamed the beach, seeking an unguarded purse or a wallet to be lifted with deft fingers.

Police officers patrolled on foot and bicycle, wearing a beach uniform of shorts and tee shirt, keeping an uneasy truce.

Ashleigh moved easily among the different worlds now, but that had not always been the case. Without Burke, she might have descended into the tumultuous maelstrom of the underworld, finally disappearing into the abyss like so many others, the victim of an overdose, AIDS, or violence.

Beside her, Bobby seemed less comfortable as they sat at the sidewalk table, drinking the champagne they had started with brunch. "We're a long way from Kansas," he said, smiling.

On the sidewalk, a pretty young woman wearing a white crocheted bikini twirled gracefully on roller blades, seemingly oblivious to those who watched. A small gold ring glinted from her pierced navel and the biceps of her left arm were encircled with a tribal tattoo, a series of sharp gray lightning bolts intertwined to form a permanent bracelet.

"What does it mean?" Bobby asked, nodding toward the skater. "The tattoo?"

"What does your tattoo mean to you?"

"That I love you."

"You see? It's very personal. For her, it can mean anything she wants. It's her statement, her initiation into the new tribalism. Some would call it modern primitive." Ashleigh paused. "Personally, I think it's an amulet to keep her tits from falling out."

Bobby laughed. "And the ring?"

"Modern man's—and woman's—search for meaning in a simpler existence. We have dehumanized society. Some of us rebel and seek expression in ways that shock what we call civilized society. Tattoos, body scarification, piercing, are all rituals as old as man. Tokens of religious significance to ward off evil and the fear of the unknown."

"And your tattoos . . . what do they mean to you?"

With a sudden kick of her leg, the woman skated away, weaving her way gracefully through the crowded sidewalk. Ashleigh watched her until she disappeared into the throngs.

"Once, I was a slave," Ashleigh said quietly. "Burke, my master, my mentor, my savior, put the bracelets on my ankles. Later, when I was ready, when he had taught me everything he could, the bracelets could not be removed, so he gave me the sunburst and sent me into the world."

"Jesus," Bobby whispered, "are you speaking figuratively or symbolically?"

"Symbolically, of course," Ashleigh said, smiling and reaching out to touch his hand. "Burke would never hurt me."

"Did you love him?"

"I worshipped him. I still do. He's the kindest man I've ever met."

A woman wearing a long flowing skirt and a white lace blouse and carrying a basket of flowers passed between the tables. "A flower for the lady, sir?" she asked.

Bobby smiled and for two dollars purchased a red rose, presenting it to Ashleigh with a flourish.

"Thank you."

"And the spider?"

"The symbolism is obvious, too obvious," Ashleigh said, smelling the rose, "the female who devours her mate, but it suits me. I don't care what others think. That was one of the things Burke taught me. I was hurt once. The spider reminds me."

"Did it hurt?"

"Terribly. My nipples are very sensitive, as you know. It wasn't so bad on the breast itself."

"It should have a name."

"Oh, it does. Its name is Woman."

Carrying her rose, Ashleigh took Bobby's hand and they strolled down the boardwalk, pausing at the tables to look at buttons, bumper strips, coffee cups, refrigerator magnets, post cards; boom boxes blared a variety of types of music. On the beach, a couple danced, gyrating wildly in the sand.

"Do you like to dance?" Ashleigh asked, and then laughed. "Of course you like to dance. It's your work."

"Temporarily."

"I meant, would you like to dance with me?"

"Now?"

"Tonight, silly. I feel like dancing. I know a club on Santa Monica Boulevard. It's different."

"I'd love to dance with you," Bobby said. "Anytime. Can we go dressed like this?"

"We can do anything we want," Ashleigh said.

* * *

They went to Bobby's apartment, a small one-bedroom unit in a three-story building off Wilshire Boulevard. As always, when told to make herself comfortable, Ashleigh went directly to the bookcases. She was delighted to find *War and Peace* on the shelf and *Anna Karenina* on the coffee table. Many of the other books had to do with acting. Several paperbacks were devoted to audition scenes for actors. The rest were mostly paperback novels, a mixture of classics and modern with a few mysteries.

Two Nagel prints hung on the living room walls. The black-haired woman in one wore a black halter over full white breasts. In the other, the woman crossed her arms over naked breasts. She wore a black bracelet on one wrist and a black skirt hung on her hips below her navel and the swell of her belly. She wore her black hair piled high on her head, the way Ashleigh did when she wanted to disguise her beauty.

Ashleigh followed Bobby into his bedroom. The picture she had given him stood on the nightstand enclosed in a gold frame, a complement to her hair and pale, sad features. Ashleigh sat on the bed and watched as Bobby undressed. When he was naked, Ashleigh said, "Come here. Let me moisten the tattoo again."

She peeled a corner of the bandage back and then ripped it off. He jumped, a natural reflex. "Baby," Ashleigh said, "that didn't hurt."

"No, but it should."

He stood in profile as she gently massaged the soothing ointment over the tattoo, obliterating the features of her face until the flame-framed portrait stared out at Ashleigh through a murky film, as though the sunburst struggled for life through the dark clouds of an overcast day.

His cock was at eye level, and as Ashleigh massaged the tattoo, it rose slowly, undulating like a cobra rising from its charmer's basket, until it stood out straight and stiff. "You're having naughty thoughts," Ashleigh said. She smiled up at him. "I hope they're about me."

He groaned when she cupped his balls and squeezed, gently at first and then harder. "Oh, yes," he said, gasping at the pressure.

"We should tie a string around it. Then, I could lead you onstage, like we'll do at the convention. Your ladies would like that, wouldn't they?"

"Yes."

"What were you thinking to make you so big and hard, Bobby?"

"Jesus, don't stop. Hold me like that forever."

"What were you thinking, Bobby? Tell Mama." She increased the pressure, enjoying the power she possessed over most men, knowing that Bobby would submit to anything she asked. "Does it hurt, Bobby?"

"Yes," he moaned, "but I don't care."

"Tell me."

"Oh, Jesus, I want you to wrap your tits around my dick and jerk me off."

"Is that all?" Ashleigh whispered. "You must really want me to do that to get so big."

"Yes, oh, yes."

"But you'd come all over my tits. Is that what you want, Bobby, to come on my nice big tits, on my spider?"

"Yes, Jesus Christ, yes."

"I'll do that for you, Bobby. I'll rub my tits all over you. I'd like you to come on my tits. My spider would like it, too. But not now . . . tonight. I want you to think about it, anticipate it. It'll be so much better that way." She leaned forward and ran her tongue along his penis, kissing its tip, tasting the milky drops of his sperm oozing out. "That's just to help you remember what's going to happen tonight." She released him.

He turned and reached out for her, but she scrambled away across the bed, laughing.

"Jesus, I love you, Ashleigh."

Standing across the bed from him, Ashleigh realized that she felt differently about him, that she was beginning to love him, despite his weakness. He wasn't like the other canvases. But he wasn't like Chance, who'd discarded her so casually.

Or Burke, who'd forced her to leave because he wanted her to live in freedom, not entangled with a man so much older.

Ashleigh hoped that Bobby's tattoo would be the masterpiece she wanted so much, that she wouldn't have to send him away, like the others. She forced herself to say it. "I'm falling in love with you, too, Bobby."

"Thank God. I thought you'd never say it."

"It's only been three days."

"I fell in love the first time I saw you. I used to stand outside looking for you. I was afraid you wouldn't come back."

"But I did."

"Dan was right. You were stalking me."

"That sounds so ominous, as though I'm dangerous. Is that what Dan thinks, that I intend to harm you?"

"I don't care what Dan thinks."

"I was looking for someone. I chose you."

"I'm glad."

"You're not afraid I'll devour you?" She smiled across the bed.

"A little. You said you could be cruel." He turned away abruptly to dress.

Ashleigh watched, admiring the tanned flesh of his back, planning the tattoo, the Lovers of the tarot card. In the original, the Lovers were depicted as Adam and Eve, watched over the by the archangel Raphael. The Lovers stood between the tree of life and the tree of knowledge of good and evil, where the serpent lurked. But she would transform the scene, make it her own, dark and erotic, as the Lovers embraced within the coils of the serpent, bound together for all time by both truth and falsehood, the reality of human love. This time the image did not fade.

"Wait," Ashleigh cried.

Bobby turned, startled, shirt in hand.

"I want to touch your back." She crossed the room quickly and adjusted his pose like an artist arranging her model. She closed her eyes and started at his neck, where Raphael would be, a strange and ephemeral figure. And lower, where Eve, head thrown back in ecstasy, open and vulnerable, curled one leg around his back, and Adam . . .

"Yes," Ashleigh whispered.

Bobby turned and took her in his arms.

"Yes," she whispered again, and opened her mouth for his kiss.

They were just passing the club when Ashleigh saw the sixth tattoo. He stood away from the line of people waiting for admittance, scanning the sidewalks in both directions. Ashleigh knew he was looking for her. They had met at the club and gone there often together, until . . .

She turned away to hide her face in the shadows of the car. "I've changed my mind," she said. "It's too crowded. I'd rather be alone with you."

Hc drove past the club and made a u-turn at the next intersection.

The sixth tattoo was still there, searching, when they passed the club again.

Ashleigh relaxed and took Bobby's hand as he turned into the hills and they began climbing toward home.

"What did you see back there?" he asked.

"Just someone I used to know. It doesn't matter."

The note was taped to the door. Bobby tore it free and handed it to Ashleigh. She recognized the way he addressed his love letters to her, underlining her name. Inside, she crumpled it and tossed it unread into a wastebasket.

"Just someone you used to know?" Bobby asked.

"He doesn't mean anything."

"How about your telephone messages?" He indicated the flashing red light on the answering machine.

"Nothing matters," Ashleigh replied, "except for you and me." For now, she thought.

Chapter Four

The colors of the elaborate tattoo were already fading in death. Guy Benjamin had never seen anything like it. It was an abstract, something that might hang in a museum if it had been on a canvas and not on a naked and deceased male caucasian.

"What a piece of shit to put on your body," Harris said.

"I think it's rather beautiful," Benjamin said, "or would have been, in life."

"Jesus, Guy, if you're going to get a tattoo," Harris persisted, "it ought to say something. Make a statement."

"A heart with mother in it?"

"Yeah. Like that. Even skinhead punks make a statement with their swastikas. 'Look at me. I'm a stupid shit.' That's what a tattoo ought to say."

"You're a philistine, Harry." Benjamin walked around the body, following the intricate course of the design. "It doesn't appear to be finished," he said. "It just stops abruptly. There on the thigh."

"The unfinished masterpiece?"

"More like a work in progress."

"It's done now." Harris laughed. "Unless somebody wants to finish it up in the morgue."

Benjamin could not take his eyes from the tattoo. The colors were bright and vivid, yet managed somehow to convey a sense of brooding helplessness. It was something that Edvard Munch might have done. What did Munch say? "The colors were screaming." Yes, that was it, Benjamin thought. The artist was screaming with blue and red and yellow squares, geometrically linked by vast areas of darkness.

"You gonna stare at that fucking thing all day," Harris interrupted, "or can we get some work done and get out of here?"

Everything pointed to suicide.

There were no signs of a struggle. Even a cursory examination of the entrance wound indicated that the victim had pressed the barrel to his temple and fired the shot. The revolver, a .38-caliber, had fallen to the floor in close proximity to the dead man's hand. The victim had apparently been drinking—an empty Scotch bottle and a glass stood forlornly on the stand next to the chair. And there was a woman involved. The rambling suicide note told them that.

Ashleigh, I can't live without you . . . we could have been so happy together, Ashleigh . . . why, Ashleigh? The spider. I love you . . .

The note ended there, reminding Benjamin of Kurtz's last words. "The horror! The horror!" What was "the spider"? Who was "Ashleigh"?

It was signed formally—"Jonathan Carver"—as though his full signature somehow added validity to his act.

It had to be a self-inflicted gunshot wound to the head, but . . .

A woman could have done it—a woman named Ashleigh.

They went through the motions anyway. After nearly twenty years working in Homicide, Benjamin had learned not to accept appearances.

He kept going back to the note, wondering what sort of woman could induce such desperate passion in a man, so much that he would kill himself rather than live without her. Benjamin believed that nothing in life could be so bad as death.

Her last name was Thomas.

The dead man's address book yielded two addresses and telephone numbers for her. The first was obviously a home address, somewhere in the Hollywood hills. The second was labeled simply, "Studio." Was she an artist? Had she perhaps put that tortured expression on Carver's body?

Nothing indicated that she had ever been in the apartment. Nothing indicated that anyone had been in the apartment when Jonathan Carver had killed himself.

Ashleigh waited patiently. It would be her last tattoo of the day and she didn't mind waiting for the young couple to make their decision. Once, she would have been impatient to get away, eager to meet Chance or Bobby, but now . . .

They had argued last night. It had started over the blinking red light on her answering machine, one of those inconsequential things that could so quickly escalate into harsh and unforgettable words, accusations, bitterness.

"Aren't you going to see who called?" Bobby had asked.

"No," Ashleigh replied. "I don't care."

"Is it the guy back there at the club, the one who left the note? You don't want me to hear the message? Is that it?"

Ashleigh turned the machine's volume to its highest setting. "Play the message, if you want."

Bobby pressed the button. The frantic plea thundered in the living room.

"Ashleigh, please, I can't live without you!"

"Who is he?" Bobby demanded.

"The sixth tattoo."

"Doesn't he have a name? Is that all I am to you? A fucking tattoo? What number am I?"

"Seven."

She knew he would be back. They always came back.

The couple had been in the studio for an hour, browsing nervously, holding hands and looking at the designs and patterns on the wall, before taking the large notebooks that contained Ashleigh's original designs to the couch in the studio's waiting area.

Once, they got up and came to the counter. The young woman lowered her voice, even though the studio was empty. "It's going to be on my breast. Is there a place . . . "

Ashleigh nodded. "There's a private room," she said.

"Is it all right if Tommy watches? It's my birthday present. I'm twenty-one today."

"Only if you want him to," Ashleigh said. "I will only give you a tattoo if it's what *you* want. It must be for you."

It was Ashleigh's standard response. The boyfriend always wanted to watch as his woman received her decoration. It was part of the ritual. Was it the pain inflicted, however slight, or the permanence that so excited them? Sir Stephen had watched as the final rings were placed in O and again when she was tied to receive his brands. O's first lover, Rene, watched as O was whipped and taken by others. Perhaps it was the same for women, but Ashleigh would never know. She could not bear having her lover tattooed by another. She wondered what emotions went through Burke's mind when he inscribed the spider on her or the butterfly on Danny.

"The tattoo was my idea," the young woman said, "and I want Tommy with me. It's kind of like childbirth. I'm Susan, by the way."

"Hi, Susan. Happy birthday."

"Thank you."

"That's beautiful," Tommy said, pointing to the framed portrait of Ashleigh posing as the warrior goddess. "Did you do it?"

"A friend of mine gave it to me," Ashleigh said, knowing that he did not recognize her as the model. No one ever did. She disguised her beauty too well while she was working, wearing little makeup and a shapeless artist's smock, pinning her hair up in a severe bun, wearing glasses she did not need. Few people—men or women—knew her true persona. Chance did. Burke, of course. Sometimes the men she had chosen to be her canvases and lovers received brief glimpses. Bobby might . . . someday. To her clients and to the world, however, Ashleigh Thomas was a mousy and nondescript tattoo artist.

No one denied her talent, though.

Susan and Tommy went back to the couch when the studio door opened.

Ashleigh recognized him immediately for what he was.

Cop.

"May I help you?" she asked.

He smiled and nodded, glancing curiously around at the tattoos on the wall as he approached the counter. "I'm looking for Ashleigh Thomas," he said.

The old sense of panic returned, but Ashleigh kept her face passive as she replied, "I'm Ashleigh Thomas."

Benjamin saw the wariness in her eyes and knew she had been in an unpleasant encounter with the police—arrested, perhaps even had done time. He showed her his badge. "I'm Guy Benjamin, Robbery Homicide. Is there a place where we can talk privately?"

"In the back." The couple giggled over one of the notebooks. "I'll be out in a few minutes," Ashleigh told them, lifting the countertop for Benjamin.

"What was it for?" he asked, when Ashleigh closed the door. Benjamin glanced around the room. It was a complete studio for those who wished to receive their decorations in private.

For a moment, Ashleigh thought of pretending not to understand the question. Then she said, "Prostitution," and the memories returned. The judge had been on a momentary moral crackdown, and instead of the usual probation, Ashleigh was sentenced to thirty days in the correctional facility for women. Ashleigh fought one bull dyke after another, but she had not been raped, and then she'd bartered the crude jailhouse tattoos for her safety.

Her pimp was waiting when she was released.

So was Burke.

Benjamin nodded. "Do you know Jonathan Carver?"

"Yes," Ashleigh said, "or rather, I did."

"Did?"

"He's dead, isn't he? That's why you're here."

"He apparently committed suicide sometime last night or this morning."

Ashleigh, please, I can't live without you . . .

"Suicide?" Ashleigh said. "Why?"

Benjamin shook his head. "There was a note addressed to you. I thought you could tell me."

"I'm sorry," Ashleigh said. "He was a client."

"And a lover?"

"Briefly. It didn't work out."

"You did the tattoo on his body?"

"Yes."

"Why didn't you finish it?"

Ashleigh shrugged. "It was a failure."

"I thought it was very good," Benjamin said.

"A failure," Ashleigh insisted.

"What is 'the spider'? It was in his note."

"I have a black widow spider tattooed on my breast."

"I thought it might be something like that. It reminded me of Kurtz's last words in *Heart of Darkness*. Have you read it?"

" 'The horror! The horror!' "

"Why do you hide it?"

This time, Ashleigh truly did not understand the question. "Hide what? The spider?"

"Your beauty. You're the woman in the portrait outside."

"You recognized me? Very few people do."

"I recognized you immediately." He turned to leave.

"Does the police department know?" Ashleigh asked.

Benjamin paused, his hand on the doorknob, and turned back. "Know what?"

"That you're gay."

"You're very good," he said.

"So are you," Ashleigh replied, "but I'm not a whore any-more."

"I know."

That night, Guy Benjamin began a journal.

Ashleigh remained in the back after the police officer left. *Ashleigh, please, I can't live without you. Ashleigh, please, I can't live without you.*

His agony echoed in her mind now. Poor Jonathan. Ashleigh tried to find pity or sorrow for him, but she was empty of any feelings she might have once had for him. Even if the tattoo had not been a failure, he would not have lasted. Like Kurtz, who looked into the abyss and found himself lacking, Jonathan lacked strength.

Ashleigh went back to Susan and Tommy.

"Have you found something you like?" she asked.

"They're all beautiful," Susan said, "but I like this one the best. So does Tommy."

Ashleigh looked at what Susan had chosen. The multicolored butterfly had its wings spread and looked as though it were about to light. Something was missing, however. "That's one of my favorites, but may I make a suggestion?"

Susan nodded eagerly.

"It needs a flower to land on," Ashleigh said. "How about if I put a rose . . . " she leafed quickly through the notebook and pointed, ". . . this rose, on your nipple?"

Susan shivered and frowned. "I don't know. Won't that hurt a lot?"

"Some, but it's not unbearable. I had one done there once. I'll show you, if you like."

"Would you mind?"

"Come on back," Ashleigh said. "Tommy, too, if you don't mind, Susan."

After closing the studio, Ashleigh went to the small bar down the street. She had found the third tattoo there. She had also found a friend.

Ashleigh had watched as Cynthia Brewster took the call, listened for a moment, and then slammed the phone down.

"Men are weird," she told Ashleigh. "The guy on the phone wants to know if I'm wearing a bra. My boyfriend wants me to get a tattoo and wear a wig for him."

Ashleigh had smiled at the young woman. "I'm an artist," she said, offering her card, "I'll do your tattoo for you, but only for you, not your boyfriend."

"He wants to watch. Isn't that strange?"

"Not always," Ashleigh said.

She remembered that first conversation now as Cynthia poured a glass of white wine for her. Tommy had been solicitous of Susan as she'd sat in the leather recliner with her breast exposed to the needle, holding her hand as Ashleigh worked. He had been embarrassed, too, when Ashleigh had displayed the spider for them, blushing furiously as he stammered, "Awesome." Ashleigh smiled at the memory. She didn't know if he referred to the spider or her breasts, probably both.

Cynthia was Irish—she had chosen Celtic runes for her tattoo—with long strawberry-blond hair. Ashleigh never understood why the boyfriend—long gone now—had wanted Cynthia to wear wigs when they made love. Cynthia's own hair was so lovely.

The boyfriend was gone, but the tattoo on Cynthia's belly remained. Ashleigh had kissed it often enough after they'd become occasional lovers, sometimes spending a night together between boyfriends, laughing as they'd caressed each other, calling it their mutual masturbation society.

The bar was quiet in the late afternoon. Ashleigh had closed early, more shaken by Jonathan Carver's death than she wanted to admit. She had seen death before, violent death on the streets and the lingering death brought by drugs. Burke had taken her away from that.

"How have you been, Ashleigh?"

"All right."

"I've been thinking of getting another tattoo. Would you do it for me?"

Tattoos, like everything else the human condition is drawn to, are addictive. "Of course," Ashleigh replied. "Do you still have the wigs?"

Cynthia smiled. "Isn't it silly? Now that Brian's gone, I like the wigs. I can be someone different anytime I choose."

"Sometimes, I feel like a different person every day."

"You haven't been in for a while. I've missed you. Have you been working hard?"

"I'm working on a new canvas. I hope this is the one. I want to enter it in competition at the convention."

"I'm sure you'll win."

"I don't know. We argued last night. I may have to look for someone new."

"He'll be back. You can't get rid of a man."

"Yes, you're right," Ashleigh said. Unless he kills himself, she thought.

Bobby was waiting when Ashleigh got home.

"I'm sorry," he cried, as she got out of her car.

"I am, too," Ashleigh said.

"I was so jealous. I wanted to kill you. I had to leave."

"There's no reason for jealousy," Ashleigh said. "You're the only man in my life." Except for Burke, she thought, who is always with me. And Chance, who would not go away, haunting and mocking her every time she saw his picture with Heather. "He's dead now."

"Who?"

"Jonathan Carver, the sixth tattoo. He committed suicide last night."

"I don't care," Bobby cried. "I don't care. He almost came between us. Jesus . . . I'm glad he's dead."

She took his hand and led him to the wrought-iron bench perched on the edge of the precipice that fell away to the city below. They sat quietly, separated as dusk fell over the city. A man stood at a backyard barbecue at one of the homes lower on the slope. Across the canyon, a dog barked fiercely to drive away some demon approaching with the night.

Bobby drew Ashleigh close.

She settled in his embrace, resting her head against his shoulder, looking out wistfully at the sun screaming at the horizon of the vast ocean, struggling for life, but fading rapidly.

Day ended as the last red flames flickered and died, slipping beneath the black horizon, but the vast city glowed brightly in the night, like a gaudily painted whore enticing the momentary lover into her arms. Like me, Ashleigh thought, as she turned to Bobby and kissed him. "It has nothing to do with you or last night," Ashleigh said, "but I need to be alone tonight."

Bobby remained silent for a long time.

Ashleigh waited for his response, not wanting another argument.

"All right," he said finally. "Will I see you tomorrow?"

"Of course, darling."

Ashleigh returned to the bench after Bobby left and tried to rid herself of memories. But they flooded over her like waves crashing against a solitary rock.

The cop, Benjamin, had disturbed her. He had penetrated her disguise, her defense against the world, so easily and stripped her naked to her soul, not because he'd desired her, but because, peering into her secret depths, he had recognized her for what she had once been. He'd frightened her as no man had since Frank, not because he was inherently violent, like her former pimp, but rather because he saw her for what she was and had been.

Burke had somehow matched Frank's savagery.

Ashleigh had stood in the bright warm sunshine outside the jail, watching as the two men had spoken, waiting to see who would take her away. Burke had spoken briefly—she could not hear what he said—but Frank had shrugged and walked away. Burke had never told her what he had said to Frank, but it had been enough to send the pimp away defeated. Burke had taken her hand and led her gently to his car. That night Ashleigh had moved into the back room of his studio, bringing only the teddy bear. Everything else had been left behind.

The next day Ashleigh began her real apprenticeship with Burke, watching as he worked, listening to his explanations, making notes that she studied over and over again, drawing and sketching her own designs. Burke paid the tuition for her first art classes she attended at night through the university extension. She read the books he gave her and they discussed them endlessly.

Looking out at the lights of the city, Ashleigh knew he was down there somewhere. If not for Danny, she would have gone to him, listened to his reassuring voice, as always. "I would be your slave, Burke," she whispered to the night, finding comfort in the possibility of total submission to another, relinquishing all responsibility. But it was too late now. He had found another.

Chance, too, was down there somewhere, with Heather. Everything might have been different if Chance had remained faithful. Instead, he had destroyed her hopes and her dreams. His only legacy was the spider. One day it would have its revenge.

Ashleigh went into the house, going from room to room turning on lights as though the artificial light provided protection from the night. Then she erased the messages on the answering machine without listening to them.

The sixth tattoo was dead.

Ashleigh wondered briefly what would happen to the seventh tattoo. Then, she went to the bookcase and stood for a moment, undecided which Bible she wanted. She chose the King James version over the modern edition. It was the Gideon Bible she had taken on a sudden whim from the shabby hotel room where she'd brought her tricks. Ashleigh did not need the Bible. It had been beaten into her from her first memories until she'd fled that moonlit night.

Ashleigh remembered the exact moment when she'd known she would leave New Mexico. It was when the minister had looked at her, exhorting her alone to step forward for Christ, pleading for her to accept Christ as her personal savior. Rebelliously, she stood unyielding, meeting his eyes, knowing that he wanted to lay his hands on her, drive Satan from her soul. He thundered for her to come forward, ignoring the others who formed a ragged line, waiting self-consciously for the laying on of hands.

Ashleigh refused.

Afterward, he had drawn her father aside on the threadbare lawn of the small church, but Ashleigh had overheard as he'd told her father to get control of his women, that they were not properly subservient in God's eyes.

But she had long ago forgiven God and His Gospel for her

childhood and she could still read Scripture with pleasure. She opened the Bible to Genesis and read again of those first lovers, driven from the Garden of Eden for their transgressions.

"And the Lord God said, Behold, the man is become as one of us, to know good and evil . . . "

Ashleigh returned the Bible to its place and took *Paradise Lost* to read "Of man's first disobedience . . . "

Today, I met the most beautiful woman I've ever encountered. She hides her beauty, but even if I hadn't seen the portrait that hangs in her studio, I'd have known. The artist loves her. I wonder who did it. Her beauty is seductive, hypnotic. She has a bright sunburst tattooed on the back of her neck and a spider tattooed on her breast. I've seen the one. I would like to see the other, not because I'm attracted to her sexually, but rather because it must be beautiful, like everything else about her.

A man killed himself because he could no longer have her.

The spider is dangerous, luring victims to its web.

She is intelligent—she recognized me immediately for what I am—a police officer and a middle-aged gay man—just as I recognized her. She is talented. The work that hangs on the walls of the studio is original and striking, not the usual collection of hearts and flowers and serpents. The dead man's tattoo was unfinished—she called it a failure, but it was not. She is too harsh in criticizing her work.

She is an outlaw, too, not in the criminal sense of the word, but in the sense of a rebel. Tattoos today, as always, mark the rebellious, those who live in another dimension—the criminals, the bikers, the young. That's why Christianity banned tattoos. The marks identified the individual as someone apart from society, signified membership in another group. In Leviticus, it is written: "Ye shall not make any cuttings in your flesh for the dead, nor print any marks upon you: I am the Lord."

Doubtless, Satan is tattooed.

And Eve. What tattoo would that first woman choose today?

She was a whore once and served thirty days. That one arrest only ten years ago. Jail would not have been easy for her. Women in the isolation of jail would kill for someone like her. Did someone protect her, or did she fight? Probably she fought. She has the strength that Jonathan Carver lacked. He should have been content with her marks on his body and the memories.

She calls herself Ashleigh Thomas, but Ashleigh Thomas is dead. I know that because I searched the Hall of Records for her birth certificate—and I found her death certificate first.

Who are you, Ashleigh Thomas?

When will I see you again?

Chapter Five

After working late into the night, sketching furiously in a futile attempt to capture the images she wanted for the Lovers, Ashleigh slept restlessly, plagued by nightmares in which Jonathan Carver's skeletal hands dragged her to the edge of an open grave. Once, she awakened, cold and petrified by fear, certain that he stood at the foot of her bed. Terrified, unable to move, she wanted to scream, beg him to leave her alone. The memory of his mocking laughter from the nightmare filled her head. She knew he wanted her to join him in death, to be with him for eternity. Finally, nearly paralyzed by the fear, she summoned the courage to reach out for the lamp. The room was empty in the sudden blaze of light. It was only a shadow, Ashleigh told herself over and over again. Her mouth was dry. Still trembling, she forced herself to get up and started downstairs for the kitchen. At the bedroom door, she stopped abruptly.

He was down there in the darkness, waiting for her.

Ashleigh turned and went into the bathroom, drank greedily from the tap, and then splashed cold water on her face. When she got into bed again, she left the lamp on and hugged Bear tightly, desperately. The big white teddy bear was a comforting presence against the chill she felt—and the fear. "Please, Jonathan," she whispered, "I'm sorry."

* * *

The bright morning sunlight dispelled fear, but not remorse. Standing naked and wet before the bathroom mirror, steamed with fog from the hot water of the shower, Ashleigh watched as the black widow slowly emerged from the mist, standing out with stark clarity, its malevolence burned into her flesh. It had struck and killed once. It would do so again and again unless she stopped it. The towel squeaked against the mirror as she rubbed hard in a futile effort to make it go away, yet knowing the symbol she had chosen to decorate her breast was appropriate. The corruption came from within her.

Dressed, she wandered through the house restlessly, unable to bear the thought of work or the presence of others. Abruptly she called the studio and left a message on the answering machine for Dean saying that she was sick.

It was true. She was sick in her heart.

She fled the house, normally her place of refuge, and descended into the city.

Disoriented and uncomfortable, Ashleigh drove aimlessly. The city by day was strange and unfamiliar. She was always more at ease with the night and its lost inhabitants, the people of the street—pimps and whores, bikers, drug dealers, petty thieves and burglars, cops, drunken johns, the restless young people seeking nirvana. That was her milieu, her inspiration, her tableau.

Until last night.

The sixth tattoo had taken his revenge.

The truck loomed large in her rearview mirror. Its lights flashed on and off angrily. Ashleigh pressed the accelerator and pulled away from the monster, looking around for her bearings. She was on the San Diego Freeway, just passing the airport. How did I get here? Where am I going? Jesus, help me.

She took the next exit and found herself heading toward the ocean. Then, Ashleigh knew. She wanted to see Burke's woman. Given purpose, the day was no longer so disconcerting and it would help her forget the night—and Jonathan Carver.

Danny's office was in one of those endless oceanside communities that dot the Southern California coastline from Santa Barbara to San Diego.

Even without the nameplate on her desk, Ashleigh would have recognized Burke's woman immediately. Danny was just as she had been in the photograph—tall, sophisticated, elegant. The blue business suit contrasted nicely with Danny's blond hair and pale complexion while it hid her secrets from the world. Ashleigh was happy for Burke but saddened and jealous of the woman who was so perfect for him in ways she could never match.

As Ashleigh opened the new account—a small money market account as an excuse for her presence—their eyes met briefly. When Ashleigh left, Danny was waiting at her office door. She smiled and approached her company's newest client.

"I'm Danielle Petersen. Welcome to our little investment family."

"Thank you." Ashleigh wanted to run.

"Burke said you were beautiful."

"How did you know?"

Danny smiled again, looking around to ensure they were alone. "I've kissed you often enough. You're always in my bed when Burke and I make love."

Ashleigh snapped her fingers. "Of course. My face is on his back . . . I wasn't thinking."

Danny nodded. "And the portrait in Burke's studio."

"I'm sorry," Ashleigh said. "I shouldn't have come, but I wanted to see you. I'm happy for Burke. And you."

"I'm glad you did. I wanted to meet you, too."

"Burke said you would be jealous."

"Oh, I am, but you exist, and I can't make you go away. I can't erase you from Burke's life, his memories."

"I'm jealous, too. He loves you very much."

Danny smiled. "I was about to go to lunch when you came in. Will you join me?"

Ashleigh hesitated.

"Please."

"All right."

They strolled along the marina to a crowded sidewalk café where Danny greeted the hostess by name.

"It'll be about fifteen minutes. Can I get you something to drink while you wait?"

"Ashleigh?"

"A glass of chardonnay, please."

"Your usual iced tea, Danny?"

"No, I think I'll have a glass of chardonnay as well. This is a special occasion." She smiled at Ashleigh again. "Two old friends meeting for the first time."

Sitting beside Danny while they waited for their table, Ashleigh found it difficult to imagine the older woman in the role of submissive, a tied and helpless slave, waiting for Burke to make love to her. Danielle Petersen was so calm and self-assured, a successful businesswoman. Ashleigh wondered how long he made her anticipate. "Are you a feminist?" she asked.

"Yes, of course. I believe in equal rights, opportunity, and compensation for women of ability in whatever endeavor they choose to pursue." Danny paused and glanced around. "But that's not your real question," she continued, lowering her voice. "You want to know how I reconcile those beliefs with Burke and our relationship."

"Yes."

Moorings creaked as gentle swells caressed the boats. Like the boats in their slips, conversations rose and fell at the nearby tables.

"Because it gives me pleasure, as well as Burke. Ah, thank you, Mary."

"It'll just be a few more minutes now."

"There's no hurry. We're enjoying our conversation." She watched as Mary went back to her station. Then, Danny raised her glass to Ashleigh's. "To old friends," she said.

"Who have never met," Ashleigh continued.

Danny sipped the wine and said, "It was inevitable. We are each, in different ways, important to Burke. When was the last time he fucked you?"

"Months ago," Ashleigh said. "When he put the spider on my breast. I've only seen him once since then."

"He fucked me last night and will again tonight."

"You're very lucky. He is the kindest man I've ever met. I wish I could have been the right woman for him."

"Yes, he told me of your quest for perfection in your art, to transform tattoos into a higher art form. He believes you'll succeed one day, but only after a great struggle and much pain."

"I hope he's right, but he could have been the best of all."

"He chose a different path. But you, Ashleigh, you are the warrior goddess of the portrait in his studio. You are the female on the warrior's journey. You must not fail. You are taking the quest for all of us."

There was a long silence. "Burke's very lucky, too," Ashleigh said finally.

Danny smiled.

It was pleasant to sit in the shade of the umbrella, listening to the waters lapping against hulls and pilings, the screech of gulls, faint laughter from a passing sailboat. Around them, men and women talked of business deals, compensation packages, insurance.

"When I was married," Danny said, "I was always free and my husband did nothing for me. I was taken for granted. With Burke, I am bound and he does everything for me. You must remember what it's like."

"I was young. Burke never tied me; he only used handcuffs on occasion."

"How sad."

"Yes."

"Burke is painting again."

"He told me. You've arranged a showing for him."

"Yes. I'm also sitting for him," Danny said. She laughed.

"Actually, I'm reclining, lying on the bed. It's a nude, although I'm wearing a mask. It wouldn't do to have my clients and friends know I posed naked. By day, I must keep up appearances. But at night, with Burke, I'm free."

"I'd like to see it. Would that embarrass you?"

"No. I like posing for him. When he's painting, I can tell what part of my body he's working on. It's as though the brush is caressing me and not the canvas. When he painted my breasts, my nipples got hard." Danny smiled. "I asked him to work very slowly. They're getting hard just thinking about it."

Ashleigh glanced down at the soft swell of Danny's bosom.

"Does it show?" Danny asked.

Ashleigh shook her head. "You're blushing, though."

"I'm not used to sharing intimacies with another woman, but it's different with you. We are linked by Burke and we bear his marks."

"But you chose the first tattoo yourself. You didn't know you would fall in love with him."

"That's true. But the second tattoo was for Burke. It was my submission to him."

"Is everything all right?" Mary asked.

"The salads are perfect, Mary, as usual."

When Mary went on to another table, Danny said, "I've asked Burke to brand me. He won't, of course, but I want to wear his initials on my ass."

"Like O."

"Exactly like O. I wish Burke could send me to Roissy." Roissy was the chateau where O had been taken by her lover to be enslaved, whipped, and possessed by others.

"Roissy can exist in your mind," Ashleigh said. "Anything can happen there." She has a glorious smile, Ashleigh thought. She's so radiant.

"Yes, exactly," Danny said. "Burke is going to tattoo his initials on me. It will be just like in the novel. I'm to be tied very tightly to a column and the tattoo machine will be my branding iron. Do you think me strange?"

"No," Ashleigh replied simply.

Danny stared out at the marina. "There's something missing, however," she said. "My submission must be public . . . will you . . . will you be Anne-Marie for me? I must ask Burke for permission, of course."

"O and Anne-Marie were lovers," Ashleigh said.

"I've never been with a woman. Have you?"

"Yes."

"There's so much I haven't done," Danny said, looking away wistfully. "Until Burke . . . "

"Anne-Marie had O whipped."

"I know. Have you ever been whipped?"

"No. I was spanked as a child. Once, I . . . "

Distant memories of a schoolgirl bending over the teacher's desk flooded back.

Mary Margaret struggled to hold back tears; girls were rarely paddled in the church school and the class was allowed to vote on Mary Margaret's punishment, the teacher polling each student individually and marking the vote on the blackboard. Ashleigh cruelly voted yes, envying Mary Margaret, wondering what it felt like to lean over the desk. The vote was close but Mary Margaret was judged guilty by the class and received six strokes of the paddle, crying and howling as the last sharp crack filled the hushed classroom. After, Mary Margaret walked back to her desk, blushing and rubbing furiously, where she sobbed quietly for the remainder of the period.

Ashleigh contrived her own punishment, stealing the teacher's pen, bragging about it to the class tattletale, knowing it would get back to the teacher. Asked about the pen, Ashleigh confessed. There was no vote. She was immediately sentenced to ten strokes, an unheard-of punishment for a girl, to be administered during the last period of the day.

She spent that entire day anticipating it.

The teacher had been remorseless when the announced time of her punishment had inexorably arrived. Ashleigh had gone to the desk and waited, bent over the desk, girlish buttocks clenching, while the teacher had delivered his homily on the sin of stealing. Her long hair had shielded her face from her classmates while she'd pressed youthful breasts and hard, tingling nipples into the desk top.

She did not cry until later, as she walked home with burning buttocks, not understanding the strange but pleasurable sensations coursing through her body. At home, she went straight to bed, pleading illness, and squirmed beneath the blankets, kneading her small, plump breasts, one hesitant hand snaking down her body to the still, sparse hairs between her legs and she exploded in her first orgasm.

"I was twelve," Ashleigh said.

"Did you cry?" Danny asked.

"Not in front of the class."

"I wonder if I would be as brave."

"I have a birthday tomorrow."

"Happy birthday, Ashleigh."

"Thank you."

"We've only talked about me. What about you, Ashleigh? Who are you?"

"I don't know." Ashleigh met Danny's eyes for a moment and then looked away, wanting Danny's approval, wanting to be liked by the older woman. "I killed a man."

If Danny was shocked, she disguised it well, saying only, "Tell me about it."

Ashleigh bit her lip, wanting confession. "He was a canvas . . . and a lover . . . he committed suicide. He shot himself. The police came to see me."

"Then you killed no one. He killed himself. The decision was his. The responsibility was his. We are each responsible for our actions. No one else."

"It was a failure," Ashleigh cried. "I couldn't stay with a failure. He would have been a constant reminder. But he kept calling and calling. I should have done something. Now . . . it's too late . . . I'm sorry."

Danny took Ashleigh's hand, stroking it gently. "It wasn't your fault."

After lunch, they walked along the marina. Ashleigh was reluctant to part, feeling unusually close to the older woman. She wanted Danny to make love to her, but that was impossible. Instead, she decided to call Cynthia, but Ashleigh wanted Danny's arms to embrace her, knowing she would feel secure then. She craved Danny's kisses, yearned for her caresses. "I'm glad I met you," Ashleigh said suddenly.

Danny smiled that radiant smile again. "I'm glad to have met you, too, Ashleigh. It was inevitable."

Driving back toward Hollywood, the smell of Danny's perfume lingered, the result of her parting kiss on Ashleigh's cheek. Ashleigh wanted to send Danny a present. But what? Something special. Flowers? Candy? No. They were too commonplace, and inappropriate for one woman to give to another when they were not lovers. What, then? Something intimate, an indication that Ashleigh understood Danny and appreciated her.

Then, Ashleigh knew.

The place where she would have to go to purchase Danny's gift might be tawdry, but the present would not be. She would infuse it with love before sending it.

Ashleigh ignored the furtive stares of the customers in the adult bookshop, all men, each standing alone as he looked at the forbidden pleasures. She went directly to the counter, leaning down to look at the array of vibrators, dildos, lotions, whips and paddles, handcuffs, and leather cuffs and straps, until she found the nipple clamps. Ashleigh chose a pair attached by a heavy silver chain. In the photographs, Danny's nipples had been large. She could bear the weight of the chain.

The clerk smirked when he pulled the clamps from the display. "You want 'em wrapped, or are you gonna wear 'em?"

"Fuck off."

The insolent young man laughed. "Have fun," he said.

Before going home, Ashleigh bought a bouquet of flowers.

* * *

Ashleigh fondled the present she had bought for Danny and regretted not having purchased a set for herself. She wanted to experience the pinch of the clamps and the weight of the chain, but there was no one to command her obedience. Bobby would do it, but Bobby would do anything she asked. It would not be the same. Ashleigh wanted to believe that her pain would appease Jonathan Carver. She wanted Burke, but Danny entered her mind.

At Danny's order, Ashleigh slowly unbuttoned her blouse and removed it.

"*Continue,*" Danny said.

Ashleigh freed her breasts from the brassiere.

"*Penance,*" Danny said. "*This is your penance for Jonathan Carver.*"

"*Yes,*" Ashleigh replied. "*I'm sorry.*"

"*Caress yourself, Ashleigh, make your nipples hard.*"

Ashleigh closed her eyes, moaning as her body responded.

"*It's time, Ashleigh.*"

The clamp was padded and adjustable. Ashleigh gasped as she placed the clamp on her left nipple and tightened it.

"*More. Harder.*"

Ashleigh bit her lip, but tightened the clamp until the pain was unbearable. I'll be good, Mother, she thought. "*Please love me.*"

Her lips glistening wetly, Danny watched as Ashleigh repeated the process.

"*Hands behind your head.*"

Ashleigh obeyed. The motion lifted her breasts. The chain was heavy, tugging at her imprisoned nipples.

"*Does it hurt?*"

"*Yes,*" Ashleigh cried.

"*Now, go and look at yourself in the mirror.*"

Again, Ashleigh obeyed.

The black widow spider was trapped in the clamp's cruel embrace. Another turn and the spider would die, squeezed of its venom.

Ashleigh watched in the mirror as Danny approached to embrace her lovingly, to absolve her of sin.

The telephone rang.

"God damn it," Ashleigh cried. She dropped her arms and quickly loosened the clamps, sighing with relief, before answering the telephone on the fifth ring.

"I was afraid you weren't home."

"Bobby. I was just . . . "

"I called you at work. Dean said you were sick."

"I just couldn't face anyone today. I had a bad night. I couldn't sleep, and when I did . . . I just wandered around today."

"I want to see you."

"I know, but . . . "

"But . . . "

"Not tonight, please. I'm not very good company. I'll be better tomorrow—I promise."

"I love you."

"Thank you."

She replaced the telephone and stroked her breast where the clamp had nearly killed the spider. She wanted Danny back, to feel the comfort of her embrace. But Danny was gone. She was with Burke now.

The note was brief. "For Danny." She signed it only with her initial.

She placed the clamps in the small box, carefully arranging the chain, on the white tissue paper, folding it over, putting the note on top. She addressed the package to Danny in care of her office, writing "Personal and Confidential" on the box, smiling at the thought of her opening it there in the conservative business surroundings.

"I don't want to be alone tonight," Ashleigh said. The words were familiar. She had said that before. When? To whom? Then she remembered. It was to Burke, after they'd made love on the night he'd put the black widow on her breast. Now he was with Danny. The sadness of his loss overwhelmed her. "Would you like to come over?" Ashleigh asked.

"I can't," Cynthia Brewster said. "My mother's visiting. I'm sorry. It would have been nice."

Disappointed, Ashleigh said goodbye.

She worked for an hour in the studio.

The image Ashleigh had seen in Bobby's apartment would not transform itself to paper. The woman demanded freedom. She would not be bound to her lover by the serpent or by her transgression. She had become a goddess, but one who eluded Ashleigh.

Disgusted, Ashleigh went downstairs and poured a glass of wine and attempted to read, but the words blurred on the page. She thought of Danny in Burke's arms and she finally discarded *David Copperfield,* something she rarely did, but there was no comfort in literature tonight. She longed for Cynthia's soothing caress and whispered endearments, anything to banish fear and doubt into the darkness.

Chapter Six

The Hollywood streets were deserted in the early morning, empty of all those who had prowled the night. Traffic on the freeway was still sparse and Ashleigh sped through the Cahuenga Pass, quickly leaving the Hollywood Bowl and Universal Studio exits behind. I would have been thirty-one today, but I'm really only twenty-six. Heading east on the Ventura Freeway, the brightening rays of the rising sun blinded her. Squinting against the glare, Ashleigh turned off and entered the vast cemetery, climbing and turning through the green rolling hills.

When Ashleigh parked, she took the bouquet and walked down the hill, through the graves, slipping once on the dewy grass until she stood before the simple headstone of her grave.

ASHLEIGH THOMAS
BELOVED DAUGHTER
SEPTEMBER 28, 1965
MARCH 22, 1966

Kneeling, she placed the bouquet on the grave and whispered, "Happy birthday, Ashleigh." Rising again, Ashleigh glanced around furtively. Once, she had gone to her grave and found a middle-aged couple standing there, still weeping after so many years. She had pretended to visit another grave until they'd left, though wanting to approach them, to comfort them and say, "Your daughter is not dead. I'm Ashleigh now.

I'm living in her place." But at that time they would not have been proud of the surrogate who had assumed their daughter's name and identity, and Ashleigh avoided them. Now she liked to think that they might feel a tinge of pride that she had left that other grim and sordid existence behind for art. She had Burke to thank for that. There had been times over the years when Ashleigh thought that Burke—and the girl buried at her feet—were her only friends. Now, there was Cynthia. And Danny.

"I've been doing all right since our last visit," Ashleigh told the grave, "but I still haven't made the breakthrough. I wish I could show you my work. I feel like I'm so close, so close, but something always seems to elude me. I thought the sixth tattoo would be the one, the masterpiece, but it didn't come to life and I had to send him away. He kept calling, but I didn't answer. I couldn't help it. Even though I liked him, and might even have grown to love him in time . . . once the tattoo went wrong . . . well . . . I would always have to live with my failure. Still, it's been for the best. He turned out to be very weak. When he called, he begged me to see him again, pleaded for me to call him. But I didn't, and now he's dead."

Below her grave, the San Fernando Valley stretched to distant mountains, made blue in the early morning haze, reminding her of New Mexico. She was still Jamie Lee then. That's why Ashleigh Thomas's name had appealed to her. In her youth, she thought "Leigh" was a more sophisticated spelling. Then, as a runaway in Los Angeles, she had prowled the cemetery, reading tombstones, until she'd found the right year, one that would make her an adult, a woman. For the price of a mail-order birth certificate from the Hall of Records, she'd become Ashleigh Thomas.

"Was it my fault?" Ashleigh asked the gentle morning breeze. "Would Jonathan be alive if I had talked to him? But he had a choice, didn't he? Not like you and me. I wonder what we died of?"

As she wandered, nameless, no longer thinking of herself as Jamie Lee, through the cemetery that long-ago day, she read the inscriptions and wondered about those people's lives.

Each had a beginning and an end, but she was left to fill in the vast middle. She could rewrite their stories any way she wanted, just as she was doing with her own life. And when she'd stood before the monument to a child's brief existence, Jamie Lee had died and been reborn as Ashleigh Thomas.

"We made a new friend yesterday. At least, I think so. Her name is Danny. She's Burke's friend. She's older than us, but I was very attracted to her. I hope Burke will allow her to make love to me. You know how I get sometimes. And when Bobby called . . . but you don't know about Bobby yet . . . there's so much to tell you . . . Bobby is the seventh tattoo, lucky seven, and I just feel like this is the one that will be a success, but I didn't feel like seeing him last night, so I called Cynthia—you remember our friend Cynthia . . . "

Ashleigh stared down at her grave. What would you think of all this if you were alive, she wondered. But if you were alive, I wouldn't be here. I wouldn't exist. Who would you be? Who would I be?

"I'm sorry, Ashleigh, I'm not saying any of this very well today. The truth is that Jonathan's death . . . no, his suicide . . . sometimes, I get so scared . . . "

Ashleigh hugged herself as though it were cold, but the early morning chill had dissipated. "But Cynthia couldn't come and I fell asleep on the couch . . . I was so afraid . . . just like before . . . you remember what it was like when I first came here . . . you remember and I don't want to . . . "

Ashleigh knelt again and rearranged the bouquet. She touched the name and dates carved into the smooth granite. "I have to go now, but I'll come again soon, Ashleigh. I promise."

Pacific Coast Highway curved along the edge of the continent, a precarious trail balanced between the unstable towering cliffs, ocean waters endlessly caressing the shore—sometimes gently, but more often relentlessly pounding, like an impatient lover demanding penetration. Today, however, the blue water was placid beneath the bright sunlight. Disguised by the beauty of the brilliant day, there was no trace of the malignance under the glowing veneer of water and land that could erupt so suddenly in savage waves, raging firestorms, angry mudslides.

Driving north toward Malibu—older residents called it "the Malibu"—away from the metropolitan congestion, her own beauty disguised by a white scarf and dark glasses, Ashleigh felt a sense of freedom that was not possible in her other worlds. She had survived the night and its dark memories just as she had prevailed over a lifetime of nights wandering the turbulent streets, fighting the undertow that threatened to drag her under.

She hadn't surrendered then. She wouldn't surrender now.

Simone Devereaux's home was on the ocean side of Pacific Coast Highway in Malibu. From the highway, the red brick house was all garage and wall, a grim fortress protecting the inhabitants. But when Simone opened the door, she ushered Ashleigh into a large and open house fronting on white sands bordered by blue waters edged with foam.

"Thank you for coming," Simone said. "I'm really excited about this." She kissed Ashleigh's cheek and took her hand in both of hers. It was like two old college friends were meeting after a long absence.

Perhaps this is what sorority sisters do, Ashleigh thought, but I wouldn't know. My sorority sisters were all whores. When Simone's hands lingered, Ashleigh again saw the invitation in her eyes, the same as when Simone had come to the studio. "I'm happy to do it," Ashleigh said, wondering who would take the dominant role.

Simone Devereaux was tall and slender, although her height did not match Ashleigh's. Her hair was black and straight, matching dark eyes. Barefoot, she wore blue shorts and a blue halter over full breasts. Her skin was smooth and tanned. An Academy Award for best supporting actor sat on a table in the foyer. Ashleigh knew Simone lived with Sam Harrington, who had won the award a few years ago. A small card rested next to the statuette. "This place reserved for Simone Devereaux," the neatly lettered message said.

"Let's have coffee on the patio," Simone said. "Would that be all right?"

"That would be very nice."

"Go on out," Simone said. "I'll just be a minute."

Ashleigh left her traveling tattoo kit in the living room, but carried the two notebooks to the patio table. A sailboat curved gracefully through the water. Near the pier, a line of surfers dotted the blue surface, waiting patiently for their waves, but the water was too calm. Down the sand, a woman wearing a white bikini sat in a beach chair reading a thick paperback.

Simone placed mugs of coffee on the table and stood behind Ashleigh. "It's a lovely tattoo," she said, lightly tracing the pattern on Ashleigh's neck.

Her skin tingled with the soft touch. "It's my sunburst. I think of it when I'm feeling good."

Simone drew a chair next to Ashleigh. "Do you have others?"

"Yes." Ashleigh waited for the actress to ask if she could see them.

Simone surprised her, however, by saying, "If you want the truth, I'm a little nervous about this, too."

"That's natural. I was nervous the first time."

"It's just that it's so permanent. Once you start, there's no going back."

"Nothing is permanent," Ashleigh said, "not even a tattoo."

A man walking a dog down the beach waved to Simone. She returned his wave. "He's some big corporate attorney," Simone said. "I wonder what he would say if he knew you were going to tattoo me."

Ashleigh shrugged. "Why do you want a tattoo?" she asked.

"For Rachel, my character, she's such a bitch," Simone replied. "She's exactly the kind of person who would have a tattoo to taunt her lovers. I'll be able to play my role better. I want to become Rachel."

"A scorpion will be perfect, then."

"You've seen the show? You know what Rachel's like?"

"I watched a few episodes after your visit. I don't watch much television. You're very good, though."

"Thank you, but I want to move on. My agent, Richard Sheridan, wants me to do a feature during hiatus, but we haven't found the right script yet. Do you know Richard?"

Ashleigh shook her head. "I've heard of him. He's the one they call "the Executioner" because he's so ruthless."

"That's him," Simone said, smiling. "I just wondered. I thought you might because of Chance. You were his girl-friend."

"A long time ago," Ashleigh said quietly. She turned away and stared out at the ocean. On the horizon, Catalina was a dark hulk, standing out ominously.

"I'm sorry," Simone said. "I shouldn't have said anything. Sometimes I talk too much."

"It doesn't matter now," Ashleigh said, ignoring the sudden pain of memories. She leafed through one notebook until she found the page she wanted. "There." Ashleigh turned the notebook to Simone. The scorpion was black and large, its tail curved and poised to sting.

"Yes," Simone said. "That's exactly the tattoo Rachel would have."

"Where do you want it?"

Although she blushed, Simone Devereaux looked boldly into Ashleigh's eyes. "On my belly . . . just above my pubic hair. Do you mind?"

Ashleigh smiled. "I don't mind."

"Where would you like to do it?"

"How about here? It's a wonderful day."

"It's not very private," Simone said. "We have a deck up-stairs, off the bedroom. I sunbathe there. It's very private."

"All right."

"Perhaps we should do it before I lose my nerve. Then, we'll have lunch."

"Rachel wouldn't lose her nerve."

"No, I guess she wouldn't. She wouldn't care about privacy, either. It's decided. First lunch, and then the tattoo. It'll be nice thinking about it, anticipating. Like making love." Simone touched Ashleigh's hand.

Ashleigh smiled. "It's exactly like that," she said.

In the kitchen, Simone stood at the counter preparing a salad. She had poured white wine for both of them. Ashleigh watched from the breakfast bar, liking that Simone was making the salad herself, knowing she was doing it for her. Heather would have had lunch delivered.

"I get lonely when Sam's away on location," Simone said. "I'm glad you're here."

Ashleigh did not want to talk about men being away on location. Chance had met Heather on location. She took a sip of her wine before going to stand behind Simone, reaching around, placing her hands on the actress's breasts.

Simone froze.

"Does Sam know you like women, too?"

"I don't," Simone whispered, "not usually."

"Do you want me to stop?"

"No."

"I didn't think so." Simone trembled in her embrace.

"When I saw you in the studio . . . I thought you were beautiful . . . I wanted you then . . . that's why you had to come here . . . when Sam was away."

"How many others have there been?"

"Only a few, in college. Now, there's just one. A friend."

"And me."

"Yes, and you."

"I have a friend, too. I wanted to see her last night, but she couldn't. Does that bother you?"

"No, you're here with me now."

Ashleigh turned Simone around and looked into her dark, gleaming eyes. Simone's tongue flicked nervously over her lips. Ashleigh stroked her face gently. "It's nice to have friends," Ashleigh said. "This is our first kiss, darling."

* * *

Sitting on the patio in the warm sunshine, the two women eating lunch appeared inconsequential to those who strolled down the beach and happened to glance in their direction, but they could not feel the sexual tension building as Ashleigh and Simone chatted aimlessly. Simone was shy and nervous, Ashleigh confident as seductress, now that their roles were defined.

After lunch, Simone bashfully led Ashleigh upstairs to the bedroom. Ashleigh went to the clock radio on the nightstand and tuned in to an FM station that played soft music. She turned to Simone, who stood waiting at the foot of the bed, and nodded.

Simone smiled and looked directly at Ashleigh as she slipped out of her shorts. She wore no panties. She reached behind to unfasten the halter and let it drop.

Ashleigh compared the actress with Cynthia. Where Cynthia's breasts were small, pale, and freckled, Simone's were full and tanned. Cynthia's pubic hair was a reddish wild tangle, but Simone trimmed her black hair neatly.

"Aren't you going to join me?" Simone asked. She reached out and touched Ashleigh's breast timidly.

Ashleigh covered Simone's hand with her own, pressing it against her so that Simone could feel her nipple growing hard. She wrapped her fingers in the long black hair and kissed her before backing away to slowly strip for Simone, moving sensually in time to the music.

"Oh, Jesus, I can't wait," Simone said when Ashleigh stood naked before her. "You're so beautiful."

They embraced, kissing, rubbing their breasts against each other.

"Now," Simone begged, moaning, "please, *now.*"

"No," Ashleigh whispered. "I'm going to make love to you at the same time I do your tattoo. Can you stand it?"

"Oh, God, yes. Hurry, though. Please hurry."

"Anticipation," Ashleigh said. "Remember?"

Ashleigh arranged Simone so she lay sideways on the bed,

legs parted, feet on the floor. She tortured Simone as she made her preparations, leaning over to caress her breast or kiss her mouth, flicking her tongue and biting Simone's lips gently.

"You can play with your tits while I work," Ashleigh said, "but you're not allowed to move below your waist. Can you do that?

"Yes . . . I don't know . . . I'll try." Simone rubbed her breasts, whimpering softly as she pinched her nipples.

Ashleigh knelt between Simone's legs and used her tongue to open Simone's pouting lips. The tattoo machine buzzed as Ashleigh licked Simone's clitoris. The insistent whir of the machine could not drown Simone's cries of pleasure. Rubbing Simone gently with one hand, Ashleigh frowned, concentrating, and then lowered the machine.

Simone screamed at the first cut. Ashleigh could not tell if the high-pitched, keening cry was from the initial pain or the pleasure.

Ashleigh had decided the scorpion would be emerging from the black wiry hairs, the huntress coming from its lair, but she had traced only half the scorpion on Simone's belly, teasing her with her tongue all the while, when the actress cried, "I'm coming, oh, God, I'm coming."

This is what I taste like, Ashleigh thought.

Afterward, the tattoo finished and both women satiated with love, they lay together on the bed. Simone's head rested on Ashleigh's breast. Her breath was soft and warm on Ashleigh's flesh. "I love the spider," Simone said. "Will my scorpion be as beautiful?"

"Yes, when it heals." Ashleigh had done the scorpion in blacks and grays. It would be poised and ready to strike. "Does it hurt?"

"Not very much now. I'm a little sore. God, I've never experienced anything like that before. I thought I was going to die."

"But you didn't," Ashleigh said, stroking Simone's tangled black hair.

"Did I satisfy you?"

"Oh, yes, couldn't you tell?"

"I'm glad. I like making love in the afternoon," Simone said. "Wouldn't that be a wonderful title for a novel? *Love in the Afternoon*. Someone should write it."

"Perhaps someone will."

Simone stroked Ashleigh's thighs. "Chance was a fool," she said. "You're beautiful. Heather is nothing in comparison to you. It still hurts, doesn't it?"

"Yes."

"I'm sorry."

"Do you have to leave?"

"Yes," Ashleigh said, thinking of Bobby. I shouldn't disappoint him again, she thought, knowing, however, that she could and he would still return. He had been bewitched by the spider. "I'm sorry."

"I want to see you again," Simone said. "Perhaps I'll get another tattoo."

Simone wrote a check for more than the price of the tattoo.

Ashleigh hesitated before taking it. "You're making me feel like a whore," she said.

"Darling, it's for Rachel's tattoo. Nothing else. Whatever else happened was between Ashleigh and Simone."

"Thank you."

But all during the drive home, the refrain echoed in Ashleigh's mind. I was a whore. I'm still a whore. It's what I do best.

While she was waiting for Bobby to arrive, the telephone rang. It was Danny.

"You're such a minx," she said.

Ashleigh smiled. "You received it?"

"Yes, thank you. It was very thoughtful, a wonderful surprise."

"Are you wearing them?"

"Oh, yes. I'm so hot I don't know how I'm going to get through dinner. I want Burke to fuck me right now, but he won't. He's making me wait. And, Ashleigh . . ."

"Yes."

"Burke's given his permission. He thought it was a wonderful idea. You *will* be my Anne-Marie, won't you?"

"Of course."

Bobby took her in his arms. "Are you feeling better? I was worried about you."

"Yes, darling, I'm feeling much better now. It was just such a shock, but I'm over it now. I've been looking forward to seeing you." It's not really a lie, she thought. I did miss him, but I'm going to have to be an actress myself tonight. Simone's soft hands and tongue had drained her of desire.

Bobby kissed her and she thought of Simone and Danny and Cynthia.

Oh, God, I'm such a slut.

Happy birthday, Ashleigh.

Chapter Seven

She lives at the top of the world, at the end of a cul de sac overlooking the great Los Angeles basin. It's an older home, small but comfortable looking. She doesn't own it. The title is in the name of Gladys Richardson, who lives in Santa Barbara. I spoke with her today—told her Ashleigh had used her as a reference. Gladys is delighted with Ashleigh as a tenant, saying that she always pays her rent on time, keeps the house up, makes improvements, never complains. "Such a pretty, sweet girl," she said. Gladys rented the house to Ashleigh because of Burke.

Burke was her mentor, took her off the streets, taught her to tattoo as his apprentice (this is apparently the time-honored and traditional way to learn the trade, although he called it "the art"), and when Ashleigh was ready, set her free. That was the term Burke used. He "set her free."

Ashleigh has a teddy bear that she named "Bear." It was the only thing she brought when she went to live in the back room of his studio. It's as though her life began at that moment. There was no Ashleigh Thomas before—only after. If Burke knows anything of her earlier life, he did not—or would not—tell me.

I was afraid Burke wouldn't talk to me.

"Why?" he asked.

"Because I want to be her friend," I replied.

He looked at me for a long time, staring into my soul—just as she did—before he said, "I believe you."

It's true. I do want to be her friend.

But why?

I wonder—is it art?

Who are you, Ashleigh?

Why do you exert this power over me?
Questions, only questions, when my life's work is to seek answers.

"It's your mysterious woman, isn't it?"

Guy Benjamin nodded, putting down his pen, sighing with pleasure as Elliott massaged his shoulders expertly. He had taken to spending his days off, at least a portion of them, investigating Ashleigh Thomas. It isn't really an investigation, he told himself. It's only satisfying my curiosity about a beautiful and mysterious woman.

"More like pursuing an obsession," his life partner said. "You're not going straight on me after all these years?"

"Of course not, Bucko. I just want to know about her. I'm a nosy cop. If you had seen her, you'd understand."

"Perhaps I'll drop by and get a tattoo. Would you like that?"

Benjamin smiled. "I wouldn't mind." He remembered the fading abstract on the suicide's body. That *was* art. But, of course, Ashleigh wouldn't do something like that on a casual customer. She would save her art for her canvases. Her victims. Jonathan Carver had suckled that breast, drunk deep from the venomous spider, and died. "But if you do, be careful. She has a black widow spider tattooed on her breast."

"How do you know?"

"She told me. And I saw it today. Only a photograph, of course. She hasn't been at work for a couple of days. But I talked to her partner at the studio. He's one of those flaming queens who talks too much. I asked if he had done her tattoos, but it turned out that she has a mentor, a man named Burke. He has a studio in Hollywood, so I dropped by there. Ashleigh apprenticed with him. I think they were lovers once. Anyway, he has photographs of his best work on display. One of them showed a woman's breasts . . ." His voice trailed off as he sat, remembering.

"You couldn't see her face . . . but the black widow was unmistakable . . . it had to be her breast . . . it was beautiful . . . deadly . . ."

"I think you'd better be careful," Elliott said.

"I will." Guy pushed away from his desk and took Elliott in

his arms, kissing him, glad once again that they had been monogamous for so long, before AIDS became a common word and the epidemic wasted and killed so many of their friends. I couldn't stand to watch him die, he thought. "I love you, Elliott," he said, looking into Elliott's eyes.

"And I love you, Guy, always and forever."

They walked to the bedroom holding hands and as they undressed, each watched the other, their eyes meeting, still smiling shyly in prelude. Naked, they approached each other, meeting, embracing, shivering, rubbing against each other, kissing, enjoying the prologue that was so important to both of them.

Elliott stood back and smiled, that same warm expression that had attracted Guy so many years before. "You've had a tough day. Let me make it better. Would you like that?"

"Yes, I think that's a wonderful idea."

"Then, I'll do it," he said, taking his lover's hand, "just for you, Guy, just the way you like it." Elliott led Guy to the bed, crooning softly, "Come with me, baby, come with me."

Elliott held Guy, stroking his body softly, tenderly, brushing at his graying hair, biting his nipples gently, driving thoughts of Ashleigh from his mind.

Guy slowly relaxed beneath the caresses, thinking again how lucky they had been to find each other—so many never found love—and then gave himself up to the distracting kisses, the caresses.

"This is my gift to you tonight," Elliott whispered.

"Don't stop," Guy moaned.

"I'll never stop, baby, never. I promise."

"God, yes, that's right. Bite me, harder. Ah."

Elliott was relentless, always promising more, backing off, starting anew, until Guy writhed on the bed, begging.

. "Do it, please, do it now."

Elliott was smiling when he finally took Guy in his mouth, slowly at first, licking, sucking, licking again. Teasing, always teasing.

Oh, Jesus, yes, I love you so much, suck me now, I can't wait any longer, please, oh, yes, that's right, yes, oh, God, yes, it feels so good, yes, yes, oh, please, don't make me wait any longer, your mouth is so hot, don't stop, I love you, I love you, yes, so much, God, yes.

Danny knelt unmoving, head down, her arms raised behind to fasten the cameo on a black choker he had given her for the occasion. The pose lifted her bare breasts for Burke to capture on his canvas. The folds of a simple cotton skirt were arranged loosely around her hips and over her legs. She smiled slightly, as though remembering some whispered endearment or a fleeting pleasure. When he asked how she managed to maintain such a beatific expression, Danny laughed and said, "I just think of you, darling."

As Burke painted, he was filled with love for this woman who loved him and gave of herself so completely. He had never been so happy. With her submission Danny had enslaved him.

"A cop came by yesterday," Burke said, "asking about Ashleigh."

"What did he want?" Danny asked, straining to maintain the pose, but knowing that conversation was the prelude to a break. "Is she in trouble?"

"Not according to Benjamin. That's his name. Guy Benjamin. It's a strange name for a cop. An old boyfriend of Ashleigh's committed suicide because he couldn't live without her. Benjamin investigated and met Ashleigh. He said he was intrigued by her.

"Intrigued?"

"That's the word he used."

"I wonder which Ashleigh he saw?" Danny said. "But it doesn't really matter. She captivates you immediately."

"Yes. Benjamin said he wanted to be her friend."

"Did you tell her?"

"Yes."

"How strange. Ashleigh told me he looked as though he wanted to punish her."

Burke put down his brush and palette. "Would you like a break?"

"Yes, please. I am getting tired." She rose and stretched, easing the aching muscles, before crossing the room to stand behind him and look at her painting. "You've made me much prettier than I really am."

"I'm not nearly good enough to capture all your beauty."

"You're sweet to say so, but I know the truth. Your brush flatters me, but I don't mind."

"You're the most beautiful woman in the world."

"Liar," she laughed. "What about Ashleigh?"

Burke stood and turned to take Danny in his arms. He smiled down at her and said, "Well, perhaps the second most beautiful woman in the world."

"Yeah, I thought so. Fickle, but I love you anyway."

Danny sighed when he stroked the curves of her buttocks where his initials would soon be cut into her flesh. Yes, darling, yes, I love you so much. She pressed against him, savoring his embrace and the feel of his shirt against her naked breasts. "I love being your model," she said.

"Another half hour?" Burke asked. "And then we'll go out. Would you like to see a movie?"

"That would be fun."

They saw Chance and Heather's new film.

"Did you like it?" Burke asked as they left the theater, emerging into the crowded shopping mall.

"Yes," Danny said. "I thought they were very good together. When they made love . . . God . . ."

"Did you want him?"

"I wanted you. I still do."

He took her hand as they walked along. "Would you like a frozen yogurt?"

She laughed. "If that's the best I can do for the moment."

"Just for now," Burke said.

"How can you love such a shameless hussy?"

They sat on a bench outside the yogurt parlor to eat.

"The eagle on Chance," Burke said. "Did you know Ashleigh did that? It's her work."

"Really?"

"They lived together before he made it as a big star. Ashleigh was wildly in love with Chance. Then, he became famous and met Heather . . ."

"And left Ashleigh."

"Yes."

Danny bit her lip. "I couldn't stand it if you left me."

"He hurt Ashleigh terribly," Burke said. "She changed after Chance."

"How?"

"She became older, harder. That's when she became obsessed with creating a masterpiece."

"All artists are obsessed. I watch you as you paint."

"I get caught up in my work, but it's not my whole life. I have you."

Danny smiled. "We have each other."

"But Ashleigh has no one."

"She has a boyfriend."

"But she doesn't love him. Ashleigh seduces the man she wants for her canvas. Each one will be the masterpiece, the perfection she seeks. But . . ." He took their empty containers and dropped them in a trash can.

"But . . ." Danny waited for him to finish his thought.

"She unconsciously creates a flaw so she can discard the canvas and go on to the next. Until Ashleigh allows herself to love again, she'll repeat the pattern again and again."

"How sad."

Chapter Eight

They drank to her success in a dimly lit restaurant for lovers. Framed paintings of elegant and seductive women—all nude—graced the walls. In a secluded booth, their glasses touched and they smiled with their eyes as they drank the chilled champagne.

"To a masterpiece," he said.

"Thank you," she replied. "To a masterpiece."

Ashleigh made no attempt to disguise her beauty. Her hair was down and she wore a claret-red velvet top and a long black skirt complemented by a wide black belt with a silver buckle. She had drawn admiring glances from the parking valet who'd opened her door, the maitre d', other diners, and even the attractive young waitress who served them.

"To a masterpiece," Bobby repeated, "worthy of its creator."

Ashleigh smiled. "What a wonderful prelude to a work of art. I'm glad we came out tonight."

"I want this to be very special for you."

"It will be. It already is." She sipped from her champagne and then leaned over to kiss him, darting her tongue into his mouth, withdrawing just as suddenly. "That was just a little something to keep in mind for later," she said.

"I've missed you."

"That's sweet."

"Are you nervous about tomorrow?"

"Some. I want it to be so good, the way I see it in my mind."

"It will be."

"I hope so."

"Don't think about it. Let it happen naturally."

"Yes, of course, that's the way to do it." But how? she wondered. How? She remembered Stein's words in *Lord Jim*. Burke had been so pleased when she'd come to the passage and brought it to him. "This magnificent butterfly finds a little heap of dirt and sits still on it; but man, he will never, on his little heap of mud, keep still. He want to be so, and again he want to be so. . . . He wants to be a saint, and he wants to be a devil—and every time he shuts his eyes he sees himself as a very fine fellow—so fine as he can never be. . . . In a dream." That's how all of us are, Burke told her, so fine as we can never be. "In a dream," Ashleigh whispered.

"What dream?" Bobby asked.

Ashleigh shook her head. "Nothing, I'm sorry. I was thinking of something else."

"Think about this," Bobby said, "I'm going to make you beg for mercy tonight."

Ashleigh smiled and took his hand. "I'll bet you can't."

"What would you like to wager?"

"Make it easy on yourself."

"First one to make a sound gets a spanking."

"Moans and groans don't count."

"The loser has to say, 'I give up.' "

"It's a bet," Ashleigh said. "Shake on it."

They shook hands solemnly.

The waitress approached their table. "Are you ready to order, or would you like a few more minutes?"

"I think we'll enjoy the champagne for a bit," Bobby said.

"Yes, we've just made a bet," Ashleigh said, smiling at the young woman. "The loser gets a spanking."

If Ashleigh's comment surprised or shocked her, the waitress did not allow it to show. "Oh, what fun," she said. "My name's Carol. Just call me when you're ready."

"Jesus Christ, Ashleigh," Bobby said when they were alone again.

"You're blushing, dear."

"My God, why don't you just make an announcement over the public address system?"

"Do you think they have one here?" she asked smiling sweetly. "Should I ask?"

"You're impossible."

"Yes, I am, rather."

"I love you anyway," he said, shaking his head.

"Flattery will not help you win."

When Bobby excused himself to go to the restroom, the waitress came up to the table. "I hope you lose," she said.

"So do I," Ashleigh replied.

Carol grinned as Bobby returned.

They lingered over coffee, drawing out the evening, anticipating what would happen next. Ashleigh told him of reading *Genesis* and *Paradise Lost,* paraphrasing the opening lines of Milton's great epic, "Of woman's first disobedience, and the fruit/Of that forbidden tree whose mortal taste/Brought death into the world, and all our woe/With loss of Eden . . ." Ashleigh paused. "She wanted to be as a god."

"But failed . . ."

"Yes," Ashleigh said. "She failed."

"But you won't. It will be a masterpiece."

"God, how did I get off on all that? It's so serious. I feel like a rapid-cycling manic depressive. Up one moment, down the next." She smiled and squeezed his hand. "Please, take me home now . . ."

"Thank you," Carol said as they left, "and have a good evening."

Bobby saw the envy in the valet's eyes as he handed over the receipt for the car and was proud to be standing with Ashleigh. He leaned close to her, smelling her perfume, and whispered, "He wants to fuck you."

"Everyone wants to fuck me," Ashleigh whispered back, "but tonight you belong to me. After I win our bet, of course."

When Bobby pulled out of the parking lot, Ashleigh said, "Stop at the sporting goods store. I want you to buy a ping pong paddle for me. I don't want to hurt my hand."

"Ha!"

"And drive carefully, darling, I'm not wearing my seatbelt." She leaned over and unzipped his trousers. "The bet starts now."

"Ted Williams hit .406 in 1941," Bobby said, "the same year as Joe DiMaggio's 56-game hitting streak. The last 30-game winner in the major leagues was Denny McLain. He won 31 games in 1968 for the Detroit Tigers . . . oh, shit . . ."

Ashleigh stood docilely in front of the fire as he slowly undressed her, raising her arms when he pulled the top over her head, shaking the hair from her eyes, opening her lips to his kiss, feeling the heat that had smoldered all evening become more intense. She sighed deeply when he freed her breasts and caressed her nipples, teasing them with the palms of his hands. She threw her head back and arched her back for his kisses.

Oh, God, yes, don't stop, not yet, yes, that's it, bite me now, harder, I love it, bite me.

He discarded her belt now and let the skirt fall away from her hips, sinking to his knees.

She parted her legs, swaying as he licked the lips between her legs and found her clitoris. She grabbed his head, entwining her fingers in his hair for balance. Oh, God, that's so good, darling, don't stop. With each caress of his tongue, Ashleigh thought she would faint from the pleasure.

"Oh, Jesus," she cried, dropping to her knees, kissing him frantically as she fumbled with the buttons on his shirt. "I don't care. You win. I want you now. Fuck me, darling, fuck me."

"Say it," Bobby commanded.

"I give up," she cried, "I give up."

Afterward, he leaned back against the couch and took Ashleigh in his arms. She snuggled in his embrace, her hand caressing the hairs on his chest as she watched the flames create random shadows across their naked flesh. "You made me forget my manners," she murmured happily. "I didn't offer you a drink."

"I didn't notice."

"Would you like one now? I have some cognac."

"If you have one . . ."

"We'll share," Ashleigh said, "like the lovers I'm going to put on you tomorrow." She rose and walked into the kitchen.

Satiated, Bobby closed his eyes, feeling the warmth of the fire, waiting. When Ashleigh returned, she knelt and offered him the snifter, holding it to his lips. Then she drank, looking at him over the rim of the glass.

"I love you," he said.

"I always pay my debts." She took another sip of the cognac. "How do you want me?"

"Just like this. It was a dumb bet anyway."

"No, I lost. If I had won, I wouldn't let you off."

"Christ, you're serious, aren't you?"

"Very," Ashleigh said. "Tomorrow, I'm going to hurt you. Tonight is your only chance to hurt me."

"Ashleigh, it was just a game."

"Not anymore."

They stared at each other. Ashleigh recognized the cruelty in his eyes and knew he wanted to inflict the pain. He was getting hard again just thinking about it. *Do it, baby, I want it, too.* She clenched her cheeks, anticipating, remembering, growing wet again.

"All right," he said finally, "get the paddle."

Ashleigh smiled, knowing she had won again. "Yes, darling." She went to the mantel. When she turned, he was sitting on the couch.

"Kneel before me."

She knelt and offered the paddle, pleased that he recognized the importance of ritual.

He took it and placed it across his knees. "Sit back on your heels, hands behind your head, and tell me why you're being punished."

Ashleigh followed his instructions immediately. "I'm being punished because I lost a bet."

"Stay like that until I finish my drink. Keep your eyes on the paddle."

"Yes, darling."

He made her wait a long time before offering her the snifter. "When you finish this, I'm going to spank you. You may take as long as you like."

Looking boldly into his eyes, issuing the challenge, Ashleigh finished the cognac in one swallow.

"Across my lap."

Oh, what a big hard-on I'm giving you, Ashleigh thought, as she arranged herself over his lap, squeezing her legs together, pressing her breasts against the rough fabric of the cushion. She was trembling with excitement and anticipation. I'm going to be spanked, she thought, just like when I was a girl.

"Give me your hands."

She crossed her wrists behind her back. His grip was firm. Her buttocks tingled as he caressed her. She tensed as he raised the paddle. You won't make me cry, she thought.

He struck her lightly.

She twisted and moaned, crying out, "Harder. Hurt me. I want you to hurt me. I'm bad. So bad."

Again, he raised the paddle and delivered a stinging slap.

"Ah, yes, just like that."

The paddle rose and fell.

"Ah, Christ, I'll be good, daddy, I'll be good. I promise."

She struggled, writhing across his lap, feeling his cock hard against her belly, but he did not release her.

Again and again, he struck.

She rubbed against the cushion, squirming and gasping with each blow. "Ah. Ah. Ah!"

Yes, I love it, yes. Hurt me. Make me cry.

"I'm getting so hot, yes, oh, Christ, yes, ah yes, ah yes, I give up again, fuck me, just fuck me now."

They slept late. When Ashleigh awakened, she touched his back lightly, envisioning the art as it would grow, finally covering his entire back.

She slipped quietly from the bed and went into the bathroom, turning to look at her buttocks in the mirror. The redness had disappeared during the night, but tingling memories remained and Ashleigh knew she had taken another sensuous step forward. She had liked the mild punishment administered, wondered at her enjoyment of pain, but accepted it, thinking she would have to discuss it with Danny. Bobby had liked it, too, but he would not—perhaps could not—admit it. Burke knew himself to have sexual tastes not readily accepted by society, but cared nothing for what others thought. Once more, Ashleigh felt the tinge of envy at the relationship Burke had found with his Danny.

Yes, Ashleigh decided, as she stood in the kitchen waiting impatiently for the coffee to brew, I will definitely have to discuss this with Danny. She will understand even if Bobby doesn't. Perhaps Bobby has too far to travel. Perhaps he is too different from me. He was willing to stop, even though it was his casual remark that started it. But once we began, I could never turn back, not until I had looked into the abyss. Like Oedipus, Hamlet, Lord Jim, Kurtz, Stephen Dedalus, I cannot stop until I know the truth about myself—even if it destroys me.

It began earlier than last night, with Danny asking if I had ever been whipped and reawakening old memories. In fact, Ashleigh marveled, it began when one or the other of her parents spanked her as a little girl and culminated with Mary Margaret and the sexuality it had aroused. And later still, when she was sent to fetch the razor strap as her father sought to break her spirit, save her soul for Jesus Christ Our Savior.

The moment when I lay across Bobby's lap began when I was a child, an inexorable succession of events shrouded in the multitudes of life, leading inexorably to that point in time last night while I waited for him to begin. Oh, Bobby, you should have savored the moment more, as I did.

I wonder what's next?

Bobby was leaning against the headboard when Ashleigh returned to the bedroom with coffee for both of them.

"You didn't say goodbye," Bobby said.

"I never say goodbye," Ashleigh said, sitting on the bed next to him.

"God, you're lovely." He reached out and touched the spider.

Ashleigh smiled. "Don't you ever get enough?"

"Of you? Never."

While the bathtub filled, Ashleigh showered carefully, cleansing her body in preparation for the solemn moment when she would begin her work. And then, still naked, she led Bobby to the tub, the goddess preparing her victim for the sacrifice.

Ashleigh washed and rinsed Bobby lovingly, putting her finger to his lips once when he started to speak, wanting him to recognize the solemnity of the occasion as well. After that, he only sighed as she washed his penis and scrotum gently. She rinsed his back before spreading the cream over him and taking up the razor. She shaved him carefully and then helped him to stand and, while the tub drained, used the shower massage to rinse his body once more. Then, she shampooed and washed his hair.

She dried him with a large bath towel, but did not touch his back, allowing it to dry naturally in the air while she blow-dried his hair. Finally, she cleansed his back once more with the cold, stinging alcohol.

The familiar rites were complete.

Bobby was stretched out full length on a reed mat on the floor of Ashleigh's home studio. His face rested on folded arms. Warm sunlight flowed through the window, providing excellent light.

Now, as she straddled his naked body, she turned the machine on. " 'And the serpent said unto the woman, Ye shall not surely die.' " Ashleigh whispered the words from Genesis as though asking for a blessing upon the work she was about to begin. The buzz of the machine drowned her words. " 'For God doth know that in the day ye eat thereof, then your eyes shall be opened, and ye shall be as gods, knowing good and evil.' "

She lowered the machine and made the first bold cut.

"Christ," Bobby said. He closed his eyes and clenched his fists, but endured. Ashleigh had warned him the pain would be most intense while she worked near his spine.

The archangel Raphael would be the centerpiece, but not so dominant as on the tarot card that had inspired Ashleigh's creation. The Lovers would be the commanding figures in the landscape of the Garden of Eden. Still, everything flowed from the archangel. Ashleigh had to begin with him.

Ashleigh worked quickly, confidently, feeling the elation as the archangel took form in Bobby's flesh. She stopped frequently to change needles. "Are you okay?" she asked in the sudden silence when she turned the machine off.

"It hurts like hell," Bobby said, "but I can stand it."

"Just another hour, and then we'll stop for the day. Can you stand another hour?"

"I could stand it a lot better if you got naked with me. You could whack off on my butt."

Ashleigh smiled, remembering Simone's wild orgasm midway through her tattoo. "Not while I'm working," she said, turning the machine on again.

"Oh, God, I love you," he cried, as the needle descended.

Ashleigh frowned in concentration.

After two hours Bobby sat up while Ashleigh applied the healing ointment and bandaged his back. "Better now?" she asked.

"It's like hitting your thumb with a hammer. It feels so good when you stop."

"It's been a very good start. I'm pleased. Thank you."

He turned to face her. "I'd do anything for you, Ashleigh."

"I know." She reached out and stroked his cheek gently. "In return, I'll try to do whatever you like."

"Take your blouse off for me. I like it when you're topless. It reminds me of our first night together."

"Yes, darling, I will."

They became like hermits for the weekend, straying from the house only once to stock up on food and rent videos to watch during the evenings. When they returned in mid-afternoon, Bobby stripped off the loose-fitting sweatshirt and leaned forward while Ashleigh removed the bandage and moistened the tattoo again with the soothing ointment. She did not bandage it again. "I want it to get as much air as possible," she explained. "It will heal better."

Bobby smiled as Ashleigh tugged her blouse from the jeans and removed it for him. Then, they went into the kitchen, and while Ashleigh put the groceries away, Bobby opened a bottle of wine.

"I love you," Bobby said.

Ashleigh turned and smiled. "I love you, too," she said, wondering if it was true.

Ashleigh lay on the couch, her head in his lap, alternately reading and dozing off while Bobby watched the early news on television.

Bobby looked down at the woman he loved, intoxicated by her presence, but troubled at her ability to control and dominate him, wishing that he could take back the careless bet, that it had not happened. She had provoked him into spanking her and he was still shocked to find how much he wanted to hurt her, making her scream with the last vicious blow. Her agonized cry had been real, unfeigned. How could you love someone and want to hurt her? He had thrown the paddle across the room, into the fire, horrified at what he had done. Then they were on each other like animals, clawing at each other, fucking. Dear Jesus, what is she doing to me?

She murmured softly when he stroked the swell of her belly. Christ, Ashleigh, who are you? What are you?

They took their wine into the secluded garden behind the house to barbecue steaks. They sat on a picnic bench, holding hands, waiting for the gas grill to heat. The garden was quiet, cool in lengthening shadows.

"Do you regret last night?" Bobby asked.

"I regret nothing," Ashleigh said, squeezing his hand and smiling.

Their lovemaking was gentle and prolonged, growing urgent and frenzied only as they neared climax.

When Bobby cried out in the night, Ashleigh was instantly awake. "What's wrong, darling?" she asked. "Bad dreams?"

"I turned over on my back. Christ, it hurt."

In the darkness, Ashleigh cared for Bobby and the emerging tattoo meticulously, cleansing it gently with a warm washcloth, applying fresh ointment. She knew every pore and ridge, every nuance, of his back now.

"There," Ashleigh said. "Is it better now?"

"Yes." Bobby sighed as she lay down beside him, her cool

fingers stroking his neck and shoulders. "I love you, Ashleigh."

"Go to sleep, darling," she whispered. "I'll take care of you."

They slept late again on Sunday morning. Ashleigh was growing accustomed to his presence in her bed, liking the comforting feel of his hand on her breast before she fell asleep. Jonathan Carver no longer haunted her dreams.

When they finally rose, Ashleigh made coffee and breakfast. Bobby did the dishes. And then he stripped and together they went to the studio, where Ashleigh worked for two hours on his back. She would have liked to work longer, but while her needle continued to hover around the spine, the cumulative impact of the pain was too intense for Bobby, although he did not complain. Still, he sighed with relief when she turned the machine off and administered the soothing balm.

Ashleigh made him take two Advil and some vitamins— zinc and B-complex—believing that they helped the body heal faster during complicated and intricate work.

"I wish it were done," Bobby said. "Not because it hurts, but because I want to be able to see it. All of it."

"It's going to be wonderful, Bobby. The very best."

Chapter Nine

When the telephone rang, Ashleigh was in the back room of the studio with Kim Lee, a shy, beautiful Asian woman with lustrous jet-black hair that fell to the small of her back. The young woman—Ashleigh thought she was perhaps twenty-four—stood naked on a reed mat, turning back and forth as Ashleigh examined her body, making notes, a quick pencil sketch, frowning as she struggled with an elusive concept.

Kim and her husband had entered the shop two days ago, asked for Ashleigh by name, and requested an oriental-style tattoo, a half body suit that would begin at Kim's ankle and curve up her leg, encompassing the entire right half of her body, both front and back. Kim's husband, Jimmy, insisted that Ashleigh do the tattoo in the traditional freehand manner and chose the most suitable design herself.

Ashleigh had protested, saying that she was not a specialist in the oriental style and asked if they would not prefer a male, a traditional master.

"While we wish to follow the traditions," Jimmy Lee replied, "we are also Americans, and Kim prefers a woman artist, as do I. You were highly recommended."

"By whom?"

"My financial adviser, Ms. Danielle Petersen." He smiled at the surprise on Ashleigh's face. "You see, I am not at all chauvinistic."

Ashleigh turned to Kim. "And why do you want a tattoo?"

"It will make me more beautiful for my husband. I wish to please him. And myself."

When Ashleigh said that such an artistic work would be time-consuming and expensive—$300 an hour—he gave her a check for $3,000 and made an appointment for Kim every Wednesday morning for as long as it would take.

Now, thinking it was Bobby calling, Ashleigh told Kim, "I'll just be a moment," and answered the portable phone she always kept in the back room.

"Hello, Ashleigh, this is Guy Benjamin."

Taken by surprise, Ashleigh did not answer.

"The police detective," Benjamin prompted. "I came to see you when—"

"I know who you are," Ashleigh said. "I was expecting someone else to call. I hear you want to be my friend."

"You've talked to Burke, then?"

"Yes. I tell him everything. He tells me everything. He is my friend and master."

"Yes, I want to be your friend, too. Will you have lunch with me?"

"When?"

"Today."

"All right."

"I'll pick you up at twelve, if that's okay."

"See you then." Ashleigh replaced the antenna.

"You have a master?" Kim said. She stood facing Ashleigh, modestly shielding her small breasts with crossed arms.

Ashleigh smiled. "I was his apprentice. He taught me my art."

"Jimmy likes to think he is my master. I act subservient, but I'm really the one in control. Men are so foolish."

"Let me see your breasts now," Ashleigh said. "Raise your arms above your head, please."

Kim slowly raised her arms and did not shrink away when Ashleigh reached out and touched her.

"I'll start here," Ashleigh said, "but I won't touch the nipple, and then we'll move around your side and go up to your shoulder."

"But won't that hurt so much, to begin on my breast?"

"Surprisingly enough, it will hurt less than if I began with your ankle or your rib cage. The needle hurts less on the fleshy parts of the body than near bones. I know because I have a tattoo on my breast. It hurt very much on the nipple, but for the rest it was nothing. The bracelets on my ankles were much worse."

"I trust you," Kim said. "Will you begin today?"

Ashleigh laughed. "No, we'll begin next week. First, I have to design your tattoo. I'd like to take some Polaroids of you. Do you mind? I'll need them for reference as I work. I'll give them to you when we're done."

"I'll do whatever you say."

Ashleigh enjoyed photographing Kim, asking her to turn, lift her right arm, extend her leg. "You're very beautiful," Ashleigh said, showing her the photographs.

Kim smiled shyly as she looked at herself. "You will make me more beautiful."

"Yes," Ashleigh said, snapping another picture. "I will."

When Benjamin arrived promptly at noon, Ashleigh was ready, hiding the nervousness she felt. A life on the streets, however brief, had created a natural distrust of police in her.

"Hello, Ashleigh." He was dressed informally, wearing gray slacks, a blue pullover, a gray herringbone jacket, and cordovan loafers. "I'm off duty," he explained.

"I feel better already," Ashleigh said.

"You have nothing to fear from me," he said smiling.

"That's good," Ashleigh said. "Have you met my friend and partner? Dean, this is Detective Benjamin."

"Please, call me Guy." He shook hands with Dean.

"Enchanté," Dean said. "Have a nice lunch."

At Ashleigh's suggestion, they went to the bar and grill where Cynthia worked. Cynthia motioned them to a booth near the back and came from behind the bar. Ashleigh and Cynthia exchanged greetings, kissing chastely, as old friends.

"What can I get you?" Cynthia asked, when they were seated.

"Iced tea, please," Ashleigh said.

"Make it two."

"I'll be right back. We have a grilled chicken Caesar salad as our special today."

"You come here often?" Benjamin asked, when Cynthia had left. "This is your regular place?"

Ashleigh nodded. "Cynthia and I are lovers occasionally. When we're lonely."

"You see," Benjamin said with a smile, refusing to be shocked. "We have something in common, although I can't imagine you ever being lonely."

"Oh, I am. Quite often."

"What about Burke? I could tell he loves you."

"And I love him. I always have, but I don't want to hurt him, destroy him. That's why we're not together, and now he's met someone new. I'm happy for him, for them."

"Are you lonely now?"

"Not at the moment."

"Another canvas?"

"Yes."

They were interrupted by Cynthia returning with tall glasses of iced tea and sliced lemons on a saucer. "Have you decided, or would you like to wait awhile?"

She nodded. "I'll have the special."

"The same."

"Two specials it is."

Benjamin squeezed lemon into his tea, shielding it with the palm of one hand. "I saw the spider," he said.

"Did it turn you on?"

"The spider did, not the breast."

"That's how I met Cynthia. I tattooed some Celtic runes on her belly. Her belly turned me on. You should be open to all experiences."

"Oh, I am," Benjamin said. "It's just that I've already had

that particular experience. I was married for ten years. I have two children. They're grown now."

"And do they accept your sexual preference?"

"Now they do. For a long time they didn't. It was hardest on Jenny, my former wife, but when I met Elliott I couldn't go on pretending anymore. She's remarried now."

"Are you friends?"

"I've only seen her once in the last ten years. She was going to remarry and she wanted me to meet him. She wanted to know if her new boyfriend was hiding in the closet. She wanted me to tell her she wasn't making the same mistake twice."

"And was she?"

He shook his head. "The kids tell me she's quite happy now." He paused. "Tell me about yourself."

"You know everything there is. I was a whore and now I'm an artist."

He shook his head gently, almost sadly. Ashleigh thought he looked a little like Burke in that moment, sensitive and mildly disappointed. "There's more," he said. "Where did you grow up, go to school, who are your parents, do you have brothers or sisters? Who are you, Ashleigh Thomas?"

"I have no family. My parents are dead. My life began when Burke took me off the streets. If you want to be my friend, don't ask me about my past. I have no past."

"All right, then. Why Burke? He's an interesting man."

Why Burke, indeed? Ashleigh wondered. Because he was there, looking out at her with his kind and melancholy eyes, surrounded by all of those vivid colors and intriguing flashes? Because I was destined to meet Burke? Because he helped me to become a woman? Because he gave only of himself, asking nothing in return, allowing me to learn on my own? Because he paid for my art and literature courses at UCLA? Because when he made love to me that first time, he tenderly led me from the bottom circle of hell, where Frank had left me, taking me through purgatory and into paradise?

Ashleigh stared across the table at Benjamin. He's looking into my soul again, she thought, as he calmly met her gaze, waiting patiently for her response. He frightens me. He sees too much of me. What do I tell him?

"Why me?" she asked.

"You remind me of someone."

"Who?"

"Years ago, right out of the academy, I used to work undercover. The vice squad. Mostly, we hung around public restrooms waiting to be propositioned by gays. We weren't quite so enlightened and called them sissies, faggots, punks . . ."

Ashleigh saw his eyes grow hard at the memory. That's what I look like when I allow myself to remember.

". . . I'm not proud of what I did then and I had one chance for redemption. There was this girl, a runaway—like you must have been—very pretty, very innocent, maybe sixteen or seventeen years old, but looked older . . . I rolled up to her corner, asked how much . . . she didn't know anything, told me right off, and I arrested her . . . she started crying and begged me to let her go . . . offered to blow me, let me fuck her . . . promised me she'd go home, but—"

"Did you let her go?" Ashleigh asked, already knowing the answer.

He shook his head sadly. "I wasn't alone, you see, and I wanted to scare her enough to get her off the streets for good . . . the others said I should have gone for the blow job . . . I truly wanted her to go home . . . but she got caught up in one of those morality sweeps, just like you did, and she got thirty days. She had an ID card that said she was eighteen, so she didn't even go to youth authority. I sent her to finishing school."

"It wasn't your fault," Ashleigh said, "she had choices, just as I did."

If Benjamin heard her words, he gave no indication. "Thirty days later, she was back on that same corner. When I tried to get her to go home, she told me to fuck off. Told me what had happened to her with . . . with the dykes. Six months later she was dead, beaten to death in an alley. Marilee Sinclair was her name. At least, that's what she said it was. Her murder was never solved. No one cared."

"Except you."

"Except me."

He motioned to Cynthia. When she came to the table, Benjamin said, "I've changed my mind. I'd like a glass of chardonnay, please."

"How about you, Ashleigh?"

"I'll stick with the tea. I have to work this afternoon."

They remained silent until Cynthia brought the wine and left again.

"How did you survive, Ashleigh?"

"I fought. I traded jailhouse tattoos for protection. Your Marilee could have done the same."

"She wasn't strong, like you."

"Then she shouldn't have been on the streets. It wasn't your fault, Guy."

"That's the first time you've called me Guy. Does that mean we're friends?"

"I suppose it does, but . . ."

"You're still unsure."

"Yes."

"I won't hurt you."

"I believe you."

There were others in the bar, laughing, ordering beer and hamburgers, while the sound system played soft rock—Cynthia's preference at a midweek lunch hour—but Ashleigh and Guy heard none of it.

"How did you become a cop?" Ashleigh asked. "Why?"

"I was still trying to prove my manhood, show that I could be as macho as anyone. Then, I found I was very good at what I was doing and I liked it. So I just kept doing it, even after I left Jenny. Then, I met Elliott and fell in love, truly in love, for the first time, the only time, really."

"You're fortunate. Many people never fall in love."

"Have you been in love, Ashleigh, truly in love?"

"Twice. Burke, of course, and . . ."

She told him about Chance and Heather.

"I'm sorry."

Ashleigh shrugged, providing her standard answer that it didn't matter, but it did. It would always matter.

"He must have been a fool to trade you for her. She's . . . she's nothing compared to you."

"Thank you."

"I knew that you were a very special person the first time I walked into your studio. There are some people who make powerful impressions. Even if you encounter them only once, you never forget them. For me, you're like that, a powerful and compelling woman."

"Are you bisexual? Do you want to fuck me?"

"I'm quite happy with Elliott," he said, "and faithful."

"I just wondered," Ashleigh said. "I like to know where I stand."

"You shouldn't be crude. It doesn't become you."

"I was a whore."

"Did you like being a whore?"

"No. I did what I had to do. I survived."

Guy nodded. "But you're not a whore anymore. You're a beautiful and desirable woman."

Ashleigh waited.

"And you are an artist."

Benjamin watched her walk to the shop, her hips swaying softly beneath the jeans, reminding him of another time when, unsure of his sexuality, he'd forced himself to be aroused, pretending that his wife's slender body was that of a boy. He could not do that with Ashleigh. At the entrance to the studio, she turned and smiled, waved, and was gone from sight.

Why did I lie to her? There was no Marilee. No, that wasn't true. There were a thousand Marilees. Some survived. Some didn't. Perhaps Elliott is right: I'm growing obsessed with Ashleigh. He got in his car and drove aimlessly for an hour before turning for home to read and await the comforting presence of Elliott.

*　　*　　*

The conversation with Benjamin troubled Ashleigh all through an afternoon that seemed to drag on forever. He had allayed her fears, her suspicions, but it was disconcerting to realize how much he knew about her. It was like walking down the street and having a man undress her with his eyes, except that Guy Benjamin looked into the very deepest recesses of her mind and soul and told her she wasn't a whore anymore.

Ashleigh wanted desperately to believe him.

She was struggling to concentrate on the sketches for Kim's body work when the punkers entered the studio, giggling loudly.

His hair was blue. The two girls with him had dyed their hair a bright florescent orange. Both had shaved the sides of their heads.

Ashleigh looked up and immediately named them Blue, Orange Number One, and Orange Number Two. It's like walking Technicolor, she thought.

All of them had tattoos. He wore earrings and a ring in his nose. Both girls wore rings in pierced nostrils.

Dean went to greet them. "May I help you?" he said pleasantly.

Blue pointed to Orange Number Two. "She wants a tat," he said. "Right there." He pointed to her shaved head.

"Yeah, a cat," the girl said, giggling.

"We have a number of lovely little pussycats," Dean said. "Let me show you into our cat house over here." He ushered them to the waiting area and a notebook filled with kittens, domestic cats, lions, tigers, panthers. "You just pick out a lovely little pussy and I'll fix you right up."

Blue was staring at Ashleigh. "No, we want her to do it."

"Ashleigh, dear," Dean drawled, rolling his eyes at her, "you have clients."

"Pick out what you'd like and call me," Ashleigh said.

The three punkers giggled and laughed among themselves for ten minutes. Then, Blue said, "We got one."

"I'll be right there," Ashleigh said. She took her time putting Kim's sketches in order. Sighing, she opened the counter and walked over to them.

Orange Number Two pointed to a black cat surrounded by a bold tribal pattern.

"Yeah, that one," Blue said, "but $200 is too much. We'll give you $150."

"It says $200."

"And I say $150," Blue sneered.

"Never haggle with your artist," Ashleigh said, "it's very poor form."

"I want it," Orange Number Two said, pouting.

"Yeah, don't be so cheap," Orange Number One said. "It's our money, too."

Ashleigh glanced over at Dean. He was sitting behind his desk, one hand resting in the middle drawer, where he kept a handgun. "Gays with guns are never bashed," he always said. He smiled at Ashleigh.

"All right," Blue said, "but I want a bonus." He reached out and touched Ashleigh's breast, pressing his hand against her. "Awesome," he said dreamily.

Ashleigh grabbed the ring in his nose, twisting it. "Hey," he cried, "I just wanted to see if it was real."

"It's real, asshole." She twisted the ring harder.

"Ow, shit, yeah, I can see that. Let me go."

"Need any help, Ashleigh, dear?" Dean asked. He was standing at the counter with the pearl-handled .38-caliber revolver, holding it pointed casually at the ceiling.

Ashleigh smiled sweetly. "No, thank you," she said, giving the ring another vicious yank.

"Ow. God damn it, that hurts."

"Get out of my fucking place, asshole." The punker scuttled along behind her, whining and crying, as she led him to the door and pulled him through it. When she released the ring, she gave him a hard shove in the face. He plopped heavily on the sidewalk and held his nose with both hands. Ashleigh could see tears in his eyes. "Next time, I'll rip it out."

She turned and held the door open for the girls.

Orange Number One scurried past her.

"Hey," Orange Number Two cried, "I just wanted another tat."

"Come back sometime when you're clean, sober, and alone," Ashleigh said locking the door behind them. She turned to Dean. "Well, that was kind of fun," she laughed, "like old times."

Dean shook his head and lowered the revolver. "I just love it when you're butch."

Bobby met her at the door, showering her with kisses while saying, "How was your day, dear? Would you like a drink? I made my famous tuna casserole for dinner. I hope you like it. Let me take your briefcase. You just sit down and relax. I'll get everything."

Ashleigh laughed and pushed him away. "What brought this on?"

"Why, I'm just the faithful househusband greeting his mate after a hard day at the office. Isn't that what people do?"

"That's what people do. But we're not people. And besides, you're not my househusband."

"We should talk about that . . ."

"No," Ashleigh said more sharply than she intended. "Not yet. It's too soon."

"But later?" Bobby asked. "We can talk about it later?"

"Yes," Ashleigh said. She stroked his cheek. "We can talk about it later. Now, you said something about a drink . . ."

Bobby sat with her on the couch as she worked on sketches for Kim Lee. He leafed through the photographs. "God, she's erotic. I love her hair."

"You shouldn't be looking at those. I kind of promised I would keep them private."

"Kind of?"

Ashleigh shrugged. "She's very shy. I feel like I should protect her."

"But you're going to put an enormous tattoo on her body,

like me. It should be seen. If a work of art is not seen, does it exist?"

"What is the sound of one hand clapping?"

"If a tree falls in the forest and no one is there to hear, does it make a sound?"

"This is getting too metaphysical," Ashleigh said, laughing, "and what's all this stuff about finding Kim Lee erotic?"

"You shouldn't bring work home, then."

"Next time, I won't." She pushed her sketchbook away and turned to him. "I better remind you of something," Ashleigh said as she lay back and drew him down on top of her. As they kissed, Ashleigh kept telling herself, I am not a whore. I am not a whore.

But later, as she knelt before Bobby, hands crossed behind her back as though wearing Burke's handcuffs, licking his balls and cock, she thought: but I act like a whore, and I don't care.

Perhaps Danny is doing the same thing for Burke right now, and she's not a whore. She would wear his handcuffs proudly and strive to please him only with her mouth, working slowly, enjoying the sounds of pleasure she gives him, just as I'm doing. It's harder this way. By taking away my hands, using only my mouth and tongue, it takes longer, drives him crazy, and I can't brush my hair away and it falls around us and it's so warm and nice, like sucking his cock in a hot little cocoon.

"Ah, Christ," Bobby cried.

Ashleigh teased him, taking only the round gorged tip in her mouth, tantalized him with her tongue, let him go to rub her soft cheek against him, feeling his heat mingle with her own.

"Oh, baby. It's so good."

She opened her mouth again, taking more this time, thinking, Don't be impatient, darling.

"Oh, Christ, I can't stand it." He grabbed her hair, tangling his fingers, and began fucking her mouth slowly and gently at first and then with greater force, harder.

He can't help it, Ashleigh thought, acquiescing, tightening her lips around him, allowing him to go deeper and deeper,

joining his frantic rhythm, stopping him only before the point
that made her gag.

When he exploded, he cried out again, and released her to
beat his fists against the couch as Ashleigh swallowed, restrain-
ing the urge to grab his balls, to milk him dry of the hot fluid.
After the first hot wonderful spurt that nearly choked her,
Ashleigh swallowed easily, sucking, wanting more, until he
was limp and shriveling in her mouth.

Only then did Ashleigh release herself and slump against
him, resting her face on his thigh, thinking, I'm such a good
little whore.

Chapter Ten

The colors—red and purple and gold—on his upper back were vivid, brilliant, and thick, like a Van Gogh painting. During the respites from her needle—insisted upon by Ashleigh—he held a hand mirror before the larger mirror in the master bathroom to better admire the mural on his back. He no longer thought of it as a tattoo. It was a painting now, and he wanted it complete. He was impatient to display her art to the world.

Bobby was as possessed by the painting as Ashleigh, insisting, even demanding, that she work on past the allotted two hours, sacrificing his back to her needle, enduring the pain and discomfort for as long as possible and then going to bed, sleeping uneasily for a day or two as his flesh healed.

Ashleigh worried as she cared for him, spreading the soothing ointment over the newest areas of the tattoo, keeping it exposed to the air as much as possible. She feared he was pushing himself—and her—to the edge.

The tattoo aroused both of them and they could not keep their hands off each other. Sometimes he began it; at other times, it was Ashleigh. When she was in the kitchen cooking, he stayed with her, watching as she worked, and when he could stand it no longer, he came up behind her to lift and caress her breasts until she turned to kiss him eagerly, even frantically. Or when he poured a glass of wine, she fondled him until he groaned and fumbled with his belt to be shed of clothing.

And slowly the work progressed.

* * *

Burke called her at the studio and invited her to dinner on Saturday. "It's a surprise for Danny," he said. "I hope you're free."

"I can be," Ashleigh replied. "What's the occasion?"

"You'll see."

"You're being very mysterious."

"It's more fun that way." He gave her directions to Danny's home. "Come about four," he said.

Ashleigh replaced the telephone and wondered if the special occasion was for Danny to receive Burke's initials. She had been expecting the call ever since Danny had thanked her for the present and to say that Burke had agreed to Ashleigh's presence. But if that were the case, why didn't Danny call herself? It would be part of the ritual, the victim inviting a witness to her sacrificial ordeal. It must be something else, then. Ashleigh decided to let herself be surprised. Burke was right: it would be more fun that way.

Finally, they argued.

Ashleigh refused to continue working. "No, God damn it," she cried, "you're rushing me. I will *not* be rushed."

"Just another hour," he pleaded. "I can stand it."

"I can't. I want time to sit back and reflect."

"But it has to be done in time for the convention."

"It'll be done. If it's not, there's always another convention." Ashleigh didn't believe that even as she spoke the words. The tattoo would be finished in plenty of time, but it would be finished right.

"It's my fucking back."

"It's my fucking work," Ashleigh cried angrily.

Ashleigh's mind overflowed with ideas for her two canvases, Bobby and Kim Lee. There were moments at work when she was so excited that she paced furiously, wishing for their presence.

Dean smiled and said, "I'm glad I'm not burdened with being an artist as well."

"It's hell sometimes, but I love it."

"Why don't you go shopping or something? Shopping always calms me down."

Burke had been so reticent that Ashleigh didn't know what to wear on Saturday. "Do you mind? I've been gone a lot lately."

"Your happiness is my happiness, sweetie."

Smiling, Ashleigh said, "I think I will treat myself then, and take the rest of the afternoon off."

Ashleigh crossed the border from tattoos to respectability simply by walking from the studio into Beverly Hills.

She enjoyed the afternoon, going from one shop to another, mixing easily with the matronly women whose husbands were doctors, corporate lawyers, television producers, and film directors, their daughters born to privilege and wealth. Dressed modestly, conservatively, Ashleigh's tattoos were hidden by clothing and hair. Only the bracelets on her ankles were visible, but the clerk who helped her try on pumps made no reference to them. Ashleigh thought the young woman was probably used to dealing with the eccentricities of wealthy customers. Ashleigh chose the black pumps with higher heels than she normally wore, feeling as she looked into the full-length mirror that they accentuated her long and slender legs.

The clerk smiled and agreed.

Unable to decide between them—and truly wanting them all—Ashleigh purchased three outfits. The first was a sleeveless tunic and short skirt ensemble in a yellow that would complement her golden hair. It was sleeveless, with a V-neck button front, and she thought it was quietly elegant. The second was a slip dress in black with lingerie straps. The bodice was fitted with princess seams and the flared skirt ended at mid-thigh. The third was a flowing summer dress that fell to her ankles. The floral print was long-sleeved and buttoned in front, but there was a lace-up tie for shaping the back.

At home, she spread everything out on the bed and tried them all on again, deciding that her favorite was the yellow combination. That is what I will wear on Saturday, she thought, delighted with her selections.

Expecting another argument with Bobby, Ashleigh waited until she was through working for the day before telling him she would be having dinner with Burke, but he actually seemed relieved, wanting a break from the growing tension between them as much as she did.

"See you on Sunday, though?"

"Yes," she replied.

Kim Lee arrived exactly on time for her first appointment wearing a baggy USC sweatshirt and jeans. She smiled shyly as she said, "Good morning."

"Hi, Kim, come on back. I've got everything ready for you. Are you nervous?"

"A little."

"That's natural. Everyone is nervous about their first tattoo."

Ashleigh showed her the sketches, a kaleidoscope alternating between swirling patterns, darkly shaded areas, and various figures—sea serpents, stylized dragons, a hooded cobra, a naked woman. "I think everything should be done in black and gray. Do you approve?"

"Oh, yes," Kim said breathlessly, turning over one sketch after another. "Are you ready to begin? Shall I undress?"

"Only if you truly want it and like it. I know what you and your husband said, that the tattoo must be chosen by the artist, but I want you, and only you, to approve."

"I do," Kim said, "I must have it." She drew the sweatshirt over her head. Again, she smiled shyly as she covered her breasts with crossed arms.

"Lie on your side," Ashleigh said.

Kim complied immediately. Ashleigh sat beside her, gently

lifting Kim's arm away from her breast. The young woman closed her eyes. Ashleigh turned on the machine and cradled Kim's breast in her hand, holding it ready for the needle. "I'm going to begin now."

"I am ready."

The only sound Kim made during the session was to sigh heavily in the sudden silence when the machine was finally turned off and Ashleigh sprayed the fresh wounds with the cold alcohol and applied the ointment.

Eve troubled her. Through all the reading and the multitude of sketches in preparation for the seventh tattoo, Ashleigh wavered on whether to portray her as a penitent or as defiantly rebellious, glad that she had released knowledge into the world despite the loss of paradise. Had the serpent seduced her by whispering those hypnotic words, "Better to reign in hell than serve in heav'n"?

That Eve was the stronger of those first lovers there was no doubt, just as Ashleigh was stronger than Bobby or any of the others. All she had to do was twitch her ass and men followed that silent siren call—except for Burke. Only Burke had the inner strength to resist her natural allure, taking her only when there was mutual need and desire. Unwilling to simply fuck her, Burke commanded her respect and earned her love. It's too bad, she thought, that I couldn't give him more of myself. It could have been so good for both of us. But I am just like my Eve, seduced by knowledge. Perhaps, someday, when the time is right, Danny will share Burke with me. I hope so.

She had never been to a zoo. Bobby didn't believe her. "Every kid's been to the zoo," he said.

"I haven't," Ashleigh replied, wondering what other childhood experiences she had missed growing up in a strict fundamentalist household dominated by prayer and the fear of punishment and eternal damnation for the slightest transgression against God's will as interpreted by her father and their minister. She was warned. God punishes those who sin. Dancing is evil. Fornication is evil. The pleasures of life are evil. But she had sinned, many times, in many ways now, and nothing happened except the discovery that the forbidden fornication gave her physical delights that she was unwilling to forgo. And God had not struck her down.

The animals greeted her. There was a kinship, a mystical bond, between them. A maned lion sleeping in the sun awakened and growled softly for her. An elephant trumpeted, lifting its trunk in salute. The giraffe and the zebra stared at her with placid eyes, contemplating her alone among those who thronged the pathways of the zoo. She imagined riding the zebra across some distant African plain, faster and faster, even catching and surpassing the wind, a pale-skinned goddess in her mysterious domain.

Ashleigh laughed and clapped her hands with delight. "This is wonderful," she cried, rushing to the next enclosure, wanting to free them all from their captivity and thinking, if it weren't for Kim, I would have never come here. When the cobra appeared in the initial sketches for Kim's tattoo, Ashleigh remembered the cobra that Burke had put between a woman's breasts so long ago. But the memory was not enough and she realized that she needed to see the cobra for herself, to be able to breathe life into Eve's tempter.

Ashleigh berated herself for not thinking of it sooner. She should have come to the zoo, to the snakehouse, as soon as she had decided upon the Lovers as the seventh tattoo to look upon Satan in his guise as serpent. Thank God, it wasn't too late.

It was forbidden to tap on the thick glass, to disturb and agitate the snakes. There was no need. As Ashleigh stood before each enclosure, the dormant forms came to life, just as they would in her art, slithering to her, tongues darting. The big diamondback rattlesnake coiled for her and buzzed, not in anger or fear, but in a solemn salutation. The black mamba, cold and deadly, followed along the edge of the glass as she moved on to the next.

And then, standing before the king cobra, Ashleigh

watched as it slowly and rhythmically rose from its coils to stand at eye level with her, hood spread majestically to seduce her once again.

Mesmerized, Ashleigh swayed and the cobra followed her movements. They danced hypnotically, as lovers on a crowded dance floor, touching only with their eyes. They *were* lovers for this moment in time. They had always been lovers.

The Lovers.

Ashleigh knew then, as never before, how to portray Eve. I am the descendant of original sin. I am evil.

"Jesus," Bobby said. "I've never seen anything like this."

The spell was broken.

The tattoo was nearing completion. The cobra gave impetus to her work, a final burst of creativity. A voluptuous and rebellious Eve blossomed from Ashleigh's needle, turning her back on the serpent, reaching, striving for the heavens while her reluctant mate waited. Ashleigh smiled at the thought of having danced with Satan like Eve, her Eve, mother of mankind.

Ashleigh, too, was now impatient to finish, to see the glorious whole of the Lovers on Bobby's body, display it for all the world, but she dared not rush it. Instead, she continued slowly, methodically.

She sometimes envied Burke his painting in oils. He could rectify his mistakes, scrape old colors from the canvas, begin anew. But there would be no thrill to painting. Ashleigh loved knowing that she had no second chance. Her work must be exact the first time. There were ways to cover up a mistake—some even specialized in transforming a tattoo no longer wanted into something else—but that was not for Ashleigh. She sought perfection. Anything less was unacceptable.

It was something Bobby failed to understand.

Only the defiant Eve of the tattoo would comprehend her need.

                              *   *   *

Ashleigh descended from the Hollywood hills into the dark murk of a smoggy Los Angeles underworld. Traffic moved at the speed limit on the freeways, slowing only as Ashleigh made the transition from the Santa Monica to the San Diego, and again as she headed south past LAX and into the South Bay curve. The traffic flow picked up again and soon she exited to drive toward the Pacific Ocean, past the huge oil refineries and strip malls and shopping centers. Then, the cityscape changed and she was climbing into a lush and wooded area. It was still a part of the great Los Angeles basin, but despite the expensive homes and developments, it was somehow isolated and remote.

Danny's townhouse was in a complex high atop the Palos Verdes Peninsula. Ashleigh stopped at the gate and pressed the numbers on the coded directory. Burke answered the intercom. "It's Ash," she said.

The gate swung open. Ashleigh drove through, turned left, and found an empty space labeled "Guest Parking" on the asphalt. She used the rearview mirror to freshen her lipstick and brush her hair before locking the car and following the walkway to where Burke waited in the open door.

"Hello, Ash."

"Hello, Burke."

Burke ushered her into a bright and airy living room. Beneath the picture window, the green landscape was dotted with red tile roofs in the Spanish style, sloping away in gentle swells to the ocean far below. The view was magnificent and panoramic, stretching along the curve of Santa Monica Bay all the way to Malibu.

"Welcome to the Peninsula," Burke said, kissing her cheek.

"I brought you some wine."

"Thank you. It's good to see you, Ash. You look lovely, as always. I like the outfit very much."

"Thank you. It's good to see you, too, Burke. Where's Danny?"

"In the bedroom. You'll see her soon. Champagne?"

"Yes, please."

"How have you been?"

"I'm working hard. And you?"

"The same. I've moved in with Danny."

"That's terrific, Burke, soon you'll be getting married."

He smiled. "Would you believe that?"

Ashleigh followed him into a spacious kitchen and watched as he popped the cork on the champagne. "It's a long commute for you, though, especially when you work late."

"Sometimes, when it's late and Danny's already asleep, I stay over, sleep in your old room."

"I always think of it as my old room, too."

"It'll always be your room. I can't go in there without seeing you when I tucked you in that first night and read you to sleep."

"You saved my life, Burke. I don't know what would have happened if you hadn't taken me away from Frank. Probably, I'd be dead now."

He handed her a glass of champagne and they lifted them in a toast. "What shall we drink to?" Ashleigh asked.

"To a special occasion."

"To a special occasion," Ashleigh said, smiling, "and to Burke and Danny."

"Let's wait for Danny in the living room."

She turned to face Burke, sitting sideways on the couch, tucking her legs under her. "My God, Burke," she cried as she noticed the painting hanging over the fireplace for the first time. "I didn't see it before. It must be yours." She jumped up and went to the painting. "It's beautiful."

"I had a good model," Burke said as he joined her. "We hung it just for you. There's a replacement for when Danny entertains. It wouldn't do for her business associates to see quite so much of her glorious beauty."

It was the painting Danny had told Ashleigh about where she reclined nude upon the sofa with a feathered mask disguising her face.

"You left off her tattoos."

"I thought the mask was enough. I wanted to portray her simply. Adding the tattoos would have detracted from the overall impact I wanted to create."

"You're right," Ashleigh said. "The focus is where it should be, on a beautiful and mysterious woman. Is she waiting for her lover?"

"She's waiting for whatever you like."

"God, you're talented, just like I've always told you."

"I'd like to do a painting of you and Danny together. Would you mind modeling for me?"

"Of course not, Burke. You know I'd do anything for you."

"I'd call it The Lovers," he said.

"How synchronistic," Ashleigh said. "My work in progress is called The Lovers." She looked up at the painting again and wondered how Burke would have them pose. But as she stared at the nude Danny, Ashleigh wondered how she would be able to maintain any pose so close to Danny. Her perfume would be intoxicating, her presence overwhelming . . . it would be so wonderful to have Danny make love to me. But, of course, she would. It was a forgone conclusion. It was going to happen tonight. Jesus, Burke, what are you doing to me? I can't wait any longer.

An hour passed quickly as Ashleigh described her tattoo and told him of the new commission for Kim Lee. They sat on the couch where Burke and Danny must have sat while he read *The Story of O* to her.

"It's good, Burke, 'The Lovers' is very good."

"Is it your masterpiece?"

"I hope it's one of them," she said.

They had a second glass of champagne and Burke, taking her hand, showed her through the townhouse. There were three levels. The living room was the second level. Downstairs were a family room, a small bedroom that Danny had converted to a home office, and laundry facilities. "The master bedroom and the guest bedrooms are upstairs. You'll see them later, when Danny's ready."

Ashleigh listened intently but beyond their voices. The residence was silent. "What's keeping her?" Ashleigh asked.

"She's waiting for you, but she doesn't know you're here," Burke said. "This is her birthday."

"Burke, you should have told me. I didn't get her a present."

"Excuse me for a few minutes. I have to help Danny now."

Burke was gone for a long time. Ashleigh poured another glass of champagne, leafed through several novels, and stared out at the beautiful, pristine view. She turned at the sound of Burke's footsteps on the stairs.

"Come to me," he said. "It's time." Burke smiled, taking her into his arms, kissing her and crushing her breasts against his chest.

Confused, Ashleigh pushed him away. She had never done that before. "What about Danny?"

"This is for Danny," Burke said, taking her into his arms again. "Trust me."

Ashleigh submitted as he kissed her again, feeling the old and powerful attraction for this man, yet guilty at their betrayal of Danny. She was breathing heavily when he finally released her.

"You *are* the present," he said. "Come, Danny's ready for you now."

"Oh, God, Burke." Her mouth was suddenly dry. She drank the rest of the champagne quickly.

"I told you, it's a surprise," he said. "Danny knows nothing of all this." Burke took her hand and led her upstairs. He opened the bedroom door and stepped aside for Ashleigh.

Danny's arms were outstretched and fastened to the bedposts by long black straps. Similar straps were cuffed to her ankles. Her legs were pulled up and back and fastened to the posts, leaving her open and vulnerable. She wore a leather hood with breathing holes for her nose. A rectangular insert built into the mask held Danny's mouth open. Ashleigh stood over her and looked down. Perhaps sensing the presence of another, Danny's tongue darted nervously within its prison.

A small leather whip with multiple strands of soft, pliant leather was on the bed beneath Danny's widespread legs.

Ashleigh turned to Burke.

"Tonight," Burke said. "You are Anne-Marie."

Chapter Eleven

The seventh tattoo was finished.

Under Ashleigh's constant attention, it had healed gloriously. Now, as she stroked and kissed and embraced her creation, it was like touching the thick oils of a painting. She felt the colors living and breathing beneath her fingertips, just as the black widow throbbed and pulsated to Bobby's caress. Even with her eyes closed, she knew every nuance, each delicate stroke raised on her canvas.

Ashleigh had taken the tarot card of the Lovers and transformed it into her own. Bold, impressionistic colors covered Bobby's back. At his neck, the golden rays of the sun danced and shimmered. The archangel Raphael emerged from thick white clouds, arms outspread in benediction. He was resplendent in royal robes of deep purple. Bright red flames formed his halo and his widespread wings were red.

A leering serpent coiled around the tree of knowledge and its bright fruits, representing each of the five senses. Another tree, the tree of life, bore twelve fruits, symbols of the signs of the zodiac.

Eve, the naked rebel, her golden hair cascading down her back, stood unashamed on the velvet grass of the Garden of Eden next to Adam, with one hand reaching out to him, but looking to the heavens. Her breasts were full and rounded, with dark ruby tips. Perhaps there was a hint of apprehension on her face, a fear of the unknown, the pain of childbirth promised Eve—and all women—by God as penalty for her transgression.

Adam, too, reached out for Eve's hand, but oblivious to the archangel's presence he looked only to Woman, his weakness emphasized by his erect penis.

In an earlier, discarded sketch, Eve had knelt before Adam, but even as she'd taken him in her mouth, her eyes had been raised to the archangel, as though she sought forgiveness for releasing the knowledge of good and evil into the world. Adam's hands were entwined in Eve's lustrous golden hair. His head, eyes closed, was thrown back in ecstasy, uncaring of the harsh judgment already pronounced upon them. It might be sacrilegious, but Ashleigh could not make Eve regret her seduction by the serpent. *If I have no regrets, how can my creation? I am Eve, too. I have always been Eve.*

And the words of Genesis still echoed in her mind.

"And to the woman he said, 'You shall be eager for your husband, and he shall be your master.' And unto the woman he said, 'Thy desire shall be to thy husband, and he shall rule over thee.' "

"Yes," Ashleigh cried, submitting as he entered her. "Ah, yes!" Like her creation, Ashleigh wanted Bobby as never before, wondering if he could master her according to the prophecy.

Ashleigh was sick of the mundane tattoos requested by an endless anonymous line of men and women who passed through the studio, each thinking it was a daring, rebellious act, but none of them understanding the power of the tattoo, its ability to transcend the ordinary, to create beauty. The bikers wanted Harleys, or the slogan "Born to Raise Hell." Housewives and sorority women wanted butterflies and flowers. A young Marine wandered in and Ashleigh put the Globe and Anchor on his biceps. At least he was cute.

"Christ," she cried, when the two giggling women left the studio, "I wish the world had never heard of Elvis. "I'm so sick of doing Elvis."

Dean only laughed. "It's better than a real job."

"Barely," Ashleigh stormed.

Thank God for Kim Lee. Without her, waiting to show the Lovers for the first time would have been unbearable. Without her, Ashleigh would have had no outlet for the restless creative energies that filled her brain like the roiling surf, waves relentlessly building to rush and pound the shore, each onslaught containing more power and force than before, until she felt she would explode. Without Kim, Ashleigh knew she would be prowling the nights seeking a new canvas.

Each time Kim Lee slowly removed her clothing, Ashleigh held her breath as she waited for the final unveiling. When she was naked, Kim raised her arms above her head and turned slowly, eyes still shyly downcast, a slight smile always parting her lips. Yes, Ashleigh thought, slowly exhaling as she viewed her work in progress—yes.

The stems that circled and grew from Kim's breast curved beneath her shoulder to explode in dark blooming flowers against a background of fern leaves. The petals were widespread, with their stamens reaching to the heavens as though seeking the sun's rays and the lifegiving rains. Beneath the flowers, which climbed to the shoulder, a seashell seemed to glisten wetly. A lover who cared to put an ear to the skin and listened closely would hear the hushed, distant roar of waves, a siren call emanating from the woman's very soul.

Always, Kim waited patiently, as a molded statue in a gallery, content to be the object of admiration, for Ashleigh to break the spell in some fashion, to give permission for her to move and the work to resume. Today, Kim trembled slightly at the touch of Ashleigh's cool fingers that stroked the curving stems of the flowers.

"It's going to be very beautiful," Ashleigh said.

Kim lifted her eyes and darted a quick smile. "Oh, yes," she said, as she reclined on the mat, "very beautiful."

"I love your hair," Ashleigh said, carefully arranging Kim Lee's black strands over her shoulder. She could have simply pushed it out of the way, but that would have been indifferent, unworthy of the creation that was growing on Kim's body.

The ritual must be maintained. Ashleigh had already begun thinking of Kim's body decoration as the eighth tattoo, regretting that it would be seen only by her husband. But it could be no less a work of art for that.

"Thank you," Kim said, "but you have lovely hair, too. Everything about you is lovely. You're very lucky. Sometimes I feel most unworthy."

"Don't be silly. You're beautiful and exotic. There are hundreds of women, even thousands, in Southern California who are much prettier than me. Blond, blue-eyed, and gorgeous."

"That's not true," Kim said quietly, hesitantly, as though fearing to contradict her artistic mistress. "Their beauty is on the exterior only. Yours comes from within, from the soul."

Ashleigh smiled. "And have you looked into my soul?"

"Oh, yes," Kim said. "I had to, don't you see? There is a spiritual bond between us now."

"What did you see there?"

"Eternal beauty. Great talent. A sensitive woman who is also a fierce warrior . . ."

"And?"

"You should not give in to your doubts, your fears. Greatness such as you seek cannot be achieved without agony and the turmoil caused by warring forces. You must not doubt your talent. I am visible evidence of that. You have given much of your soul for me, to me."

Kim Lee turned on the mat and touched her small breast. "The seed which begins here gives life to your creation. All else flows from this nourishing symbol. I feel the magic and power of your needle. Its sting is nothing, the pain merely a minor irritation that must be endured for beauty. You must teach me."

"How to be?" Ashleigh asked before turning on the machine.

"Yes," Kim cried, her black eyes glistening as she awaited the day's first cruel caress, that initial pain when their souls fused, becoming one for a time.

Ashleigh worked longer at each appointment, consumed by her new canvas, wanting to see the creation finished, but regretting that moment when Kim would leave her, never to return.

Kim endured the pain silently, gracefully, as the cobra spread its hood for her.

Waiting.

Simone called. "It's beautiful. Would you like to see it?" she asked.

"I'd love to," Ashleigh said. "I want to take a picture of it."

"This afternoon?"

"I'm free after four."

"I'll come then. We can have a drink together."

"I'd like that."

Ashleigh waited.

Ashleigh introduced Simone and Dean and then led the young actress into the back room. Ashleigh closed the door and turned to take Simone in her arms.

"I've thought of you a lot," Simone said, after their long and lingering kiss. "It was a wonderful afternoon."

Ashleigh smiled and stroked Simone's hair softly, thinking of Danny and Cynthia, and feeling like an unfaithful whore. "Yes, it was. We'll do it again."

"Oh, yes."

"Now, let me see this beautiful scorpion of yours."

Simone kicked off her loafers and pulled her blouse from the jeans, unbuckling a wide belt. "God, it itched, but I followed your instructions exactly and it healed exactly as you said it would. I couldn't stop looking at it. I must have spent two weeks in front of the mirror, just admiring it."

When she had slipped off the jeans and panties, Simone

gathered her blouse, holding it beneath her breasts, and looked down at herself. "Isn't it wonderful?" she cried.

Ashleigh was pleased. It had turned out just as she'd planned it. The scorpion, a dark and predatory huntress, emerged from its lair, tail raised and curved menacingly, poised to strike. "Does Rachel like it?"

"She loves it. Everyone on the set keeps complimenting me on my work, thinking I've reached back for something extra. I just smile at my little secret." Simone paused. "Do you like it?"

"Oh, yes. It's one of my best."

"I'm glad."

As Ashleigh looked at the scorpion through the viewfinder, the huntress was framed, frozen in time, and Ashleigh wondered how many victims it would claim.

They went to the Century Plaza Hotel and sat in the lobby bar, listening to a pianist, dressed formally, play soft show tunes. The bar was not crowded, but a steady stream of men and women passed by, their day's business either concluded or continuing. Two men sat nearby, making notes on napkins. At another table a woman sat alone, waiting for someone or something to enter her life.

Perhaps she's just waiting, Ashleigh thought—like me.

"Sam loves it, too. He's been insatiable ever since he first saw it."

"Tattoos are very erotic for some people."

"I'll never forget yours. Sometimes, when Sam is making love to me, I think of you and I see the spider hovering over me, getting bigger and bigger." Simone shuddered. "You should give me a picture. You have one of me now."

"I'll send you one," Ashleigh said.

"I'll keep it in my secret place. No one will ever see it. Do you have a secret place, somewhere to keep very special things, somewhere to go when you're depressed or upset?"

Ashleigh nodded.

"I have a little room at the top of the house. Sam never goes there. It's only for me. That's where I keep my high school yearbooks, pictures of old boyfriends, love letters they wrote. Where do you keep your secrets?"

"Only in my mind," Ashleigh said.

"Nothing else?"

Ashleigh shook her head. Once . . . she shook her head again, refusing to remember.

"I'll show you my room next time. We'll make love there. Then, it'll be *our* secret place. I don't mind sharing, not with you."

Her wait continued.

Making love with Bobby, Ashleigh fought the urge to rake her long red fingernails across his back, ripping and slashing until the masterpiece was destroyed. Instead, she devoured him like the black widow, riding him like a demented woman until he was empty and then demanding more, screaming with the ecstasy of each successive orgasm until she fell limp in his arms, pleading silently to be allowed to sleep, only to rise after an uneasy hour to go downstairs.

She stood at the window, looking out at the twinkling night lights of the great city stretching to the ends of the world and beyond.

Bobby found her there and embraced her from behind, feeling the rise and fall of the spider's agitation. "Come to bed," he said.

"I can't sleep."

"You have to. You're going to make yourself sick."

"Haven't you ever felt like the greatest performance ever— Hamlet, perhaps, or Cyrano, or Oedipus—was right there, waiting to burst forth for all the world to see and applaud? That's what I feel like all the time."

"I've always wanted to play Willy Loman," Bobby said quietly, stroking her belly, nuzzling the sunburst on her neck.

"You're too young to play Willy Loman."

"If you can hide your beauty, I can hide my youth. A little makeup and I can be sixty years old."

"I never want to be sixty."

"Then come to bed."

Ashleigh complied, but she did not sleep. As she lay in Bobby's arms, visions danced in the shadows of the room, elusive shades of works to be, if only she could capture them, freeze them for all time, as in the frame of her camera.

The seventh tattoo would be displayed tonight.

"Don't worry," Bobby told her on the telephone. "It's going to be great. They'll love it."

"I can't help it. You don't know what it's like," she said, knowing that wasn't true. Bobby knew. Rehearsals ended and an actor or a dancer had to appear in public, performing for audiences and critics, eager for even perfunctory applause and acceptance. Writers could rewrite only so many times before their works left their hands to be read by others who might or might not understand the agony that accompanied each printed word. An artist added the last tiny splash of color and declared a work finished and allowed others to look upon it.

"Trust me," Bobby said. "It's great. You're great."

"Break a leg," Ashleigh said.

"You, too, babe. I'll see you tonight. I love you."

Ashleigh would have preferred revealing the seventh tattoo for the first time at the convention, but that was impossible. Bobby had to return to work. If he hadn't been such a popular dancer at the club, he'd have been replaced already.

Ashleigh had not been to the club since the night she'd chosen Bobby for her canvas. She'd planned to go alone, but a growing apprehension over how the seventh tattoo would be received demanded company, and so she called Cynthia. "I don't want to be alone when he comes out," she said.

"I have a date," Cynthia said, "but I'll break it."

"Oh, don't do that. I'll survive. It's just that I'm so nervous about it. No one has seen it yet except for me and Bobby."

"I didn't really want to see this guy, anyway. I was just bored when I said yes."

"I won't be able to stay with you afterward. I'll have to be with Bobby, no matter what happens."

"That doesn't matter. I can hardly wait to see it. I'm sure it's going to be beautiful."

"God, I hope so."

Now, Ashleigh and Cynthia sat at a small table near the back of the club, sipping wine and waiting for Bobby's first appearance. Around them, the other women in the audience grew less inhibited and more raucous with each new drink and each successive dancer, cheering every suggestive movement and any gyrating thrust of a pelvis on the runway.

"These guys have great bodies," Cynthia said, during a brief intermission. "Do any of them have brains, too?"

"I don't know," Ashleigh replied. "I've never met them."

"What does Bobby say?"

"We've never talked about them." No, since the moment I picked him, Bobby has been consumed with me. There was no reason to talk about the other dancers or his friends. I stayed away from such involvement deliberately. It was easier that way. There was nothing I could share in return . . . nothing I wanted to share.

The voice from the loudspeaker boomed. "And now, ladies, the moment you've all been waiting for." A drum roll rattled through the club. Women pounded fists on table tops.

"Here he is, ladies. *Bobbyyyyyyy Cole!* King of the exotic dancers."

Ashleigh licked her lips nervously as the room went dark and the spotlight fell on Bobby, wearing tight jeans and a tee shirt that stretched over tight muscles. He stood motionless in the glare, eyes closed, seemingly oblivious to the screaming adulation of the women. The music built.

"Oh, God," Ashleigh whispered. "Let it be good."

Cynthia took her hand and squeezed.

His dance was alternately arrogant, then strutting, and then soft and sensual, making each woman in the audience feel his performance was for her alone, teasing her, promising to share unspeakable delights.

Only Ashleigh and Cynthia knew the woman he danced for.

"He's good," Cynthia whispered. Again she squeezed Ashleigh's hand.

Ashleigh waited. Christ, this is unbearable. Why didn't I do something else? Anything except the Lovers. What if they don't like it? This is what it will be like for Burke when his exhibit opens. This is what it's like for every artist, waiting for the reaction from an unworthy audience.

She wanted to flee, but she forced herself to stay and watch.

Women were going wild, cheering as he slowly removed his jeans, throwing them carelessly into the darkness beyond the glaring light focused on the runway. A woman shrieked as she won the scramble for the jeans.

"Oh, yes, lover," a woman screamed, as Bobby fondled the bulge in his bikini briefs. "Do it to me!"

And then it was time to remove the shirt. Bobby prolonged the moment, playing with it, lifting it over his stomach, drawing it down again.

Each time, Ashleigh tensed, a heavy weight building in the pit of her belly. Do it, God damn it, just do it!

Bobby ripped the tee shirt over his head with a practiced movement. It sailed into the darkness as he froze on the stage, facing away from the women.

The silence was abrupt, stunned, brief, before the room erupted in cheers and catcalls, delighted laughter, applause.

"My God," Cynthia said, "it's beautiful."

Ashleigh nodded. She was devoid of emotion.

It was over.

Bobby danced for another ten minutes, lowering himself on the runway as women stuffed the dollar bills into his briefs, but for Ashleigh it was over. That moment would never return.

As the lights went up, Ashleigh listened to the excited chatter around her.

"My God, why would someone do that to himself?"

"Oh, I don't know," her companion said, "I kind of like it."

"But what does it mean?"

"Who knows?"

"Who cares? Did you see the dick on that guy in the tattoo? I wouldn't mind having one of those at home all the time."

"I'd rather have the dick on Bobby."

"Oh, that's probably just padding."

They left after the first show. Ashleigh's ears throbbed in the sudden silence as the door slammed shut behind them.

"I would say it was a mixed reaction at best," Ashleigh said, when they were in the car.

"You're not going to go by what a bunch of drunken women said, are you?"

"No, I suppose not. The reaction at the convention—that's what will count."

"It was beautiful, Ashleigh. I mean it." Cynthia leaned over and kissed her, touching her breast lightly.

"You're sweet." Ashleigh pressed Cynthia's hand. "I wish I could stay with you tonight."

"Don't worry about it. It wouldn't be the same, anyway." Cynthia laughed. "All those male bodies turned me on. It's dildos and vibrators for me tonight. Bobby's a hunk, though. I'm jealous. Are you going to keep him?"

Ashleigh gripped the steering wheel, squeezing it tightly. "I don't know," she replied, knowing that it was happening again. The tenuous love she had for Bobby was already fading. Now that the seventh tattoo had been shown to the world, the familiar doubts had entered her mind, just as with all the others. It was what had driven Jonathan Carver to suicide. "Bobby's nice, but . . ."

"But there's always another canvas."

"Yes." It was true. There *were* other canvases, a lifetime of canvases for her creations. "Let's go get another drink somewhere."

*   *   *

Climbing through the dark streets toward home, Ashleigh was exhausted and relieved. The seventh tattoo had been seen in its first exhibition. It is good, Ashleigh thought, no matter what they said. Cynthia's right: I don't have to listen to a bunch of drunken women whose minds are on dicks.

At home she paced the living room nervously, impatient now for Bobby's arrival. She wanted to see the Lovers, touch it, reassure herself that it existed, that it still lived and breathed as she created it, that it had not been tainted by others.

Chapter Twelve

Ashleigh and Bobby meandered down the coastline, avoiding the freeways as much as possible, driving slowly through what had once been small and insular beach communities, but were now just part of the nearly endless metropolis stretching from Los Angeles to the Mexican border.

They could have driven to San Diego in less than three hours, but it was Ashleigh who wanted to make a day of it. The idea had come with the full moon when she'd remembered, as she always did, the night she'd fled New Mexico. During the three days and nights Billy took to get to Los Angeles, she saw nothing but truck stops, rest stops, and the cab of his truck. It didn't matter so long as they were in the desert, but when they reached San Diego and Billy turned north along the coast, the vast ocean and the little towns clinging to the edge of the continent intrigued her and she vowed to take the time one day to reverse the trip, see what she had missed riding high in the cab above the freeway.

But there had never been time or opportunity before—until now. Before Frank, she survived. With Frank, she whored. With Burke, she learned. She had traveled with Chance, of course, but they always flew—to San Francisco, to Las Vegas, once to Phoenix, uncomfortably close to New Mexico. For too long her world had been restricted to Los Angeles and its seething netherworld, a vast city of shades. She was ignorant of her surroundings, and she couldn't tolerate it.

Today, Ashleigh felt as she had when Burke had met her at

the jail, and again when she'd met Chance—free, and beginning a new phase of her life, whatever that might be.

Now, Ashleigh and Bobby drove through Belmont Shore in Long Beach, a street filled with trendy shops, and crossed over the bridge into Naples, a small island interwoven with canals where it was still possible to take a romantic night cruise on a gondola, serenaded by the oarsman. Turning at the marina, they took Pacific Coast Highway south into Seal Beach. Ashleigh was tempted to stop at a tattoo studio, but there would be tattoos enough during the long weekend. The highway was crowded with restaurants and surf shops. They passed Huntington Harbor, a wealthy enclave of homes and boats.

Then they were in Huntington Beach, going between preserved wetlands on one side and a long expanse of beach on the other. The parking lots were scattered with campers and recreational vehicles, arriving for a weekend of beach parties, swimming, and barbecues.

The Huntington Beach pier was crowded with fishermen dangling long lines into the water below. People of all ages skated along the sidewalks or bicycled, following an asphalt path along the beach.

Newport Beach was a crowded haven for the rich in their luxury homes with boats docked at private slips. It was a growing commercial center for Orange County as well, with hotels and high-rise office buildings encircling the shopping center at Fashion Island.

But there were places along the old Coast Highway where development had not yet destroyed the gentle rolling hillsides, still denuded and recovering from devastating wildfires. South of Newport and Corona del Mar, where state parks protected some of the area, cattle still grazed on land once a part of an old and massive Spanish land grant and now owned by the Irvine Company.

Bobby drove Ashleigh's Mustang. The top was down and their hair flew in the breeze. To those who saw them, they were the perfect California couple, handsome and beautiful, young and tanned, hair bleached by the sun. Sitting beside him, Ashleigh enjoyed the sun, the sense of freedom, the rushing air. In no hurry to reach San Diego, the convention, and the tension that would accompany entering the Lovers into competition, Ashleigh relaxed and listened to Sinatra sing of Scotch and soda.

The day was warm and bright, cloudless. Close to the shore, the Pacific waters were turquoise where kelp floated beneath the surface, but beyond, the color deepened into a rich blue.

"Look," Ashleigh cried suddenly, pointing to a little rocky inlet between Corona del Mar and Laguna Beach. "Let's stop."

Bobby pulled to the side of the road. Ashleigh jumped out of the car. "I want to climb down. Do you mind?"

"We can do anything we want today," Bobby said.

They followed a winding dirt path down to the inlet a hundred feet below. Protected from the larger waves, the waters of the inlet lapped gently at scattered rocks and swirled in little eddies. Down the beach, a couple with two small children, a boy and a girl, explored along the edge of the water. The little girl, wearing a pink swimsuit, carried a small pail and shovel.

Ashleigh jumped from rock to rock, pausing to stare intently into a crystal-clear tide pool. A tiny crab scurried into a crevice in the rock. "Look, Bobby," she said laughing, pointing, "a starfish."

"Haven't you ever played in a tide pool before?"

"No, this is wonderful."

"Where did you grow up anyway?"

"Please, Bobby, don't ask. Never ask me that."

"I'm sorry."

Ashleigh smiled to soften the harshness that had been in her voice. "It's not your fault I'm such a mysterious woman."

"It's all right. I don't mind being in love with the enigmatic Ashleigh Thomas."

She looked back to the starfish and remembered the cold, clear nights of New Mexico, while she waited for her wish to be granted. "Star light, star bright," she chanted, "first star I see tonight . . ."

"I think that only works at night," Bobby said.

"It can work anytime," Ashleigh said, "you only have to believe." She looked down at the starfish again and whispered, "Wish I may, wish I might, have the wish I wish tonight . . ."

She stood and took Bobby's hand, leading him back to the shoreline. But what wish do I want? she asked herself.

The little girl waited for them. "Are you in love?" she asked solemnly.

"Why, yes, I am," Ashleigh replied.

"My mother says love is the best thing in the world."

"Your mother is right. She must be a very smart woman."

"She helps me with my homework. I'm a very good speller. Can you spell?"

"I'm pretty good," Ashleigh said, "but probably not as good as you."

"You can be, if you work very hard. Is that what your mother told you?"

"My mother . . . yes, that's what my mother told me."

"Maggie, don't bother anyone," the girl's mother called.

"That's good. I have to go now." She ran back to join her parents and brother.

Ashleigh looked after her. "She's cute."

"Do you want children? We've never talked about it."

Ashleigh hesitated, remembering a hardscrabble ranch and the thin, drawn woman who'd been her mother, struggling always to please her father. "I don't know," she said finally. "Perhaps . . . someday."

They waited for their patio table at the bar of an old hotel in Laguna Beach, a landmark to times past, when life had been simpler. The beachside art community was crowded with tourists. The Pageant of the Masters, a popular art festival where living individuals recreated great paintings on stage, attracted thousands each summer weekend.

Sharing a bottle of chardonnay, they drank to her success at the convention. Ashleigh had put the despondency behind her, telling herself over and over again that the women who congregated at the club were not proper judges of her work. Finally, she convinced herself. The judges who were her peers in art would be the final arbitrators. No one else mattered.

"On vacation?" their waitress asked.

"Just driving through," Bobby said, "on our way to San Diego for the weekend."

After lunch, they wandered through several art galleries, all tastefully arranged with seascapes filled with rushing waves, one still life after another of flowers or bowls of fruit, portraits, abstracts. There was one nude study that reminded Ashleigh of Burke's portrait of Danny, although it was not nearly so good. She lingered there, knowing she would soon pose with Danny for Burke's own version of the Lovers and she shuddered at the thought of kissing Danny's breasts again. Oh, God, what an evening. While Burke showed her the townhouse and they drank champagne and talked, Danny had waited submissively in the bedroom, alone, not knowing what was about to happen . . .

"I wish I could paint," Bobby said, taking her hand as he looked at the nude. "You would be my model always. Like Wyeth's Helga."

"Wouldn't you get tired of me?" Ashleigh asked, glad for the interruption. The memories of Danny were still too powerful. She had fallen deeply in love with a woman for the first time in her life and believed Danny returned that love. *How will Burke arrange us?*

"Wyeth never seemed to tire of Helga, and you're much prettier."

"Just pretty?" Ashleigh teased automatically, still thinking of Danny.

"Beautiful," Bobby said, "eternally beautiful."

"I'll grow old."

"We'll never be old."

Holding hands, they joined the tourists on the crowded sidewalks. "I love you," Bobby said.

"I wish we could stay here forever," Ashleigh replied.

Browsing in a small bookstore, Ashleigh found a paperback

copy of Richard Henry Dana's *Two Years before the Mast* in the local history section.

As they drove south along the coast again, Ashleigh read of old California to Bobby. " 'San Juan is the only romantic spot on the coast. The country here for several miles is high table-land, running boldly to the shore and breaking off in a steep cliff, at the foot of which the waters of the Pacific are constantly dashing. For several miles the water washes the very base of the hill, or breaks upon ledges and fragments of rocks which run out into the sea. Just where we landed was a small cove which gave us, at high tide, a few square feet of sand beach between the sea and the bottom of the hill. This was the only landing place. Directly before us rose the perpendicular height of four or five hundred feet. How we were to get hides down, or goods up, upon the tableland on which the mission was situated, was more than we could tell.

" 'There was a grandeur in everything around, which gave a solemnity to the scene, a silence and solitariness which affected every part! Not a human being but ourselves for miles, and no sound heard but the pulsations of the great Pacific . . .

" 'Having landed, the captain took his way round the hill, ordering me and one other to follow him. We followed, picking our way out, and jumping and scrambling up, walking over briers and prickly pears, until we came to the top. Here the country stretched out for miles, as far as the eye could reach, on a level, table surface, and the only habitation in sight was the small mission of San Juan Capistrano, with a few Indian huts about it, standing in a small hollow, about a mile from where we were.' "

Ashleigh closed the book. "I wonder what he would think if he saw what man has done to the land."

At Dana Point, they backtracked to San Juan Capistrano and went to the old mission, first dedicated in 1776, but damaged by earthquakes in 1806, 1918, and 1994. Still it survived, and the most recent repairs were completed, the scaffolding gone—until next time.

It was cool in the garden and the church. Still hand in hand, they walked in Dana's footsteps, exploring the old mission, and Ashleigh again read to Bobby from a brochure, telling him the history of the mission and the legendary swallows that returned each spring to nest in the old ruins left over from Spanish colonial times. She read, too, of the black robed Franciscan ghost who prowled the twilight shadows of the garden and the bells that mysteriously tolled while their ropes remained motionless and coiled upon their pegs.

In the small museum, as they looked at old vestments and relics, Ashleigh read of the young Indian girl, a neophyte, who had died with the last reverberations of the self-tolling bells and wondered what she'd died of, just as she often wondered what the real Ashleigh's cause of death had been.

Ashleigh hated religion, but she did not blame God for what men did in His name, the harsh retributions exacted in the cause of goodness. But standing there in the midst of the old mission, Ashleigh thought of the Indian girl and speculated on what she thought of the alien beliefs she had embraced. There had been times when Ashleigh longed for the harmony and discipline of a strict religious order, imagined herself sworn to silence and chastity, devoted only to learning and the love of God.

"Let's get out of here before I become a nun."

"Ha!" Bobby snorted.

The vast Marine Corps Base at Camp Pendleton, home to the First Marine Division between wars and deployments, was still mostly an undefiled coastline for some seventeen miles between San Clemente and Oceanside. After the nuclear power station at San Onofre, the coast and inland areas were broken only by a few scattered installations visible from the freeway.

And a rest stop.

She had stood there once, long ago, wistfully gazing across the freeway at the calm waters of the Pacific while Billy napped in the truck. He had fucked her there for the last time. "Just a little quickie for the road," he said, laughing. Ashleigh turned and looked back at the trucks and cars parked among the trees. They looked like cottonwoods from a distance.

"What did you see?" Bobby asked.

"Nothing," Ashleigh replied, turning back again.

At Oceanside, they got off the freeway again, driving down Hill Street past all the shops and stores catering to Marines. The sunwashed street was uncrowded and only a few young Marines, instantly recognizable by their short haircuts, were in town on a workday, most of them carrying laundered camouflaged dungarees or green dress uniforms from the cleaners.

Ashleigh ruffled Bobby's long hair, tugging at his curly locks, and laughed. "I wonder what you'd look like with one of those haircuts."

"I don't think it's my style."

Finally, inexorably, they arrived at the convention hotel in San Diego. Waiting on the sidewalk while Bobby gave the car to a valet, Ashleigh looked at the hotel, knowing that her future, their future, would be decided here. Wish I may, wish I might, have the wish I wish tonight . . .

Bobby checked them into the hotel.

Ashleigh registered for the convention.

It was one of a dozen or more tribal gatherings each year around the western and southwestern states, a place for initiates to congregate. Artists gathered to share ideas, display their work, examine new equipment and techniques. It was a trade show, like any other trade show—the American Bookseller's Convention, a computer expo, a small business fair, the National Rifle Association's annual meeting—except that the participants were beyond the norm of society in their devotion to tattoos.

The manufacturers were set up in one ballroom. In an adjoining ballroom, hundreds of tattoo machines blended into a deafening roar as new disciples received their first tattoos and others added to their body decorations.

For the straights staying at the hotel, the conventiongoers were a bizarre collection of rebels, their bodies heavily decorated with tattoos, wearing rings through pierced navels, nostrils, lips, and ears.

Even Bobby, who displayed his body nine times each weekend for the enjoyment of women, was awestruck at the casual exhibition of near nudity in the hotel lobby, hallways, elevators, and convention halls.

Once in the room, Bobby cried, "Jesus, did you see that woman getting off the elevator?"

"Which one?" Ashleigh asked innocently, smiling. Attending a tattoo convention for the first time was an experience.

"The jangling one with all the rings in her ears and the chameleon on her boob."

"Which did you notice first?"

"What do you think? You should enter the spider," Bobby said. "They must have a 'best breast' category. You'd win for sure."

"The black widow is very good," Ashleigh said seriously, "but it's not the kind of design that's entered into competition. It was done only for me."

"Who cares about the spider? You'd still win for best tits."

"Yes, I probably would."

Ashleigh rarely stayed in hotels except when she went to an out-of-town convention. Her memories were of sordid motel rooms, rented by the hour, and she found it pleasant to spend time in a clean room, filled with little luxuries for the guests—real soap, shampoos, body conditioners, guidebooks to tourist attractions and nightlife, clean sheets, big, fluffy pillows, an honor bar, color television with cable movies that could be brought up with the flick of a button, room service menus.

Ashleigh kicked off her shoes and bounced on the bed.

Bobby laughed. "You're just like a little girl."

"Sometimes I think I was *never* a little girl."

"Like the one on the beach today. She was so serious."

"I was like that," Ashleigh said, "but not tonight. Let's stay in and order from room service, watch movies, have fun, just like rich people."

Bobby smiled. "It's good to see you like this for a change. You *have* been too serious, ever since I went back to work."

"I know . . ." She kissed him. "It's better now."

Bobby went out again to find a liquor store.

"Don't get distracted by anyone," Ashleigh said, "just remember who's waiting for you here."

"Can I look?"

"Just so long as you hurry back."

Their room was on the seventh floor—lucky seven for the Lovers—and there was a small balcony with two chairs and a patio table. The view overlooked the bay. Ashleigh took a split of champagne from the bar and carried it to the balcony. While she waited for Bobby, she tried to empty her mind of thoughts and enjoy the deepening red hues of the sun as it built momentum for the sudden rush beneath the horizon. A pleasant and cool breeze blew off the water to play with the strands of her hair. She sipped champagne and refused to remember.

When Bobby returned, he had two bottles of champagne, a chardonnay, and a cabernet sauvignon. He opened one of the bottles of champagne and put the other to chill in the room's ice bucket before joining Ashleigh on the balcony.

"This is decadent," he said, as he refilled the water glass from the bathroom and poured his own.

"No, not decadent, *trés élégant*," Ashleigh said. "I love it."

They ordered hamburgers and french fries and sat crosslegged on the bed, eating and watching a rerun of *City Slickers II,* laughing and giggling all the way through it.

Ashleigh watched, chilled and fascinated when the rattlesnake filled the screen, yet laughing when its victim begged for someone to suck the poison out. Unconsciously, she stroked the serpent of the Lovers.

"Biggest damned rattlesnake I ever saw," Bobby said. "If I get bit on the butt, will you suck the poison out?"

"Count on it, lover boy."

After the movie, they wrestled playfully over the last french fries. Ashleigh grabbed the plate and ran behind a chair. "They're mine," she said, sticking it in her mouth, sucking it in slowly. Ketchup ran down her chin and she wiped it off with one finger and licked it clean.

Bobby chased her and they fell on the bed. He tickled her ribs and she laughed and cried hysterically, begging him to stop.

It was late when they undressed. Bobby stretched out on the bed as Ashleigh uncapped the small vial of oil and approached him solemnly. "Just a very light coat," she said, working the oil over his back and the Lovers, "a preparation for tomorrow night."

In dozens of other rooms throughout the hotel, there were wild and drunken parties in progress, but Ashleigh and Bobby made love slowly, tenderly, each trying to please the other until they cried out in unison at the unbearable pleasures they had created.

Ashleigh awakened only once during the night. Naked and uncaring, she went out to stand in the cool night air on the balcony. She stared up at the stars for a long time before returning to bed. Star light, star bright . . .

Chapter Thirteen

Ashleigh wished Burke—and Danny—had decided to attend the convention. It was Burke, of course, who took her to the first, introducing her to other artists, telling each that she would soon be the best of them all. Since then, however, Ashleigh had made no attempt to maintain friendships with artists other than Burke and Dean, telling herself she did not want her work influenced by other styles, other creations.

Still, she dutifully went through the manufacturer displays, but saw nothing she wanted or needed, believing that state-of-the-art equipment was no substitute for creativity and talent—or tradition. The truly gifted artist could create from old and primitive equipment. She had done good, even excellent, jailhouse tattoos with little more than contraband straight pins and black ink. Without the gift, however, tattoos were mere scratchings on the skin, graffiti for the body.

She guided Bobby through the vast ballroom where dozens of artists plied their trade. Some who knew her nodded slightly in recognition. Ashleigh smiled politely, nodding in return, but remained aloof. She knew they called her "the Bitch," but she didn't care.

The Lovers—or Bobby's tattoo—were entered in the competition. He was number nineteen, although Ashleigh would have preferred number seven. She told herself again that a number didn't matter, only the work itself, and the work was good, perhaps her best, but the doubts lingered throughout the long day.

Bobby was still overwhelmed at the diversity of tattoos on exhibit everywhere. They ranged from the sublime to the grotesque. He tried not to stare but couldn't help himself.

"It's all right," Ashleigh said. "They're here to be seen."

Hideous skulls, pierced by daggers and makeshift wooden crosses, were popular, as were images of Elvis in glittering suits and Madonna wearing metal cones and sucking on a cigar. Tribal patterns, including dark lines of lightning bolts, decorated men and women alike. Elaborate oriental patterns were everywhere.

Bobby liked the traditional style—the nude pin-up girls of old calendars from the forties and fifties, convertibles, even an art deco drive-in restaurant with roller skating carhops and a neon sign that read *"Vaqueros."* A man in his forties had a 1951 Mercury tattooed across his back. It looked just like the car James Dean had driven in *Rebel Without a Cause.*

One dark-haired woman had flowers that began at her elbow in bright colors that climbed to her shoulder. She wore metal horns that seemed to grow from her head and a ring in her nostril.

"Jesus, she looks evil," he whispered to Ashleigh.

Close scrutiny showed that the palm of a hand was a skull.

A woman, her back turned, wore thigh-high boots and a leather jacket. She stood, hands on hips, her bare ass naked and inviting. That was on a man's arm. On another arm, lovers embraced. They were both women.

Frankenstein glared from a man's back; a furry kitten stared mournfully from a woman's back.

Shaved heads were decorated in a variety of ways—the tribal designs, colored swirls and eddies, sunbursts.

A framed portrait of Custer's last stand covered another back. Spaceships from *Star Wars* battled endlessly on another. A matador, resplendent in his suit of lights, performed a graceful veronica on a charging bull.

"Look at that," Ashleigh said, pointing to a man who wore only a strap between his cheeks and a cloth cup over his genitals. He had a full oriental body suit with a beautiful geisha in a red brocade gown and a fat, Buddha-like lover. They sat in the midst of a vast, brightly colored garden that covered his entire body. There were ponds and waterfalls, wooden footbridges, and multitudes of plants and flowers. "That represents hundreds of hours of work."

"I can't believe it," Bobby said, turning to look at a young woman whose tattoo was of a bare-breasted woman, hands bound behind her, daydreaming of herself as a black-corseted whip-wielding dominatrix. The tattooed images looked like Betty Page, a famous pin-up of the forties and fifties. Bobby knew of her because he had once rented and watched a video entitled *Betty Page in Bondage*, a grainy black-and-white production taken from old 8-mm films.

"I give up," Bobby said, as a portrait of Albert Einstein passed. "Let's get out of here. Have a drink. Eat lunch."

"I told you it would be different," Ashleigh said, taking his arm.

The parade of tattoos followed, but none matched the Lovers. "I want to tear my shirt off and show them a real work of art."

"Not until tonight," Ashleigh said.

"I'm impatient."

Again they shared a bottle of wine. Both ordered seafood salads and watched the passing cavalcade of body art.

The wine made Ashleigh drowsy. "I'm tired," she said after lunch. "I think I'll go up and take a nap."

"I'm going to stay down here and wander around some more. Do you mind?"

She shook her head. "Not at all. Have fun."

"I'll be quiet when I come in."

A bouquet of flowers waited in the room. A small envelope nestled among the blooms was addressed to Anne-Marie. The card inside read, "Break a leg tonight." It was signed, "Danny and Burke." Ashleigh smiled as she read it and smelled the flowers. How sweet, she thought, wishing again for their presence, biting her lip as love and desire filled her with warmth.

Ashleigh undressed slowly, quietly, as she had that night when Burke had left her alone with the woman he loved, becoming Anne-Marie once more, remembering how Danny had waited in her bonds, not struggling, resigned to the darkness, yet eager for the pleasures she knew would eventually follow. Ashleigh had forced restraint on herself, savoring the delicious moments of anticipation, knowing that to hurry would be to break the mood, cheat Danny of her yearnings.

Ashleigh didn't know how long Danny had waited. Neither Burke nor Danny had told her. At least an hour or two, perhaps more. Had Burke kissed her before placing the hood? Of course he had. It would be a part of their loving ritual. Did Danny know of the whip placed beneath her outstretched legs, or was that meant as a surprise? Again, Ashleigh didn't know. Once Burke closed the door, she knew only her role.

She was Anne-Marie and Danny was O.

Naked, Ashleigh positioned herself in the center of the hotel bed. Eyes closed, she imagined what Danny felt as Burke tied first one arm and then the other. He would do it slowly, perhaps caressing the soft underflesh, before turning to her legs. Oh, Danny, I wish you were here. Spread wide and open, like Danny, Ashleigh tugged at imaginary bonds, not fighting the straps that restrained her, only testing the limits she was allowed, like Danny, and remembered.

As Ashleigh stood over Danny, she realized how small and delicate the butterfly and the flower were. The photographs did not do justice to Burke's work. Startled, Danny moaned, her tongue fluttering helplessly in its prison when Ashleigh touched her breasts. Will she hear me if I tell her I love her? Ashleigh wondered. It doesn't matter, she will know, even when I whip her.

Ashleigh's breasts caressed Danny's when she leaned over to touch her tongue with her own. The strange gag prevented a true kiss, but Danny squirmed, arching her body, as she ran her tongue over Ashleigh's lips.

Danny moaned and whimpered, shaking her head frantically—the greatest movement allowed her—while Ashleigh kissed her breasts, her belly, her thighs. Danny's orgasm came almost as soon as Ashleigh's tongue parted and invaded the lips between her legs. But overwhelmed with love and wanting desperately to please, Ashleigh continued relentlessly, allowing no respite from the spasms that convulsed Danny.

After a long time, Ashleigh wet two fingers in Danny's vagina and placed them in her mouth. Danny licked them eagerly. Then, Ashleigh dried her fingers on Danny's breast before leaving her.

Ashleigh explored Danny's bedroom, easing dresser drawers open, smiling when she found the nipple clamps lying on a pile of lace brassieres in black and red and green and white. She went through the closet; it smelled of Danny's scent as she buried her face in the blouses and dresses hanging there.

Danny moaned. Ashleigh turned to look at her. Did she think she was alone now? Did she know what was to happen next? Did she care?

Ashleigh took the clamps from the dresser. Danny moaned again when Ashleigh—no, not Ashleigh, she was Anne-Marie now—teased her nipples to full erection and tightened the clamps.

The thongs of the whip were soft against Ashleigh's hand. She held out her palm and raised the whip. The crack was loud and the blow stung her hand, but the pain was bearable, much less than when Bobby had spanked her.

If Danny heard the sharp crack, she gave no sign, but she shuddered when the thongs trailed softly over her thighs, her belly, her breasts.

Ashleigh took the chain and lifted it, pulling Danny's breasts taut. Danny whimpered and moaned when the whip curled around the soft, pale flesh.

Ashleigh unfastened Danny's legs and then her arms, helping her to sit up and turn so she could unfasten the leather hood that held her in darkness.

"I knew it was you," Danny cried when she was finally freed. She fell in Ashleigh's arms, kissing her hungrily, greedily. "Oh, God, you were wonderful."

Ashleigh stroked Danny's damp and matted hair. "I love you," she whispered.

Burke found them like that, both spent from their lovemaking, but still holding each other, caressing, kissing.

Together, Burke and Ashleigh bathed a still shuddering Danny, soap-

ing and rinsing her with tenderness and love, drying her as Danny turned to each of their commands.

Then it was Ashleigh's turn, and she luxuriated beneath the hot, stinging jet of waters from the shower and the caresses of Danny and Burke.

But it was not over.

Burke fastened the collar around Danny's neck, kissing her both before and after. Then he drew her arms behind her and snapped the handcuffs tight around her wrists.

Burke took one of Danny's arms. Ashleigh, dressed now, took her other, and they guided her downstairs. Danny gasped when she saw the preparations Burke had made.

A white column and ropes awaited her. Burke's tattoo machine was in readiness for the symbolic branding.

Danny bit her lip as she looked from Burke to the Anne-Marie who had loved her and whipped her and loved her again.

"Do you consent to wear his marks?" Anne-Marie asked.

"Yes," Danny said. Her mouth was dry and she licked her lips nervously.

The handcuffs were removed then, but only so Danny could embrace the column. They tied her as tightly as O had been, with ropes at her waist and knees, drawing her belly tight against the column, causing her buttocks to protrude for the needle. They tied her wrists and ankles.

Danny could have looked back to watch Burke make the final preparations, but she didn't. Had the ropes not held her in a cruel embrace against the cold column, she might fall to the floor in a faint.

Anne-Marie held her face with both hands and kissed her roughly as Burke prepared her flesh for his initials, cleansing her one last time with alcohol. When she released her, Danny's face was stricken and Ashleigh wanted to untie her, shower her with kisses, beg forgiveness, but Danny did not want mercy. Her fear was feigned. She wanted to feel as O had at the warmth of the approaching iron and the searing pain. Ashleigh believed at that moment that Danny would have submitted to the branding iron, even preferred it, if only Burke would allow it.

Anne-Marie had counted to five during O's branding and Ashleigh counted slowly for Danny as Burke made the first cut. Danny took her breath in sharply, but did not cry out. Tears of joy rolled down her cheeks and Ashleigh kissed them away, tasting the salt, before resuming her count.

When it was done, Burke released Danny and carried her to the couch.

Her arms were around his neck and she kissed him. "I love you, darling, I love you."

"Happy birthday," Burke said.

"It's the best birthday I ever had."

Bobby awakened her gently, kissing her cheeks, stroking her hair. She murmured and reached for him sleepily. "Who sent the flowers?" he asked.

"Friends," Ashleigh whispered, still sluggish, disoriented.

"That was nice."

She pulled away when he kissed her. "Wait," she said, "I want to brush my teeth."

Closing the bathroom door, Ashleigh stood before the mirror and saw Danny. She splashed cold water on her face and the other woman was gone, vanished into the dimension where dreams and memories and nightmares wait to be summoned. She had tried not to think of Danny and Burke and succeeded in forcing them from her thoughts for much of the time since their evening together, fearing that it might not happen again, knowing it would be up to Burke.

After brushing her teeth, Ashleigh was alert, senses heightened by Danny's presence in her dreams. She applied perfume between her breasts and on a whim took her lipstick—once forbidden—and defiantly colored her lips and nipples for Bobby, even as the windswept plains of the high desert danced and shimmered in the mirror.

Oh, Mommy, why did you tell? I just wanted to be like the girls in town.

He pushed her through the door of the unused storage room in the barn. She sprawled on the floor, weeping, her face raw and stinging from the rough soap he had forced her to use to clean the last vestiges of lipstick away.

"On your knees, girl," he roared, "and pray to God for mercy and forgiveness."

Tears ran down her face as she struggled to her knees and clasped her hands in supplication to God, knowing she would receive no mercy from her father. "Dear heavenly Father," she stammered.

The door slammed shut and she heard the heavy padlock click shut and she was left in darkness with a scattering of hay for her bed and a slop pail for her physical needs.

When she was sure he was gone, she huddled in the corner of the small room and wept bitterly.

He kept her there for a week, allowing her out only to go to church on Sunday, where she sat between her parents, her eyes downcast, shamefaced and blushing furiously during the interminable sermon, knowing that her father had spread the word of her transgression.

After she changed from her church dress, he marched her back to the barn. Her mother said nothing. She, too, had been sentenced to solitary confinement on more than one occasion when she had dared speak her mind.

Each dawn and sunset, he brought her two crusts of bread and a bottle of water and read awkwardly to her from the Bible while she ate hungrily, uncaring of the words she heard.

The punishment seemed to go on forever, until Jamie Lee hallucinated, fearing that she was condemned to the tiny prison for the rest of her life. She maintained her sanity by staring out at the forbidden world through a small knothole. At night, she strained her eyes to seek out a star in the clear sky.

Star light, star bright . . .

Bobby knocked at the door. "What are you doing in there? Are you all right?"

"Just making myself pretty for you. I'll be right out."

Bobby was lying naked on the bed when Ashleigh closed the door on her memories. She plucked a red carnation from the bouquet and held it for Bobby to smell as she knelt beside him on the bed.

"It smells good," he said, "like you."

"But I shouldn't have taken it," Ashleigh said. "Now it's dying." She scratched his chest and belly with the short stem and used its petals to caress his penis, smiling as it grew for her, the cobra emerging from its charmer's basket, rising and swaying to the music of a distant flute.

Ashleigh straddled him then, supporting herself with her hands, letting her breasts dangle for him to taste the lipstick.

She threw her head back and cried out as he squeezed her breasts and began to suckle.

The wilting carnation fell to the floor.

There was no thought of hiding her beauty that night. Ashleigh dressed in black leather—boots, miniskirt, halter. The black widow climbed above the edge of the revealing halter in stark contrast to the pale swell of her breast.

"My God," Bobby said, "why don't you dress like that all the time?"

"Because every asshole biker in the hall is going to hit on me, but for tonight I don't care. I want everyone to know the artist matches the work."

The crowd in the hall was loud and boisterous.

Bobby found his own way to take his place in the line of men and women entered into the "best back" competition. Ashleigh took a seat near the front, ignoring the eyes and comments that followed her.

"Jesus, look at that, will ya?"

"That's the bitch from L.A. Nobody gets close to her."

"How would you like to have those legs wrapped around you?"

"Fuck the legs. See those tits, man?"

"She's probably a fucking lesbian."

"Fucking lesbians all over the place. Did you see the dyke with the Harley on her ass?"

Ashleigh sat quietly, staring at the judges seated at a table. Three men and two women.

"You entered?"

Ashleigh turned to find the man next to her staring at the black widow. She shook her head.

"Too bad."

Ashleigh waited, concentrating, trying to make herself be at one with the moment, to think only of the Lovers. But the ebb and flow of the noisy room filling quickly destroyed her focus.

Looking around, Ashleigh knew she was one of their cult, yet apart, somehow vastly different. The room should be hushed in quiet homage and appreciation for works of art, not filled with rowdy drunks aching to party through the night.

She renewed her lonely vigil in the midst of a growing bedlam.

The preliminaries began with the best black and gray and continued through best sleeve, best leg piece, best traditional, best portrait. Finally, it was time for the best back, time for the Lovers.

Ashleigh watched as one back after another was displayed.

There was wild applause, followed by shrill whistling, foot stomping, and catcalls when a nearly nude woman—number seven—pulled her black panties down to her knees to display a tribal pattern that began on her buttocks and traveled all the way to her neck. She lifted her hair to display the entire work and wiggled her ass, grinning back over her shoulder at the audience.

There was polite applause for a galloping unicorn and slightly more for a red oriental dragon breathing fire and smoke, less for the Four Horsemen of the Apocalypse . . .

Ashleigh closed her eyes when applause for number eighteen—a prowling Bengal tiger—died away.

"Number nineteen—Bobby Cole, Los Angeles. The artist—Ashleigh Thomas, Los Angeles."

Ashleigh tried to gauge the applause for the Lovers. It was loud and sustained, but was it more than number twelve or number seven or number fourteen? Ashleigh could not tell. It would be up to the judges. They would have to recognize quality, not applause.

"Number twenty . . ."

Ashleigh opened her eyes. Bobby stood calmly, back to the audience, displaying the Lovers. One of the judges took a second look and scribbled on the pad before him. That was a good sign, Ashleigh thought.

*   *   *

"And the best back is Christie Wilson of Tucson, Arizona. Her artist is Stormy Waters of Tucson."

God damn it, she was the ass-twitching tribal pattern.

"Second place is . . ."

"Taking third place in the 'best back' competition . . ."

Ashleigh's wish was not granted.

The Lovers received nothing, not even an honorable mention.

Flashes

Chapter Fourteen

The underworld awaited her return, beckoning seductively, calling her from murky depths that even the gaudy neon night could not penetrate. They were all there, riding the roller coaster of hell—the young men and women seeking their dreams, thrill seekers, prostitutes, bikers, petty thieves and pickpockets, scam artists, dealers and their addicts, gang bangers, derelicts—the damned and those few who fought to save them.

They lived down there, drifting through dimly lit bars, nightclubs of leather and rough trade, health clubs and gyms, private clubs catering to every taste, sex shops, movie theaters that smelled of sweat and semen and despair.

He was down there somewhere, wandering, waiting for her—the ninth tattoo, the tenth, the eleventh . . .

His initials still excited Danny, never more so then when she passed through her office, smiling and knowing how her flesh swayed beneath her dress in eternal enticement, causing the men among her investors and clients to turn their heads surreptitiously to follow her passage. They had healed beautifully—two capital letters done in an elaborate old English style. All Burke had to do now was touch one or another of the brands—she never thought of them as tattoos; they were deeper and more permanent than that, her offering to him for all time—and she wanted him. Oh, what a lovely secret I share with my two lovers.

Had it been so long ago now?

She could not remember without feeling a weakness in her legs and an insatiable craving to make love to Ashleigh. Their shared kisses and caresses had been too brief after Ashleigh had released her. Danny hungered for more and had a new role for Ashleigh to play, that of Jacqueline, the woman O had seduced for Rene and Sir Stephen in order to send her to Roissey. When told of Roissey and what would befall her there, however, Jacqueline was reluctant, willing only to see what it might be like. Unlike O, who had chosen her fate, accepted it willingly, Jacqueline would have to be forced. No, Danny decided, she could not condemn Ashleigh to Roissey. That was a choice she must make for herself.

As I did.

Still, the vision of Ashleigh bound to her bed, open and helpless, just as she had been, excited Danny, and she wanted to return the pleasures she had received. It was not that she loved Burke any less; indeed, she loved him more now for giving her to Ashleigh, but even O had been allowed to make love with other women, to wield the whip on occasion.

Did she know when I cried out at the first blow that I wanted her to strike harder, to make me scream with ecstasy? Did she like whipping me?

Danny stared at Ashleigh's telephone numbers. Burke had given her both the studio and the home number. "Why don't you invite her for the weekend?" he had asked. "I'd like to begin painting the two of you."

"Won't she be with her boyfriend?"

"Not after the convention. He'll be gone by now."

"Even if the Lovers won?"

"Especially if the Lovers won."

Her administrative assistant tapped lightly on the door. "I have some letters for you to sign," she said.

Danny nodded. "Come in, Helen." She was glad for the interruption. Not having seen or talked with Ashleigh since *the* night and unsure what Ashleigh's reaction might be, Danny was hesitant to call now. It's silly, she thought, as she quickly scanned each letter before adding her signature, the evening must have been as important for Ashleigh as it was for me.

"Thanks, Helen."

Danny waited until the door was closed before lifting the telephone and pressing the numbers for the studio. "Is Ashleigh in?"

"May I tell her who's calling?"

"Yes, tell her it's Anne-Marie."

Danny waited on hold for a long time. Finally, she heard the click of the receiver and Ashleigh said, "Hello, Danny."

"Hello, Ashleigh."

"I'm sorry I kept you waiting. I wanted to come into the back room. How are you?"

Danny thought her voice was soft and doubtful, like her own.

"I'm fine. And you?"

"I was hoping you'd call. The flowers were lovely. Thank you."

"I'm the one who should thank you . . ."

"Did I . . . hurt you?"

"No more than I wanted."

They were silent for a moment.

"We'd like you to come for the weekend. Burke wants to begin the painting. He's going to call it *The Kiss* now."

Silence.

Dear God, please let her come. I want to see her so much. "Ashleigh?"

"I'd love to," Ashleigh said. "I was just thinking about *The Kiss*. He's doing it for us, you know."

"Yes."

"The thought of posing with you, touching, kissing . . . you know I love you."

"Yes, and I love you."

Now that Elliott had met Ashleigh, he looked forward to hearing more of her. As Benjamin wrote in his journal, Elliott waited impatiently, eager for the tale of the beautiful and mysterious woman to unfold. They had fallen into a new routine with Guy reading each entry aloud to Elliott when it was completed.

"It's like a soap opera, isn't it?" Elliott said. "I can hardly wait for each new chapter to arrive."

"Shh, I'm almost done," Guy said, "and then I'll read." He disagreed with Elliott's assessment, however. It was not a soap opera. For Guy, it was an unfolding novel that he hoped would end happily; but he feared tragedy for the heroine he was growing to love.

Ashleigh gave Bobby away.

It was not so much that she had grown tired of him. She told me she loved him, at least as much as she could love any of her canvases, but he was a failure and she could not bear to live with a failure, a daily reminder of the heights to which she aspired, heights she'd failed to achieve.

"I would prefer not to hurt him," Ashleigh said in a strange echo of Melville's tortured scrivener. I went back after that and read of Bartleby again and was struck by similarities. When questioned by his employer on his place of birth, his background, Bartleby always replied, "I would prefer not to." Of course, at the end of the tale, the reader learns that Bartleby came from the dead letter office. What a despairing image.

And I am nothing but a poor scrivener myself, copying what little I know of this woman into my humble ledger.

What dead letter office sent Ashleigh to us, so reluctant to reveal anything of her own birth and background? It is as though she did not exist before that night when she appeared at the window of Burke's tattoo studio, a frightened waif. But of course, she didn't exist.

I have seen her grave.

Ashleigh, why do you prefer not to exist? What terrible memories do you have?

The memory of Jonathan Carver haunts Ashleigh, although she does not discuss it anymore. I suppose she prefers not to. But that is the reason she gave Bobby to Cynthia. She knows the power she has over men. She has always known that, but now she has learned to fear it.

A parting gift to alleviate his pain. Or did she give Cynthia to Bobby?

They argued bitterly, as lovers always do when a relationship ends, but in the end, Bobby accepted it much better than Jonathan Carver. There were no threats of suicide or violence beyond the usual "I'll make you regret this."

Even though it's beyond my realm of experience, I suppose it was Bobby's male ego. What man could resist when told that an attractive and desirable woman wanted him? Bobby must have felt the allure of the new and the different, even with the loss of Ashleigh. And Bobby and Cynthia do have a great deal in common—both want to act, both are well read and literate, both have made love to Ashleigh. Do they discuss it, now that some time has passed? Does it matter anymore?

Not to Cynthia.

The last time I had lunch with Ashleigh, we went to Cynthia's place. (Isn't that strange? It has a name, but I think of it only as Cynthia's place.) When Ashleigh went to the restroom, I asked Cynthia.

"Because he's nice," Cynthia said. "He's not a creep, like most of the guys I've dated. He treats me with respect. He's a kind and considerate lover. As much as I care for Ashleigh, I think she was dumb to break up with Bobby, although I'm glad she did. I'll marry him if he asks me."

But what does Bobby think? Does he miss Ashleigh? Cynthia, too, bears a mark, but can it match the deadly thrill of coupling with the black widow, knowing she must one night turn and devour you? How could he not miss her?

"How deliciously kinky," Elliott said.

Has Ashleigh read *Bartleby?* Guy wondered. I must ask her.

Chapter Fifteen

Ashleigh went back to doing the flash—one of those inconsequential stock patterns and designs that hung on the walls of every tattoo studio in the country—for the young Marine. She had done nothing but flashes for weeks now, an endless series of the vapid and mundane. No one seemed to want an original work, and her search for a new canvas had been unsuccessful so far. Without Kim Lee and the eighth tattoo, Ashleigh knew she would be crazed. She needed a new canvas. Soon.

The first Marine had chosen the Marine Corps bulldog, wearing a World War I helmet cocked at a raffish angle. The other Marine wanted the Globe and Anchor on his biceps. The tattoos were just two more flashes for Ashleigh, but for the two young men, each no more than nineteen years old, they were important proofs of their successful initiation into the fraternity of warriors, and Ashleigh was determined to make the flashes somehow exceptional, something each could display proudly. But it was difficult to concentrate after Danny's call. The words still echoed seductively. *And I love you and I love you and I love you . . .*

Her voice is honey, thick and sweet, like the nectar flowing from her body. Burke is so lucky. He can taste and drink of Danny whenever he desires.

"Does it hurt?" Ashleigh asked.

"Shoot, no, ma'am. I'm a Marine."

Ashleigh smiled. They were so polite and earnest, refugees

from the deep South—Georgia or Alabama or Mississippi. "What do you do in the Marine Corps?"

"We're infantry, ma'am. Bravo Company, Fifth Marines, but we have orders to Force Recon."

"And what's that?" Ashleigh asked.

"The best of the best, ma'am."

"Just like you, ma'am," the waiting Marine said. "That's why we come here. We heard you was the best of the best."

After the two Marines left, the afternoon and a week of afternoons stretched endlessly before her. It seemed now that Friday, and the magic moment of reunion with Danny, would never arrive. But when it did, Ashleigh wondered how they would react—as old friends and lovers, or would they be as casual acquaintances, pretending on the surface there was nothing out of the ordinary about their relationship? No. That could not be. And I love you and I love you and I love you . . .

They would smile at the pleasure of being together again, embrace briefly, kiss, and look to Burke for guidance. Burke was their master. He loved them both.

In her loneliness, Ashleigh went to a bookstore after closing the studio, not one of the large chains, but an independent shop that had somehow survived the onslaught of competition and price-slashing discounts. At another time, perhaps she would have called Cynthia, but that was no longer possible. It would be too incestuous. Unfair.

After a time, Bobby had accepted his fate quietly, with resignation. Ashleigh was grateful to be spared the prolonged arguments and shouting matches, recriminations, protestations of undying love, the telephone messages that invoked misery. Thankfully, there would be no replay of Jonathan Carver. She had told him of Cynthia's interest, taken him to the bar, introduced them. When she'd left unnoticed, Bobby and Cynthia had been talking animatedly, laughing. Perhaps he was tired of me. I hope so.

Ashleigh found comfort in browsing among the narrow

aisles and crowded shelves, seeking the book that would speak to her alone, offer solace and companionship for an evening or two. She found it in the literature section, a small volume of D. H. Lawrence's short stories, squeezed in among his novels and nearly hidden. The book fell open to a story entitled "The Woman Who Rode Away." Intrigued, feeling a sudden kinship with the woman of the title, Ashleigh bought it.

But once she was home, Ashleigh left the book unopened on the couch as she poured a glass of wine and carried it upstairs, sipping occasionally as she changed into shorts and a tee shirt, still thinking of Danny. Questions flooded her mind. Will Burke tie her? Will he tie me? What roles will we play this weekend? Am I still Anne-Marie? When Danny called, she was Anne-Marie. Am I to be O now? Perhaps Jacqueline . . .

"The Woman Who Rode Away" called her, but Ashleigh delayed reading the story. There were restless hours yet to fill before she could sleep. The book was for later, to be savored as she read herself into the respite provided by blessed oblivion.

Downstairs again, she went into the kitchen and refilled her glass before beginning a salad. Chopping radishes, green onions, avocado, bell pepper, and tomato distracted her for a time. She added lettuce and dressing to the bowl before tossing the salad with her hands, licking the dressing from her fingers afterward. Placing it in the refrigerator to chill, Ashleigh went outside into the cool shadows of the garden.

The days were growing shorter as summer slipped into fall. Soon it would be winter and the nights would be chill and crisp. Will I still be alone? For the first time, Ashleigh regretted sending Bobby to Cynthia's arms. Are they happy together? Will they make love tonight? Do they talk of me?

Ashleigh heard the faint ring of the telephone from inside. She thought for a moment of letting it ring, but then decided any human contact, even a wrong number, would provide a brief interlude from the loneliness she felt.

The answering machine had just picked up. "Ashleigh, it's Simone . . ."

"I'm here, Simone. How are you?" she asked eagerly.

"I'm fine, Ashleigh. How about you?"

"A bit down," Ashleigh admitted.

"I'm sorry. What's wrong?"

What is wrong? Danny and Burke love me. Simone is my friend and lover.

"Ashleigh . . ."

"I'm still here. I was just trying to figure out why I'm depressed, and there's no real reason. I'm not working on anything I care about. I guess that's it."

"Well, I have something to cheer you up. We'd like you to come to a costume party."

"Oh, how fun. I've never been to a costume party. What shall I wear? What are you wearing?"

"I don't know yet. Last year I was a harem girl. That's why I'm inviting you so early—you have weeks and weeks to decide. The only rule we have is that you must wear a mask. Plan to spend the night. That way you won't have to drive home so late. You can bring someone, if you like."

"I'll see. There's no one right now."

"I wish Sam was out of town. I'd like to see you."

"That would be nice."

"We should make a date to get together soon."

"I'd like that."

"I'll call you."

Ashleigh hung up hoping that Simone would call, but feeling uneasy about meeting the actress again, knowing it would violate the intense emotion she had for Danny. Simone was a friend. Their encounter was a pleasant interlude. It could never be anything else.

But Danny was more, a passionate recipient of Ashleigh's caresses, if only once; they shared secrets, affection, love. Ashleigh did not want to be unfaithful to Danny and knew she would have to tuck away her love for Danny, keep it in a very special place, like the place Simone kept her secret things.

After eating the salad, Ashleigh finally took the book to the loft and curled up on the loveseat. She leafed through the pages and still felt the one story calling out to her, but she resisted for a moment, reading "The Horse Dealer's Daughter" and "The Princess" first. Both were strange little tales of unhappy women craving to fulfill their sexuality who, once taken, remained unsatisfied.

The lights of Los Angeles far below glowed in the window as Ashleigh turned to "The Woman Who Rode Away," feeling its allure as she read of yet another unhappy woman living in Mexico with her husband.

A casual remark prompted the woman to ride into the mountains to seek the Indians who lived there in isolation. Seeking their gods, the woman found her destiny. Ashleigh identified with the unnamed woman, blond and blue-eyed, thirty-three. Ashleigh would have been thirty-three, the age of Jesus at the Crucifixion.

Ashleigh knew mountains like them, distant hulks in a blue haze. She had stared at them from an insurmountable distance, as though they possessed a secret knowledge that could never be shared, until, despairing, she too rode away into a primitive wilderness as forbidding and dangerous as the untamed land encountered by Lawrence's California girl from Berkeley. Except, Ashleigh thought, the savages here are not so civilized as the Indians found by the woman who rode away. There was order and faith to their lives even as they served a cruel god, passing the legend and the power from one generation to another.

The woman who rode away fulfilled her destiny. Had she remained at home, she would have been among the living dead, trapped by marriage and her children, grown old in isolation, and dead without ever tasting her emancipation. Only in her sacrifice to primeval gods could she find ultimate freedom.

The woman who rode away knew what would happen to her as they kept her a prisoner in solitary splendor, dressing her in blue, the color of the wind, the color of the dead.

No longer reading, Ashleigh watched as the woman, drugged and unresisting, was carried to a cave high above the village and displayed naked to the silent people below, her long blond hair streaming down her back.

She was purified by the priests and when she was worthy of going to the sun, they laid her on the altar. Ashleigh lay upon the cold stone of the altar, wondering why they held her so tightly. She had no intention of struggling, of flight. But still they pressed her to the rough altar, limbs open and wide-spread, waiting, a willing offering to the sun.

Behind her closed eyes, there was no darkness. Ashleigh saw the light descending to the luminous point when the sun would penetrate her heart, possessing her for all time.

And I love you and I love you and I love you . . .

And she died.

Ashleigh sat in the loft, still drugged hypnotically, the book trailing from her fingers. Finally she shook herself from the trance and went to the studio to record the vision before it fled.

Ashleigh sketched furiously with colored pencils, one scene after another. The wait, the purification, the examination, the journey, until the priests carried their sacrificial victim to free-dom while dancers—ominous and surrealistic stick figures wearing feathers and the masks of wolves, panthers, coyotes—circled the waiting altar with graceful steps.

The woman in the sketches alternated between Danny and Ashleigh. It was Danny who stood naked before the people below. It was Ashleigh's body probed by the priest. Once, Ashleigh tried to include Simone's likeness, but her fingers would not obey.

And it was Ashleigh who awaited the sun upon the sacrificial altar.

"My sister would like to meet you," Kim Lee said. "She would also like to be decorated by you."

"I'd be happy to meet her and do whatever she'd like."

"Sue should wait until she is married, but she is very head-strong. She does not yet realize the importance of patience."

"Few people do," Ashleigh said. During many of their conversations, Ashleigh felt that Kim Lee offered oblique instructions, sometimes reversing their roles, always, though, with great humility, as though apologizing for her temerity.

"When you are working, we become as one. We are connected by the needle, the pain, and the great art you are creating for me. You give of your soul. It is a great sacrifice on your part. In return, I give what little I can. My love and my gratitude. It is not enough."

"It is more than enough."

"Our spirits dance together and I sense a growing impatience in you. This is true."

It was not a question, but Ashleigh answered. "Yes," she said, thinking, I am impatient for the next canvas, for the weekend, for Danny and Burke, and love, and tomorrow and all of the wonders it will bring. "But there is one thing I wish would never end."

Kim Lee smiled shyly. "That is why I am giving you my sister. We will still be together in that way."

Oh God, Ashleigh thought, is that why I gave Bobby to Cynthia, so we could still be together?

"Have I troubled you?" Kim asked.

Ashleigh smiled quickly, shaking her head. "No, it was an alien thought that intruded. It does not belong here with us."

"Good," Kim said. "I am relieved."

"Now," Ashleigh said, "it is time to begin."

"I have a confession," Kim said.

"And what is that?"

"I, too, am sometimes impatient. All the time we have been talking, I was eager to show myself to you. You have made me so beautiful, I cannot wait to share it."

An actress now in a stylized ritual, Kim slowly and gracefully disrobed, removing each article of clothing, never once meeting Ashleigh's eyes, until she finally stood naked and unmoving, a work of art sculpted by her artist's needle.

The cobra had become the centerpiece, rising gracefully from its coils, spreading its hood in a hypnotic dance, mesmerizing its victims for a final, deadly kiss.

"Is your sister as beautiful?" Ashleigh asked, reaching out to stroke the cobra, feeling its chill.

Kim trembled at Ashleigh's touch, but she did not pull away. "Not yet," she replied, eyes still downcast, "but when you are finished with her, she will be more beautiful than I could ever be."

"I cannot believe that."

"It is true. You will see."

"You are exquisite."

"Thank you," Kim said, "even if it is not true."

"Believe me," Ashleigh said, turning away reluctantly, ready to begin work.

"Please . . ."

Ashleigh turned back to find tears streaking Kim's cheeks.

"Kim, what's wrong?"

"Please, may I see you today?"

Ashleigh was silent. She replied by unpinning her hair and shaking her hair loose before reaching for the top button of her blouse.

They emerged from the back room shortly before noon.

"Thank you," Kim Lee said.

"You're welcome. See you next week."

"I'll bring Sue."

At the door of the studio, Kim offered her hand formally, as she always did. "Goodbye."

Dean was grinning when Ashleigh went to her desk. "You were back there a long time today. What were you doing?"

"Working."

"I didn't hear the machine for ages. Were you branching out just the teeniest little bit in your sexuality?"

"You have a dirty mind. Nothing happened. Kim was curious. She wanted to see my tattoos."

"Come on up," Dean trilled, "and I'll show you my tattoos."

"It's your turn to get lunch. What do you feel like?"

"Chinese. What do *you* feel like?"

* * *

Between flashes, Ashleigh studied the sketches from the night before. They were of excellent quality, she thought, each deserving of a canvas of its own, depicting a moment in the long journey of the woman who rode away. She would take them to Burke and Danny.

"Dean, let me buy you a drink after work," Ashleigh said. "I want your advice on something."

"Another tat for your tit, interior design, jewelry, cosmetics, a new outfit?"

Ashleigh laughed. "Don't stereotype yourself."

"But dearest, those *are* my best areas for offering advice."

"A new outfit, then. I've been invited to a costume party by Simone Devereaux."

"Oh, what fun! I know the best little shop in all the world for costumes."

I can be whatever I want, whoever I want, just like before, when I met the real Ashleigh for the first time. Queen, belly dancer, witch, houri, cowgirl, mime, Lady MacBeth, showgirl, Little Bo Peep, Cleopatra, vampire, high priestess, warrior goddess—what shall I be? A mannequin in the window wore a dress of royal purple and a crown. Another wore only an imitation animal skin. Ashleigh looked at Dean, her eyebrows raised in question.

"Please, *I* am your costume consultant. I will not have you running about in a scanty animal skin, looking like Raquel Welch at the beginning of time. You'll catch your death."

Ashleigh laughed and moved on, past suits of armor, swords, and lances, to another aisle of magician's robes and clown outfits, bulbous noses and oversized shoes.

"I think not," Dean said, shaking his head. "All those actors and actresses and television people will be there. You must be the belle of the ball. Don't be impatient, Ashleigh, dear. You'll see. We'll find the perfect thing."

Wigs of all colors and lengths. Ashleigh stroked long and soft black hair—a stark contrast to her own, the hair of a witch. Dean shook his head.

Masks. Red and black masks for the eyes, unadorned. Others sparkled with jewels and feathers. One, the feathered mask of an owl, reminded Ashleigh of the mask worn by O when she was taken to the party, leashed by rings piercing the depilated lips between her legs and displayed naked for the pleasure of the partygoers and the boy who showed O to his date, a very young girl, and told her he would do the same to her.

Sensing her interest in the elaborate mask—a headpiece, really—Dean said, "But there's nothing to go with it."

Ashleigh nodded, wondering if he had read *Story of O* and knew what such a mask would entail. Ashleigh was vaguely disappointed when they moved on.

They both stopped when they saw her.

Standing on a pedestal in a corner of the shop, resplendent in the light that played upon her pale skin, was Marie Antoinette. She wore a beautiful dress of the period and a powdered wig, a dimple upon her cheek and another on her breast. Her glass eyes sparkled, but Ashleigh thought she could see a sadness there too, as though the queen knew she was doomed.

Ashleigh's flesh crawled with the thought of the condemned woman riding in the tumbrel through the rough cobblestoned streets of Paris to finally climb the steps to the guillotine. But surely a woman of such royalty and regal bearing would be granted the privilege of a private execution. Surely she would not be subjected to the taunts of the rabble. She would die like the woman of Ashleigh's sketches, with dignity and acceptance of her fate, her destiny.

Ashleigh's fingers went to the tingling sunburst on her neck, feeling it bared by the executioner for the waiting blade. She didn't care. I am Marie Antoinette. I will be the queen.

Ashleigh turned to Dean, ready to argue if necessary.

But Dean only nodded. "You'll be a beautiful queen," he whispered.

Flashes.

Chapter Sixteen

This time it was Danny who waited at the door. "I was getting worried," she said, pleasure and relief evident in her smile, her eyes, as she kissed Ashleigh's cheek and offered her own.

"The traffic was horrible on the 405. I thought I would never get here."

"You should have waited until rush hour was over."

"I couldn't," Ashleigh said. "I wanted to see you."

"I'm glad you didn't. Let me help you with your things." Danny took the overnight bag and a cosmetic case from Ashleigh. "I'll just put them on the stairs for now. Later I'll take you up to your room, but let me get you something to drink first. A glass of wine, or would you prefer something else?" She turned and faced Ashleigh. "Are you as nervous as I am?"

Ashleigh nodded slowly. Where is Burke? "Oh, yes. I thought the week would never end, and when it did, I panicked. I almost called to say I was sick. I was afraid things would be different, that you wouldn't like me . . ."

"It's silly, isn't it? I was afraid of the same things. But I *do* love you."

"And I love you," Ashleigh said, watching as Danny crossed the room, admiring the older woman's beauty as she had so many times in her daydreams. Danny had not changed from work. She wore a white blouse, a black skirt, and a green jacket that complemented her hair and eyes beautifully. Gold hoop earrings were her only jewelry. Ashleigh was glad now that she had decided against dressing too casually, choosing a brightly patterned summer dress that bared her shoulders, and white pumps.

Ashleigh waited, swallowing as Danny approached in slow motion. She was so cool and elegant, tall and powerful, a woman of great self-assurance. But she was O, too, a willing slave to her lover and to Anne-Marie. Ashleigh wanted to cry out, Who am I?

"Now, let me greet you properly," Danny said, finally taking Ashleigh in her arms.

When Danny kissed her, Ashleigh knew the answer and submitted willingly, happy to have her decisions taken away, her choices eliminated, murmuring softly as she opened her mouth and pressed against Danny, smelling the freshness of the other woman's hair and the faint scent of her perfume. They kissed for a long time, slowly, parting only reluctantly, breathlessly, still holding each other lightly.

Danny's breath was warm on Ashleigh's cheek as she said, "You are the first woman I've ever kissed like that. I've wanted to do it for the longest time. I couldn't return your love the first time. Now I can." She took Ashleigh's hand and pressed it beneath the jacket against her breast. "Can you feel my heart pounding?"

"Yes."

"Now, what about that drink?"

"A glass of wine would be fine," Ashleigh replied, her voice shaking like her knees. She licked her lips and tasted Danny's lipstick, wanting more, yet knowing now that she had only to follow Danny's lead. The script had already been written.

Ashleigh followed Danny into the kitchen.

"I have a nice bottle of champagne," Danny said, kneeling gracefully before the open refrigerator. "I've been saving it for you . . . for us."

Ashleigh dared not ask.

Danny smiled, her eyes twinkling, as she rose and brought the bottle to the counter. "It's just us girls tonight. Burke's working late and he's going to spend the night at the studio."

"A present," Ashleigh said. "To us."

"Yes," Danny said, "isn't he sweet? I love him so much, just as you do."

"Yes."

In the living room, Danny curled her legs beneath her. Ashleigh sat next to her, relishing a nervous anticipation of the evening ahead. Burke's absence added a dimension Ashleigh had not expected.

"How have you been?" Danny asked.

"All right, but a little restless. I need to work on something big again."

"I'm sure you were disappointed when the Lovers didn't win."

"That's behind me now. There's always another canvas."

"Have you found him yet?"

Ashleigh shook her head. "I've been doing some sketching, though. Would you like to see them?"

"I'd love to."

Ashleigh went to her bag and took the drawings from a heavy folder. One by one, she handed them to Danny.

"They're very good," Danny said. "Better than that—excellent. You have real talent."

"Thank you."

"But why didn't you put me on the altar?" Danny asked.

"I didn't want to hurt you."

"But that's who I am."

"Usually," Ashleigh said, "but not always, not tonight."

"No," Danny said, "tonight it is my turn to give you pleasure."

"Who are we?"

"I am O, always O."

"And am I always to be Anne-Marie?"

Danny stroked Ashleigh's cheek, softly, tenderly, brushing a strand of hair away. "No," she whispered, "now you are Jacqueline. I'm going to seduce you for Burke."

Ashleigh nodded, thrilling to hear her fate spoken. "Jacqueline is such a pretty name, but I never liked her in the novel.

I've always wished for a sequel in which Jacqueline was sent to Roissey. I wanted to see her dance under the whip, to hear her cry and plead for mercy."

"Are you so cruel?"

"She deserved it."

"Would you go to Roissey in her place?"

"With you?"

"With anyone."

"No," Ashleigh answered after a long pause. "I would only go for someone I loved very much."

"Burke?"

"No. He belongs to you now."

Danny smiled. "Yes. By becoming his slave, I have made him mine forever."

Ashleigh sipped from her wine. "I have another present for you," she said shyly.

"And I have one for you."

Ashleigh smiled. "Mine first."

"All right."

"It's in my bag. I'll get it."

"No. Let me show you your room. You can give it to me there."

Danny took Ashleigh to a second bedroom, adjoining the master bedroom. Ashleigh glanced in as she passed the open door. The bed was neatly made, but she would always remember a helpless and vulnerable Danny waiting for her.

Danny placed the bag on the bed. "Do you like the room?"

"Oh, yes," Ashleigh replied.

"Think of it as yours. Always."

They sat on the edge of the bed as Danny removed the ribbon and the wrapping from the box.

"Oh, it's lovely, Ashleigh. Burke will like it very much. Please, put it on for me."

Ashleigh took the black choker and cameo. Danny lifted her hair as Ashleigh fastened it about her neck. Together, they went to the mirror and looked at their reflection.

"It's beautiful," Danny said touching the cameo.

"I'm glad you like it."

"You give me such lovely presents," Danny said, meeting Ashleigh's eyes in the mirror. "They must be what you would choose for yourself."

"I don't know."

"I do," Danny said.

"When I bought the nipple clamps, I tried them first, but I was disappointed." Ashleigh paused, still looking at Danny's reflection. "I wanted you to put them on me."

"Are you ready to play such a part?"

Again, Ashleigh replied, "I don't know."

"Get them," Danny commanded coldly, in their ever-shifting reversal of roles. "You know where I keep them."

Ashleigh blushed, remembering how she had explored Danny's bedroom, wanting to know her secrets. "You knew I peeked through your things?"

"I sensed it. I would have done the same. Perhaps I will one day."

"Perhaps."

"Now, go. I'll wait for you downstairs. When you return, I'll give you your present."

Ashleigh entered Danny's bedroom slowly, feeling as she had long ago when she'd been sent to fetch the razor strap for her father. But that was different. She hated her father and he hated her because she would not bend to God's will as he interpreted it. He stopped beating her only when he discovered that she preferred pain to the terrible isolation of her long and maddening confinements in the barn.

They were in the dresser drawer, waiting for her. Ashleigh wondered if they had been used on Danny since that night. The whip was there, too. Ashleigh knew that it had been unused. Burke could not bear to hurt Danny, even though she liked it, wanted it. Ashleigh was proud that he loved and trusted her enough to whip Danny in his place.

"Kneel there." Danny pointed to the floor in front of the couch.

Ashleigh did as she was told, her hand going automatically to the buttons of her dress.

Danny stopped her. "No, let me."

Ashleigh sat back on her heels, arms at her sides. She closed her eyes when Danny stroked her breasts, her fingers moving in tiny circles over the nipples.

Danny unbuttoned Ashleigh's dress slowly, slipping it from her shoulders, letting it fall around her waist. Danny unfastened the brassiere and tossed it aside before touching and kissing the spider as in homage.

Ashleigh murmured when Danny touched her nipples again, making them even harder, and winced as Danny tightened the small screws, imprisoning first one red bursting nipple and then the other.

"There," Danny said sitting back. "Lovely."

Ashleigh looked down. The chain was cold against her belly.

"Now, put your dress on and come sit next to me while you open your present."

In a dream, flesh tingling, Ashleigh opened her gift and turned to Danny in surprise. "It's beautiful."

"I wore it for many years while I waited for Burke. I want you to have it now. You are very much like me. One day, you will meet your master and you will give yourself to him as I have submitted to Burke."

Ashleigh nodded, looking down at the thick gold bracelet. She held out her wrist. "Will you put it on me?"

Danny fastened the bracelet on Ashleigh's left wrist. It was heavy, like the weight that pulled at her breasts. Ashleigh extended her arm to admire it. "It means I belong to you now."

"Yes, for tonight, you belong to me."

During dinner, neither made reference to the adornments they wore. Danny touched her choker frequently with evident pleasure. Ashleigh's chains were hidden beneath the dress but evident nonetheless as her aroused nipples pushed at the material with her every movement. And the bracelet was heavy upon her wrist.

Danny told Ashleigh of a complex investment she had concluded only that afternoon. In turn, Ashleigh related stories of the flashes she had been doing and of the costume she and Dean had chosen for Simone Devereaux's costume party.

"Oh, you must take a picture so Burke and I can see how lovely you are."

"Of course."

"We must do something really special for Burke tomorrow. Would you like him to fuck you? I wouldn't mind."

"Whatever he wants," Ashleigh answered carefully. "And you."

"Well, tomorrow's a long way off. Right now, I think we should have a nightcap. A cognac, to celebrate our love."

"Yes, I'd like that," Ashleigh said, as they went into the living room. "But let me get them. You've been doing everything."

"If you like," Danny said, nodding toward the bar.

When Ashleigh returned, Danny was leaning back against the couch, eyes closed, lips parted in a slight smile.

"What are you thinking?" Ashleigh asked.

"Oh, a jumble of things. You . . . Burke . . . how happy I am." She sat up and took the heavy crystal snifter and swirled the dark liquid. "How strange this would all seem to others."

"I think only of how normal it is. Two women who care for each other, love each other, should express it."

"Yes." Danny sipped and then put the snifter down. Leaning over, she unbuttoned Ashleigh's dress and bared her breasts for the second time. "You haven't complained," Danny said, lifting the chain.

"It was my choice."

"When I wear them, I think of you."

"Then I hope you wear them often."

Danny smiled. "Oh, I do. Shall I take them off now?"

"If you like."

"What do they feel like?"

"Love." The answer came quickly, naturally, but it was

true, Ashleigh realized. The constant pressure, shifting with her every movement, kept her warm and pleasantly aroused, reminding her always of Danny's passion and the impending moment when she would be taken in love by the older woman.

"Then you should wear them a little longer."

Ashleigh felt like a virgin, a character in some obscure nineteenth-century English novel, going to her marriage bed as she followed Danny up the staircase and into the second bedroom.

Danny turned and took Ashleigh into her arms. "You're trembling. Are you afraid?"

"No," Ashleigh whispered. I can't wait any longer. I love you so much. I want you to love me.

All through the long evening, Danny had teased her relentlessly with kisses, a caress, a casual touch, until even a glance or a smile drove Ashleigh to abandon.

Please hurry, darling.

But Danny undressed her slowly, discarding dress and chains, kneeling to kiss her belly as she drew the panties down, allowing Ashleigh to step out of them.

Ashleigh moaned as Danny kneaded her buttocks and pressed her face to carefully scented pubic hair. Ashleigh entwined her fingers in Danny's hair.

Hurry now please hurry now.

Danny led Ashleigh to the bed and then slowly undressed for her, smiling as she removed the blouse and skirt, lifting the slip over her head with crossed arms. Even when she was naked and Ashleigh opened her arms, Danny prolonged the moment by turning and going to the switch, dimming the lights before finally approaching the bed.

"I want to see your reaction," Danny whispered, "as I make love to you. I want to watch your pleasure. And hear you. I don't want to miss anything."

Danny was relentless.

Ashleigh's face contorted. She gripped the rails above her head. She cried and moaned. She screamed and beat her head against the pillows and screamed again, arms flailing wildly. Burning sweat ran into her eyes, but she was oblivious to everything except Danny's tongue, lips, hands. Her flesh rippled and she gasped for breath as one orgasm ended and another began. She saw Burke's initials burned into the pale flesh and they became as one. Ashleigh reared her head and thrust her tongue deep into Danny even as she grabbed at Danny's tits, slippery with sweat, and held on as Danny's moans joined her own and the sweet taste of Danny filled her mouth.

Afterwards, limp and exhausted, filled with love, they held each other and cried, tears streaming down their faces, mingling, becoming one as they had been, as they still were, as they always would be.

When Ashleigh awakened, it was cool and the first streaks of light were just filling the bedroom windows. Sometime in the night, Danny had turned away from her and she could clearly see the initials Danny wore so proudly. She touched them lightly, not wanting to disturb her lover and friend. Then she moved closer and put her arm around Danny, cupping her breast as her lovers had so often done for her. Danny stirred but did not awaken, and Ashleigh fell asleep once more, her hand filled with the pleasing weight of another woman's breast.

When Ashleigh awakened again, sunlight streamed in and Danny's face, still streaked with tears of joy, was beside hers on the pillow, smiling. "Good morning."

"Good morning, darling," Danny said.

"I don't want to get up. I want to stay here with you forever."

Ashleigh could not help but feel regret and envy when she saw the joy on Danny's face as she ran to greet Burke at the first sound of his key in the lock. "Good morning, darling," Danny cried, as she kissed him.

Good morning, darling. Earlier the words had been for

Ashleigh, but the interlude was over. Good morning, darling.
Ashleigh wished she could love a man as Danny loved Burke.
One day you will meet your master, Danny had told her. Will
I? Will he love me as I love him? Will we be happy, like Danny
and Burke?

"Hello, Ashleigh," he said, smiling sadly as always.

"Hello, Burke." She kissed his cheek.

After her initial greeting, Danny resumed her role of submissive in Burke's presence. The dominant of the night before
had vanished. Ashleigh wondered if it was unconscious, a second nature.

A casual visitor, perhaps a neighbor dropping by for a cup
of coffee, would see nothing unusual in the relationship between Danny and Burke. The neighbor would see only a
woman and a man for whom the exciting freshness of their
love had not yet worn off. An observant neighbor might see
Danny as too solicitous, instantly refilling Burke's coffee cup,
or too eager to please in other little ways, but that would pass
in time. For his part, Burke exhibited a familiarity with household chores, rinsing the breakfast dishes before placing them
in the dishwasher, wiping the counter and sink clean of even
the tiniest of crumbs, squeezing the sponge dry. That, too,
would pass, the visitor would think.

Without knowing its meaning, that same person would believe the cameo choker Danny wore too formal for a Saturday
morning at home. Ashleigh, however, was no casual visitor.
She saw the way in which Burke gripped Danny's wrists—not
her hands—in another slight reminder of her slavery as he
drew her close for a kiss. And Ashleigh wondered if Danny
would be restrained in some fashion tonight, perhaps tied or
chained. She hoped so and thought, I'm acquiring a taste for
discipline.

Ashleigh stared at Burke's brushes and his palette and the
colors arrayed there, just as she so often stared at her machine

and the brightly colored vials of ink. Somewhere in the mystery of the combination oil and brush, ink and machine, all the masterpieces of the future and past lurked, waiting only to be released by the chosen.

It was strange to undress for Burke after last night. Ashleigh glanced over at Danny and was certain she must feel the same self-consciousness. Danny was dressed casually, barefoot, wearing shorts and a tee shirt from a Don Henley concert. She undressed quickly, tossing the garments aside, smiling.

Ashleigh wore only a long tee shirt that fell almost to her knees. She lifted it over her head slowly. For a moment, Ashleigh covered her breasts and loins modestly before deciding that was absurd. She had given more of herself to Burke than any other man. He knew her as intimately as one person could know another. Still, Ashleigh blushed as she averted her eyes from Burke—and Danny.

But Burke was the professional artist as he arranged them in the pose he wanted, ignoring their nudity as he stepped back to look. "Danny, tilt your head a little more. No, the other way. That's it. Good. Ashleigh, you're looking down into her eyes. Open your lips. A little more. Good, remember, it's your first real kiss as lovers. You're both anticipating it. Looking forward to it. Good. Perfect."

For *The Kiss*, they knelt close to each other, Danny sitting back on her legs, Ashleigh leaning over her, the tips of their breasts just touching. Ashleigh's hand hid Danny's face from the sight of Burke's brush, a protection of her identity. Ashleigh's face was obscured by her hair, but it didn't matter. If Burke wanted to display her to the world, she would consent gladly, in any obscene position he wanted. She owed him that—and more.

Their lips brushed and they smiled at each other with their eyes. "I love you," Ashleigh whispered.

"And I love you," Danny replied.

There was no need to whisper. Burke understood their devotion to each other and accepted it, secure in his own position with the two women who loved him, each in different ways, as he loved them.

It was a quiet Saturday afternoon and the residents of the complex went about their activities. Outside, children played, laughing loudly as they rollerbladed up and down the sidewalk. A mail delivery was made; letters dropped into the box and the lid clanged shut. Somewhere in the distance a siren wailed, an ambulance racing to an emergency medical situation. It was replaced by the sound of running water as a man washed his car down the street. Next door, the muted voices of two women discussed a flower garden. There was a *ping* of an aluminum bat on a ball as a father shouted encouragement to his son. It's all so normal, Ashleigh thought. Except . . .

Inside, two naked women posed, prolonging a phantom kiss for a man who had fucked them both.

When Burke signaled a break, Ashleigh and Danny stretched. Neither made any attempt to go behind the easel. Both knew Burke didn't like them to see the work until it was further along.

Danny slipped into her shorts and shirt. "I'm just going to get the mail," she said.

"How's it coming along?" Ashleigh asked, standing on tiptoe, reaching for the ceiling.

"Pretty good. Would you like some more coffee? I'll make a fresh pot."

"Yes, I think I would. I'd forgotten how tiring it is to pose. I'm getting sleepy." She slipped her own tee shirt on and followed Burke into the kitchen, watching as he rinsed and refilled the pot and reached into the cupboard for a new filter.

"I should be doing that," Ashleigh said.

"Why?"

"To please you, to do a little something to thank you for last night."

"Posing for me is enough."

"Why, Burke?"

"Because both of you wanted to be alone with each other. You needed it. It was another step on your journey."

"You always know the right thing, don't you?"

"Sometimes. Not always."

"We're going to be married," Burke said.

"Oh, Burke, that's wonderful. I'm so happy for you, for both of you."

"It's nothing fancy. Just a judge, but we want you to be there."

"I'm honored, Burke." She went to him and embraced him. "I want you to be very, very happy."

"Sorry," Danny said when she returned. "I got trapped by that horrid Henderson woman from the homeowners' association. She's still trying to get me to run for the board. I told her no. Again."

Ashleigh embraced Danny. "Burke told me. I'm very happy for you."

"Isn't it wonderful? I'm so lucky."

For another hour they maintained the pose silently, wanting Burke to do his best work. But then, Ashleigh suddenly stuck her tongue between Danny's parted lips.

Danny giggled.

"Keep still," Burke said. "I'm concentrating."

"Sorry, darling."

"Sorry, Burke."

Danny made a face, grimacing. "Artists," she said.

They giggled some more, like two schoolgirls complaining about their parents.

"Jesus Christ."

"We'll be good," they chorused.

And they were. Until a strand of Ashleigh's hair brushed against Danny's nose.

"That tickles," she cried, trying to blow it away without moving.

Ashleigh joined in.

"I can't stand it," Danny cried, breaking the pose to scratch her nose furiously.

"I'll give you tickle," Burke cried, rushing across the room to grab Danny's foot. She laughed hysterically as he tickled her sole, struggling to break away. "Please," she cried, "I'll be good. Ashleigh, make him stop, please make him stop."

"She's next," Burke said, pulling Ashleigh close, tickling her rib cage, as she wrestled to get away, laughing, crying, "No, Burke, please. Oh, stop it, please."

Danny jumped on his back and pulled him down. "Get him," she cried. Still laughing, Ashleigh joined the struggle and they soon pinned him to the floor, Danny astride his chest, Ashleigh holding his legs.

"Give up?" Danny asked.

"Never," Burke said laughing.

"Get his pants off," Danny said.

"Okay, okay, I give up."

"Too late," Danny said leaning down to kiss him. "Now, it's your turn."

Ashleigh watched, feeling like a peeping tom, as Burke put his arms around Danny and returned her kiss. She wanted to leave, started to leave, but Danny took her hand and refused to let her go. Their eyes met and Danny nodded permission.

"Oh, Burke," Ashleigh whispered, before she kissed him.

Outside, children laughed.

They took turns.

Ashleigh fed him her breasts and moaned as he sucked first one nipple and then the other while Danny licked him to erection. Ashleigh closed her eyes when she took him in her mouth and listened to Danny's whimpering cries of pleasure. But it was Danny who swallowed his sperm greedily while he moaned and cried even as he kissed Ashleigh frantically.

When it was over, they sat beside him, stroking his chest and face. "We love you," Danny said.

* * *

He arranged them side by side, their bodies touching, as for another painting, with cushions from the sofa beneath their buttocks. Danny held Ashleigh's hand tightly, her smile turning to a sudden gasp as Burke kissed her breasts.

Ashleigh waited, watching her lover bite her lip as Burke made love to her. The wait was brief. Burke showered them both with kisses and caresses, alternating between them, driving them into a frenzy as they writhed and moaned, their cries indistinguishable. When his legs imprisoned theirs—Ashleigh's right, Danny's left—their bodies were wet with perspiration and their excited, distraught kisses tasted of salt.

"Oh, Jesus, God, yes, yes," their cries filled the room as Burke fucked Danny with his tongue and Ashleigh with his fingers.

They drove to San Pedro for dinner, winding along the narrow blacktop road that shifted uneasily in a landslide-prone area. The rugged coastline was marked with small coves and inlets beneath steep bluffs. They ate bouillabaisse sitting on the veranda of a restaurant overlooking a portion of the harbor where fishing boats and pleasure boats bobbed gently side by side in their moorings.

Danny and Burke exchanged a glance as they entered the house. Burke nodded. Danny turned to Ashleigh and said, "Would you excuse us for just a moment?"

"Of course."

"Why don't you put some music on? When I come back I'll pour a cognac for all of us."

When they returned, Danny was dressed only in chains. She wore them proudly. Ashleigh was envious as she held the glass for Danny to take delicate sips.

*   *   *

Still wearing her chains, Danny watched with fascination as her two lovers fucked, thinking, "This is how Burke and I look as we make love.

In the morning, as Danny opened her legs to Burke, Ashleigh thought, This is how I looked and sounded last night.

Sunday night, when Burke cried for mercy, Danny and Ashleigh made love again.

The weekend passed all too quickly.

Chapter Seventeen

As he danced, Bobby always looked behind the footlights, watching for her, daring to hope that one night she would be there again, to see what she was missing, but she never was. And that made him want to hurt her all the more.

Cynthia watched the eleven o'clock news as she waited for Bobby to come home from his last show. June McCormack, the anchorwoman, chattered breathlessly with the weatherman and the sportscaster between accounts of two private airplane crashes, the disappearance of a woman feared kidnapped, a drive-by shooting, a battered woman who shot her husband with his own gun, another disgraced politician, arrested while soliciting a prostitute, the winning lottery numbers. It was a way to pass the time until Bobby arrived.

During all the weeks they had been going out now, Cynthia had competed fiercely with a shadow for Bobby's affection. Cynthia knew Bobby still loved and missed Ashleigh, but she didn't care. Cynthia understood the depth of his emotions because she, too, missed Ashleigh, their friendship, their occasional playful encounters. But it was lessening—for both of them. Time, that blessed magician, and her own deep and growing love for Bobby, would eventually erase the pain—for both of them.

She wasn't nearly as beautiful as Ashleigh. Bobby kept two pictures of Ashleigh hidden away in a bottom drawer of the dresser. Sometimes, when she was alone and waiting for him, Cynthia took them out and made the comparison, always knowing that any man who had possessed Ashleigh even once would long for her.

Ashleigh's face was of a classic beauty. Cynthia's was fresh and girlish. Cynthia wore her reddish hair in a ponytail that added to her youthful appearance. She was nearly as tall as Ashleigh, but slender, with long, coltish legs. Her breasts were small in comparison, but rounded and firm, with nipples that popped up when ever Bobby looked at her with that smile that said, "I want you." Her shoulders and the upper swells of her breasts were decorated with pleasing freckles that Bobby liked. Looking at the twin photographs propped against the mirror, Cynthia decided for the twentieth or thirtieth or fortieth time, I look like an Irish milkmaid with perky nipples. It will have to be enough.

But one advantage belonged to Cynthia: she loved Bobby and wanted him. Ashleigh did not.

Cynthia knew she was winning the competition when Bobby asked her to spend the weekend at his apartment and they had made love for the first time. Before that, they had only fucked. It wasn't the same as that wonderful, prolonged evening when he had loved her slowly, tenderly. She cried when he said, "I love you," and he kissed the tears away.

Since then, she had spent every weekend with him, working hard to please him without surrendering too much of herself. She would not be an imitation lover for any man. At first, knowing how Ashleigh kissed and caressed her lovers, Cynthia tried to avoid any similarities between them, but it only made her stiff and awkward in bed with Bobby.

One afternoon, she said, "I want to discuss sex."

Bobby smiled. "A good topic, one of my favorites."

"Don't tease. I'm serious."

"All right, let's talk about sex."

Blushing, thinking, "What would me Mum say," Cynthia said, "I want to know everything that pleases you."

"Even if it's kinky?"

"Especially that."

"And in exchange?"

"I suppose I must tell you my secrets."

"And what are they?"

"No, you first."

"All right. I like the way you kiss. I like it when you touch me in public and take my arm. I like it when you call me 'Sweetie' . . ."

"But what do you want me to do that I'm not doing?"

"I want to give you an enema, a hot boiling enema."

"All right," Cynthia said seriously. "You can do that."

"Jesus, you mean all this?"

"It's important, God damn it, tell me what you want me to do."

"Cyn, baby, I want to please you. That's what I want."

"Then tell me what I should do."

"There is one thing . . ."

Once he began, there were other things as well, and when it was her turn, Cynthia found hidden delights that shocked her roiling from her subconscious to her lips. Oh, dear, sweet Jesus, what would me Mum think?

Cynthia turned the television off. Bobby would be home soon. She went into the bedroom and removed her sweater, folding it neatly. That was one of the things he liked best, for her to go around the apartment naked to the waist. "Sometimes," he told her, "I think about you working in a topless restaurant, or maybe tending bar."

Without telling him, she had gone to one of the clubs and applied for a job, wincing in the manager's office when he said, "Let me see the tits, honey," wanting to say, "I'm not your honey, asshole," but stripping anyway, cringing again when he said, "A little small, but they'll do."

Now she was a topless bartender two nights a week. Bobby dropped her off and returned an hour before her shift ended to sit at the bar, watching as she served expensive drinks to a variety of men. When they got home again, he was always insatiable. After overcoming her initial shame, Cynthia decided it was worth it. And the tips were good.

God, isn't life strange and wonderful? she thought, as she went into the kitchen to check the Irish stew simmering on the stove. Perhaps tonight is the night he'll fuck me in the ass. Cynthia still blushed when she remembered asking if he would do that for her. He was making her wait, though, to anticipate. He had learned that from Ashleigh. The war for Bobby's heart and love still wasn't over.

Cynthia waited for Bobby to close the door before she ran to greet him. "Hi, sweetie." She stood on tiptoe and kissed him.

"Honey, there's something we have to talk about," Bobby said.

The chill of a sudden fear ran through her, but she smiled and tried to answer casually as she turned and went back into the kitchen. "What's that?"

Bobby sat in a kitchen chair and drew her down on his lap, holding her as he said, "I want another tattoo. I want Ashleigh to do it."

Cynthia leaned against him, averting her face. Please, don't let me cry. Let me say the right thing. "What would you like?"

"Another tarot card. I haven't decided yet. Something to go with the Lovers." His hand stroked the smooth, warm flesh of her back.

"All right." She hoped he didn't notice the tension that had taken over her body. "Where are you going to put it?"

His hand shifted, moving softly over her belly where she wore the marks put there by Ashleigh Thomas. "On my stomach. We'll match then."

"Yes."

"I want you to be there," Bobby said.

Thank God. It was going to be all right, Cynthia thought, as he nuzzled her breasts. "Don't you want to eat?" she asked.

"I am," he said.

Cynthia held his head as he licked her breasts like twin ice cream cones, thinking, Please, God, let it be all right.

Chapter Eighteen

Without true seasons, the passage of time in Southern California is marked by natural disasters and the biannual change to and from Daylight Savings Time. The hot and smoggy months of summer and fall are punctuated by the raging wildfires—usually manmade—that destroy brush and homes, filling the sky with thick smoke clouds. When the winter rains finally cleanse the skies and shining snow-capped mountains are visible to the east, torrential mudslides and flooding, as destructive as any fire, roar over the recently denuded lands. Local wags are fond of adding riots and earthquakes to fires and floods to make up four seasons for Southern California.

For some, there are only two seasons. There are the long, lingering summer days when darkness does not fall until after eight o'clock and the fortunate take their evening cocktails on poolside patios while others crowd beaches and parks for relief from the heat. But as the year wears on, the days grow shorter and more urgent. Life must be lived fully before the death that comes with the autumnal equinox.

Ashleigh, however, marked time by failure. There were now twelve tattoos in the distinctive portfolio she kept only for her own, very special, creations. Of those, only the eighth and ninth Tattoos—Kim Lee and her sister, Sue—were judged adequate by Ashleigh, but they would never be seen. Of all the others, the Lovers and Death came the closest to the perfection Ashleigh sought, but ultimately they did not match the clarity of the mind's vision.

The sketches of the Woman Who Rode Away were there, too. One of them—Ashleigh's naked figure high above the waiting throngs—would be beautiful on a canvas, etched with her machine into the perfect skin. But Ashleigh was beginning to think it would never be transferred to flesh.

She turned the page from beauty to Death.

Kathleen again selected the Queen of Wands to represent Ashleigh, who sat quietly watching fate unfold as the cards were dealt. All life was before her, if only she could understand.

"You must remain open to all possibilities," Kathleen said. "I see great work and a powerful love looming. There are choices to be made, but a grand adventure lies before you. There are those—past, present, and future—who are your allies and your enemies. You must choose among them carefully, wisely. The power is yours. Always."

"What is the great work?"

"Remain open," Kathleen said smiling, "accept what is to be, what must be. Do not force it."

"And love?"

"Accept," Kathleen replied gently. "Be open."

But I want to know! her mind screamed. "I will," Ashleigh said.

"Be open to all choices, all possibilities."

Ashleigh was surprised and shocked when Bobby called her at the studio.

"I'm fine," she replied warily. "And you?"

"Working, auditioning, acting classes. The same."

"How is Cynthia?"

"Fine. She's right here. You can say hello in a minute." He paused. Ashleigh heard him take in his breath. "I'd like another tattoo," he said.

"Really?"

"I'm afraid you've hooked me on body decoration. I want something to match the Lovers."

"What were you thinking of?"

"Death."

Behold a pale horse; and his name that sat on him was Death, and Hell followed with him . . .

"From the tarot?"

"It matches the beginning of life for the Lovers."

"Yes. If you're sure . . ."

"The first was for you. This is for me," Bobby said. "We'll come to the studio. You can do it there."

We. He would bring Cynthia. There could be no harm in that. It wouldn't be a repeat of Jonathan Carver. "Yes, that'll be fine," Ashleigh said.

They made an appointment. "Now, here's Cyn," Bobby said.

"Hello, Ash."

"How are you, Cyn?"

"Happy."

"I'm glad. I've missed you."

"You should come by for lunch again one day. We'll catch up."

"Yes, I'd like that."

"Perhaps, after Bobby's tattoo is finished. We could do it then."

There was no attempt to disguise her beauty as she went into the night in search of the thirteenth tattoo. Ashleigh wore leather—black boots that folded over her knees, a short tight skirt that fell to mid-thigh, a supple blouse molded to her breasts. Her hair—she thought it the color of Death's horse now—was down, falling nearly to her waist.

She sat at the bar drinking mineral water, coolly appraising the possibilities, rebuffing one attempt after another to buy her a drink. They were all unsuitable. Too drunk, too glib, too flashy, too eager to impress her, too old.

"I'm waiting for someone," she said.

When she left, the remark followed her into the night.
"Lying bitch."

Ashleigh tipped her way to a good table at a rock club and allowed herself two champagne cocktails during the set. The lead singer would have been perfect, Ashleigh thought, as she followed his athletic movements around the small stage. His voice was good, his body even better, hard and muscled. The sweat glistened on his bare chest as he performed. But his eyes
. . .

There was nothing there.

Cocaine, Ashleigh decided, or something else. It didn't matter. She wasn't bestowing her talent on anyone whose most important part of each day and night came from a powder.

After the set, she went to the ladies' room, walking slowly past those who sat at the bar. No one. The thirteenth tattoo wasn't present, not tonight.

The invitation was simple and elegant, worthy of the full-color reproduction of *The Kiss* which graced the inside. Ashleigh thought it beautiful and erotic when Burke had finished and she stood beside Danny, admiring the work. Now, looking at the invitation to Burke's opening, Ashleigh thought it even better. It's as though Burke captured all of our love and placed it within the frame. Burke, I'm so happy for you.

The first session was awkward. Bobby insisted on Death. Ashleigh suggested a card less ugly and more life affirming— the Sun, or the Moon, or the Star, with its beautiful maiden, the earth mother. She did not say that Death made her uneasy, despite Bobby's argument that all renewal came from Death.

"Winter is death," he said, "Spring is life in the endless cycle. Any survey course in literature is filled with examples."

Cynthia listened impassively.

Ashleigh shrugged. It was his body again. She no longer had any rights over it. "I'll give you the very best I can."

"I know that," Bobby said, taking Cynthia's hand. "That's why we're here."

Ashleigh pretended she was an attorney, dressing in fashionable business suits, like the deputy district attorneys who were sometimes on the television news, wearing black outfits with short skirts—cool, professional, and sophisticated, like Danny. She carried a slim briefcase and told herself that she had just come from court after a brilliant cross-examination of a recalcitrant witness. He would recognize her for a very special person, knowing only that she had just accomplished some incredible feat, and come over to offer his congratulations, buy her a drink in celebration. She would accept his compliment gracefully, modestly, invite him to join her.

They would smile and laugh and she would signal with her eyes, a smile, a casual brush of her fingers. Later, they would have dinner. Over coffee, he would say, "I want to see you again."

"I'd like that," Ashleigh would reply, her eyes sparkling only for him, "very much."

"Where's Cynthia?" Ashleigh asked.

"She's working."

"At this hour?"

"She didn't tell you?"

"Tell me what? We haven't really talked lately."

"She has a part-time job now. She's a topless bartender."

"Jesus Christ, Bobby, you let her do that?"

"She did it for me."

"I don't care. She's not that kind of woman."

"What kind of woman is she, Ashleigh? You're so goddamned smart, tell me."

"She deserves better than that."

"That's really good, coming from you. Don't you think she deserved better than a hand-me-down boyfriend of yours?"

"It wasn't like that. She liked you, wanted to meet you."

"And it sure solved your problem. Let's get rid of Bobby so he doesn't make a scene, give him away to Cynthia. Well, I'm glad you did. Cynthia's a real woman with real feelings and real emotions, not some ball-breaking *machine*. One of these days, you're going to get yours, and when it happens, I'll be right there, laughing and reminding you of what you did to that other poor son of a bitch and me and Cynthia."

"You're a bastard."

"Well, fuck you, too. I'll get someone else to finish the tattoo."

"You can't do that! It's mine."

"No, Ashleigh," he said coldly, "it's mine."

Guy Benjamin escorted Ashleigh to Burke's opening. "I'm glad I called when I did," he said, helping her from the car.

"I am, too, Guy. I didn't want to come alone, for some reason. It was perfect timing." She took his arm as they strolled down the street. The days were much shorter now, and it was nearly dark as they entered the gallery.

It was a small gallery near Danny's office. Fifteen or twenty people were there, scattered about the room, drinking champagne and looking at paintings. The walls were given over entirely to Burke's paintings.

Benjamin signed the guest book for both of them as Ashleigh looked for Danny and Burke. She found them standing by an antique desk, chatting quietly with another couple. "I was going to say I'd introduce you to the artist, but, of course, you already know him."

"Yes," Guy said.

"You're kind of cute when you're looking sheepish," Ashleigh said, smiling. "Come on, I'll introduce you to Danny. They're going to be married."

"Thank you for coming," Burke said, as the other couple moved away.

"This is wonderful, Burke," Ashleigh said, as she kissed his cheek and turned to Danny. They smiled and kissed chastely. "Guy, this is Danielle Petersen, Danny for short."

"It's very nice to meet you."

"Thank you for coming."

"Isn't it exciting?"

"I love it. Our Burke."

"Congratulations."

"Everyone has been very complimentary about his work."

"I had no idea, Burke. When did you find time to do all this?"

"It's only a baker's dozen. That's the complete works. Thirteen."

"You're one ahead of me."

Although the other paintings—a variety of seascapes and landscapes—attracted more than polite attention, the two nudes were the centerpieces of the showing. Hung on opposite walls, they captivated their audience—men and women alike.

The Mask, as Burke had renamed the reclining study of Danny, seethed with eroticism. Ashleigh thought the plumed mask a brilliant touch that added mystery and allure to the woman waiting for her lover. The delights of the flesh were offered willingly, but the true essence of the woman was yet shrouded, promising more revelations of the soul to the lover who dared remove the predatory mask. Ashleigh wondered how many of the women present would be wearing masks when they next appeared before their lovers.

Turning to admire *The Kiss* again, Ashleigh remembered that she would be a masked Marie Antoinette soon. Perhaps I'll keep the mask for another time, she thought. No, I'll borrow Danny's. I'll go to Simone's as a hawk, not Marie Antoinette. Yes. A female hawk.

The Kiss, too, was highly erotic, filling Ashleigh's mind with memories and her body with renewed desire for Danny. Even looking at the painting with a detached and critical eye, Ashleigh felt the heat emanating from the canvas, the thrill of anticipation as the moment of *The Kiss* neared. It was as though the warm breath of the two lovers filled the room.

"Were you one of the models?"

"Yes," Ashleigh said, turning to the woman beside her. She was tall and slender, perhaps forty or a little more. She wore a black cocktail dress and was heavily laden with expensive jewelry.

"I've never met a model before. Is Danny the other woman in the painting?"

"No," Ashleigh said, "just another model."

"Too bad," the woman said, moving away. "You'd make a lovely couple."

She knows, Ashleigh thought, and she's jealous.

Ashleigh stood apart, sipping a second glass of champagne, watching as Burke accepted one compliment after another from the room filled with well-wishers. Danny was at his side.

This is what it would be like to own a gallery of my own, Ashleigh thought, rearranging her own canvases in her mind. Heather would be relegated to an obscure corner now, with Chance banished entirely, perhaps. Ashleigh was surprised that Chance and Heather came to mind so suddenly and that her desire to punish them was still so strong. Yes, they would be present, but only as footnotes to her important work, like Bobby and the others.

The worthiest, Kim Lee and Sue, would stand at opposite walls, their pedestals elevating them above the visitors who marveled at their beauty, so enhanced by the art they wore—Kim's half body-sleeve, all dark and elegant swirls amidst the menacing coils of the cobra and the wild, tangled garden that grew on Sue's belly, petaled breasts sprinkling new life with tiny droplets of blood. But who would be the centerpiece?

The thirteenth tattoo.

Or Danny.

How would I decorate her? Let me count the ways.

Danny saw Ashleigh standing alone and excused herself,

touching Burke's arm lightly, before crossing the room, nodding and smiling as she weaved through the groups clustered about each painting.

"You're wearing the bracelet," Danny said, smiling and touching the cameo at her neck.

"For you."

Danny smiled. "For the moment." She looked around at the crowded room. "Everyone's so enthusiastic about Burke's work."

"He deserves it."

"What were you thinking? You looked so serious over here all by yourself."

"About a gallery of my own, a place to display my art."

"A human gallery?"

"Yes, and if it were possible, you would be the centerpiece."

"And how would I be displayed, hung upon the wall?"

Ashleigh shook her head. "On a pedestal, as you deserve, but there would be no masking your beauty."

"Naked, for all the world to see."

"Like tonight."

"But they don't know it's me."

"They suspect." Ashleigh pointed out the woman who spoken to her earlier.

"Oh, Sandie Westerman. Long ago, before I met Burke, she made overtures to me. I was horrified at the thought of a woman touching me. I've certainly changed, but I still wouldn't want Sandie making love to me."

"Good, I'd be jealous."

"What would you put on me to show the world?"

"I don't know. Something beautiful."

"I think I might like another tattoo. I must ask Burke."

"And what would it be?"

Danny smiled and touched Ashleigh's arm as she had touched Burke's earlier. "Your initial," she said. "Just above my pussy. I'd have Burke shave it for you."

*   *   *

They were climbing the dark road to Ashleigh's home when Guy asked, "What about you, Ashleigh? Wouldn't you like to paint?"

"Someday, perhaps. But right now I have my own work."

"Danny's a very beautiful woman, not like you, but in her own way. I'm glad to have met her. Burke's lucky."

"And talented."

"Yes, he is. Would you like to come in for a drink or some coffee?"

"Coffee would be nice."

They were standing at the door when a car started down the street and quickly pulled out. They turned at the abrupt interruption of the night's silence. For a second, Ashleigh thought the outline of the car looked like Bobby's, but that was absurd. He would be at the bar, watching Cynthia flaunt her tits for the customers. The bastard. "You remember my friend Cynthia?" Ashleigh asked, as she opened the door and switched on the lights.

"Yes, of course."

Ashleigh told him of Cynthia's new job as she made the coffee, and about the argument with Bobby. "I finished Death, but he was nasty whenever we were alone. Obsessed with the tattoo. He seems all right with Cynthia, thank God."

"But you're sorry you introduced them."

"Yes."

"And you miss Cynthia, even though you have Danny now."

"You know everything about me, don't you?"

"I know everything and nothing."

Ashleigh smiled and poured the coffee. "Come on, I'll show you my special album."

"I'd like that."

Ashleigh brought out the portfolio and placed it before Guy. "This is who I am," she said. "This is the sum total of my life. There is nothing else."

Guy turned the pages reverently, studying each photograph, each tattoo, glancing briefly at Ashleigh with appreciation. "Good," he whispered, "so very good." He passed by the fifth tattoo quickly, without comment.

It was Ashleigh's turn to whisper. "I'm sorry."

"I know," Guy said.

At the seventh tattoo, he said, "They should have given you everything."

"What?"

"It's an old album I listened to as a kid. I wanted to be a bullfighter. I thought I would look good in the suit of lights. Instead, I became a cop."

"You should have a suit of lights. It's not too late. It's never too late to fulfill your dreams."

"Barnaby Conrad was the narrator. It was about the death of Manolete. He was a very famous bullfighter. He was gored, and before he died, asked if the crowd had given him an ear of the bull." Guy was silent for a moment. "They gave him everything."

"They gave me nothing."

"They will." He turned the page. "My God," Guy exclaimed. "They're beautiful and the work is so exquisite, so detailed."

"But the work will only be seen by a few."

"I'm honored to be one of them. You really should paint."

Guy admired the sequence of the Woman Who Rode Away, recognizing its source immediately. "Why did you alternate between yourself and Danny?"

"I don't know," Ashleigh replied, shrugging.

In Death, an armored skeleton rode his pale horse over a fallen king as he approached a cowering child and mother. The woman turned away fearfully. It was Cynthia's face.

"It reminds me of Hieronymus Bosch."

"That wasn't my intent, but you're right. I don't like it very much."

"It's good, but I don't like it, either. He should have been content with the Lovers."

*   *   *

Ashleigh walked him to the door. They embraced briefly, exchanged kisses on the cheek, said goodnight. She waved as Guy pulled out and watched until his headlights disappeared down the hill.

Inside again, Ashleigh stared down at the open album. On the left was Death. On the right the empty page awaited the thirteenth tattoo.

Chapter Nineteen

She circled high above, wings spread, riding the air currents, gliding gracefully through darkening skies, patiently seeking her prey, waiting . . .

Descending the staircase into Simone's living room, Ashleigh was the hawk she portrayed. She wore a black evening gown and the black mask, plumed with feathers and narrow slits for her eyes, each lined with tiny stones that might be diamonds. It was fringed with beads that hung over her cheeks, ending above her lips, brightened by a deep red lipstick. Eyes turned upward and a hush fell over the room, only to be broken by excited whispers.

"Who is she?"

"Nobody. Some friend of Simone's."

"She's gorgeous."

"Jesus, what does she have on her tit?"

"It looks like a spider web."

The gown rustled softly as Ashleigh walked to greet Simone.

"This is the last time I invite you," Simone whispered. "You've stolen the spotlight from me and every other woman in the room. God, you're beautiful."

"Thank you."

"Make yourself comfortable. You know everyone by their costumes. At midnight we unmask. Until then, we are our characters. I'll introduce you formally after midnight."

Simone and Sam were Batwoman and Batman.

Robin Hood was accompanied by Maid Marian. A Friar Tuck in a brown cassock carried a crooked staff. One couple came as clowns with matching costumes, floppy shoes, and sad frowns painted on their faces. Wonder Woman was there with a grizzled cowboy. Superman was fat and aging.

Men and women, all dressed formally in black tie, gowns, and masks, served drinks, passed among the guests with trays of canapes, carved roast beef.

Ashleigh moved among them, pausing to chat a moment, smiling before moving on. Men clustered around Ashleigh, trapping her near the bar while their wives watched over them warily, whispering cruel jibes about the rival who had suddenly appeared in their midst.

"Who is she really?"

"She's some sort of tattoo artist."

"I suppose we must be nice to her because of Simone and Sam."

"That spider. It's just too bizarre."

The men, given their opportunity to peer down her gown and mentally strip and fuck her, drifted away one by one until Ashleigh flew alone, circling, waiting.

"They're not really so bad," Wonder Woman said, taking two champagne flutes from the tray of a passing waiter. She handed one to Ashleigh. "You made quite a stir with your grand entrance."

"It was unintentional," Ashleigh said. "It's just an evening gown."

"It's the mask. You *know* it's the mask. It's just so goddamned sexy and erotic. I'm jealous."

When lovers first meet, they have spent a lifetime hurtling through the intricate maze of time and space to that final clash when individual spirits collide, instantly fusing into one. To the lovers, everything is in slow motion, but within the endless scope of history their journey is as meteoric as any flaming passage across the night sky. At the moment of impact, time stops abruptly, the planets cease to move in their orbits, and nothing can ever be the same again. They are the chosen.

Ashleigh, not daring to breathe, recognized him immediately, just as Danny had said. One day you will meet your master . . .

No!

He came late, dressed as a medieval executioner, naked to the waist, wearing black tights and a black mask. He carried a headsman's ax, a prop borrowed for the evening from a studio or costume rental. A coil of rope hung from his belt. He was tall, and his slender body was muscled and tanned.

Ashleigh watched enviously as Simone greeted him, laughing at something he said, touching his chest, and pulling at a hair playfully.

He stood in the foyer for a moment, looking over the room, a slight smile on his lips, cruel and mocking, as though he disapproved of those he saw.

"Who is he?" Ashleigh asked.

"Oh, that's Richard Sheridan," Wonder Woman said carelessly. "Dressed appropriately enough, I see. I'd be careful if I were you. I wouldn't want to play to his executioner."

Simone's agent. The man known throughout the industry as the Executioner. Their eyes met from behind their masks, the female predator and the Executioner.

"Excuse me," Wonder Woman said, as he crossed the room.

I'm not dreaming. He felt it, too.

"I want to see your face," Ashleigh said, when he stood before her.

"That's against Simone's rules."

"You care nothing for rules."

"Have we met?"

"Just now."

He nodded and pulled the mask from his face and stood smiling down at her.

Ashleigh looked into his eyes and knew. Slowly she lifted

her own mask, baring her soul for his approval, feeling the weakness in her legs, no longer the impervious bird of prey. Without the mask in place, she stood before him, more naked and vulnerable than if he had stripped the gown from her.

"I'm Richard Sheridan."

"Ashleigh Thomas." She lowered the mask again, regaining her strength. When he replaced the mask, Ashleigh reached out and adjusted it slightly.

"Ashleigh Thomas," he repeated, "I'm the agent for half the people in this room, most of whom are afraid of me and loathe me for their fears; I'm considered powerful and wildly successful; I'll be forty next month; and I want very much to make love to you."

"Richard Sheridan, I'm a tattoo artist; the only person I know in this room, really know, is Simone; sometimes I'm twenty-seven, sometimes I'm thirty-three; and I would like you to make love to me. Very much."

He smiled. "Perhaps we should have a drink first."

"Yes, I'd like that." She took his arm and they went to the bar.

"Champagne?" he asked.

"Please."

"Champagne for the lady, and I'll have Johnny Walker Black on the rocks."

They took their drinks and retreated to a corner of the room.

"Are you always so direct?" Ashleigh asked.

"Yes. And you?"

"Only when it's important."

As party guests talked of development deals, scripts, productions beginning and ending, projects in turnaround, they watched Ashleigh and Richard, waiting to see what the Executioner would do with the latest addition to his collection. The boldest among them interrupted briefly to pay homage to the powerful agent. Richard eased them away quickly with offers of breakfast meetings or lunches. "We'll get together soon," was his constant refrain.

"Richard, I'm so glad you met Ashleigh."

"Simone, darling, you should have introduced us sooner. We've wasted so much time."

"I see you're making up for it now," Simone laughed, dancing away to join another group.

"How did you become an agent?" Ashleigh asked.

"I was a writer, but I couldn't get published. When I grew tired of rejection, I became an agent. Now . . . I no longer care."

"Do you still write?"

"Occasionally."

"Will you write something for me?"

"I already have. I'll write more, just for us."

"Will you change our names?"

"If you like."

Between interruptions, Ashleigh said, "I'd like to tattoo you."

"All right."

"Just like that?"

"There would be an exchange, of course."

"All right."

"Just like that?" He smiled.

Ashleigh liked his smile. It had none of the insincerity he showed to the others. They *were* afraid of him, even those who addressed him as old friends. "Yes," Ashleigh said.

"I'm going to make you a slave."

Ashleigh stared at him for a long time, knowing a choice must be made, a decision that would alter her life forever. Then, she smiled and crossed her wrists, holding them out to him, not caring what the others in the room thought of her sacrificial offering, her immediate submission, her challenge.

The room was quiet as the other guests watched to see what the Executioner would do.

Ashleigh, too, waited, curious to see if he would meet the challenge, knowing she would be disappointed if he didn't.

The rope dangled loosely from his hand. "Behind your back," he said. "It's more appropriate for the condemned prisoner, don't you think?"

Ashleigh turned without hesitation.

He tied her wrists quickly, expertly. Simone bit her lip and frowned as she watched. Sam's eyes flashed behind his Batman mask. Ashleigh thought the other men regretted their lack of boldness and now longed for her body; they must be filled with jealousy and envy. What if I . . .? But they hadn't. The Executioner had. Ashleigh raised her eyes and looked to a point on the far wall, dismissing the gathering. They no longer existed.

Ashleigh pulled at her bonds. The rope was tight around her wrists. He didn't ask her if it was too tight—she liked that. She turned and met his eyes again.

"Shall we go?" he asked.

Ashleigh nodded. "You'll have to help me. My things are upstairs."

"Of course."

The guests parted as he guided her through the room to the staircase.

While she waited in the center of the bedroom, he repacked her suitcase quickly, expertly, going to the bathroom with her cosmetic case without being asked. "Is that everything?"

Ashleigh nodded.

Downstairs, still the center of envious attention, Richard said, "Thank you so much, Simone, it's been a lovely evening."

"Richard, don't you think this has gone far enough?"

"Not at all. It's just beginning, isn't it, Ashleigh?"

"Yes. Thank you, Simone. It *was* lovely."

"Call me," Simone said nervously, kissing Ashleigh's cheek.

"When I can." Ashleigh smiled at Richard.

At the door, Richard draped the cape over her shoulders,

fastening the clasp at her neck. Ashleigh thought he would kiss her then and parted her lips, but he only turned away to take her bags into the vestibule.

A light rain was falling as they waited for the chauffeur to bring his limousine. "My car . . ."

"We'll get it tomorrow," Richard said.

"All right," Ashleigh said.

The chauffeur—a tanned young man—held the door open as Richard helped her into the car. If the young man noticed her awkwardness, he gave no sign. "Thank you, John."

"Of course, sir."

"I'm going to have another drink," Richard said, opening the bar. "Would you like more champagne? It's not far."

"No, thank you," Ashleigh replied. "I'll wait, but may I have a sip of your Scotch, please? It'll take the chill away."

"Certainly. Do you prefer blended or malt?"

"Whatever you're having."

He poured and then held the glass to her lips. As she sipped, a little of the warm liquid trickled down the side of her mouth. He wiped her chin with his finger and then licked the Scotch from it.

"It's awkward, at first," he said, "you'll get used to it."

"Yes."

"Are you frightened? Shall I untie you?"

It was a test. He would be disappointed if she asked to be released. "I'm not afraid," Ashleigh lied. She feared—and thrilled—to this man's sudden exertion of power over her.

"Good." He settled back against the seat. A motorcycle, going too fast for the weather, roared down Pacific Coast Highway toward Santa Monica. Its headlight lit the interior of the limousine briefly and then it was dark again.

Again Richard held the glass to her lips as they drove through Malibu, past the pier. "Thank you," Ashleigh said. She turned and looked out at a couple embracing at the door of a restaurant while they waited for the attendant to bring their car. The woman was free and unfettered. Ashleigh suddenly pitied her.

"What are you thinking?" Richard asked.

Ashleigh looked at the window between them and the chauffeur.

Richard pressed a button and raised the window.

"I felt sorry for that woman back there," Ashleigh said.

"Why?"

"I'm not sure . . ." Ashleigh paused. "What are you going to do to me?"

"Does it matter?"

It was happening too fast. Ashleigh looked out the window as they climbed the hill past Pepperdine University. The ocean water was dark, forbidding, like her thoughts, as she fought a swelling panic. For an instant, she wanted to stop time, like Faust, and return to the moment when he'd crossed the room to her. This time, she would not accept his challenge. She would simply turn away and take another champagne flute from a passing tray, compliment Simone on her party, and when she turned back to him, they would talk of the mundane. And then none of this would be happening. Not to her. Not tonight. But she had offered herself, crossing her wrists for the bite of his rope. It was too late to turn back. She had chosen.

"Does it matter?" he repeated.

"Not so long as you love me," Ashleigh heard herself say, knowing that she would accept any cruelty he offered. Oh, Burke, what am I doing? Is this what Danny does for you?

"I will," Richard said. "I do."

He kissed her then for the first time.

Ashleigh wanted to return his embrace, hold him close to her for comfort and reassurance, but she was helpless and reveled in the strength that flowed from him. When he released her, the limousine had stopped in a dark wooden glen above the ocean. She didn't know how long they had been there. She didn't care.

"We'll have to walk from here." It was the first time he was apologetic.

"I don't mind."

He helped her from the back seat and his grip was firm on her arm as they followed the chauffeur's flashlight through the rain down a long and steep driveway inaccessible to the limousine. Animal eyes reflected from the bushes once. A rabbit, Ashleigh thought, or perhaps a fox.

Waves crashed against the shore as they walked down a sidewalk past a garage and across a tennis court, descending again to the house itself.

The chauffeur put her suitcase at the door.

"Thank you, John, that will be all for tonight."

"Yes, sir."

She waited as he opened the door and switched the lights on. He placed her suitcase inside the door and took her cape. "Make yourself comfortable while I hang this up."

She shivered both from the chill in the room and the titles neatly arranged in the bookcases built into the wall. Another man would have secreted them away in a dresser drawer, like her father had hidden magazines whose pages were filled with naked women. *Justine* and *Juliette*, *The Story of O*, *Exit to Eden* and the Beauty trilogy, *The Image*—all works of pain and refined cruelty.

Ashleigh stepped back, startled, as he knelt at her feet and lit the gas in the artificial fireplace. When he removed her mask, she felt suddenly naked. She was disappointed when he untied her, taking her wrists and massaging the ligatures from them.

The house shuddered from a large wave breaking on the shore.

"Go upstairs and change. You'll find everything you need."

"How would you like me?"

"Surprise me. I'll make the drinks."

Ashleigh nodded and carried her bag up a staircase lined with framed photographs of women in bondage. Ashleigh wondered who they were, if Richard had taken them, if her portrait would join theirs . . .

In the master bedroom, Ashleigh realized the front of the house facing the ocean was all mirrored glass. Floodlights now bathed the rain and the swirling surf. She put her suitcase on the bed, not at all surprised to find that it was a four-poster king-sized bed. *How soon will I be tied there?*

Handcuffs, open and waiting for her, lay on the dresser. There was no key.

Ashleigh turned away and slowly removed her clothing. Naked, she went into the bathroom and removed the pins from her hair, brushing it out. When she was satisfied, she returned to the suitcase and slipped the rich blue satin gown over her head. The lace bodice clung to her breasts and her leg was bared by the high slit as she crossed to the dresser for the handcuffs. They were heavy and cold in her hand.

There is still time to change my mind, she thought.

Ashleigh took the handcuffs downstairs.

"You're the most beautiful woman I've ever seen," Richard said as she crossed the room.

"Thank you." Ashleigh held the handcuffs out. "I want you to do it."

When her wrists were joined before her, she lifted her hands and touched his chest. "Aren't you cold?"

"I'll run up and change now," he said, giving her a glass of champagne.

Alone, Ashleigh stood at the window and stared out at the rain and the roiling surf of the deserted beach. Holding the champagne flute with both hands, Ashleigh emptied the glass and went to the bottle. She poured slowly, awkwardly, allowing the bubbles to subside before tipping the bottle gently again. When her glass was full, she took it and stood before the fire. The chill had left the room, but still Ashleigh shivered. Her legs trembled as they had when he'd crossed Simone's living room, approaching her for the first time, and Ashleigh had known she would do whatever this man asked of her.

When Richard returned, he was dressed conventionally, wearing gray slacks and a white shirt open to his chest. A gold chain was around his neck. "Can I get you anything?" he asked.

Ashleigh shook her head, not trusting her voice. She wanted him to throw her to the floor, take her there in front of the fire, fuck her until she screamed with pleasure. But he only nodded in return and sat on the couch, patting the cushion beside him, granting her permission to join him.

Her gown fell open, revealing her legs, as she immediately complied.

"Tell me about your work," he said, closing the silk over her legs.

"I am an artist."

"Specializing in tattoos?"

"Yes."

"And you want me to be your canvas?"

"You will be my masterpiece."

"I will be your canvas," Richard said, smiling, "but you must grant me three wishes in return."

"Yes," Ashleigh replied immediately. She could deny this man nothing.

Richard reached out and touched the spider. Ashleigh shuddered and arched, raising her breasts for him. "What if I had come to Simone's party in a different costume?" he asked. "Would you still want me for your canvas?" He slipped the strap from her shoulder, uncovering one breast only.

"Oh, yes," Ashleigh whispered. "From the moment I saw you."

"Have you read *The Story of O?* And *The Claiming of Sleeping Beauty?*"

"Yes."

"Then you know what I want from you."

"Yes." Ashleigh hesitated, but, like O, she had to know. "Will I be whipped?" she whispered.

"Does it matter?"

Again, Ashleigh hesitated. She saw herself in a drawing room, surrounded by strangers. Chains raised her arms above her head and she looked back over her shoulder as she waited for the cruel caress. "No," she said softly.

He smiled and kissed her for the second time, pressing her back against the sofa, holding one naked breast, squeezing gently as he explored her mouth.

Again, Ashleigh wanted to put her arms around him, but

they were shackled and trapped between their bodies. This is what it feels like to be a slave, safe and secure and loved. This is how Danny felt when I made love to her, helpless to do anything except her master's—her mistress's—bidding. Oh, God, what's happening to me? I want him so much, this stranger I've known forever.

The rain fell harder, streaking the windows as the house shuddered and they danced to the breaking waves, kissing softly. Her arms were around his waist and the chains that joined her wrists held him captive as well.

Sometime—she didn't know when—Ashleigh lifted the hem of her nightgown with both hands, drawing it up until her hands were over her head and she was able to shrug free of the garment. She stood proudly before him, staring into his eyes, while the fire warmed her back.

Sometime—she didn't know when—her hands were freed and they lay together before the fire, each stroking and caressing the other until the pain of separation became unbearable and they fused into one helpless shuddering entity, moaning and crying out their love.

Sometime—she didn't know when—he carried her upstairs effortlessly. Drowsy, trusting, she put her arms around his neck with no fear of falling and murmured, "I love you." He placed her gently on the bed and awakened her with kisses.

Sometime—she didn't know when—the night ended.

The Thirteenth Tattoo

Chapter Twenty

The flowers—thirteen long-stemmed red roses—arrived in the early afternoon. Instead of a note, there was a letter, sealed with red wax. She had never received anything sealed with wax before.

"A new admirer?" Dean asked, arching his eyebrow.

"Yes," Ashleigh said.

She took the letter and the roses to her desk. Breaking the seal of the envelope, Ashleigh read his letter.

Dearest Ashleigh:

Like boots, lipstick, perfume, a choker, a silk blouse, a black slip, a lacy bra, or earrings, the implements of your submission—soft ropes, handcuffs, chains, leather, a collar like that worn by O, perhaps a red or white or black corset—are only decorations to enhance your beauty and your acceptance of a different kind of love. The deviation is exciting, erotic.

How shall we decorate you and love you? There are so many ways.

While I want to dress you in ropes and chains, I also want to give you elegant dresses, delicate perfumes, jewelry. There are mannequins dressed in negligees. One wears a plumed mask of a bird of prey, as you did the night we met (was it only two wonderful glorious days ago?), the other a jeweled black mask. Perhaps that is where we shall shop.

Ashleigh is a beautiful woman, wearing an exquisite dress—and handcuffs.

We talk and drink, as though the evening is normal and it is—except for the handcuffs you wear as jewelry. After a time, your position is changed, your wrists are locked behind your back. It is another step to the inevitable, an increasing helplessness.

But later, this night—or another—the decorations multiply. Soft white ropes bind your wrists. Other ropes encircle your breasts, lifting them, holding them for my kiss. You shudder as I paint your nipples and their aureoles with lipstick. They fill with passion and stand out while I give them a deeper color, only to kiss it away again. Your role is simple—to enjoy the intensity of our mutual seduction, our companionship, to writhe and moan or cry out, knowing that my purpose is to give you pleasure, even as I receive it. These moments are our cherished gifts to each other.

Wearing your beautiful dress (or is it a black slip?), you are tied to a post. Now the ropes encircle your ankles, your knees, your hips. Other ropes are placed above and below your breasts. Your helplessness is kissed, until you are so aroused that you must beg for freedom—and love.

Another time, you will stand facing the wall. Your arms are drawn above your head by silken black straps and tied to a hook in the ceiling. Your back is bared. You wait and grow impatient, looking over your shoulder. That is the signal for me to approach, to stroke your back, kiss your neck, and let your uplifted breasts fill my hands once again, as I kiss the nape of your neck, nuzzle your earlobes, and caress your naked back.

There will be a time when we begin in the living room, slowly removing your clothing. For the moment you are free, but when you are naked, we adorn you with other things. A black collar is fastened loosely around your neck. The leather leash hangs between your breasts. When your hands are cuffed behind your back, I kneel before you and slip the black heels on your feet. It is then that I lead you to the bedroom. You are tall, statuesque, and beautiful in your captivity. Another woman might feel humiliation being led to the bedroom at the end of a leash, but you should not, for it is a brief journey and the heels and leash will be quickly discarded for new pleasures. You will be fastened anew, with soft cuffs and silken black straps as you lie upon the bed, arms and legs outstretched and tied to the posters of the bed. And this, too, is the time to add a blindfold. Each touch, each caress, each kiss, will come as a surprise to you, never knowing where the next sensation will appear—your sweet lips, your rouged nipples, the swell of your breast, your belly, your thighs, the soles of your feet, waiting, waiting, waiting, until finally, I find your clitoris with my tongue and go down on you, drinking the juices of your explosive climax. This, too, is my gift to you.

Until tonight.
I love you.

It was signed with his initial.

Thirteen roses—one each for her failures and one for her success. He would be the thirteenth tattoo. All she had to do was agree . . .

But to what? He would not tell her, saying only, "You will understand soon enough."

It was so easy to submit when they were together. But here in the studio, she wondered if she could be so happy. Did she dare? Memories told her yes. Her heart told her yes. But it defied all reason . . .

She had awakened to the sound of the crashing surf. The sky was gray and the rain fell steadily, beating against the bedroom windows. She turned her head on the pillow and found Richard smiling at her. "Good morning, my love," she said.

"Good morning, darling. You sleep beautifully. There's a wonderful smile on your face, like the Madonna."

"You put the smile there."

"I'm glad."

She kissed his cheek before going to the bathroom. When she started to close the door, he said, "No. I want to watch you."

"Have I surrendered all privacy, then?" she asked.

"Yes."

Nodding, she sat on the toilet, staring down at the beach, blushing as she felt his eyes on her. The rain looked as if it would never stop. Offshore, a single powerboat fought its way through rolling swells under the gray skies.

When the flow of water started, gushing from her body, Ashleigh's cheeks burned with embarrassment. No one had ever watched her in the bathroom before. She turned slightly and met his gaze, biting her lips at the sound she made, thinking it would never stop.

Squatting over the toilet to wipe herself, tears filled her eyes.

Ashleigh felt humiliated, but she had agreed. She was a slave. She belonged to him now.

After washing her hands, she walked back to the bed, feeling exposed as never before, all jiggling tits and ass, wanting to cover herself, as though she had never been naked in front of a stranger, but he was not a stranger. Now now. What else would he demand of her?

But he only reached out for her, taking her hand, drawing her gently back into the bed. She hid her face against his chest and cried as he embraced her, stroking her back lightly. Her cheeks were still hot and flushed. "I love you," he said.

"And I love you," she whispered, still crying softly, frightened at the power he exerted over her, but even more afraid of her willingness to submit.

And later they had walked down the deserted beach through the rain. Beneath her cape, Ashleigh was handcuffed again. She wondered if he would release her when they reached the restaurant. With another man, she would have taken his hand as a reassuring touch, a closeness, but with her hands imprisoned behind her back she felt an even greater intimacy. She was owned.

Of course, he released her. A hundred yards from the restaurant, he stopped her for an affectionate hug and as he kissed her, he freed her hands. They entered the restaurant then as any normal couple, except perhaps for their new love glowing on their faces.

After brunch, Richard dropped her at Simone's. "I'll see you back at the house," he said.

"Thank God, you're here," Simone said. "I couldn't sleep last night," Simone said. "I kept thinking of you, wondering if you were all right."

"Richard is very gentle and considerate," Ashleigh said.

"There are so many stories about him, though. Did he . . . did he keep you tied?"

"Some. I was handcuffed. I didn't mind."

"Well, I must say, your exit created quite a stir, but anything Richard does is so . . . so different. The party broke up quite early. The men were absolutely horny. I wonder how many of the women went home to find ropes waiting for them."

"Did Sam tie you?"

Simone blushed. "Do you know how hard it is to find rope in the modern household? We used his ties."

Ashleigh smiled. "Did you like it?"

"I've never seen Sam so huge. He got bigger just carrying the ties across the bedroom." Simone paused. "I really think I must visit the hardware store today."

"I have to go," Ashleigh said. "Richard's waiting for me."

"What are you doing today?"

"Whatever he wants. I belong to him now."

She raised her eyes from the roses to find Dean smiling at her.

"Really, Ashleigh, you look absolutely beatific," he said. "You simply must tell all."

"I met the most wonderful man at Simone's. I'm in love."

Ashleigh took a single rose—the thirteenth—home with her, placing its vase on the mantel.

The manuscript was delivered to her home that evening by messenger. When she was alone again, Ashleigh read his cover note in which he instructed her what she must do before reading the story.

Ashleigh followed his orders exactly, lighting the fire and pouring a glass of champagne before stripping naked, luxuriating in the fire's warmth on her flesh. Impatiently, she waited for the clock to strike eight, when she was allowed to begin reading. He had told her to pass the time by fondling her breasts, but under no circumstances was she to bring herself to orgasm. That was to wait for his arrival. When Ashleigh finally began reading, she was in delicious agony.

WAYLAND THE CRIPPLE

by
Richard Sheridan

    Bitter winds sing of Wayland the craftsman, warrior, hero, and god taken in treachery by the greed of Nidhad the king.
    Bitter winds sing of Wayland's revenge.
    In the wretched hut, Wayland the craftsman lays his crippled body to rest, but his mind broods. The vow is made and the mind will not sleep. Wayland fans his hatred as he fans his craftsman's fire. Treachery will be repaid a thousand times and more. Let Nidhad the king go to his bed in agony. Let Nidhad search for solace in the monstrous teats of Bodvild, his queen. He will find no comfort. Their limbs will intertwine futilely—too late, too late. Her womb is barren. Their line will die with them. They will go to death in dishonor. There will be no ship to carry them from this world, no servants to accompany them on their last journey. They will have only the memory that they are grandparents to the bastard child of Wayland the craftsman.
    The bitter winds chill the island, screaming out of the north to buffet the walls of the hut, but Wayland is not cold. Hatred keeps him warm.
    "I am a god," Wayland says.
    The bitter winds moan in reply.
    "I am a god treated like a peasant slave."
    The winds cry their sympathy.
    "I am Wayland, a god, and I will have my revenge. Their house is cursed from this moment. Nay, their house was cursed from the moment Nidhad summoned his arrogant courage and gave life to his plan. I will destroy Nidhad and all his family, even the beautiful Beadohild, who looked upon my plight with compassion, shall feel the wrath of Wayland the god. I have spoken. It will be so."
    Now the bitter winds calm, their anger passing. Wayland the god had spoken. It would be so.
    Yet even against his will, the hard lines in Wayland's face

soften, for he remembers Allwise the swan maiden, his beautiful lover. Wayland remembers the softness of her bosom, paleness tinged with crimson at the pleasure of his caress. Her arms draw him close until the weight of his body threatens to crush her and they cry out the joys of their love.

The winds, too, remember Allwise. The winds, too, miss her, for they took great delight in her company, swirling about her, tugging gently at her skirts, caressing her golden hair, until her face gloried with love for Wayland.

For seven years they loved—Wayland and beautiful Allwise—but in the eighth year, Allwise grew melancholy, longing to return to her own land. In the ninth year, she fled.

But Wayland did not despair. He waited in the forest clearing that was their home. He did not let the flame of his forge die. Instead, he made beautiful jewelry for his lover, exquisite presents for her return. He hunted. He worked. He waited. Time passed slowly.

The winds mourned her absence with Wayland the god.

One lonely afternoon, Wayland returned to the clearing with the carcass of a bear slung over his shoulder. He renewed the fire and set a piece of the meat to cooking. Then, as usual, he went into the hut to count his rings, necklaces, bracelets. The fame of Wayland the craftsman was widespread and the intricacies of his beautiful jewelry were coveted by all.

He counted the rings once, twice, three times, but it was gone. A thief had visited the clearing in Wayland's absence. The most beautiful of all the rings, wrought only for the delicate finger of Allwise, was missing.

What manner of thief would take but one treasure from a host of treasures? What thief would risk the wrath of Wayland for a solitary ring?

No.

Surely, it was Allwise returned. She had come home to her lover and found the ring as evidence of his love. And now, she wore the ring, hiding in the forest, observing his joy, yet teasing him playfully, as a lover will.

Wayland joined her game. He sat near the fire, his heart pounding with happiness. The meat sizzled on the coals, dripping grease, forgotten in Wayland's exhilaration.

Lost in thoughts of his beautiful Allwise, Wayland failed to hear the muffled clank of armor in time. They fell upon him swiftly, leaving him no chance for defense. Disarmed, bound hand and foot, Wayland the craftsman was carried through the dark forest, rudely, roughly.

The court of Nidhad mocked his helplessness.

Nidhad himself wore Wayland's sword, forged so cunningly in the smithy's fire.

Bodvild the queen defiled the lover's ring, forged so cunningly in the smithy's fire. She polished the ring against her teats until the noblemen of the court cast desirous glances at their women.

Wayland's jewelry was gone, vanished into the secret coffers of Nidhad the greedy without so much as a small gift to his sons or to his beautiful daughter, Beadohild.

"See, husband," the queen said, "how he hates us. His teeth are bared like those of the hungry wolf. He would tear the flesh from our bones."

"He is helpless, wife," Nidhad replied. "He can do us no harm."

Bodvild's eyes glinted as she turned to her husband. "Ensure that he is powerless to bring harm to our persons. Cripple him."

"As you wish," Nidhad said. "It will serve our purpose all the more."

Wayland's own sword was slowly drawn from its jeweled scabbard. The sword was wondrous to behold. Heavy of purpose, its hand guard intricately decorated with the most precious metals of the land. The blade shone brightly, even in the flickering light of candles. Its sharpness was unmatched by any blade in the kingdom, or even the world. The sword was a work of art cunningly wrought by Wayland, the greatest craftsman, unrivaled by any thing by man or god.

Yet Nidhad the king despoiled his stolen treasure. He gave the sword to a retainer.

"Let it be done," Nidhad commanded.

Wayland the craftsman was flung to the floor and pressed into the dirt.

Bodvild smiled as the honed tip searched out the first tendon and with a flick of the retainer's wrist, the tendon was severed.

Wayland struggled, but strong hands imprisoned him. Pain burned his leg, but he did not cry out.

The beautiful Beadohild pressed forward with the rest. Her eyes shone, her lovely bosom heaved with excitement.

Once more the sword, Wayland's own sword, searched out a tendon. The wrist moved.

Wayland the craftsman winced, not from pain, but from anger. Each time the sword accomplished its bloody work, the useless tendon shriveled. The strength was being taken from his legs.

Wayland's eyes met those of Beadohild. He saw sorrow in her eyes, but there was excitement, too. Her tongue flicked over dry lips.

Eight times the sword pierced his skin, the blade raising the tendon, and it was done. The tension in Wayland's legs was gone. He was hamstrung like the cattle before the slaughter.

The retainer wiped the sword carefully before returning it to Nidhad, who flung it home in the scabbard with a crash that rang through the court.

"Let him be known henceforth as Wayland the cripple," Bodvild said.

The court laughed as Wayland was lifted to his knees. Now he was like the scabrous cripples in the marketplace, crawling about, wailing their pleas on hands and knees cushioned by leather pads to ease the pain of rough surfaces.

Wayland the cripple disdained the court. His eyes passed over the royal family, as he burned their images into memory, he vowed there would be no pads to soften his journey. Let the pebbles and stones scratch and bite him. The blood drawn would remind him of the debt that Nidhad and all his family—wife and sons, beautiful daughter—had incurred. Only Beadohild displayed sympathy, but she would suffer with the rest.

Nidhad the king addressed his court. "First, let Wayland the cripple be taken to the island of Saevarstod. There he will do work of my bidding. Second, let no one visit him save myself. This I command."

Wayland the cripple was pulled from the great hall, his feet dragging helplessly behind.

The court dispersed to their various amusements.

The winds pitied Wayland, crying out in sorrow, mourning for this noble man and god crippled through the capriciousness of evil. So the winds screamed their anger as they rushed over the island prison of Wayland, watching and waiting.

Chapter Twenty-One

Ashleigh paused, shivering like Wayland with the chill winds, wondering what message Richard sent with his story. She knelt before the fire, looking down at her shrunken nipples. As she warmed, she caressed herself into hardness again, longing for his presence. When the shivering stopped, she went back to the couch, turned the page, and continued reading of how Wayland thought of his gentle Allwise even as he lusted for revenge. And finally, Nidhad's greedy sons came to the island and were killed by Wayland, their bodies buried in a dung heap where the worms and maggots would clean the flesh from their skulls in preparation. Ashleigh turned the page only to pity the beautiful Beadohild.

"Where is Wayland the craftsman?"

Wayland crawled from the hut.

Her beauty illuminated the gray day. Her hair attracted light, seeming to pierce the low clouds, drawing the rays of the hidden sun to her. The golden tresses that fell to her shoulders reflected on the crippled body at her feet.

"Your father ordered that none save he would visit my prison."

"Will you tell him?"

"It is not my concern."

"My father is selfish. He would hide your skill. He does not show the marvelous treasures you make for him. My mother is equally selfish. She has hidden your ring."

"What of your brothers? Are they selfish, too?"

"*They drowned. They were coming to visit you. They would not bring me.*"

"*That was fortunate for you.*"

"*Yes.*"

"*You wish to see evidence of my skill?*"

"*What woman would not wish to adorn herself with jewelry made by Wayland the great craftsman?*"

"*You watched when they crippled me. You should have left the court.*"

"*I'm sorry,*" Beadohild said gently.

Wayland nodded. "*I will show you my work. Come into the hut.*"

"*I would help you with your cloak, but I cannot stand.*"

"*Poor Wayland.*" Beadohild removed her cloak.

"*Sit there,*" Wayland said, "*on the bearskin.*"

Beadohild sat gracefully, spreading her cloak about her legs. "*It's cold in here,*" she said.

"*I will stir the coals a little,*" Wayland said. "*I have wine. It will warm you.*"

"*No,*" Beadohild said.

"*You will drink it from a silver goblet, inset with many precious jewels. Your father ordered that I make it for his pleasure alone. You will be the first to drink from it.*"

"*In that case, let me have some wine.*" She laughed and clapped her hands with delight. "*It will be a fine trick upon my father, who is so selfish.*"

A flush spread through her bosom as she took the goblet. "*Wayland,*" she whispered, "*it is the work of a god.*"

"*Drink,*" Wayland said. Despite himself, Wayland was pleased with her compliment. Regret passed through his mind, but he eliminated any thought of mercy.

"*I thought your mother would come to visit me.*"

"*My father watches her too closely. She must be satisfied with only one ring of Wayland.*"

"*I will give you two rings.*"

"*You honor me, Wayland,*" Beadohild said. Her eyes glistened. "*I will wear them always.*"

"*Yes.*" Wayland would have wished the queen to come to his prison first. Instead, poor, beautiful Beadohild had dared the sea to visit him. Now, she must be punished in her mother's stead.

"It is warm," Beadohild said, although Wayland had not stirred the fire to life.

Wayland watched as she lay back on the skin and slowly brushed a lock of hair from her forehead. The drug was working. Soon, she would be helpless, as though bound by the rough ropes of a condemned prisoner. He crawled to her, to lie with her.

Beadohild murmured no protest as he stroked her cheek gently. "Wayland," she whispered.

His lips touched hers and she surrendered, opening her mouth for his warm and loving kiss, accepting his tongue in that first symbolic penetration. She could do no else. Beadohild was the prisoner of Wayland the god.

Despite the drug in her wine, Beadohild responded, smiling as he slipped the dress from her shoulders, baring her bosom for new kisses, new delights. The brown tips of her pale breasts rose to his caress. Slowly, slowly, she forced one slender arm to obey her command to encircle his neck and press his face into the softness of her perfumed breasts.

Wayland was kind as he parted her thighs and kissed the pale, silken hairs that decorated her loins, seeking out and finding that secret spot of womanhood.

"Ah," Beadohild cried.

She cried again as he entered her, taking her maidenhead painfully as his warmth filled her belly.

He loved her well, then, as he would love his own Allwise, not as the daughter of his sworn enemies. He wanted to give her pleasure as well as pain to remember for it would be the last time the beautiful Beadohild would lie with a man. No prince would marry her now. Were she not of royal blood, the women would strip her naked and cruelly beat her from village to village, suffering the fate of the wanton whore.

Poor Beadohild.

She shuddered with pleasure as Wayland thrust deeper and deeper into her belly. She fought the drug that bound her and raised her body to meet his, arching her hips and returned thrust for thrust to her lover, crying out her pleasure as Wayland pounded her loins. She loved her crippled Wayland.

Other lovers speak tender words, but Wayland left her, skirt and bodice bunched about her waist, nipples swollen with the memory of his gentle caresses. Her legs remained widespread, helpless to close, as she yearned *for the return of her lover—cruel lover. Within her, their seed joined. "I love you," Beadohild said.*

Wayland the lover returned, dragging his crippled body across the dirt floor of the hut. Her eyes brightened as he gently caressed strands of her golden hair, stroked the slender neck, touched each of her breasts in turn, kissed the teats that would suckle his child.

He showed her golden rings, delicately engraved with tiny patterns of scrollwork.

"These rings were made for your mother," Wayland said. They came apart in his hands, sections not yet permanently joined.

Beadohild smiled, happy to have his touch upon her body.

Now, Wayland showed her a long needle used for sewing leathers. It was sharp and shining with the care he gave all his tools.

The winds peeked through crevices and cracks in the hut. The winds pitied poor beautiful Beadohild, but Wayland must have revenge. It was just. Poor Beadohild.

Beadohild's eyes filled with horror as Wayland pulled at her nipple, stretching the skin taut. "No," she pleaded, closing her eyes as he placed the needle to her engorged nipple, "I love you."

He pierced her breast.

Beadohild screamed with the sudden pain, and again when the ring was closed. Wayland wiped droplets of blood away as Beadohild sobbed. When Beadohild opened tear-filled eyes, she wore Wayland's ring in the breast that hung over her heart.

"Your teats will grow heavy with milk for my child. He will feel this ring and know of his father, Wayland the craftsman, a god. Your father will rage when your belly grows fat with my son. Tell him that it was Wayland who took his daughter."

Beadohild moaned as Wayland turned his attention to her other breast, but she did not cry out when the needle pierced her flesh for a second time. She would bear his pain silently and wear his rings proudly. Beadohild loved Wayland, her craftsman.

When the second ring was in place, movement returned to Beadohild and she knelt before Wayland, looking down at the rings he had given her. They were heavy in her breasts. "They are beautiful, Wayland."

Relenting for a moment, Wayland said, "Almost as beautiful as the woman who wears them."

"I will stay with you as your prisoner, as your devoted slave. Beat me *daily if you like. I will gladly cut the rods for your hand, but do not leave me. I love you."*

"I must go." Wayland crawled away, only to return with a wooden chest. He placed it beside Beadohild. "Take this to your mother," he said. "Inside are the jeweled skulls of your brothers. They did not drown. I killed them. Let your mother place my gift on her mantel and tell all who visit that Wayland the craftsman decorated the heads of her sons with jewels."

"My father will kill you."

"I will not be here to witness his anger. I have wings to carry me from my prison."

"Please, Wayland, take me with you. I will honor you."

"You must remain. Your parents must be reminded each time they see you that they made me a cripple and still I took my revenge. Let them listen to the cries of our son and be reminded of Wayland the cripple."

Beadohild cried long after Wayland had left her. Finally, she dressed and gathered the chest in her arms. The heavy weights in her breasts told her that already she carried Wayland's child in her belly. And already a lifetime of despair and loneliness was upon her.

"They are beautiful rings," she whispered to her departed lover.

Nidhad the king gnashed his teeth in helpless fury. He himself went to the island and caused all the land to be searched for Wayland. None ever claimed the reward offered for the head of Wayland.

Bodvild mourned her sons but coveted the jewels. Secretly one night, while her husband raved against Wayland, she removed the jewels and hid them away, refusing to tell her husband their location.

None saw Beadohild save an old servant who attended her.

"Let her be taken from my sight," Nidhad cried. "She is no daughter of mine. Let her bear and suckle her bastard child in perpetual solitude."

Beadohild mourned her Wayland as she paced the floors of her tiny prison.

Wayland and Allwise, the swan maiden, were reunited, loving each other fully. But in the darkest part of the night, Wayland sometimes thought of the beautiful Beadohild who wore his rings and felt remorse. Poor Beadohild.

The bitter winds still sing of Wayland's revenge.

Ashleigh's mouth was dry when she put down the manuscript. It's the most sensuous story I've ever read, she thought, knowing at the same time what he expected of her. Ashleigh's nipples were erect and bulging, awaiting his caress. Would she grant his first wish? Again she touched her nipples, biting her lip and moaning softly at the sensations that swept through her. And if she allowed him that first wish, what would he expect of the second and the third? Do I love him that much?

She stared into the fire and waited.

At nine o'clock, Ashleigh rose and went to the door, waiting less than a minute before hearing the roar of his Corvette as it topped the last crest and turned into her driveway. She switched off the lights, knowing that the flames danced skillfully over her body, enhancing her beauty for him.

When Richard entered and embraced her, Ashleigh summoned her courage and whispered, "Yes."

Without speaking, he led her to the fire, where he took her from behind, plunging deep within her, fondling her breasts, while she pressed against him, crying out her acquiescence, "Yes, yes, yes. Don't stop, please, don't stop. Ah, yes!"

Ashleigh would discover that it was always like that with Richard. There would be days and weeks of normalcy, when their relationship was like any other, where both individuals worked, following their own careers and paths, meeting each evening for dinner in casual conversations that were the hallmark of routine.

"I did nothing but flashes today. I'm exhausted. How was your day?"

"Meetings all day long and nothing got done, as usual," he might say with disgust.

They would eat dinner, read—Richard always had a neverending stack of screenplays that required his attention for one client or another—go to bed, usually to make love, but often enough only to hold each other as they awaited sleep.

But then, like tonight, after preparing her from afar with mental foreplay, he would take her suddenly, without preamble, making love to her in the kitchen, the loft, on the staircase, until she could stand it no more and pleaded with him to stop.

Ashleigh reveled in the unpredictability of her love.

In his arms now, Ashleigh said, "You sure know how to make a girl beg for mercy."

He smiled and pushed a sweat-matted strand of hair from her brow. "I thought the day would never end. It's been so long since I saw you."

Ashleigh laughed. "It was just this morning. We kissed in the rain."

"An eternity."

"Are you hungry? Would you like a drink? I stopped for Scotch."

"The answer to both questions is yes."

"I'll fix your drink and then I'll give you the tour of the house."

"Put something on first. I don't want you getting sick."

Normalcy again.

"You have a lovely home," Richard said after dinner. "May I stay tonight?"

"Of course, I want you to." She thought the request strange. Doesn't he know I'm his, to do with as he pleases? Gravely, she offered him a key to the house. "I had this made for you today."

"Thank you. I have a key for you as well. It's in the car with a few other things. I'll just run out and get them."

Expecting something quite different, Ashleigh was disappointed when he unpacked the garment bag and she discovered it contained nothing but clothing and toilet articles. "I loved your letter," she said tentatively.

"And the story?"

"Oh, yes."

"And you accept?"

Ashleigh nodded.

"I want to hear you say it."

"I accept."

"You'll be very beautiful."

"When?" she asked, knowing instinctively that he would do it himself.

"Soon."

She went to him then. "Please hold me," she said.

Chapter Twenty-Two

"Slavery becomes you," Richard told her.

Ashleigh agreed, realizing that submission came naturally to her. Without being told, Ashleigh began dressing so that she was always accessible whenever they were to be together, discarding jeans and pants suits, the tight black leather skirts and blouses, going without underwear—unless he suggested otherwise.

Ashleigh also realized that she liked her new state of being.

When she was tied or otherwise restrained in one fashion or another, he pampered her beyond belief or expectation. Ashleigh might have been a most favored houri in some sultan's harem and Richard the eunuch charged with tending to her every need, bathing and perfuming her, giving her food and drink, entertaining her, applying rouge to her lips and nipples, placing a fabulous jewel in her navel, or veiling her charms in preparation for a visit to the royal bedchambers.

Except that Richard was no eunuch.

Sometimes, not often, in the evenings, he dressed her in silver collar and manacles that locked about her wrists and ankles with matching chains, beautiful delicate links that joined her wrists and ankles. A long chain equally exquisite fell from the collar, hanging between her breasts, linking neck, ankles, wrists. It was then that Ashleigh played slave girl to Richard's master. The chains tinkled softly as she prepared dinner or freshened his drink or knelt on the floor beside him and she always thought, I sound like wind chimes.

Ashleigh would have done it for him anyway. She had always enjoyed cooking for her man and making his drink. What did it matter if she dressed conventionally or wore the silver ensemble, as she had come to think of it? It pleased him. And it pleased her.

Another woman, desperate to renew her husband's interest and attention, might greet him one evening wearing a filmy negligee or a red garter belt, stockings, matching red pumps, and still be rebuffed. Ashleigh had no need for such subterfuge. In accepting her slavery, she had Richard's complete regard always.

Ashleigh knew how beautiful and attractive he found her in chains. He loved watching her as she moved about the kitchen or the living room. The chains restricted her movement, forcing her to take short, dainty steps, and she could raise or lower her hands only to her breasts or to her belly. So restricted in her movements, Ashleigh loved sipping champagne as Richard held the glass to her lips as he had that first night in the limousine.

Nor was there anyone but Richard to see her in slavery.

"This is my refuge," Richard said. "Very few people ever come here. When it's necessary to entertain, I do it in town."

And the mirrored glass of his home shielded her from the world, those who walked the beach or trotted by on horseback. Even if the light was right and the mirrors were penetrated, Ashleigh cared nothing for what they might think.

It is my choice.

Only Danny knew how far she had traveled in accepting Richard's domination. Danny was so very pleased when Ashleigh called to tell her of Richard.

"I am a slave, too." It thrilled her to say the words, especially to Danny. It was an affirmation of her new life.

"I just knew you were like me. Oh, Ashleigh, I'm so happy for you. Isn't it exciting and wonderful and glorious to walk around in total freedom all day, always wondering what new surprise the evening will bring?"

"Yes. It makes me so horny I can't stand it."

"And it makes Burke so inventive and imaginative. I hope Richard is the same."

"Oh, yes."

"Has he whipped you?"

"No."

"Will he? Do you want him to?"

"I don't know." Again, she imagined herself in a drawing room, arms raised above her head and tied, awaiting the first stroke of the whip. She wondered why the vision always took place in a drawing room. Perhaps it's more elegant, she thought.

"I goaded Burke into spanking me."

"Really? Burke?"

"He was trying to paint and I kept telling him the colors were wrong. He got really pissed, but I kept it up anyway. Finally, he threw me across his lap and spanked me really hard for a change. I'm getting hot just thinking about it. Afterward, he made me stand in a corner for an hour holding my dress up with my panties down around my ankles. I was crying just like a little girl. God, I loved it."

"Why, Danny?"

There was a long silence on the telephone. Finally, Danny said, "I don't know, really. I just do. I've given up trying to analyze myself. I'm different from other women. So are you."

"Yes."

"After he spanked me and the hour was up, we fucked ourselves crazy."

"We must get together for lunch soon."

"Shall I drive up? I've never seen your studio. I'd like to."

"If it's not too much trouble for you."

"Of course not. It's been too long since we've seen you. We'll have you and Richard to dinner as well."

Slowly, they revealed their secrets.

Richard was an accomplished photographer. Ashleigh had discovered that in asking about the portraits of bound women that lined the staircase to the master bedroom. He had taken them all.

"Tell me about them. Were they lovers?"

"Some, not all."

"I'm jealous. Who were they? Will you point them out?"

"If you like. This is Susan. You didn't see her without her mask, but she came to Simone's as Wonder Woman."

"No wonder she left so quickly when you came over. She didn't seem to like you very much."

"She doesn't. It ended badly."

"I hope you left her like that for a long time," Ashleigh said. In the photograph, Susan knelt on some kind of platform. She was tied to a smooth and polished plank attached to the platform. She wore a flowered summer dress that left her shoulders bare. Ropes encircled her waist and thighs, cinching her tightly to the plank.

"Long enough," Richard said. "She didn't like it."

"How sad for her." Ashleigh pointed to a woman lying on a blue carpet with wrists and ankles tied. "She was your lover, too. Who is she?"

"Paula. She moved to New York."

"Did you love them?"

"No. I love only you."

"And will you photograph me? Will I hang in your gallery as well?"

"In time, you will be the only one. We'll keep a record of your journey."

"Our journey, darling."

"Yes."

Pleased, she kissed him.

In her own turn, Ashleigh shared her work, her secret portfolio, her own lovers of the past, told him of Cynthia and Simone.

"My Ashleigh has hidden depths," Richard said with a smile. "I never suspected."

She even told him of Burke and Danny, and her relationship with them. "I'd like you to meet them."

"I'd like that very much," he said.

But despite her happiness, Ashleigh was troubled, knowing that she was dishonest with him, that she could not continue the lies she had perpetuated throughout her adult life. What would he say and do when he knew the truth, learned she had been a whore? Would he turn from her in disgust? Tell her to leave? Beat her? Richard, her heart screamed, I'll submit to anything to be with you. Punish me if you must, but please don't leave me. I couldn't bear to lose you, just when I've finally found you.

For the first time, Ashleigh regretted the maze of deceit she had created.

Ashleigh sunbathed on the redwood deck, reclining on a lounge chair, while she waited for Richard to return from his run on the beach. She wore a red crocheted string bikini, a concession to those who passed the house on their walks along the beach, but as she applied tanning lotion, Ashleigh thought she might as well have discarded propriety for all the suit concealed. But Richard had picked it out and she wore it gladly for him.

He enjoyed shopping with her, for her. She loved emerging from the changing room to turn gracefully before him, showing off whatever garment they had chosen, awaiting his approval, his eyes tiny mirrors reflecting her beauty and their love.

He would be returning soon. Ashleigh rose and drew the hooded matching cover-up over her shoulders and went to the deck's railing. The beach was not crowded and she could easily pick him out, a tiny distant and dark figure running steadily, effortlessly, at water's edge. As he drew closer, Ashleigh waved. He did not return the wave, but he angled away from the water to run directly at her through the heavy, thick white sand.

Now he was running to her, for her.

Oh, God, I love you so much.

Ashleigh renewed her acquaintance with Cynthia, stopping by the bar to talk as in the old days before Bobby when they had been true friends and sometimes lovers.

They were both eager to be companions and confidants again, but Bobby always hovered between them.

"Bobby doesn't say anything, but I know he's haunted by you. I'm a poor substitute."

"Don't be silly. You're a very desirable and beautiful young woman. You give him something I never could—your love. In time, he'll come to appreciate that."

"He's good to me. I think he loves me as well as he can right now."

"You're good to him, too. You work topless for him."

"It's exciting for him, and I don't mind. The money's good."

Ashleigh wanted to tell Cynthia to quit that job, that it cheapened her, but she thought it far too ironic. Who am I to advise her on cheapness? I'm nothing but a former whore and a slut who would do far worse to please Richard.

In the end, Ashleigh confessed, taking Richard to the grave, saying, "This is who I am." There, sitting on a shaded bench, Ashleigh told him of New Mexico and running away. Speaking in a dull monotone and with tears filling her eyes, she told him of whoring and of meeting Burke, of reading endlessly in a struggle to educate herself, of devoting her life to art, of the men she had taken for her canvases after Heather had stolen Chance, of discarding them heartlessly with each failure. She told him everything. No one, not even Burke, knew so much of Jamie Lee and Ashleigh.

During the tormented hour Ashleigh spent with Richard there, other visitors to the cemetery passed them on the way to graves of loved ones. They might think the handsome young couple sat on the bench mourning the loss of a child. And I am, Ashleigh thought.

She fell silent for a long time and sat there looking down at her grave. Finally, she asked, "Can you forgive me?"

"Let's go home, darling, I want to make love to you."

She smiled then, a little wanly, but still the smile pierced her unhappiness. "I have to say goodbye first," she said, nodding toward her grave.

Richard watched as she knelt at the grave, sitting back on her heels as she whispered to her namesake, to herself.

They were quiet as they drove the canyon road back to Malibu. Without speaking, they followed the path down to the house, crossing the tennis court, descending again. When the door was unlocked, Ashleigh went upstairs, dropped her purse on the dresser, and turned to face him.

He undressed her slowly, kissing her all the while, making the heat grow and burst into flame. She returned his kisses, frantically, crying, tasting the salt of her tears, giving herself with wild abandon. When he penetrated her, she wrapped her legs around him, squeezing tightly, never to let him go.

He never mentioned what she had told him, not directly.

But when she next came to Malibu, a big white teddy bear was propped against the pillows of the bed they shared.

Ashleigh wept as she clutched it gratefully.

At work, Richard was never far from her thoughts. They talked several times during the day. He gave her his private number, allowing her to bypass the gatekeepers who guarded his time jealously. And when he called her, Ashleigh always interrupted whatever flash she happened to be working on at the time. Often, their conversations were no more than to say, "I was thinking of you" or "I love you."

Between flashes, Ashleigh worked on concepts for the thirteenth tattoo, but none was satisfactory and all were relegated to her place of lost ideas. There was no room for error. Oh, God, if ever perfection were required . . . Ashleigh knew she would recognize the thirteenth tattoo when the time was right. There was no other way. It had to come to her magically.

On the increasingly rare occasions when they spent the night apart, one or the other called to say goodnight and they fell asleep with longing and with whispers of love still floating through their bedrooms.

One room had been converted to a small movie theater. It was there they watched the film that had brought Chance and Heather together. As the closing credits rolled on the screen, Ashleigh sat quietly, tight-lipped, wondering why Richard had chosen that film for their entertainment. She loathed it the first time she saw it. Seeing it again now brought back all the terrible memories—the wracking jealousy, the sense of loss that persisted for months, the anger, the hatred.

Richard turned to her and asked, "Do you still love him?"

"No!" she exclaimed. "How could you ask that after . . . I hate both of them. I love only you."

"Can you be in my office tomorrow at eleven?"

"I think so. Yes, of course. I'll just tell Dean something's come up. Why?"

"It's a surprise."

It was the first time she had been to his Century City office. Ashleigh rode the elevator to the twenty-seventh floor nervously and gave her name to one of the two receptionists fielding a barrage of telephone calls. Christ, they're gorgeous, Ashleigh thought.

"Sheridan Agency."

The refrain echoed in the waiting room.

"Sheridan Agency."

A supply of the day's trades—*Variety* and the *Hollywood Reporter*—waited on coffee tables for visitors to this dealmaking seat of power.

"Yes, he's expecting you, Ms. Thomas," the receptionist said with a dazzling smile. "I'll show you right in."

She tapped lightly on the door and immediately opened it. "Ms. Thomas is here, Richard."

"Hello, darling." He came from behind his desk to meet her halfway across the huge office. They kissed briefly.

"Can I get either of you anything?"

"Ashleigh?"

"Nothing, thanks."

"We'll be fine, Pamela. Thank you."

Outside, they could hear the other receptionist say, "Yes, he's expecting your call, but he's on the other line. I'll let him know you're waiting."

"Thanks, Joann. Five minutes and put them through."

"Please, don't let me interrupt," Ashleigh said.

"Oh, they'll wait," Richard said. "They're expecting me to offer them a fifteen-million-dollar deal."

"Jesus, Richard, who?"

"Why, Chance and Heather, of course. How do you like my office?"

"Richard, what's going on?"

"Isn't the view magnificent?"

"Richard, please?"

He smiled. "Come sit on the couch with me. We'll take the call there. I've been packaging a deal. The property is perfect for Chance and Heather. They'd kill for the opportunity to make this film, but I'm going to let you make the decision."

Jesus!

The telephone rang. Richard put the call on the speaker. "Hello, Chance, Heather. Sorry to keep you waiting, but you know how it can get crazy around here." Winking at Ashleigh, he continued, "Sorry to put you on the horn, but I've got some contracts to sign that just won't wait."

"No problem," Chance said. "I hope one of those contracts is ours."

"Richard, darling, how are you?" Heather said. "It's so good to hear your voice."

"You, too, Heather. It's always a pleasure."

Richard doodled something on a yellow legal pad and held

it up for Ashleigh to see. He had drawn a heart with their initials inside.

"This really is the perfect property for us, Richard. We're excited about it."

Smiling, Ashleigh took the pad and wrote, *I love you.* "I don't know, guys. We've had some second thoughts . . ."

"If it's a question of money," Chance interrupted, "we might be willing to talk about a little less going in and a little more in gross points."

"That's not it. Everyone knows you're a bargain at this price, but . . ."

"But what, Richard?" Heather demanded angrily. "What the hell's going on here?"

"There's some concern now at this end that perhaps another Chance and Heather film is going too far, that it won't do the business this script deserves. And frankly, although I don't believe this for a minute myself, there's a concern that . . . well, perhaps Heather is getting a little too old for the role, that she might just be getting a little too flabby in the tit department."

Ashleigh stifled a laugh with her hand.

"Jesus Christ, Richard, what are you saying? I've been exercising. My tits are as firm as ever."

"Yes, I'm sure that's true. But my principals are also worried that they've been overexposed. Like Madonna's. Everyone in the world's seen them now. My people are looking for someone younger, perhaps a little more bountiful. You've met Pamela, my receptionist. She's tested very well. There are some who think she could very well be the next Heather Johns."

"A fucking receptionist?" Heather screamed.

"We can be there in an hour," Chance said. "You can see her tits for yourself. Play with them, for all I care."

"Jesus, Chance."

"Shut up, Heather."

Richard held the pad up for Ashleigh. *Yes or no?* he had written.

Ashleigh took the pen and circled the *no.*

"Sorry, guys," Richard said. "We're going to have to pass on this one. Stay in touch, though."

"God damn it, Richard, don't hang up on me."

"I have an old friend of yours with me, Chance." He nodded at Ashleigh.

"Hello, Chance. Heather."

"Ashleigh?"

"Yes, Chance. How have the two of you been?"

"God damn it, Ashleigh. You're behind this. You fucking no-good bitch . . ."

"Got to run," Richard said. "Our table's waiting." He broke the connection.

He took her to Harry's American Bar. "I've been entering the Bad Hemingway Contest for years," he said lightly, as they were shown to their table, "but I've never come close to winning. I think maybe I'll have to become a judge."

"Thank you, Richard."

"How did it feel?"

"That's what it's like to exercise power, isn't it?"

"Yes."

"I loved it."

One evening, Richard took her to a part of the house she had not seen before. Oh, she had noticed it, of course, when they'd returned from the restaurant that first morning and after each of their walks upon the beach, but thinking it probably a storage area, she had made no comment.

It was below the house at the foot of the steps leading from the deck to the beach. Richard unlocked the sliding glass door and stepped back for Ashleigh to enter the darkness. When he closed the door behind them, she could see nothing, hear nothing but the sound of their breathing, which seemed to overwhelm even the gentle waves that broke upon the beach scant yards away.

Ashleigh waited, anticipating, knowing she was about to be shown something very special.

The sudden flash of light blinded her for a moment. When she regained her sight, she was in a fantasy world of Richard's creation.

So this is where it will be done.

Chapter Twenty-Three

It was a strange and different realm she entered of her own choice. He opened a door and she stepped through willingly, with just the slightest hesitation, looking back only to ensure he followed.

Choices.

So many choices—to run away from home, to find Ashleigh, to whore and then not to, and enter Burke's exotic underworld, to sacrifice all for education, art, Chance, to turn right instead of left at a freeway exit and find Danny, to cross her wrists for the Executioner's rope.

But that was not an alternative, an option. She had been compelled to make that decision. All choices ultimately led to destiny, that one moment in time when the incomprehensible became suddenly clear.

Where are we? she asked. What is this place?
Wherever we like, he answered. It is whatever we want.
We?
Of course.
Roissey?
If you like.
If?
Of course, he said again. He appeared quite surprised that she did not understand.

The Castle or the Village? she said, *referring to the places where Beauty was taken to be subjugated to the will of others and punished.*

This time, he only nodded.

Outside, an occasional wave, bigger than the others, crashed against the beach, sending a shudder through the underground chamber and her heart.

Choices.

Sometimes, Ashleigh wished he would force her, relieve her of decisions, make her do his bidding, leave her no alternative but to accept *his* will. But, of course, he did force her—to make choices.

Together, holding hands, they strolled through their secret place as she quickly came to think of it. It was a curious mixture of the modern and the medieval. Everywhere she turned, she saw her reflections in the mirror-lined walls.

Sometimes, it was a photographic studio. She saw the platform where Susan had been tied so beautifully and the blue carpet for Paula.

It could be an exercise room. There were a variety of exercise machines and weights and small barbells.

The flick of a light switch or the laying of a fire in the fireplace instantly transformed it into a dim chamber of torments. An innocent exercise board became the whipping bench she had seen described in a variety of erotic novels.

She took a riding crop from the wall and tested it against the palm of her hand. Could she stand it if—no, when—he asked? She must.

She touched the soft white silken ropes so neatly coiled, awaiting the moment when they would grace her body.

She turned to him. She said, We'll have such pleasant times here.

Choices.

Guy Benjamin called. "I want to make an appointment for your professional services," he said formally.

"Oh, Guy, you?" Ashleigh laughed delightedly.

"Why not?"

Still laughing, she said, "Why not, indeed?"

When Guy arrived at the scheduled time, Ashleigh greeted him with a kiss, smelling the subtle scent of his cologne and aftershave. "I like it," she said.

"I like your perfume. How have you been?"

"Wonderful. Oh, Guy, I have so much to tell you."

"You're in love."

"It shows that much? I'm disappointed. I can never surprise you with anything." I might shock you, she thought, but I can't surprise you.

"We're too much alike," Guy said. "You can't hide from me, nor I from you."

"Well, I'm in love," Ashleigh said, pretending to pout, "and I'm going to tell you all about him anyway."

"I want to hear everything."

And Ashleigh told him almost everything. "He came as an executioner and I was a beautiful bird of prey . . ."

Guy listened, smiling occasionally, nodding. She's so much in love, he thought.

"Are you horrified?" Ashleigh asked, when she was finished.

"No. Remember, S and M is a part of my culture, too. Leather bars, rough trade." He shrugged. "It appeals to some. Just be careful."

"I'm still the black widow."

"And Ashleigh?"

"Yes?"

"I wish you all the best. You deserve it." He embraced her.

"Thank you, Guy, thank you."

They held each other for a long time.

"But you're here on business," Ashleigh said finally. "We shouldn't spend all our time talking about me. You really want a tattoo?"

"Yes. But it has to be something macho. I'm still a cop."

"I can do macho," Ashleigh said smiling. "What did you have in mind?"

"You." He pointed to the warrior goddess. "Would you

mind? Other cops would see it. Laugh and make obscene comments about fucking you."

Ashleigh shook her head. "I'd be flattered to do it for you, but . . . what does Elliott say?"

"He agrees. He knows how much I care for you. He's not suddenly threatened by your presence. After all, some of our best friends are women."

"Why, Guy?"

"Because I don't see you often enough. This way, you'll be with me always."

"I am truly, truly flattered, Guy. I'll give you my very best."

"I know you will."

He wanted it in miniature, on his arm, from his shoulder to his elbow. Ashleigh worked carefully, providing the greatest detail possible in the limited expanse of skin she worked with, even adding a minute black widow for him.

After leaving the studio that same afternoon, Guy Benjamin began asking around about Richard Sheridan.

The next day Ashleigh closed the studio at noon, after Danny's arrival, drawing the curtains against the outside world. At her request, Dean had taken the day off.

"I thought we might eat in," Ashleigh said. "It'll give us more time together."

"Minx. That's not what you had in mind at all."

"No." Ashleigh smiled. "What did you have in mind?"

"Do you have Richard's permission?"

"Yes. And you?"

Danny nodded.

"Richard thinks you're very beautiful. I showed him the photographs of *The Mask* and *The Kiss.*"

"You must thank Richard for me."

Ashleigh smiled. "He asked me to thank *you.* For lending me the mask. He said he got hard just seeing me in it. He knew immediately, just as I did."

"I'm so happy for you, Ashleigh. Burke is, too."

"Richard wants to commission Burke. He thinks he's very talented."

"What does he want Burke to do?"

"Another painting of you and me. Two paintings, actually, one for you and Burke, and one for us. In our natural state, he said."

"Meaning we would be tied."

"Isn't that our natural state now?"

"There's not much to see," Ashleigh said, as she showed Danny around the studio. "It's almost the same as Burke's"

"I want to see everything, though," Danny said, "because it's yours." She leafed through each of Ashleigh's notebooks, looking at original designs and flashes alike. At Ashleigh's work space, she picked up a framed photograph of Richard. He was on the beach, hair blowing in the sea breeze, smiling for Ashleigh's camera. He wore jeans and a white pullover. The arms of a red cashmere sweater were tied loosely around his neck. He was barefoot.

"He's very handsome," Danny said, taking the photograph from the table. "Are you going to tattoo him?"

"Oh, yes. He will be the thirteenth tattoo. My masterpiece, but first, I must grant him three wishes."

"What are they?"

"I've already given him the first. You'll see." Ashleigh restrained the urge to touch her breasts.

"And the others?"

"I don't know. I've already said yes. I trust him. I'll do whatever he likes."

"Yes, trust is a very important part of relationships like ours."

Danny walked through the studio again, touching things as though committing them to memory, pausing before Burke's portrait of Ashleigh. "I love this rendering of you," Danny said. "You must remember that you are still the warrior goddess. You make the quest for all of us in your art."

"Even in slavery?"

"Especially in slavery."

Ashleigh opened the champagne while the Chinese food—orange-flavored chicken and beef with broccoli—heated in the small microwave. They ate lunch in the reception area. Ashleigh told Danny about Guy Benjamin's visit and the tattoo he wanted.

"He made a very good choice," Danny said.

Choices.

Danny took a piece of chicken with her chopsticks and held it out for Ashleigh to take. Ashleigh returned the gesture and they finished their lunch, each feeding the other.

Danny cleared the coffee table and returned with the champagne, filling their glasses again. "This is wonderful," she said, as she sat beside Ashleigh and took her hand.

"Yes," Ashleigh agreed, "isn't it nice?"

"I've taken the afternoon off. We have the rest of the day together." Danny held her glass for Ashleigh to sip. Then, she leaned over and kissed her, slowly, gently, running her tongue over her lips, into her mouth. When she sat back again, Danny said, "I love to kiss you when your lips are cold from the champagne. I love to warm them."

"You certainly did," Ashleigh whispered. "I'm so glad you're here."

They kissed again, but when Danny reached for her breast, Ashleigh pushed her hand away. "No," she said. "I want to show you something first."

Ashleigh stood, turned away, pulled the sweater over her head, and reached behind to unfasten the bra.

When she turned, Danny gasped. "Oh, Ashleigh, my God, they're beautiful."

They chose the rings together.

He allowed her to keep them in her purse. Frequently, she took them out and opened their box to look at them, lifting them, hefting each in her hands. As time wore on, they seemed heavier each time she took them out.

But she had given her consent. She would not—could not—turn back. She only wondered when he would choose to do it.

"Did it hurt?"

"Excruciating."

"Did you scream?"

"I wanted to, but I asked Richard to gag me. I was afraid he would stop if I cried out. He's like Burke. He doesn't want to hurt me, not really." There was another reason she had asked for the gag. It prevented coherent speech and she would be unable to tell him she had changed her mind, beg him to stop. Her choice was then irrevocable.

"Were you tied?"

"Oh, yes. I thought of you." Ashleigh stroked Danny's skirt, imagining she could feel Burke's initials burning against her palm.

She noticed, too late, that she was unable to watch. He had already filled her mouth with the red ball gag and fastened the straps, not behind her head, but behind the exercise bench on which she reclined. It held her head immobile between her raised and outstretched arms pinioned by ropes tied off on a hook somewhere above and behind. The positioning raised her breasts for him in willing sacrifice. She stared at the ceiling where the mirror should have been. I must tell him later, she thought, on another occasion.

Danny reached out tentatively, withdrew her hand suddenly. "May I?"

"They don't hurt anymore. I was amazed at how quickly the pain went away."

Ashleigh jumped when Danny touched her. "Oh, God, that feels so good. They're more sensitive than ever now. Richard can make me come just by playing with them a little. I've had orgasms just from the friction of one of my sweaters. I wear it whenever I can now, but when I go out I have to wear a bra. Otherwise, everybody can see them sticking out."

"Were you frightened?"

What's taking so long? Panicked, she strained against the straps around her ankles, her thighs, her waist. Is this what Danny felt like? Then, brilliant light illuminated her body. She felt the warmth on her skin and then cold as he bathed her nipples with alcohol. She felt the pressure of a small padded clamp that helped elongate her nipple.

Now it was happening too fast.

Wait, she cried, wait. I'm not ready.

Her eyes bulged and sweat popped from her pores as she bucked against her restraints, screaming silently at the searing, indescribable pain.

And then it was done. As the pain subsided, she felt the tiny weight hanging against the swell of her flesh. Richard looked down on her and with his handkerchief wiped away the humiliating saliva drooling from the corners of her mouth. She thanked him with her eyes.

He disappeared from her sight.

Oh, God, it's going to happen again.

"I'm sure you've thought of all the wonderful possibilities they offer," Danny said, gently pulling Ashleigh to her.

"I have two little heart-shaped lockets that I wear for him sometimes."

"And a leash?"

"Of course. And a chain."

"We're two very depraved women."

"Would you have it any other way?"

Danny answered with a kiss.

He filmed the ritual with two video cameras, editing scenes from each into one. The film was like wedding pictures. Someday, Ashleigh thought, we'll watch them and remember how we were when we were young and so much in love.

Watching the film was like watching another person, except for the heavy gold rings that tugged at her nipples, keeping them in a perpetual state of erection now, a constant reminder of her sexuality and the man who loved her.

"Undress me," Danny whispered huskily. "Please. I have a surprise for you, too."

"Oh, Danny, you did it."

"I've never felt so naked."

Danny moaned as Ashleigh kissed her, running her tongue against the grain, feeling the rasp of tiny whiskers. It's like

Richard's cheek after he's shaved, Ashleigh thought. She's so exposed, inviting.

Someone knocked on the door, rattled the knob, went away.

"Oh, God, yes, Ashleigh, darling, do it to me."

Ashleigh held Danny the way Richard held her after making love. It felt strange having her arm around the older woman's shoulders with Danny's face cradled against her breast. Strange, Ashleigh thought, not because I'm with a woman, but only because I've never had such a lover. Danny toyed with the rings, heightening the sensations that were with her always now.

"Do you find it unusual for me to hold you?" Ashleigh asked.

"No," Danny murmured. "Why should I?"

"It's just that you're older, wiser. I don't mean this in a bad sense, but you're old enough to be my mother. It must feel like your daughter making love to you, holding you after."

"Yes, if I had you when I was eighteen, you could be my daughter, but I think of you as a very cherished younger friend," Danny said, "someone I love very much."

"Sometimes," Ashleigh said, "when Richard puts me in chains, I feel like a filly being saddled and bridled. Do you ever feel like that with Burke?"

"Do you find it humiliating?"

"No, I just think I'm a very lucky filly to have an owner who loves me so much."

"There are bridles for women. And black leather corsets and helmets with manes. I've seen them in catalogs."

"Would you like to be a pony girl?"

"I suppose, if Burke wanted."

"We could race."

"You'd win. I'm too old to run."

"Richard runs. Six miles every morning."

* * *

Danny stirred in her arms. "It's time, darling."

Ashleigh traced the letter on Danny's plump, smooth pubis. "I'm honored," she said.

"I'll wear it proudly," Danny said. "Always."

Ashleigh walked Danny to her car. They kissed chastely. "Give Burke my love."

"I will. You do the same for Richard. Tell him how happy we are for both of you."

"Thank you."

Ashleigh watched her drive off, waving once before turning to her own car and Malibu.

Ashleigh ran to greet Richard as he entered the house, throwing her arms around his neck, kissing him.

"How was your day?" he asked.

Ashleigh laughed. "Oh, the same old thing. How about you?"

"Same old thing."

Ashleigh awakened to the gentle caress of her lover before she learned what would befall her in the room. He stroked her flanks gently and touched her buttocks. For a time, she feigned sleep as he fondled her body, enjoying the soothing caresses wondering what her lover planned for today, but again her body betrayed her. Already she had become his slave once more, entering into her servitude willingly. Her nipples filled as he played with the rings and the warmth spread within her when he manipulated that tiny pleasure spot of her loins. She moaned helplessly and turned to embrace him, but gently he pushed her back, continuing his exploration of her body until she cried out with the pleasure.

After, lying in his arms, Ashleigh said, "What a lovely way to begin our day together."

Richard smiled. "I like to give you pleasure."

"And pain." She touched her rings. Oh, God, it feels so good.

"Pain is often pleasure. You will hurt me in time with the tattoo."

"Yes. It is a fair exchange," Ashleigh said before asking, "When will you write something more for us? I want to know what happens next."

"Are you so impatient?"

"Eager."

Richard smiled and stroked her hair. "I'll give it to you today."

"Mmm," Ashleigh murmured. "That will be nice. Can you feel me purring?"

Chapter Twenty-Four

Ashleigh read his story that afternoon after lunch. He sat with her at the patio table. A sailboat was anchored offshore, its crew diving into the water, swimming about the gently bobbing stern. Further out, someone on a jet ski headed for the distant point. Long blond hair flew in the breeze, but the jet skier wore a black wetsuit and Ashleigh could not tell if it was a man or a woman.

Richard read scripts as she turned the pages slowly, placing each beneath a small piece of driftwood she used as a paperweight. He had changed their names as she'd requested. It was called simply *The Story of Caroline*.

In the beginning, Caroline fled.

But one evening, shortly after her return to Phoenix, Caroline's lover took her to a dinner party. They dressed formally, unusual for the desert community. Christopher was elegant in his tuxedo and Caroline stunning in a full-length black evening gown. For the occasion, Christopher had presented her with a single strand of pearls which he fastened about her neck.

"They're beautiful," Caroline said. She thanked him with a kiss.

"Not so beautiful as you," he replied.

In the car, Caroline said, "Tell me about the dinner party."

"You must not interfere with anything that is said or done tonight."

"What is going to happen?"

"John Evans is our host. Lauren, his wife, has displeased him. She will be punished."

Caroline wondered at the sudden thrill that passed through her body. She licked her lips nervously, tasting her lipstick.

Again, Christopher took her hand, squeezing gently. Caroline returned the pressure with her own hand, turning to smile at Christopher with an assurance that she did not feel.

The last to arrive, Caroline and Christopher were greeted at the door of a large southwestern-style home high in the mountains above the city. Caroline was shocked to recognize their hostess, a television newscaster on a local station. Lauren wore a red evening gown. Full white breasts swelled above the low-cut bodice. Her hair was long and blond, falling softly to the small of her back. Lauren wore handcuffs on her slim and delicate wrists.

"I'm delighted to meet you," Lauren said, raising her hands in unison to take Caroline's. Christopher has told us so much about you." Lauren turned to Christopher. "She's beautiful, Christopher. You're very lucky," she said, offering her lips to him.

"I know," Christopher replied.

They gathered around the pool in the back. In the distance, the city's lights penetrated the gathering twilight. There were two other couples along with John and Lauren and Caroline and Christopher. Lauren introduced Caroline to Edward and Jacqueline first and then to Morgan and Anne. All were older men with younger and very beautiful women. But their beauty was nothing when Caroline stood beside them.

As Lauren circulated among her guests, offering champagne, gracefully balancing the tray on her chained wrists, Jacqueline and Anne gathered around Caroline.

"It's so nice to have you," Anne said. "Christopher has spoken of you often."

"Yes," Jacqueline said. "He loves you very much."

"I know," Caroline replied.

Her duties as hostess fulfilled for the moment, Lauren joined them, leaving the men to stand at the poolside bar. Caroline wondered what they were talking about in this strange setting.

"You're lovely tonight, Lauren," Anne said.

Jacqueline smiled at Lauren and tugged at the handcuffs, drawing her near, kissing her lips. "Yes, you're very beautiful, dear. I always wonder what your viewers would say if they saw you like this. You'll be squirming tomorrow."

Caroline thought she heard a note of spite in Jacqueline's voice. Did she imagine it?

"Oh, I won't be working tomorrow," Lauren said. "John and I have other plans."

Lauren spoke lightly, casually, but there was a tremor in her voice and she paled slightly.

"And what entertainment has John planned for this evening?" Jacqueline asked.

"I don't know," Lauren said. "He never tells me."

"Morgan always tells me in advance," Anne said. "He likes me to anticipate. I hate it," she said, shuddering and shaking her thick red hair. "But in the end, it's better. My imagination always has it much worse than it actually is."

"It doesn't stop you from howling," Jacqueline said. "You begged so prettily last time."

"I remember a time or two when you cried rather lustily," Anne said.

Jacqueline ignored her, tossing her own long blond hair haughtily, turning to Caroline instead, asking, "Has Christopher initiated you yet?"

"No."

"I'll enjoy hearing about it when he does," Jacqueline said. *She left them and joined the men at the bar. They laughed at something she said. Then she whispered in Christopher's ear. He smiled and nodded, touching her arm. Caroline felt a twinge of jealousy and she wondered what Jacqueline had said to Christopher.*

"Don't mind her," Lauren said. "She's a little bitch at times. Next month, it's her turn. That's what's really bothering her. Edward can be very inventive."

"I always enjoy it so much when it's Jacqueline's turn," Anne said. "She deserves everything she gets."

"Anyway, it's lovely to have you here," Lauren said to Caroline. "And always remember how much Christopher loves you. And now I'd better check on dinner. I don't want to antagonize John any more than I have."

Dinner was served by Juanita, a woman of Spanish and Indian descent. She was dressed in black and her hair was pulled back into a severe bun. She was of an indeterminate age, with a stocky figure, the heritage of a strong peasant stock. Conversation during each of the courses ranged from horses—all owned horses, as Christopher did, it seemed—business, and mundane matters. There were polite inquiries of Caroline: How do you like the desert? Are you glad to be back? Will you be working? What do you do?

Caroline answered each question shyly. It was difficult for her to keep her mind on either the superb food served or the shifting conversations. Caroline found her eyes turning to Lauren more and more. The hostess performed admirably, entertaining those on either side. Occasionally, Lauren smiled at her husband. Was she asking for mercy? Caroline wondered. Or perhaps she was prolonging the dinner, putting off whatever was about to happen next.

Finally, John said, "It's time, darling."

"Of course," Lauren replied, acquiescing immediately. She rang the tiny bell and nodded when Juanita appeared in the doorway of the dining room.

Caroline's throat was dry as she watched Juanita unlock the handcuffs that had held Lauren prisoner throughout the evening. When she was free, Lauren lifted her long blond hair and bowed her head, allowing Juanita to fasten a black leather collar about her neck. A chain fell from a ring in the collar to hang between her breasts. Then she rose and said formally, "Please excuse me." Lauren did not resist as Juanita drew her arms behind her and once more locked the handcuffs around those slender wrists. Lauren winced as the cuffs were tightened. Caroline watched, transfixed, as Juanita took the chain and led a docile Lauren, eyes downcast, from the room.

"Why don't we have cognac while we wait," John said. "Christopher, may I escort Caroline?"

"Of course, John." Christopher's hand squeezed her thigh before they rose from the table.

"I'm sure everyone has been telling you how nice it is that you've returned," John said, offering his arm. Caroline took his arm and followed as they left the room.

Caroline smiled nervously. "It is good to be back."

"We're all going to look forward to seeing you again. I'm sure it will be often."

They went to the far side of the large, rambling house and entered a room that might have been added on after the original construction. Caroline could not tell. The walls were mirrored. Caroline saw a dozen reflections of herself. The room itself was comfortably furnished with leather chairs and a leather couch. A small bar was well stocked with a variety of liquors. Above a fireplace at the far end of the room, there was an oil portrait of Lauren, beautifully rendered by the artist.

Jacqueline and Edward lounged on the couch. Jacqueline smiled at Caroline as Edward caressed her breast. Anne and Morgan took adjoining chairs. Caroline noticed that they were holding hands, even as Christopher took her own hand, drawing her apart of the others to chairs opposite the couch. Everything was arranged in a half-circle around what appeared to be a vaulting horse. It was also covered in black leather.

John poured cognac in large crystal snifters for everyone before taking a chair and raising his glass. "To good friends," he said. Then he took his seat and pressed a button.

Caroline sat frozen as Lauren followed Juanita into the room, hurrying to match the servant's pace. She was naked. This time she was led by a chain that passed through the golden rings that pierced erect nipples. Lauren knelt awkwardly before her husband. Her arms were bound behind her with strands of silken rope around her wrists and elbows, forcing her arms together, making her breasts stand out prominently.

Lauren's eyes, Caroline saw, were wide and frightened now, her cool demeanor vanished. Lauren started to speak, wet her lips, tried again. She looked up at her husband. "I beg forgiveness, darling."

"Do you deserve punishment?"

"Yes, darling."

John Evans nodded at Juanita, who had waited impassively. Again, the tug pulled at Lauren's breasts. She struggled to her feet, crying out when Juanita suddenly pulled the chain from the ringed nipples. A gag appeared from within the folds of Juanita's dress. It was a red ball with thin straps.

"Wait," John said. He went to his wife and kissed her long and passionately, holding her tightly. Releasing her, he said, "I love you."

Juanita forced the ball into Lauren's mouth before she could reply, filling her mouth, distending the tender lips. She fastened the straps behind the young woman's head.

"Since we have a new guest tonight," John said, "it should be her decision as to the nature of your punishment. Caroline, what is your wish? Shall Lauren's punishment be moderate or severe? Or will you pardon her entirely?"

Lauren's eyes above the gag pleaded with Caroline. The others in the room waited expectantly. Lauren waited, still beseeching Caroline.

"Severe," Caroline said, suddenly filled with the desire to hear Lauren's muted cries of anguish, to see her writhe in pain and watch the tears stream down her cheeks.

Lauren slumped when Caroline pronounced sentence upon her.

Driving home, Caroline said, "It is Jacqueline's turn next month?"

"Yes."

"And then?"

"Anne," Christopher replied, offering no more, knowing the next question, but cruelly making her ask it.

"And me?"

"The month after Anne."

"What will you do to me?"

"You will be whipped, but only if you love me, and only if you request it. You must make the choice."

Caroline was silent, staring out at the dark shadows of the passing desert—mesquite, stately saguaro cactus. To be whipped or not . . . She played idly with the lovely strand of pearls hanging about her neck, falling to her bosom. A coyote stood at the side of the road, watching the car brazenly, and then it was gone. Caroline recalled the punishment of Lauren as from a dream, hearing again the crack of the multithronged short-handled whip Juanita wielded. Juanita had whipped Lauren slowly, methodically, pausing between strokes, as though gathering strength for the next blow.

Caroline turned to look at her lover in the dim light of the car. The dashboard illuminated Christopher's features slightly.

"I love you," Caroline said.

Christopher pulled to the side of the road, stopped. He leaned over and kissed her awkwardly in the cramped confines of the car. A console was between them. "I have another present for you," he said, opening the console. He handed her a small rectangular package.

"What is it?"

"Open it."

Caroline carefully removed the ribbon and the wrapping paper. Inside the box, a pair of handcuffs rested on a satin wrap.

"They will look lovely on you," Christopher said. "They suit you."

"Yes," Caroline said.

He took the handcuffs and unlocked them. "Lean forward."

Caroline did as he ordered, placing her arms behind her. The cuffs clicked shut with a finality. Caroline sat back awkwardly, leaning against her arms. She turned to him. "I truly belong to you now."

"For all time," Christopher replied. Again he kissed her.

"I have another question," Caroline said.

"Yes?"

"What did Jacqueline say to you?"

"She asked if she could have you for an afternoon or an evening."

"And will you give me to her?"

"Perhaps," he said, starting the car again, easing to the blacktop again from the shoulder.

Caroline could see his smile in the dim light cast by the dashboard. "Jacqueline would be very heartless with me," she said.

"Yes."

"Will you be as cruel as Jacqueline?"

"Yes," he replied, "but not tonight."

The story ended there.

"Why Arizona?" Ashleigh asked, when she had finished reading. She tapped the manuscript pages neatly into order.

"Can you take a few days off a week?"

"Yes."

"Would you like to go to Arizona with me?"

"To Lauren and Jacqueline?"

"No, silly, I have a ranch there. It's small, only twenty acres, but I still call it a ranch. It's another refuge."

She reached out and touched his hand. "Yes, I'd like that," she said smiling. "I think."

Richard laughed then. "It's just a story, darling."

Ashleigh would not question him further. Wayland, too, had been only a story and now she bore the weight of his rings—her rings. She looked across the blue waters, so placid in the afternoon, to Catalina and wondered who she was. In the beginning, she had been Caroline, but then she had become Lauren, feeling the heavy strokes applied by a serving woman, and back again to Caroline, who might or might not be given to another woman. There were so many wonderful possibilities.

Ashleigh was positive of one thing only. It was not just a story. One day, he would be cruel to her, but not tonight. That's too bad, she thought, as she leaned over and blew her warm breath softly into his ear as he liked. "I love you," she whispered.

"And I love you," he said. "You must always remember that."

"I know, darling, I will."

Chapter Twenty-Five

They boarded last. The flight wasn't crowded and the coach passengers were already through the first-class compartment when they entered the aircraft. They had packed lightly—a garment bag for each that a flight attendant had hung in a compartment. Ashleigh returned the attendant's smile, glancing down at her name tag, finding her name was Barbara.

They were the only passengers in first class. As soon as they were seated, Barbara offered them drinks.

"Ashleigh?" Richard said.

"Oh, what a pretty name," Barbara said.

"Thank you. I picked it myself."

Barbara looked confused.

Ashleigh smiled up at her. "Never mind. It's a long story. I'll have a glass of champagne, please."

"Of course. And you, sir?"

"Scotch. On the rocks. A double. Johnny Walker Black, if you have it."

"We do. I just unpacked it myself."

The aircraft was already backing away from the gate. Those left behind waved from terminal windows.

"It's our first vacation together," Richard said.

"I'm looking forward to it. We'll have a wonderful time, darling."

They took off to the west and banked south, flying parallel to the coast for a few minutes. Ashleigh looked down at the

Peninsula for Danny's home, but it was lost in a maze of tiny red-tiled buildings. When they turned east to head inland over Long Beach, Ashleigh saw the *Queen Mary* at permanent anchor. As they climbed, the ground was soon lost, covered by a brown smoggy blanket.

"I'm very lucky to have a week alone with the most beautiful woman in the entire world."

"Why, thank you, kind sir."

"Now, can I have your honey-roasted peanuts?"

Desert winds buffeted the aircraft on its slow descent into Sky Harbor Airport. Ashleigh gripped Richard's hand tightly, nervously. She hadn't flown enough to be a seasoned and nonchalant flyer. Richard held her hand and waited casually for landing.

A limousine took them north of the airport. Ashleigh wasn't sure how far, perhaps twenty or thirty miles. When they left the freeway, they were on a two-lane road that cut through the desert scrub, heading east toward distant mountains.

"I bought the place because it backs on government land. My twenty acres is really thousands of acres. I don't know how many. You'll see."

His pride of ownership amused Ashleigh. It was a trait she hadn't seen before. Although the home in Malibu was probably worth millions, he didn't show the same animation or excitement about it as he did about twenty acres of desert.

Ashleigh wondered how much he would pay if she stood naked on some trader's block, chattel for sale to the highest bidder. The idle scenario brought a smile.

"Someday, soon, another five years or so, and we'll retire here," he said, adding quickly, "if you like it."

"I'm sure I will," Ashleigh replied. But it really doesn't matter, she thought. I belong to you and I will, must, do whatever you want.

"We're getting close now."

They turned left at a traffic light and shortly after that,

turned left again, onto a corrugated dirt road curving into the desert.

"This is it," Richard said, as the driver pulled into a dirt driveway.

Ashleigh saw nothing but desert, populated only by stately saguaro cactuses, their arms uplifted in supplication to the cloudless blue sky; and then they burst into a clearing and parked in front of a small southwestern-style house.

The front door opened and a dark-skinned woman of perhaps fifty ran into the yard, wiping her hands on her apron, calling over her shoulder. "Miguel! Señor is here, Miguel!"

Richard hugged her. "Juanita, how are you, my love? You're as pretty as ever."

Juanita!

Ashleigh stared.

The woman didn't look at all like the "Juanita" in the story. How could this round-faced woman with such a pleasant smile be the one who would . . .

"Juanita, I want you to meet a very special lady. This is Ashleigh."

"Oh, Señorita, I am so pleased to meet you."

"Buenos tardes, Miguel, *como esta?"* Richard shook his hand and then threw his arm around Miguel's shoulders. "It's good to see you, *amigo."*

"It's good to see you, *amigo.* Everything is ready for you."

"Miguel, this is Ashleigh."

"Señorita," he said shyly.

Ashleigh smiled and shook his hand.

Juanita fussed over Ashleigh, showing her through the house, while her husband took Richard on a brief tour of the ranch, showing him what work had been accomplished, what needed to be done in time.

Inside, the house was spacious and cool. The living room was furnished around the big stone fireplace. The bookcases held a smattering of novels, but there were a great many more books on Arizona and the southwest—its history, its flora and fauna, works on native Americans, biographies of early settlers.

Juanita hung their bags in the closet of the master bedroom. A desert landscape hung over the dresser and another on the opposite wall. Ashleigh touched the smooth oak of the poster bed.

"I am glad you're here," Juanita confided. "He comes too often alone. This one, he needs a good woman to look after him. All men do. You will give him many strong babies. *Si?*"

Ashleigh laughed. *"Si,"* she said, turning away from the bed self-consciously.

Ashleigh followed Juanita down the hall past a guest bedroom. "This is his office. He works too much, even when he is here."

There was a telephone console on the desk, a computer and printer, a fax machine. The only decorations on the walls were framed degrees—a bachelor's and a master's from the University of Southern California.

"Come, I will show you everything in the kitchen."

Through the kitchen window, Ashleigh saw Richard and Miguel in the yard. They were drinking beer from cans. She had never seen Richard drink beer before.

"We are going to visit our daughters in Tucson," Juanita said.

"That's nice," Ashleigh said.

"Si. Do you cook?"

"Yes."

"Good. You must fatten him up. He's too skinny, all the time running. But tonight, there is no cooking for you. I have made enchiladas and refried beans and rice. Just heat it up."

"That's very kind. Thank you."

"Remember, many babies. You can start tonight."

"Would you like the grand tour?"

"Yes. I want to see everything."

"Let's get a beer, and some carrots for the horses. Do you ride?"

"Yes," Ashleigh said. "Richard . . ."

"Yes?"

"Would you like children?"

"With you, yes."

Flowers lined the house, but beyond the flagstone patio, the yard consisted of the desert's natural vegetation. In the evenings, as they sat with their drinks watching spectacular sunsets, small rabbits hopped boldly to the edge of the light to play while awaiting their handouts of carrots and lettuce leaves. Ashleigh fed them and laughed at their antics.

The stables, a small barn, and a big corralled arena were below the house, near the edge of a dry creek bed. Richard told her that sometimes fierce waters, flash floods, roared through the creek.

Richard introduced her to their horses.

Sultan and Scheherazade.

"I call him Molasses. He's old and slow, and the perfect horse for me. I'm not a very good rider."

"But Sultan and Scheherazade are such perfect names for us," Ashleigh said. "Did you know I would come to you one day?"

"I only hoped I would meet you."

"And then we did. What a pretty love story we have." And I will tell you stories of Ashleigh's submission and of her great love.

But Ashleigh balked at entering the barn. "Please, Richard, don't lock me in there. You can do anything with me but that. I couldn't stand it again."

"Again?" he questioned solemnly, and then listened quietly as she told him of long-ago torments. When she was finished, tears filled her eyes. "Please, Richard," she pleaded.

He parted the barn doors, sliding them back with a crash, filling the barn with light. He walked through the barn quickly then, throwing open doors as he passed, and opened the doors at the other end. He turned and stood, framed in the light, beckoning. "It's just a barn," he called.

Slowly, shivering with fright, Ashleigh walked through, glancing neither right nor left, until she fell, gasping for breath, into his waiting arms.

No, Father, please . . .

Together they made the return journey. He stopped her before each storage room. "This is for our tack. This is for tools. We keep the feed here." As they emerged, he said, "It's just a barn, Ashleigh, not a prison. It will never be your prison," he promised.

"Thank you," she said, brushing the tears from her eyes.

The night was quiet. It was strange to be in a place where the house did not shake as waves crashed against the continent, or where muted sounds of the city drifted high into the hills.

Richard had drifted away first, leaving her alone to fight sleep, fearing the nightmares that come from old memories. He stirred but did not awaken as she touched his back lightly, wondering what beautiful creation she would put there. She kissed the back of his neck before easing from bed.

He did not awaken as she dressed quickly, slipping into jeans and loafers, pulling a sweater over her head. She walked through the strange house, going into the night by the patio doors to follow the moonlit path down to the barn.

The horses whinnied and snorted in greeting, and she patted and whispered soothingly to them—to herself—before she turned and confronted the demon.

Jezebel, he always thundered.

Father, no!

It's just a barn, Richard had said.

She forced herself through the crack in the doors left ajar.

He was there . . . in the darkness.

Jezebel!

Ashleigh hugged herself, telling the frightened girl within that it was only the chill of the night, knowing it was a lie.

He was there.

Waiting.

Ignoring his presence, she went to the storage room and closed the door behind her. Standing in the darkness she thought, You can't make me cry again.

But he did.

As she lowered herself to the hay-strewn floor, the first warm tears streaked her cheeks. She wiped them away with the back of her hands and sat in the darkness, remembering.

Her fists pounded the door. *No, Father, please don't leave me here.*

Jezebel!

"Yes, fuck you, yes!" she whispered vehemently. "I fuck men and women and paint my face and to hell with you and salvation. I don't care anymore!"

Please, Father, no.

"Ashleigh. Ashleigh!"

His cries awakened her. Where am I?

She remembered.

Oh, Jesus. I didn't mean to stay so long. "Richard, I'm here." She rushed out of the barn, stopping as he ran down the path toward her.

"Ashleigh, my God, what happened? I woke up and you were gone. I thought you'd left."

"I had to face him," she said as he hugged her tightly in the cold first light of day. "I'm sorry."

"He can't hurt you now. He can never hurt you again. I won't let him."

"I know."

"Don't leave me, Ashleigh. I love you. Please, never leave me."

"I won't darling. I'm yours. Always." How very strange, Ashleigh thought, taking his hand to walk back to the house, by consenting to become his slave, I've enslaved him.

They went into the small town a few miles from the ranch and purchased a pair of boots for Ashleigh. Afterward they went to a western bar and ate hamburgers and french fries and drank beer from long-necked bottles while listening to country western songs—George Strait, Garth Brooks, Kathy Mattea, Willie Nelson—from a jukebox that was never still for long.

The locals knew him. The bartender came over to shake his hand. "It's been awhile, Richard."

"Too long, Tom, too long."

"Who's this pretty lady?"

"This is Ashleigh."

"Well, I'm pleased to meet you, Ashleigh. You just let me know if this ol' rascal gives you any trouble. I'll take him out back and teach him what for."

Ashleigh smiled. "I'll keep that in mind, Tom, but I think I can handle him."

"I just bet you can, at that."

The waitress who took their orders said, "Give me a kiss, Richard. We ain't seen you in forever."

"Donna, you know you broke my heart the last time."

"And didn't you just fix me? How *do* you *do!*" she said, holding her hand out to Ashleigh. "I'm Donna, and don't you believe a word he says—you hear? He's just like all men. Ain't no good for nuthin'."

Donna hustled away, circling around tables, deftly avoiding the big paws that wanted to pat her backside.

"They like you," Ashleigh said.

"Yes, I think they do. They know who I am, what I do, but they don't care. I like that."

They saddled Sultan and Scheherazade. Ashleigh turned in her saddle and looked back at the ranch, feeling very much like the Woman Who Rode Away. Turning back, she looked at the nearby hills and urged Scheherazade forward, following Richard on Sultan into the desert.

Ashleigh wished he would tie her wrists behind her and take Scheherazade's reins, leading her to whatever lair he might have. She would ride proudly, defiantly, helplessly, to her fate. It became a recurring fantasy, just as she now imagined his examination as she stood naked on the block waiting to be sold. Sometimes, she was alone. At other times, Danny joined her and they were auctioned as mother and daughter, to be led away in chains.

But as Christopher had treated Caroline with courtesy upon her return, Richard was kind and solicitous, a gracious host, making love to her gently, striving to please her in every way. One night, lying in his arms, she asked, "How much would you pay for me in a slave market?"

"Whatever it took," he replied.

Richard told the truth. She was much the better rider, casually at ease on horseback, while Richard swung into the saddle awkwardly, relaxing only after the first half hour or so. But Sultan was a good horse for him, living up to his nickname, patiently following Richard's commands, tossing his head occasionally, as if to say, Is this what you really want to do?

On that first ride together, Richard led the way high into the hills until they reached a clearing that faced east, overlooking a vast emptiness.

Sitting at the edge of the clearing, drinking beer, Richard told her, "You are the chatelaine of all you see."

"Isn't it nice to think so?" Ashleigh said.

It became their custom to ride into the desert in the late afternoons when the shadows began to lengthen, following one trail or another into the hills. Cottontails peered curiously at them and an occasional jackrabbit raced away in looping curves through the brush.

Once, when Ashleigh was leading, they happened upon a bad-tempered rattlesnake, out late for the season, coiled in the trail. Ashleigh pulled Scheherazade to a halt and patted her neck, whispering, "Easy, girl," as the snake buzzed angrily. Ashleigh backed her away.

"Where's reverse on this thing?" Richard called out.

But Sultan took his lead from Ashleigh and backed away, snorting and shaking his head at the disturbing sound.

"He's gone now," Ashleigh said, watching the snake slither away. She turned and looked back. "Did you see it?"

"No."

* * *

Although she rarely watched the evening news at home, Ashleigh flipped through the local television channels. There were enough blond and beautiful anchorwomen to choose among. Ashleigh wondered which was Lauren.

She passed her time by reading, sketching, and wondering when she would meet the characters of his story and what they would do to her then. Anything, Richard. For you, my love, anything.

Richard called his office each morning and responded to one development or another, answered questions, provided directions, but otherwise, they were free to do as they pleased.

One afternoon, they drove to Scottsdale and wandered through the trendy streets, browsing in the art galleries. Although there were a great many nudes, Ashleigh saw none that were better than *The Mask* or *The Kiss.*

"How will you have us pose?" Ashleigh asked in one small gallery.

"Kneeling," Richard said, "as in *The Kiss,* but you and Danny will be tied, arms raised above your heads, your breasts touching, kissing."

Ashleigh turned to find the young saleswoman staring at them in horror. She smiled and said, "Don't worry, I want him to do it, and Danny is a woman I love very much."

The woman blushed and stammered, "I couldn't help hearing."

They laughed as they walked down the street, holding hands. "We're terrible," Ashleigh said.

"We've probably given her new ideas for her boyfriend."

Another afternoon, they drove to Apache Junction and beyond to Lost Dutchman State Park and stood at the edge of the immense, brooding Superstition Wilderness. Ashleigh shivered as she imagined riding, a woman alone, into the dark and trackless wasteland in search of destiny, final fulfillment.

More and more, Ashleigh thought the thirteenth tattoo

would be the Woman Who Rode Away, a personalized varia-tion that would please Richard as much as herself.

But first, the two remaining wishes must be fulfilled. Then she would tell him.

One evening, after they had dressed to dine out, Richard presented her with a single strand of pearls, fastening them around her neck.

Just as in the story, Ashleigh thought, and so it begins. I must thank him with a kiss. "They're beautiful," she said.

"Not so beautiful as you."

It will happen tonight.

In the car, Ashleigh said, "Tell me about the dinner party."

Richard smiled. "It's not what you think. We're having din-ner in a restaurant."

"Really?"

"Yes, really. Are you disappointed?"

"I don't know," Ashleigh replied truthfully.

Together, they worked to clean the pens, pitching the ma-nure into a wheel barrow, pushing it to the manure pile. Later, it would be spread in the arena and disked in to make the dirt soft.

They wiped sweat from their brows and leaned on pitch-forks, talking and laughing. When they were finished, they would go and sit on the patio and drink beer and watch the sun fall behind the distant mountains, before going into the house to make dinner, eat, read, make love . . . always to make love.

Later, Ashleigh would think their week together passed all too quickly.

* * *

Late in the week, they rode back into the desert to the clearing that had become their special place to camp out.

After making camp for the night, Ashleigh stood at the clearing's edge, looking out at the great expanse. When darkness fell, distant lights might twinkle, revealing human presence, but for the moment, they were alone in the universe.

The loop fell over her shoulders and he pulled the lasso tight around her waist, pinning her arms to her sides. Laughing, she struggled against the rope as he pulled her to him and then backed her against the tree, winding the rope several times around her waist and arms. Still laughing, looking over her shoulder as he tied the knot pinioning her to the tree, Ashleigh cried, "Richard, what are you doing?"

He circled her once, twice, admiring her beauty, brushing a strand of hair from her forehead, touching her cheek, smiling.

She joined his silence, waiting, watching to see what he wanted of her.

He stood behind her and stroked her belly until her breathing quickened. When he touched and lifted her breasts, she bit her lip, determined not to utter a sound until he did. Her rings—their rings—betrayed her, though, and she was glad she had removed the bra worn for support while riding. But for the rope, she would have placed her hands over his and pressed him to her.

When he stood before her, she met his gaze, licking her lips, waiting. He kissed her, placing one hand behind her head, protecting her from the rough bark. Ashleigh moaned a second time as he probed and explored her lips, her mouth.

He stood back and looked at her for a moment. "Oh, God, you're so beautiful and I love you so much."

Ashleigh shuddered as he unbuttoned her shirt, tugging it from her jeans and from beneath the ropes, spreading it to bare her breasts. He leaned over and pulled gently at a ring with his tongue, lifting her breast until she cried out, "Oh, God, Richard, don't stop, please, don't stop."

He tortured her relentlessly, punishing her with kisses, moving from her lips, her neck, to her breasts and belly, caressing and kissing her until the little clearing filled with her cries and whimpers. Her flesh burned to his every touch.

Even then, he did not stop, kneeling in the dirt to unfasten her belt buckle and slowly push her jeans down, kissing her thighs all the while. She kicked her boots off to help, shaking her head, groaning louder as he placed her legs on his shoulders and nuzzled the pale moist tendrils of hair.

Even nature conspired to further her sweet agony as her back pressed against the bark that scratched and bit her as a second lover while Richard filled her body with sensations, driving her to a place of oblivion where nothing else mattered and her cries became an uncontrollable litany of delighted suffering.

"Yes, Richard, yes, oh, God, yes, Richard, yes."

Helpless, his face between her open legs, she hung against the tree, her weight eased by his shoulders, her body wracked by spasms, once, twice.

"Yes!" Ashleigh screamed. "Yes!"

Only then did he allow her respite, bringing her slowly back to their little clearing in the desert, allowing her to stand against the tree as he kissed her lips and eyelids and stroked her matted hair and nibbled gently at her nipples.

Ashleigh looked down and pulled against the ropes, yearning to take hold of him, caress and kiss him as he had done for her, but she could not free herself.

Finally, he stood back and smiled.

Disheveled, her shirt wet and bunched around her shoulders, Ashleigh wiggled helplessly for him and thought, My God, he's going to do it again.

He released her then and carried her to the waiting bedrolls. Her arms were around his neck and she kissed him as he lowered her to the ground.

No more. I can't take any more, she thought, watching him undress, opening her arms and legs to receive him. "Yes," she cried, "yes."

*   *   *

They cooked on an open fire and ate sitting cross-legged on the ground, drinking chilled white wine in thermos cups. Smiling at her friend and lover and master, Ashleigh thought it was the best wine she had ever tasted.

Satiated with love, they were content to hold each other in the cold night beneath stars that watched with benign approval. Warm and secure beneath their covering, wrapped each in the other's arms, Richard asked for his third wish.

"Will you marry me, Ashleigh?"

"Oh, Richard, yes. Oh, yes. Yes. A thousand times yes."

In her happiness, Ashleigh did not think to ask of his second wish. It would not have concerned her in any case. She would be his wife no matter what he might ask of her.

Two days later, they returned to Los Angeles.

Only then did Ashleigh meet Jacqueline.

Chapter Twenty-Six

"Ashleigh, that's wonderful. I'm so glad for you."

"Oh, Danny, I'm so lucky. I still can't believe such happiness."

"Now, I really can't wait to meet Richard."

"Oh, you'll like him. He's wonderful and terrific and . . . and . . . just wonderful." Ashleigh laughed at herself. "I still can't believe it. I'm going to be married."

"We're looking forward to spending the day with you and Richard."

"It'll be so much fun. We'll just relax, walk on the beach, catch up, have dinner."

"It will be nice. Ashleigh?"

"Yes."

"Remember, I love you, too. We both do."

"And I love you, Danny."

Richard Sheridan is an interesting individual. He is a powerful agent, a superagent, respected for his ability to make deals, to create packages from among his many clients—stars, directors, writers. Twice, years apart, sheriff's deputies from the Malibu Station responded to 9-1-1 calls from his home. The first call was from his former wife, the second from a girlfriend. Domestic disputes, both resolved when the women involved said they had overreacted. His DMV record is spotless, not even a parking ticket. Before Ashleigh, he was occasionally seen at an opening, always with a beautiful woman. Beyond that, he seems a man who works hard and long and then keeps to himself. There is no recollection of lavish parties at his home or any of the other trappings that go with wealth, power, and status in the film and television industry.

Those are the facts.

But there are rumors.

The girlfriend who made the 9-1-1 call told the operator she was being held against her will. Overreaction?

He is called "the Executioner" for his cold ruthlessness in business.

The nickname sticks in rumors and innuendo about his sexual tastes and proclivities, that he dominates his women in a variety of ways. Attracted by the aphrodisiac of power (as well as by wealth and good looks), there was never a shortage of women willing to be dominated. I have looked through back issues of newspapers and seen their photographs in the society and entertainment pages. His friends wear chokers, thick necklaces, and heavy bracelets that might be collars and manacles . . . or simply jewelry.

Ashleigh says he is kind, gentle, loving, and intelligent, and always treats her with consideration and courtesy.

They are to be married next year. Elliott and I are to be invited, along with Burke and Danny and Dean and his life partner. Ashleigh says we are her only true friends.

Oh, Ashleigh, be careful.

After the two police officers—called by some prying neighbor—left, the argument resumed, became quiet, but more intense, filled with a greater fierceness than before, when they were shouting and screaming at each other.

"You don't need her," Cynthia hissed finally, her tiny balled-up fists hammering futilely at his chest.

Wanting to hurt Ashleigh, Bobby nearly lashed out and hit Cynthia then, all of the pent-up resentment and animosity transferring to her as she became the object of his loathing.

Cynthia saw the intent in his eyes, the cold fury, and fled, slamming the bedroom door, locking it.

Now, Bobby paced and brooded, his anger simmering and growing more with each new anguished cry from the bedroom. The wracking sobs battered him, forcing remorse to mingle with the anger and the hatred, diluting them momentarily, only to well up again.

The bitch. The no-good bitch. How could she refuse to tattoo him? After all he had done for her, sacrificed for her, given to her?

"You'll have to find someone else," Ashleigh had told him calmly. "I won't do it again, but I can recommend someone else."

God damn her, anyway!

I'll show her. Her and her goddamned precious tattoos. Her fucking art. She was nothing but a prick-teasing slut, using men until she no longer needed them, tossing them aside then like some piece of garbage.

Oh, shit, what have I done? What am I doing?

He slumped against the wall next to the bedroom door, slid down, and sat in the hallway, head hanging in his hands, listening to Cynthia cry. Oh, Jesus, God. What . . . am . . . I . . . doing?

"Cyn, baby, I'm sorry. I don't know what gets into me sometimes."

"Go away," she cried, bursting into renewed wails.

"Please, Cyn, don't be like that. You're right—I don't need her. I'll find someone else if I want another tattoo. Please, Cyn, let me in. I love you." Bobby knew he lied to this woman who loved him, but he couldn't help it. He *did* need Ashleigh. So long as she consented to be his artist, there was hope. She would come to her senses, realize how wrong she had been about their relationship, their love. So long as he offered his body to her machine . . .

But now.

God damn it!

He slammed his fist into the wall, bruising it badly, but was scarcely aware of the pain.

Slowly, the apartment grew quiet, the throbbing pain in his hand and the pulsating anger in his mind the only reminders of the vicious argument that had raged.

He sat there helplessly for a long while, his anger receding, wanting to cry, but unable to summon the tears.

The key turned in the lock and the door slowly opened. "Do you mean that?" Cynthia asked, looking down at him through burning eyes that could no longer fill with tears, but her chest still heaved with dry sobs.

He hugged her legs, pressed his face against her legs. "I *do* love you, Cyn."

"Not that," she said. "The other. That you'll find someone else. Forget about . . . her."

"Yes, baby, yes."

She pulled away and went into the bathroom. She was splashing cold water on her face when Bobby came in and sat on the toilet seat.

"Forgive me, Cyn, please."

"I never want to fight like this again," she said, looking into the mirror at her ravaged face and baggy, red-rimmed eyes. "Not ever."

"No," he said. "I couldn't stand it, either."

She turned to him then and pressed his face to her belly, stroked his long hair. "I love you, too, baby. I love you, too."

Cynthia took his hand and led him to the bedroom. They lay on the bed kissing and stroking each other, spent from their wrath, too tired to make love.

"Go to sleep, baby," Cynthia crooned when he turned over, putting her arm around him, pressing her breasts against the Lovers, stroking Death. "Go to sleep, baby, forget all about it. Mama's here. Mama'll take care of you, baby. That's right. Sleep now. Forget all about it."

Chapter Twenty-Seven

It began as a perfectly ordinary day with two couples gathering in new friendship to spend an afternoon and evening at a beach house. They planned to sit on the deck, perhaps go for a walk on the beach, relax in the Jacuzzi, have cocktails and dinner, and finally part only after setting a date to get together again. Hundreds of thousands of couples across the country did the same thing each weekend in one fashion or another.

But Ashleigh quickly realized—they all did—that there was nothing ordinary about it. They shared too many secrets about one another for a prosaic meeting of friends. From the initial introductions, a sensual excitement and anticipation pervaded the atmosphere and there was unspoken acceptance of a new relationship. Richard and Danny appraised each other as they shook hands and smiled. Ashleigh knew they felt it just as she did with Burke's embrace and affectionate kiss on her cheek.

And what of Richard and Burke? They were casual in their greeting, instantly at ease with one another, knowing that they shared common interests, knowing that they were devoted to the women who were their slaves.

There would be an exchange of women today. Ashleigh wondered how it would come about.

Slowly, the photographs of other women had been replaced by her own. As Ashleigh showed them to Danny, they climbed the staircase slowly, looking at the record of her journey. Each provoked loving memories of a prolonged seduction in which silken ropes or delicate silver chains caressed her in tight embrace as he whispered endearments, praising her beauty, proclaiming his love, before kissing her again or teasing a body impatient for his attention.

In one, her arms were raised and the camera captured her beauty as she looked over her shoulders as though to see what new torment might await. Her expression was imploring, as though she were begging for release from agony. But the camera could not reveal what had gone before. Ashleigh did not know or care how long she had been tied. He made her drink of lethean waters with long, lingering kisses and caresses that burned her flesh. She needed no command when he stretched and elongated her breasts, holding them for her to kiss taut ringed nipples with her own flicking tongue. When he finally turned to the camera, she was spent, exhausted, wanting only to sleep in his loving arms.

In another, Ashleigh went to the post willingly, looking back to ensure that he followed. Smiling, she stood against the post and placed her hands behind it. His touch was gentle as the first strands of rope encircled her wrists. Would he stop there? No.

Other ropes went around her ankles, her thighs, pinning her to the post, making her one with an obscene lover. The ropes held her tight. Behind, her fingers fluttered in a futile gesture against her bonds.

She returned his kiss, straining to thrust her tongue deep into his mouth. When he drew away, Ashleigh struggled yet to reach his lips. From behind, Richard caressed her breasts, her belly, her thighs as she writhed helplessly and moaned with increasing desire.

Later, as the camera snapped photograph after photograph, Ashleigh thought it was like being tied to his prick and she wished she could shrink like Alice and be tied there forever in loving permanent embrace.

"They're beautiful photographs, Ashleigh. You're beautiful. I'm so envious. I wish Richard could take some of me as a present for Burke."

"Why not?"

"Would you mind?"

Ashleigh shook her head. "Would Burke?"

"I'll ask. I'm getting wet just thinking about it."

Ashleigh smiled. "It's inevitable, you know."

"Yes, I suppose it is."

"I like your friends," Richard said.

They were in the kitchen. Ashleigh arranged hors d'oeuvres on a platter—cheese, crackers, small slices of melon, grapes. Richard opened a bottle of champagne.

"I'm glad. They like you, too, but what's not to like?" Ashleigh kissed his cheek. "What's not to love?"

"Thank you. Danny's a very striking woman. I see why you love her."

"Would you like her?"

"Is she yours to give?"

"She wears my initial, too."

"So you are both slave and mistress."

"For Danny, yes. For you, only a slave."

"Would Burke consent?"

"He already has," Ashleigh said, nodding to the window. On the deck, Danny smiled and hugged Burke. "She wants a photograph to give Burke. Will you?"

"I'd be honored."

They sat on the deck beneath the shade of the umbrella, sipping wine, eating, exchanging small talk. For a time, the men discussed the paintings Richard would commission of Burke, talking of their women as though they were not present, knowing that Ashleigh and Danny would be excited by their very exclusion.

"They should be kneeling," Richard offered.

"Arms raised and tied."

"Straining to kiss and rub their tits together."

"Crying in frustration."

"If Danny's nipples were pierced, we could fasten them by their rings."

"We might have to do that." Burke turned to Danny. "Would you like to wear rings like Ashleigh?"

"Whatever you desire," Danny replied, eyes downcast submissively, "I desire." She wanted to cry out, Oh, Jesus, yes, Burke, please.

With their presence again acknowledged, Ashleigh and Danny joined the conversation, but they were disappointed when the topic was changed to books and films.

For another hour, Richard and Burke extended the conversation. When talk threatened to flag, one or the other mentioned a new title and the dialogue resumed.

Beneath the table, Ashleigh and Danny held hands, communicating by touch, each feeling the other's growing urgency, each wanting it to begin. Let it happen now.

They're such bastards, Ashleigh thought, dragging this out, making us wait like this, knowing that they're torturing us with uncertainty. I'll bet Danny's as excited as I am. I don't care who fucks me, just as long as someone does. Soon.

Finally, Richard glanced over his shoulder at the lowering sun and said, "We should probably get started if we're going to have time for the Jacuzzi before dinner."

At last!

"Yes," Burke said, "I think you're right."

"Danny?"

She rose and looked down at Ashleigh and Burke and then to Richard. "Whatever you say, Richard."

"Let's go downstairs, then."

Danny glanced back at Burke, smiled hesitantly, blew him a kiss, said, "I love you." Then she turned and followed Richard down the steps.

"I wonder how he'll pose her," Ashleigh said, after hearing the door slide shut behind two of the three people she loved.

"It'll be a surprise."

"Yes. That's what makes it so exciting. Oh, Burke, when

we're both married, we're going to have so much fun together."

"We already are."

"That's true. Don't you wonder what they're doing?"

"Yes, just as I often wonder what you and Richard are doing. Don't you think of us at night?"

"All the time, especially when Richard is tying me. I always hope you're doing the same for Danny."

"I usually am."

"She loves you so much."

"Let's go inside. I want to see your rings."

"Yes, Richard said I should do whatever you asked."

While Burke fondled her breasts, Ashleigh tried to pretend he was as much a stranger to her as Danny to Richard, but it was not the same. He was Burke and she loved him, had always loved him. Still, she found it exciting to be touched by another man while Richard was downstairs with another woman.

"When I'm given to you," Ashleigh said, "will you surprise me?"

"You know?"

Ashleigh repeated what she had told Danny earlier. "It's inevitable."

"Yes, of course I'll surprise you."

"It'll be like old times," Ashleigh said, "only better. Shall I show you what else you can do with my rings?"

"I've never been tied by another man before. Only Burke."

"Are you nervous?" Richard smiled reassuringly.

"Yes, a little," Danny admitted. "A lot, actually. I should have gone to the bathroom first."

"Over there," Richard said. He indicated a door at the far end of the vast room.

"Thank you."

"Would you leave the door open if I asked?"

Danny stopped and turned to face him. "Do you watch Ashleigh?"

"Sometimes, yes."

"I am to do as you say."

"I know."

Danny smiled. "It's a conspiracy then? Between you?"

Richard nodded and returned her smile.

"Are you going to fuck me, too?"

"Do you want me to?"

Danny paused. "If that's what Burke wants."

"One day, after you're married, you'll be sent to me for a weekend and Ashleigh will be sent to Burke."

"Will you be cruel?"

"If you like."

Danny turned and went to the bathroom, leaving the door open, looking at Richard as she unbuckled her jeans and lowered them to sit on the toilet. "You're the first man ever to watch me pee."

"What are your feelings right now?"

"Powerless. Helpless."

"And do you like it?"

"Oh, yes," Danny said, blushing and looking away, realizing why Ashleigh was instantly attracted to this powerful and domineering personality.

Richard closed the door.

Danny told herself it would be just like modeling for Burke, knowing all the while that it was different. In a moment or two, a few minutes, she would stand naked before a stranger, submitting to his will. It thrilled her and she loved Burke even more for sending her with Richard. He would only do it because he loved her. Still, she lingered before the mirror, wishing she had brought her brush and lipstick and wondering what Burke and Ashleigh were doing. Finally, she could delay no longer.

"Thank you," Danny said when she returned, "but you could have stayed."

"I know."

"Are those for me?"

He nodded.

The pumps were red with stiletto heels. The stockings were

white. The garters matched the bright heels. The corset was black. The accoutrements of a whore, Danny thought, or a slave. Oh, Burke, you're so wonderful, always adding to my pleasures. I hope you're getting the same from Ashleigh.

Danny undressed slowly, blushing, but meeting his eyes, as she shed the veneer of prominent businesswoman to become an obedient and desirable female who had surrendered her will to another.

By choice.

"Lovely."

Her mouth dry, clenching her thighs, she waited for his inspection.

She trembled when his hand cupped the mound where the letter A was displayed.

"Are you familiar with the works of John Willie?"

"The Adventures of Sweet Gwendoline."

"Yes. For now, you will be Gwen."

After fastening Danny, he transformed her into another woman simply by placing a black wig on her. She looked at the stranger who faced her in the mirror and wondered why mirrors were so important to the ritual. Burke used them, too, so she was always able to watch what was done to her.

"You like women," Danny said as he brushed her long artificial hair. "You're gentle and strong, so loving and tender. And yet . . ." She shook her wrists helplessly. They were strapped to either end of a wooden rod and raised high above her head. Other straps pressed her ankles and thighs together.

"A woman is never more beautiful, more desirable, than when she wears the decorations of the men who love her."

"And do you love me, then?"

"Oh, yes, from the moment Ashleigh told me of you. Knowing that you had possessed her and Ashleigh you, I felt it was destined. I could not help loving any woman Ashleigh loved. I knew you would enslave me as she did."

Danny wanted him to say it. Again she shook her wrists.

"But I am helpless. Your prisoner. You can do anything to me and I could not stop you."

"You are the prisoner, but I am the slave."

Yes. He understands, just as Burke does.

"Ashleigh told you how we met?"

Danny nodded.

"The moment she crossed her wrists, daring me to tie her, I was helpless. With each successive submission, my devotion, my love for her, becomes more profound, deeper. I would do anything for her. Anything!" He stopped brushing her hair and circled to stand before her. "I ask you, who is the true slave?"

Yes. And now you belong to me as well.

"May I kiss you?"

Danny smiled at his request. "I want you to."

She swayed against him, opening her mouth, feeling his strength as he held her close. He stroked Burke's initials and then Ashleigh's. He left her nipples wet and glistening. Had she not been held upright, stretched into a rigid Y by her bonds, Danny would have collapsed when he released her.

"I want you to fuck me," she said, as he went to get the corset.

"Soon."

His arms encircled her, placing the corset against her belly, arranging her breasts in the cups, and began lacing.

Danny sighed. It was pleasantly tight, constricting. The cups lifted her breasts, but did not hide her nipples. When he finished lacing the corset, her figure was pleasingly molded. The heat in her loins and belly burned against the garment that contained it until she felt as though she would explode.

After snapping a dozen pictures or so, Richard summoned Ashleigh and Burke.

Danny blushed as they circled about her, admiring her pose and the way the corset lifted her breasts in offering to anyone who cared to touch or kiss them, how erect she was forced to stand, the loveliness of the garters, the choice of colors.

"You're absolutely beautiful, my darling. I'll treasure this gift always."

When Burke went with Richard to the darkroom, it was left to Ashleigh to release Danny—or not.

Alone, Ashleigh said. "Burke's right. You're truly beautiful like this. Did he kiss you?"

"Yes."

"And touch your breasts?"

"Yes."

Ashleigh smiled. "Burke wanted to see my rings. He led me around by my chains."

"Will you release me now?"

"Did Richard hold your tits up so you could lick your nipples?"

"No."

"Would you like to?"

"If that would please you."

"First, I'll have to get this corset off."

Ashleigh unfastened the straps around ankles and thighs and lowered the bar only enough so Danny could spread her legs.

Richard glanced briefly at Danny as she stepped into the Jacuzzi, easing into the bubbling waters. "You're very beautiful," he said.

"Thank you," Danny replied. She smiled shyly when her body was submerged. Beneath the water, she took Ashleigh's hand and squeezed.

"Yes, very beautiful," he repeated. "Burke will paint wonderful portraits of you and Ashleigh together. Two, actually. One will be a wedding present for you. That way, we'll always be together." He raised his champagne in a toast. "To new friends," he said.

"New friends."

"Good friends," Ashleigh added. "Very good friends." She pressed Danny's hand in return.

* * *

"We'd like to have you to our home," Danny said, as they lingered over coffee after dinner. "Perhaps next weekend?"

Ashleigh looked to Richard.

"We have plans next weekend," he said. "How about the next Saturday?"

"Two weeks it is."

Ashleigh smiled at Danny. "And the weekend after that, you'll be married. We all have so much to look forward to."

They walked Danny and Burke up the hill to their car.

"Thank you for a wonderful day, Richard," Danny said. "The photograph is beautiful."

"I'm glad you like it. I was afraid I might not do you justice."

Danny turned to Ashleigh and embraced her. "Thank you again," she said. Then, she whispered, "You're very lucky."

Ashleigh only smiled and nodded before kissing Danny goodnight.

Later, when they were alone in front of the fire and he had finished undressing her, Ashleigh snuggled against him and said, "Will you tie me tonight? It's been so long."

Richard laughed. "Not that long, only a few days," he said.

"It seems like forever. Please."

"You're jealous of Danny's afternoon."

"Yes, I suppose I am."

"I could never love her as I do you."

"But you do love her?"

"I told Danny I could not help but love someone you cared for."

"I'm glad." Ashleigh smiled as he rose and went to the mantel, where Burke had left the handcuffs.

For the second time that day, Ashleigh was handcuffed and followed the tug on her leash, holding back just enough to feel and enjoy the pressure on her nipples as she was led upstairs to the bedroom.

He slipped the loop of the leash over the poster of the bed and Ashleigh watched and waited impatiently as he made the preparations for her looming impalement.

Bear Junior was taken from the bed to sit on the dresser. Richard threw the bedspread back and arranged the pillows, one for her head and one in the center of the bed to raise her hips and loins to his kisses.

Oh, hurry, Richard, please hurry.

Tethered to the bedpost, Ashleigh shook her leash and moaned softly at the self-inflicted pleasure, remembering the quiet Sunday morning in Arizona when they'd ridden into town for breakfast, leaving Sultan and Scheherazade tied to a hitching rail. Through the restaurant window, Ashleigh had seen Scheherazade pull at her reins and paw the ground, eager to run free. But I don't want to be free ever again.

He delayed as always, lingering as he placed the coils of rope at each corner of the bed, pausing to pat her buttocks as he passed.

What a good Scheherazade I am. I'll tell you such wonderful stories, darling, if only you'll hurry and ride me to distant mountains.

"What are we doing next weekend?"

"It is time for the second wish."

"And what is your wish?"

Ashleigh listened quietly, secure and happy in her bonds, as he told her what would happen the next weekend, how she would be given to a lesbian couple, one a demanding disciplinarian, a dominatrix, and confined until Sunday evening, when she would be whipped.

When Richard concluded, Ashleigh asked, "How many?"

"I will be the thirteenth tattoo."

There was no need to explain further. Instead, Ashleigh asked, "Is her name Jacqueline?"

"Her name is Alice. Her slave is Vanessa."

"And then it will be my turn," Ashleigh said.

"Yes, and then it will be your turn," Richard said, smiling. "Do you consent?"

"Could there be any doubt?"

"Are you frightened?"

"A little."

"You can change your mind at any time."

"Would you love me less?"

"My love for you can never diminish, only grow."

"Will you be the one to do it?"

He reached for the knot at her wrist.

"No," Ashleigh said, "leave me like this for a while yet, please."

"All right." He lay beside her and rested his cheek on her breast and absently stroked her belly.

"Will you do it?" she asked again.

"No."

Chapter Twenty-Eight

Ashleigh worked faster and better than ever before. The images were transferred effortlessly from her mind to Richard's flesh, appearing as she ordained.

Although Richard never complained, Ashleigh discovered she enjoyed hurting the man she loved, not emotionally—she would never do that, not intentionally—but inflicting physical pain, making him endure some small semblance of what she had willingly suffered. Each stifled groan brought a small smile to her lips as she exacted no small measure of retribution. And there was another who would yet feel the sting of the black widow's fangs. Ashleigh counted the days, relishing each passing moment now, as she had dreaded them so recently.

But after each session, Ashleigh was solicitous of his comfort, caring for each new mark. It was then, after the day's work was complete, that Ashleigh told and retold of her ordeal, reciting each detail, narrating an extended love letter almost as much for herself as for him.

"This is the story of Richard and Ashleigh," she always began, "who loved each other very much. And one night, after Richard had made love to Ashleigh, driving her to new heights of pleasure, he told her that she must be punished, not because she had displeased him in any way, but because he loved her. Although Ashleigh had a choice, there was no question of refusing and she accepted because she loved him very much. If her pain would give him pleasure . . .

"Even though she admitted to being frightened, the words

thrilled Ashleigh. I am going to be whipped. I am going to be whipped. I am going to be whipped . . .

"They did not speak of it again, but all through the long week that followed Ashleigh could think of little else and when the time finally came . . .

"It happened as in a dream. It, too, was all so normal and ordinary, as though she had accepted an invitation to a society tea party—in fact, high tea was served in the garden—yet the very banality heightened the ritual until her nerves screamed with anticipation.

"Ashleigh was shown the room where it would take place and the instruments that would be used. Unlike the drawing room of her fantasies, it was a booklined study with comfortable leather chairs arranged around the platform. Sliding glass doors overlooked another portion of the lush garden where they had taken tea.

"Alice might have been a real estate agent showing Ashleigh a home she might wish to purchase. And over here, dear, is the perfect room in which to whip a woman.

"Ashleigh had been ready more than an hour before the appointed time. She waited, pacing nervously, watching the clock, knowing there was still time to change her mind. All she had to do was pick up the telephone. Darling, I don't want to do it. There would be no recriminations. Richard would still love her. Twice, her hand went to the telephone. Once, she picked it up and listened to the dial tone before replacing it.

"Ashleigh wanted to caress her nipples and satisfy the relentless heat in her loins, but it was not allowed. That was part of the ritual.

"Finally, Ashleigh took a long bath, luxuriating in the warmth. She had dressed slowly, then, adjusting the garter belt before carefully smoothing each black stocking over her long legs.

"Richard had chosen well. Strapless, the bustier neckline accentuated her breasts. The elegant and full-length evening gown was slit to mid-thigh. The pale flesh of her swelling breasts and the hourglass flash of red contrasted beautifully with the black gown. The heels were higher than Ashleigh was accustomed to wearing. She wondered if it had been Richard who'd insisted upon such high heels.

"And then it was time to wait, a continuation of the ritual that was such an integral part of the sensual game they played. She felt the thrill of the unknown. But as she tried to empty her mind of thoughts, the refrain echoed through her mind.

"I'm going to be whipped."

No.

"Ashleigh closed her eyes, trembling. The bargain had been made. Ashleigh could not—would not—go back on it. She wanted to be beaten and only regretted he would not do it himself.

"She heard the limousine before the headlights flashed across the window.

"Still trembling, she licked her lips nervously, tasting the fresh lipstick. It was his favorite. 'Richard,' she whispered, 'I love you.'

"When the door opened, Ashleigh knelt submissively, head down, wanting desperately to look at the face of the woman who would be her torturer, but that, too, was against the rules.

" 'You are obedient,' the woman said. 'That's good.' The woman's voice was quiet, feminine. Ashleigh had not expected that.

"Ashleigh remained motionless, staring down at the black boots the woman wore.

"The woman used a riding crop to lift Ashleigh's face. It was covered in black leather, matching the pants the woman wore. 'Richard said you were beautiful. I didn't believe him. Men always exaggerate so. I shall enjoy this.'

"The woman was striking—tall, with red hair, and dressed completely in black leather.

"Ashleigh shuddered and pulled away. She did not protest when the black scarf was tied tightly over her eyes.

" 'I'll turn out the lights and lock the door for you,' the woman said, guiding Ashleigh into the cold night. 'I'll just be a moment.'

"Ashleigh shivered as she waited for the reassuring touch of Vanessa's hand on her arm. When it came, she walked awkwardly to the limousine, stumbling once in her blindness before settling against the cushions. She wondered who was driving, whether it was a man or a woman who looked at her in the rearview mirror."

The memories stayed with her as she worked, smoldering within, reawakening desire until all she wanted to do was close the studio and rush home to be with Richard, to share thoughts and emotions. She was closer to this man than she had ever been with anyone, even Burke. But why not? she thought. I've given myself to him completely and without reservation. He owns me. I've never been owned by anyone before.

"This is the story of Richard and Ashleigh," she began, "who loved each other very much. . . ."

"Did you hate me?" Richard asked.

"No, of course not. How could I ever hate you?"

"Not even when you screamed?"

"Not even then."

" 'I was beginning to worry.'

" 'I'm sorry, Alice, darling. We were delayed. But we're here now. Isn't she beautiful?'

" 'She is, indeed. We'll have a wonderful time together. Take off her blindfold so I can appreciate her fully.'

" 'Of course.'

"Ashleigh blinked at the sudden light and shook her head as though that would help her see clearly.

"Alice was a handsome woman in her early fifties. Her dark black hair was cropped short and flecked with gray. She wore a dark business suit with a subdued tie. 'Oh, you are beautiful, dear,' she said, kissing Ashleigh's cheek, offering her own in return. 'Welcome to our home.'

" 'Thank you,' Ashleigh said.

" 'Let's go into the library for our cocktails. I was just thinking about making a nice pitcher of martinis before dinner.'

" 'I'll just run up and change for dinner,' Vanessa said.

" 'Yes, do that. Ashleigh and I will have a nice little chat.' Alice took Ashleigh's arm and guided her into another large room.

"Three walls were lined with books, broken only by the crackling flames in a large fireplace.

" 'Oh, what a wonderful collection,' Ashleigh exclaimed.

" 'Yes, we're quite the readers around here. You go ahead and make yourself comfortable. Feel free to browse, dear, while I fix a nice batch of martinis.'

"The library contained an excellent collection of classics, modern novels, and poetry behind glassed bookcases. One section held works of psychiatry, analysis, abnormal psychology, and a variety of medical texts.

" 'Come,' Alice called. 'Join me by the fire.'

" 'Where are we?' Ashleigh asked as she sat self-consciously.

" 'Why, Beverly Hills, of course,' Alice replied. 'But you were expecting some tawdry little mock-dungeon, weren't you?'

" 'Yes,' Ashleigh admitted.

" 'We're quite fortunate. With my psychiatry practice and Vanessa supplementing her teaching salary with her quite delightful avocation, we're very comfortable here. I'm constantly amazed that people are willing to pay so much to be beaten when there are so many individuals who would be willing to do it for free. But that's the human condition, isn't it?'

" 'I suppose so.'

"Alice poured a martini and handed it to Ashleigh. 'Do you like martinis?'

" 'I've never had one,' Ashleigh said.

" 'Oh, then you must have only one. We don't want you to get tipsy. They're very potent.'

"Ashleigh sipped. 'That's very good.' She thought it tasted like castor oil.

" 'The spider is lovely. I find it highly erotic. The symbolism is not lost on me, but we're all women here. May I?'

"Ashleigh nodded, sighing as Alice freed her breast from the bodice and stroked her gently.

" 'It's very smooth. I would have thought there would be some slight scar tissue.'

" 'Not if it's done properly,' Ashleigh said.

" 'I wonder . . . Perhaps Vanessa would like one, although she has no choice in the matter, but I think I would prefer something less ominous. Would you do it for me?'

" 'Yes, of course.'

" 'We'll discuss it at dinner, then.' "

Burke and Danny were married in a quiet civil ceremony with Ashleigh and Burke as the only witnesses. Afterward, Richard took them to a celebratory luncheon before taking them to the international terminal at LAX to catch their flight to Paris.

Ashleigh embarrassed them by throwing rice as they entered the departure area.

"We'll see you when you get back. Have a wonderful time."

"Love you. Thank you."

"It was like a dream," she repeated. "After dinner, Alice and Vanessa undressed Ashleigh, and then fastened her face down to an examining room table to purify her for the rites. Ashleigh gasped when the lubricated nozzle was inserted and the warm liquid slowly began to fill her bowels until she thought she would burst.

"Thankfully, they allowed Ashleigh to rush to the bathroom alone after her release, entering only later to bathe and perfume her, and then, still naked, showed her the training belt she must wear.

"It was a chastity belt, Alice explained, as she fastened the

first strap around Ashleigh's belly, to prevent her from mastur-
bating. The strap that went between her legs was fitted with
hard rubber dildos for her vagina and anus and, after being
lubricated, they entered easily, filling Ashleigh's orifices completely, swelling as though they possessed a life of their own.
Alice fastened the strap behind her back. As a last cruel refine-
ment, Ashleigh's wrists were cuffed to the sides of the chastity
belt.

"Alice smiled as she said, 'I know you'd like to be able to
play with those beautiful rings, but we don't want that.'

"They escorted her, then, to another wing of the house.
Alice and Vanessa, one on each side of Ashleigh, held her
arms firmly, leaving no doubt as to her status."

"Did Ashleigh think of flight?" Richard asked.

"She did not want to disappoint her lover," Ashleigh replied, smiling down at him. In an early stage of a woman's
quest, *The Sacrifice* stared back at Ashleigh. Based on the
sketches of the Woman Who Rode Away, Ashleigh had transformed them into something entirely different, made it her
own.

Richard lay on his back and his erection grew as she told of
their love story. Ashleigh squeezed his cock gently, making
him groan.

"Don't stop."

Ashleigh smiled again. "Our story, or what I'm doing?"

"Both."

"They took Ashleigh to a small room, barren of furnishings
except for an army cot and an old-fashioned clock on the wall
above. It was ten o'clock. The only window in the room was
barred.

"Vanessa went to the clock immediately and began winding
it. As she did, Alice indicated that Ashleigh should sit on the
cot. The blanket was olive drab and scratchy to the touch.
Alice sat beside her and said, 'You must love him very much.'

" 'I do,' Ashleigh replied.

" 'I've been instructed to tell you that it will happen at five P.M. tomorrow. You have nineteen hours to think about it.'

"Ashleigh nodded and could not stop herself from glancing at the clock. Already a minute had passed.

"The clock ticked loudly as they threw back the lone blanket and the sheet. Ashleigh thought they would chain her then, but they only tucked her in like a child. Alice and Vanessa both kissed her before closing the door and switching off the lights from outside.

"Her mouth was dry and Ashleigh wished she had asked for a glass of water before they'd left, but it was too late. Even if she kicked at the door or screamed, they would be unable to hear her.

"Ashleigh felt very lonely and afraid and wondered what Richard was doing and if he thought of her . . ."

One evening, Richard took her to the Great Western Forum for a game between the Los Angeles Lakers and the Detroit Pistons. It was another new experience for her. Ashleigh had never been to a professional sporting event before, just as she had never been to the zoo or explored a tidepool— or been whipped.

As John chauffeured them down Pacific Coast Highway, she met his eyes in the rearview mirror. Ashleigh smiled and wondered if he had been the driver who'd delivered her to Alice and if he'd thought of how she had been tied that first wonderful night when she had surrendered her very soul to Richard.

Richard had given her so many new experiences and promised more, but Ashleigh thought of Bobby, too, and the zoo, walking on the beach with him, the old mission, San Diego. He had been so filled with anger and violence when she'd refused his request for another tattoo. She worried about him and Cynthia, thinking she had made a terrible mistake. Cynthia was reluctant to talk, and it saddened her. Ashleigh hoped Bobby would take out his anger on her rather than on

Cynthia. It wasn't her fault Ashleigh could no longer stay with him. The fault belonged to no one.

"What are you thinking?" Richard asked handing her a glass of champagne. "You look so serious."

"Oh, nothing, really, I'm just happy to be with you."

Ashleigh found the basketball game strangely erotic, but she found everything Richard introduced to her seductive and titillating. There were so many big men charging gracefully up and down the court, twirling and flying through the air, jamming the basketball through the hoop. During timeouts, the Laker Girls danced suggestively, twirling, hair flying, hips shaking.

Richard leaned over and whispered, "You're more beautiful by far."

They were in preferred seating, some twenty rows above the court. Waitresses plied the aisles, taking drink and food orders, sending them to a concession stand electronically. "It's a better view of the complete game up here than courtside," Richard said.

Richard pointed out a tall man standing in a tunnel to their left watching the game. "That's Jerry West, one of the greatest players the Lakers ever had. He's the general manager now."

Ashleigh nodded politely. She had never heard of him, but she was amused at Richard's enthusiasm.

"A few years ago, this would have been one of the great games of the season. They played for championships then. Now . . . both teams are rebuilding."

"I don't care," Ashleigh said. "It's fun anyway."

The Lakers made a furious charge at the end of the fourth quarter, coming from nine points behind to send the game into overtime. With Richard, Ashleigh stood and cheered and applauded each steal, each dunk, each three-point basket. But the pace seemed to take something out of them and the Lakers lost by three points in overtime.

* * *

The next day, Ashleigh returned to the Beverly Hills Estates as a professional and an invited guest. Vanessa greeted her sullenly. She did not want the tattoo and had resisted until Alice had said simply, "But, dear, I want you to have one."

It was strange to return, even with different circumstances. Ashleigh looked about—as in a dream. There was the library where she had sipped her first martini while Alice had kissed and caressed her. There was the hallway that led to her tiny cell. And there . . .

Ashleigh knew Vanessa's choice of room was deliberate, a spiteful reminder of what had taken place, who had wielded the cruel lash. The chains that had held her were still in place, or had Vanessa replaced them in yet another malicious reminder . . . ? She recalled Vanessa's words and thought, I'm going to enjoy this.

Ashleigh readied her equipment while Vanessa stood defiantly in the center of the room, her arms crossed protectively. She wore a white blouse, flowing gray flannel skirt, and black boots. "I'm going to be ugly and hideous," Vanessa said.

"Nonsense. You'll be more attractive for Alice."

"Like that spider you wear?" She spat the words out.

Ashleigh shrugged. She was ready. Turning, she said, "Please remove your blouse."

Vanessa hesitated and then slowly complied, turning away. "We brought the couch down from Alice's office," Vanessa said.

We, Ashleigh thought, or you? "No," she said. "I think over here."

Vanessa turned to find Ashleigh nodding to the waiting chains. "No," she said.

"Shall I call Alice?" Ashleigh waited while Vanessa made her decision, nodding when Vanessa walked slowly to take her position.

Ashleigh enjoyed fastening the cuffs around Vanessa's slender wrists, tugging each tight, forcing the hook to reach an extra eyelet. It was more than was necessary to restrain her.

When Vanessa's arms were high and widespread, Ashleigh

dug her fingernails into Vanessa's right nipple, lifting the breast, slapping its soft underside.

Vanessa gasped and cried out.

Ashleigh smiled and slapped her again. "You should never anger a black widow spider."

"You liked it," Vanessa cried. "I know you did."

"Yes," Ashleigh said raising her hand, "but I like this more. So do you."

The thorny tangle of roses twisted around Vanessa's breast in bright splashes of red and green. Intertwined among the flowers were the capital letters A and S. That had been Ashleigh's contribution.

Alice had clapped her hands with delight. "It's wonderful. 'Alice's Slave.' She'll belong to me forever."

Vanessa had glared then.

Now she sobbed quietly while Ashleigh blotted the last droplets of blood and applied the ointment and bandage.

After repacking her equipment, Ashleigh went to the telephone and dialed Alice's office number, expecting to get a recorded message, but the doctor answered herself. "It's done," Ashleigh said, smiling across the room at Vanessa. "I think you'll like it."

"I'm looking forward to seeing it," Alice said.

"I think you should know that Vanessa tried to seduce me."

"The little bitch. I'll make her suffer for that. Thank you for telling me."

"No," Vanessa cried. "I didn't, Alice, she's lying."

Ashleigh was still smiling as she replaced the telephone and went to pick up her things.

"You're not going to leave me like this?" Vanessa cried. She shook her arms helplessly.

"Remember, follow my instructions exactly. You want to heal perfectly and be beautiful for Alice. Have a nice afternoon."

Ashleigh chuckled all the way to the car. Getting even was so much fun.

Chapter Twenty-Nine

Each day now, Ashleigh soared like Icarus, daring to climb higher and higher, effortlessly approaching the sun in ever-widening spirals, diving and swooping when she pleased, gliding for a time and then, with a powerful beat of her wings, spiraling upward again in the quest for perfection, fearing nothing. She flew confidently, exuberantly, knowing her wings were real and would not melt to plunge her into the sea far below. As she worked on the Sacrifice, coming closer and closer to completion, she repressed the rising elation at her creation, knowing that it was good, the very best of her work.

The masterpiece.

"This is the story of Richard and Ashleigh," she began once more, "who loved each other very much."

Richard sighed as Ashleigh soothed the pain, applying the ointment gently as she spoke in what Richard had come to describe as her Scheherazade voice, calling it deeper and more seductive. Ashleigh had not done it consciously, but listened to herself and realized he was right. Somehow, she had transformed herself into a captivating temptress, the black widow weaving a tale of forbidden delights for her master, enslaving him more with every telling, binding him in her silken web.

But it was her story, too, and each recounting of the details carved the tale deeper and more indelibly into memory, a vivid and growing record both of her ordeal and of their time together. She had taken to recording this tale. They would have it always then, even when they grew old together and their memories faltered.

And there were other stories yet to tell—of their first meeting, of choices made, of rings and submission, of rides into the desert, and the many marvelous tales yet to unfold of Richard and Ashleigh. Ashleigh and Richard. An oral history, a long, never-ending account of their passion and devotion to one another, a love story . . . many love stories . . . so many.

Ashleigh turned the tape recorder on and spoke softly as she worked the healing balm over the fresh wounds of the Sacrifice, his sacrifice to their love.

"Ashleigh slept fitfully throughout the long night, waking often to the relentless inexorable ticking. Like Faustus, she would have stopped time, if only that were possible. For a brief span, Ashleigh counted the ticks, stopping always at thirteen, the chosen number.

"Once, Ashleigh rose awkwardly and went to the window. If unrestrained, she would have gripped the bars of her prison, but they were beyond the cold pane of glass where she rested her cheek and she could only stare into the dark shadows of the beautiful and elaborate garden where lighter pathways led into a murky and ominous maze.

"When she finally returned to her spartan bed—surely it, too, was to make her more aware of her lowly position and the punishment to come—Ashleigh thought again of her lover, wondering if he slept well and dreamed of her.

"It was then that Ashleigh transgressed and, rolling over to her belly, rubbed the rings against the pillow, and thought of the plugs that filled her as belonging to Richard—as she did. It helped to pass a few minutes of the long, lonely hours and reminded her of her love and how much she wanted to please him. By consenting to wear his rings—their rings—she accepted love and offered all she possessed in return. She would give herself over to him, to do with as he pleased, so long as he returned her love always."

"Did Ashleigh regret wearing his rings?"

"Never." She touched their rings now and sighed at the tiny spasms she caused to ripple through her body. The story aroused both of them. *Oh, Christ, I want him so much. I love him so much.*

As she continued the story, she rose and slowly undressed, smiling with her eyes all the while.

"The dawn slowly filled her cell with light. Above her head, the clock ticked away, but Ashleigh did not bother to glance at the time. Instead, she strained to hear other sounds in the house, some slight noise to indicate that she had not been abandoned . . ."

She knelt and pressed her breasts around his cock, squeezing them, imprisoning him in their softness.

"Again Ashleigh went to the window and looked through the bars to the beautiful garden. In the growing daylight, the ominous maze had disappeared, leaving behind shrubbery and beautiful flowers, a place for lovers to meet in hidden tryst. She thought of Richard and wondered if he slept yet, or if he had awakened with thoughts of his lovely Ashleigh and her lonely penitent's vigil.

"Who would make his coffee? Who would greet him when he returned from his run on the beach? What would he do while he waited to bear witness to her punishment, her total submission to his will?"

* * *

She interrupted the story to take him in her mouth, feeling the pulsating, throbbing life as it swelled and filled her, leaving him wet and glistening with her saliva. She straddled him then, throwing her leg over him, mounting him as she would Scheherazade, and slowly descended, guiding his entry, impaling herself, forcing him deeper and deeper. Sighing and smiling at the anguish on his face and the pleasure she gave him, Ashleigh went on with the story.

"Only eight hours remained when they finally came and released her from solitary confinement. Tired, hungry, desperately wanting to go to the bathroom, Ashleigh marched willingly between them."

Oh, yes.

"This time they watched as Ashleigh sat astride the toilet, blushing, staring at the frosted patterns on the shower door."

Yes.

"It was Alice who tended to Ashleigh's needs. It was Vanessa who locked the handcuffs on Ashleigh."

Oh, God, yes.

"At breakfast—juice, coffee, cereal, rye toast, as Ashleigh had requested, fruit—they took turns feeding her, wiping her mouth delicately with a napkin . . ."

"Oh, Jesus," Richard groaned.

Story forgotten, Ashleigh rode his cock, moaning and crying out as she forced him deep within her, leaning forward, allowing her breasts to dangle for his lips. Oh, Jesus, yes, darling, that's right, swallow my tits, fill your mouth, oh, God, yes, I love you . . .

He bucked against her hips as she pumped up and down. She lost him once and scrambled furiously, his cock wet and slippery with her juices, to get him inside again.

"Ah, ah, ah, ah! Yes! Now, darling, now!"

*   *   *

Benjamin called, asking if she was free for lunch.

"For you, always," Ashleigh said.

When he came by the studio, he suggested going to Cynthia's.

"No," Ashleigh said. "Our relationship is a little strained right now."

"I'm sorry to hear that."

"It's not Cynthia. It's Bobby. He wants me to give him another tattoo, but I refused. He keeps calling, demanding, threatening."

"Like Carver."

Ashleigh nodded, but thought, no—not like poor Jonathan. Worse. Jonathan only begged. Bobby is angry, very angry. "He followed me home one night. We had quite a scene. Thank God, he left before Richard got there."

"Perhaps I should stop by, have a little talk with him."

Ashleigh shook her head. "He'll give up eventually. I'm not afraid. He won't hurt me."

Instead of Cynthia's, they went to a small restaurant—a coffee shop, really—where they sat on a patio filled with greenery and potted plants.

Benjamin was still vaguely troubled by the gossip that lingered about this powerful agent they called the Executioner, but he said nothing because Ashleigh was so radiant, so obviously deeply in love. He could only hope that it worked for her as much as it had worked with Elliott. Twenty years later, he thought, and we're still in love. He wanted the same for Ashleigh. "When are you getting married?" he asked.

Ashleigh smiled. "We already are."

"What?" Benjamin exclaimed, quickly masking the disappointment he felt. "When?"

Ashleigh touched his hand reassuringly. "Spiritually, silly. I wouldn't get married without you being there. Richard is my soulmate. We've always been married, in other lives, in lives yet to come. The ceremony will merely formalize it once more. We have already exchanged our vows. Many times."

It's true, Ashleigh thought. I wear his rings, our rings. My body has carried the stripes he inflicted through Vanessa. I

only regret they faded so quickly. He bears my marks permanently, for all time. Yes, our souls are truly intertwined. Forever and ever and ever.

"That's better," Guy said. "Spiritual, I understand. Not re-
ceiving an invitation . . ."

"Next spring," Ashleigh said. "At the solstice. That's when
we'll be married."

"The beginning of life, the rebirth."

"Yes. Isn't it romantic? I'm so happy."

Ashleigh had filled two ninety-minute tapes and started on
a third. There was so much to tell, so many exciting details,
and when she was finished, it would be Richard's turn. He
would tell her more and more of his thoughts and activities
during the long night and day while she was imprisoned,
awaiting the pain he wanted her to suffer.

Afterward, he carried her to the limousine, their tears mingling as he kissed her over and over, telling her how much he
loved her. Wrapped in a terrycloth robe, still wearing his
beautiful collar, she clung to him and all during the drive back
to Malibu he soothed her pain with kisses, adding to the flame
that had been building throughout their separation. Had it
been less than forty-eight hours?

He carried her upstairs and when he kissed her again,
gently, with great tenderness, Ashleigh tore at his clothes, crying, "Fuck me, fuck me now, I can't wait."

She crouched on the bed as he took her like a bitch in heat.
But the flame only flickered and then burst into new life, raging within, until she begged for more, knowing that she had
found countless aphrodisiacs in pain.

"As they entered the room, Ashleigh heard a clock strike,
chiming five times. She blinked against bright footlights that
bathed a platform. Beyond, the room was dark, but she heard
the music played by ice in crystal glasses.

"Voices asked and said, 'Who is she? So beautiful. So vulnerable.'

"Ashleigh had not been told there would be strangers present and for a moment considered rescinding her agreement—it remained her choice, now and always—but she had come too far on this strange, frightening, wondrous journey. And what did it matter? If Richard chose to have her beaten in the presence of others, if it heightened his love? She had made her choice long ago and did not regret it.

"Ashleigh would not disappoint Richard.

"She could not disappoint herself.

"Ashleigh followed, ascending the stage and stood proudly, defiantly, trying not to wince in the glare of the lights, as Vanessa removed her leash from Richard's gift, the beautiful collar with the heart-shaped ring. She was left alone while cocktails were freshened. Whispered conversations drifted to her, as though from a great distance.

" 'Only thirteen . . .'

" 'It is enough to make her scream . . .'

"Ashleigh wondered if perhaps the woman spoke from experience and told herself, I will not scream.

"The clock struck the quarter hour.

"She tried to look past the lights into the darkness, seeking his reassuring presence, but she could not pick him out from the other shadows who moved about the room.

"Ashleigh waited for a long time, alone with her thoughts, as in a dream, until it seemed they had forgotten her presence, and she thought she might awaken soon to the sounds of crashing surf with Richard by her side, but slowly the room grew quiet, hushed with expectation.

"The clock had struck the quarter hour again, and perhaps again. Ashleigh lost track as she waited.

"Vanessa was by her side then, turning her, urging her to the waiting chains. Vanessa released her from the handcuffs and waited as Ashleigh automatically massaged her wrists, although the handcuffs had been loose enough.

"Ashleigh saw that Vanessa's eyes were bright and glistening with excitement.

"Her right arm was raised and fastened. Ashleigh looked at the length of her arm, stretched and spread. It was happening now as she'd always imagined it. She turned and watched as Vanessa buckled the second leather cuff tightly around her left wrist. Without the stiletto heels, she would have stood on tiptoe, flesh taut against her ribs, her body forming the letter Y.

"They had lied and made her wait longer than the allotted time. The clock struck six as Vanessa loosened the clasp of her gown and drew the zipper down, kneeling to help Ashleigh step from where it fell about her ankles. Perhaps she handed it offstage to a waiting hand. Ashleigh couldn't tell because Vanessa forced her legs apart, wider and wider, to waiting cuffs until she was spread obscenely wide for the admiration of her audience.

"But Vanessa wasn't through. She embraced Ashleigh from behind, stroking her belly and breasts, pulling at the rings until Ashleigh gasped. When Vanessa stepped away, it was only to part Ashleigh's hair, draping it over strained shoulders to caress her breasts lightly, leaving her back naked and unprotected for the whip.

"Ashleigh looked back—she could not help herself—and saw Vanessa raising the thronged whip. Vanessa smiled at her before striking.

"She grunted with the force of the blow that rocked her in her chains, but she did not cry out.

"That would come later.

"But now, as the pain spread across her back and seared her soul, Ashleigh thought only of the humiliating sound she had made. It had been a sign of weakness where she wanted to demonstrate the courage of a warrior queen."

They went back to the waterside café where they had gone on the day of their meeting—two elegant and statuesque women who drew admiring glances from men and instilled envy in their women.

They were seated by Mary. Ashleigh was pleased she remembered the young woman's name, but she remembered everything about the day she'd met Danny. It had been warm and the air was filled with the sounds of boats creaking and pulling against their moorings.

Danny smiled and said, "You're just bubbling over. You want to tell me something."

Ashleigh nodded. She took three cassettes held together by a rubber band from her purse. "I made these for you."

"How nice. What are they?"

"Oh, just a story I told Richard. No, that's not true. It's more than a story. It's true." Ashleigh paused and looked about. Other diners were engrossed in conversations. She turned back and took a sip of her wine before saying, "I've been to Roissey now. Richard sent me there to be whipped."

Danny's brow furrowed as she frowned and bit her lip.

Ashleigh waited, surprised at Danny's reaction. She had expected something . . . something quite different.

"I know," Danny said finally. "I'm not supposed to tell you, but I was there."

"And Burke?"

Danny nodded slowly, smiling at last. "Oh, God, Ashleigh," she burst out, "you were so lovely and beautiful and brave. I don't know how you could take it, standing up there for so long. Waiting. I couldn't take my eyes off you. I was on fire. And we were there for nearly two hours before they brought you in. We had cocktails in the garden, and it was all so polite and civilized, except . . ."

Ashleigh smiled. She was happy that Danny and Burke had been witnesses to her final test, her sobbing, tortured reply to Alice's question.

Do you accept Richard Sheridan as your master, now and for all time? Yes, oh, God, yes!

"Except . . ." Ashleigh prompted, wanting Danny to share everything.

"I knew you were in there somewhere, being prepared. Waiting. I kept looking at windows, wondering, imagining what was being done to you, what you were thinking."

"It was a beautiful ceremony, wasn't it?"

"I'd never thought of it like that, but it was a ceremony. A woman's rite of passage into a new and higher realm." Danny reached out and took Ashleigh's hand, uncaring of what others might think. "My Anne-Marie, my beautiful Anne-Marie. You didn't whip me nearly hard enough. I wanted to tell you, but that gag . . . I'm glad they didn't gag you. You struggled and screamed so beautifully."

"It's difficult for me to remember. Did I beg her to stop?"

"Never."

"I wanted to. It was in my mind from the first stroke. I'm glad I didn't say it. It seemed like she would never stop."

"Only thirteen," Danny said. "Thirteen lovely strokes."

"I thought it was a hundred—and none."

"It was more. One hundred and seventeen to be exact. I counted the thongs on her whip. She was terribly cruel. Burke thought she went too far, especially when the tips caught your breasts. I want Burke to send me there, but he won't."

"Poor Burke. He doesn't understand, not completely."

Danny smiled shyly. "Oh, yes, he understands. Afterward, I gave him a blow job right there on the San Diego Freeway. It didn't faze him. He came and came and I couldn't swallow it all. And then when we got home, we couldn't even wait to get into the house. We fucked in the garage, in the back seat, like teenagers."

"I couldn't get enough of Richard, either. He can have me whipped anytime, so long as he fucks like that."

"I'm going to be whipped, too. It's just that Burke wants you to do it. He thinks you'll be even crueler. Will you be?"

Ashleigh nodded slowly, smiling, loving this woman, this sister in bondage and slavery and pain. "Yes."

"Thank you."

Richard submitted as she had done so often, feeling the steel close about his wrists as she handcuffed him to the bed.

She wanted him to know exactly how she felt when she was tied or handcuffed or otherwise restrained, and the joys of being helpless and trusting while he made love to her.

Ashleigh laughed as she sat beside him, stroking his arms now stretched above his head, telling him what she was going to do, watching his cock grow, leaning over to kiss him occasionally, adding finally, "But I'm not going to let you come for the longest time. You'll beg and plead, but I won't care. I'm just going to go on making love to you forever."

Ashleigh kissed Richard's body, torturing him with caresses, using her breasts as tantalizing weapons, pulling away when he strained to kiss her nipples, laughing, wagging a finger. "Naughty, naughty. First, you must say, 'Please, Ashleigh, may I suck your nipples?' "

"Please, Ashleigh, may I suck your nipples?"

"Do you like sucking my nipples?"

"Oh, God, yes, more than anything in the world."

"Better than fucking me? Better than when I go down on you? Better than when I sit on your face? Better than having me whipped? Be honest, or Mama will be cross."

"I love all of those things, but I love you most."

"What a nice answer. As a reward, I'll let you have one nice big tit, but just for a moment or two. You mustn't be greedy." She straddled his body on hands and knees and threw her head back as he bit her gently. Ah, that feels so good. Oh, Christ, how does he stand it, making me wait so long? I just want to fuck him. Now, right now.

She pulled away. "That's enough for now. If you promise to be good, perhaps I'll let you have the other one."

"I promise," he groaned.

Ashleigh smiled down at him. "I wonder what I should do next?"

"Please, anything, just hurry. I can't stand it. I want you so much."

"Yes, that's what I always say."

At times, it was like making love to herself.

What had begun with the Woman Who Rode Away, Ashleigh had made her own.

* * *

The Sacrifice began in miniature on Richard's left side, with a girl standing on the steps of a stark ramshackle church staring out at dark hulks of tiny distant mountains. Another scene unfolded with the girl imprisoned beneath the church with naught but a pitiful pallet of hay for her bed. Even in the tiny, delicate strokes of the artist's machine, the child's anguish had been captured for all time.

Then, the girl fled into a grotesque urban hellscape, her chariot a truck with flames and smoke erupting from its wheels, to stand, ugly and misshapen with grotesque breasts, beneath a dozen or more street lights, all casting deathly hues.

Growing in stature as it curved around his chest and belly and right side, the woman, Ashleigh now, soft and beautiful, dressed in black and wearing plumed feathers, stood with bound wrists held in offering to a brilliant light. And again Ashleigh was bound, arms raised high and fastened to the chandelier of her dreams. She looked back, smiling, waiting.

And then, on his back, two lonely figures on horseback, the woman leading, climbed barren slopes to an idyllic clearing, their clearing, where they had made love and would again.

The woman—the Sacrifice—Ashleigh—stood above them, resplendent in naked exultation with all the world below her feet. Her arms, free and unrestrained, were raised to the fiercely burning sun. Tribal markings adorned her cheeks and forehead—dark and jagged horizontal slashes—an acceptance of the savagery that had freed her.

Their journey was complete. They had given themselves to one another, completely and without reservation, submitting their bodies, sealing their love once and for all with pain in permanent loving dedication.

"Oh, God, no more," Richard cried, "I love you."

Oh, and how I love you, my darling, Ashleigh thought, as she said, "Just a little longer, darling, you can stand it just a little more, and then I'll set you free."

Chapter Thirty

With the completion of the thirteenth tattoo, Ashleigh was content, blanketed with a gentle happiness. The old restlessness that dominated her upon completion of a work was gone. The urgent need that had always driven her back to the underworld, desperately seeking a new canvas, a new creation, was absent. She had flown to the sun now, seen its wonders. There was no need for more.

The thirteenth tattoo was a masterpiece. It would be displayed—or not—at a convention, but the judgment of others no longer mattered. Ashleigh knew she had succeeded at last. Richard, Danny and Burke, Guy—they had all congratulated her. Burke had given her the highest accolade of all. "You did it," he said simply—the awe was obvious in his voice—before hugging her proudly.

She had already begun her first tentative lessons in photography with Richard. Ashleigh discovered he was a patient teacher as he displayed the thirteenth tattoo, their roles reversed for a time in the studio where she had so often been the subject of the cameras. He explained lighting, the capabilities of different lenses and films, composition, and focus. And, in the red light of the darkroom, as they developed the photographs of the thirteenth tattoo together, Ashleigh discovered new heights of artistic elation as she watched the images emerge, her images, swimming lazily beneath the developing fluids.

Richard gave her a new camera and she carried it everywhere, taking roll after roll of film—in the studio, on the beach, the streets, even when she shopped.

Danny and Ashleigh went on a nature walk one Saturday morning on the Palos Verdes Peninsula. The walk, sponsored by a local conservancy group, attracted some thirty men and women, couples mostly, who were split into groups of ten, each following different trails into an unstable and undeveloped area of the peninsula. Their walk leader, an enthusiastic and knowledgeable woman in her early forties named Gayle, spoke of the land's history, the geologic forces that made it unstable and prone to landslides, and pointed out the varieties of flora and fauna.

Throughout the easy three-hour walk, Ashleigh snapped picture after picture—she was the only one in the group who had brought a camera—and looked forward to developing them. Near the end of the walk, Gayle suddenly motioned for the group to stop and hushed them to silence with a finger to her lips. Then, she beckoned to Ashleigh to come forward. Slowly, she mouthed.

When Ashleigh reached her side, Gayle pointed to a blue butterfly fluttering over the scrub. "Please," she whispered urgently, "get a picture of it."

Ashleigh zoomed in on the butterfly. It was big and centered in her viewfinder. Ashleigh put the camera on automatic and followed the butterfly's erratic path until the roll of film ran out.

Gayle sighed heavily and then cried, "Look everyone, quick. It's the Peninsula Blue butterfly. We thought it became extinct ten years ago, and it's back. It's back!"

After the walk, when they were back at the small park atop the peninsula, Gayle gave Ashleigh her card and said, "Please, would you send me copies of the Peninsula Blue? I'll pay for them, of course. I'd like to send them to the Department of Fish and Game. This is so exciting."

"I'd be happy to," Ashleigh replied. "It was really extinct?"

"We thought it was gone forever," Gayle said. "We sponsor walks every month. I hope you'll come again. You're good luck for us."

* * *

While posing with Danny once more, Ashleigh decided she would take up oils and watercolors, too, and like Burke, focus her creative energies there. She would not give up her profession. She would still be a tattoo artist, always, but there was no longer any need to seek out new canvases; her masterpiece was finished. There might yet be others, but they would come to her like Kim Lee, those few individuals who truly understood the spiritual mystique of the tattoo as both art and representation of the soul. And when they were married and went to live in Arizona, Ashleigh thought she might open a small studio, doing flashes while waiting for the next Kim or Sue, but there could never be another Richard.

While Burke tied her wrists, Ashleigh asked, "Will you teach me to paint?"

He nodded. "After I saw the Sacrifice, I thought that might be coming."

"I'll never be as good as you, but I'd like to try."

"I think that's wonderful," Danny said, holding her wrists out for Richard. "It'll be a new world for you to conquer."

After their ankles were tied, Richard and Burke helped them to kneel together, arms raised above their head, their wrists joined by a single strand of rope tied to a ring bolt in the ceiling.

When they were pressed together, their breasts crushed against each other by the rope around their waists and the first waves of heat were beginning to build, Danny asked, "Will you paint me? I'd love to pose for you."

"Of course, I'll paint you." Ashleigh kissed her. What a wonderful way to spend the afternoon, she thought.

"Hello, Ashleigh, I brought you some nice flowers."

Ashleigh placed the bouquet at the headstone, touched the etched letters of her name, as always, and then sat back on her heels. The cemetery was still and hushed, although the day was bright and clear and the view of the vast valley expanse was untarnished.

"I really should visit you more often. It's not that I don't want to come or that I don't think of you, but so much has happened . . . since I brought Richard to meet you . . . since I told him the truth. And now that he knows, I'll never be Jamie Lee again. I'll always be Ashleigh Thomas."

"I am a slave now, serving a wonderful and devoted master. I wear our rings in my nipples . . . I wear his chains proudly . . . when he places me in bondage, I see nothing but adoration and love in his eyes . . . even when he sent me to be whipped— yes, I submitted gladly, choosing to accept the pain for him— he did so with love."

Ashleigh fell silent for a moment, remembering the moment when Vanessa had paused and she'd thought the ritual strangely incomplete, but the respite had only been to allow Alice to approach. "You're doing beautifully, dear," Alice had said, kissing Ashleigh, embracing her in her bonds, fondling the rings, touching her clitoris, exciting her despite the burning pain that seared her buttocks, making her moan and cry out as Alice finger-fucked her to orgasm and she forgot the pain until Alice kissed her lovingly and said, "Only six more. Count them and remember when you get to six, Richard will take you away. He loves you very much."

"Do you think me strange, Ashleigh? I hope not. I'm very happy as a slave. I'm not a masochist. The pain is nothing, something to be endured only for the great pleasures that follow. I love it when Richard does so many wonderful things for me, to me. I'm secure in who I am now. I'm not afraid to admit it. I pity all the poor women who do not have a master to serve, to receive his love, pleasure, and pain."

She stood and stared down at her grave for a moment.

"We're going to be married next year and one day soon, we'll go to live on a small ranch he owns in Arizona. I'll always come to visit you, although perhaps not so often," Ashleigh said, laughing, "but I haven't been very good lately anyway, have I? I'll never forget you, Ashleigh. You gave me life, your life. I wish I could share it with you."

* * *

In the evenings now, Richard told their story. After dinner, they took their coffee to sit before the fire.

"The wait was just as long and agonizing for Richard," he said, "as for Ashleigh." He smiled at her as he paused.

Ashleigh sat beside him on the couch, her legs tucked beneath her, touching his shoulder lightly, already engrossed in his story, eager to hear what would happen next.

"And when Alice called to tell him everything that had been done to Ashleigh—how she had been purified and cleansed, how she wore the training belt, how she was to spend the night alone in her cell—his love for this wonderful woman who consented to be his slave overflowed. The very thought of Ashleigh's submission to others for him drove him wild with excitement, as it did Alice.

" 'She's very beautiful,' Alice told him. 'You're so lucky to have found her. A truly submissive woman is a very rare and wondrous creature. There are so many dominant men that submissive women quickly meet their masters. For those men who are left, usually, they must find women to be trained to accept their roles. Ashleigh needs very little training. I'm so glad you sent her to us.'

"Alice's voice grew harsh then as she said, 'Unlike Vanessa, who constantly needs to be reminded of her station. I caught her kissing Ashleigh without permission.'

"Alice paused then and Richard heard her say, 'Tell Richard where you are and what's going to be done to you.'

"Vanessa's voice was faint, but Richard heard her say, 'Please, mistress.'

" 'Tell him.'

"There was another pause, but when Vanessa spoke again, her voice was strong and clear. 'I'm tied to the foot of the bed, bent over, my hands cuffed behind me, and my mistress is going to spank me with a cane. It's very long and flexible and I hate it.'

"Alice took the phone then and said, 'Would you like to listen while I punish Vanessa?'

" 'Oh, yes,' Richard replied.

"Alice was very severe. Throughout, Vanessa cried, begging her to stop, telling her she would be good. And while he listened, Richard could only think of his beautiful Ashleigh."

"Did you regret sending me there?" Ashleigh asked.

"No."

"I'm glad." Ashleigh snuggled closer to him, content to be in his arms for the moment, but saying, "I love being trained by you."

The story went on and on each evening, until it seemed it would never end.

Ashleigh sat on the deck, drinking coffee, sketching a beach scene, wondering what to get Richard for Christmas in addition to the very special gift she was having custom made. After her return from Alice's and his promise to whip her himself, Ashleigh had designed a leather covered whipping bench to which she could be tied in a variety of ways. Only six weeks away, she wanted their first Christmas to be memorable. It would be, she thought. She could hardly wait to feel the cold leather against her flesh.

Richard came out wearing only shorts and running shoes. He liked to run bare-chested now, displaying the thirteenth tattoo. He leaned over to kiss her. "When I get back," he said, "I'll continue with Richard's story."

"Give me just a hint." Ashleigh smiled and touched his chest and the thirteenth tattoo.

"All right," he said. "Richard's story opens like this: This is the story of Richard, who loved Ashleigh so very much, worshipping her more than the sun and the moon and the stars and the night and the oceans . . .' "

"What a lovely beginning," Ashleigh said. She didn't care that she had heard it before. Today, he would tell her of Ashleigh's training.

Training.

They both found the very word exciting, erotic.

Ashleigh stood at the deck's railing, leaning her elbows on the redwood, watching as he stretched his muscles in preparation for his run. When he was warm, Richard blew her a kiss and headed for the distant point.

Ashleigh watched Richard run until he was a tiny, distant figure approaching the restaurant where they'd gone for brunch that first morning together. Her reverie was interrupted by the portable telephone on the patio table.

"Hello."

"Hello, darling."

"Danny, what a nice surprise."

"I've been thinking of you all morning and just wanted to say hello. Burke's been working on our painting. It's coming along very nicely, but we thought we'd like to get out later, go for a little drive. Would you and Richard like to meet us halfway for a drink? Maybe in Santa Monica."

"Sure, that would be fun, but let me ask Richard first. He's out running, but I'll call you when he gets back."

"Great, I'll talk to you then. I love you."

"I love you, too."

Ashleigh replaced the receiver and smiled, thinking of Danny's Christmas present, a training belt like the one she now wore quite often. It was already purchased and wrapped. With the adjustable cuffs that could be easily removed, it could be worn beneath a dress. Ashleigh hoped that Burke would make her wear it to work.

She continued sketching until she sensed it was time for Richard's return.

Ashleigh took the binoculars and went to the railing, raising them to scan the distant beach. A couple walked toward her. Another figure, his features indistinguishable even with the powerful binoculars, stood at surf's edge. Ashleigh turned the glasses to search the horizon for the gray whales that had already begun their annual migration to the south. Quite often, it was possible to see their water spouts . . . but nothing today.

Ashleigh lowered the binoculars for a moment and then

raised them again, smiling when she found Richard running past the restaurant again. He would be with her soon and after a quick shower, he would resume the magnificent story of Richard and Ashleigh. Even as he neared home, he still ran with power. He was close enough now for her to make out his features and see the bright colors of the thirteenth tattoo. Again she lowered the glasses. Without them, he became a distant stick figure, now joined by another. Someone was running after him, gaining on him, perhaps challenging him to a sprint. Ashleigh laughed. He would have to be a very good runner to beat Richard.

Quickly, Ashleigh put the binoculars to her eyes. Richard had turned, looking back to the other runner, waiting, jogging in place. Ashleigh adjusted the focus on the other man.

Bobby!

Jesus Christ. Not again!

As she watched, Bobby slowed and approached Richard, raising his hand suddenly.

Oh, Jesus.

Ashleigh dropped the binoculars and ran down the steps to the beach. She ran, the thick heavy sand grabbing at her feet, like quicksand threatening to drag her into the abyss. She slipped and fell, scrambled to her feet again. Running, screaming.

"No!"

No! Please, no, God.

Ashleigh reached the smooth, hard-packed sand at water's edge and ran faster now, but she was already growing short of breath. Her vision blurred, cleared. Richard was on the ground. Bobby stood over him, cutting and slashing with the knife again and again.

Oh, Jesus, oh, Jesus, oh, Jesus . . .

Gasping and panting, sucking air into her lungs, she slowed as she approached. Ten feet away she fell to her knees and bit on her fist in horror.

His arteries gushed blood for the greedy sands to suck up.

Ashleigh crawled to Richard and covered the spurting wound in his neck with her hand, uncaring of the sand clinging to her, pressing against the flow. "Call an ambulance!" she screamed. "Please, someone call an ambulance!"

Bobby stood quietly, covered in blood, holding the knife at his side.

"You should have done the tattoo," he said.

Epilogue

Ashleigh Thomas is serving a life sentence without the possibility of parole, condemned to go through the remainder of her life always knowing the enormity of her loss, always thinking of what might have been.

"You should have done the tattoo."

They were the last words Bobby Cole spoke to Ashleigh.

Ashleigh blames herself, of course.

We tried to tell her—Danny, Burke, and I—throughout the prolonged media frenzy that surrounded the trial, we tried to convince her there was nothing that she could have done, nothing that anyone could have done.

Ashleigh was called by the prosecution as a key witness. She testified quietly, stoically, breaking down only at the end. From the very beginning the defense put her on trial, portraying Bobby as the victim of the black widow.

"Isn't it true that you served thirty days for prostitution?"

It began there. Eventually, the defense called the second and fourth tattoos, both still harboring jealous grudges against Ashleigh, both eager to tell their stories to anyone who would listen, anyone who would pay.

The media loved it, calling Ashleigh "the Black Widow" and "the Tattoo Queen." We protected her, shielded her as much as possible, but it wasn't enough.

Cole was found guilty and received a lesser sentence than he might have otherwise. He'll probably be out in six or seven years. He told the court that he didn't intend to kill Richard Sheridan, that he only wanted to destroy the thirteenth tattoo.

"I should have done the goddamned tattoo," were the last words Ashleigh spoke to me.

If only I had investigated the right man. Instead of Richard Sheridan, the man who dominated her, who sent her to be whipped, who loved her all the more for it, I should have concentrated on the other, but who could know?

The toll was enormous. In killing Richard Sheridan, Bobby Cole did more than destroy the thirteenth tattoo. He killed love and shattered our lives—Cynthia's, Ashleigh's, his own, the single murderous act spiraling down to Danny and Burke, to Elliott and me.

The Reader's Digest *used to have a regular feature called something like "The Most Unforgettable Person I Ever Met"—perhaps it still does. For me, Ashleigh Thomas was—is—the most unforgettable person I ever met, one of those rare individuals who, once encountered, can never be forgotten. She is always there, just within the realm of consciousness, bursting forth at strange moments. I've met two or three others like her, none of them having anything to do with my sexuality . . . my ninth grade English teacher. Ashleigh had—has—an inexplicable presence about her. It's not just her beauty, although that is part of it.*

I look at her likeness every day and night of my life, trying to understand.

Ashleigh was . . . Ashleigh.

I suppose that's why Jonathan Carver killed himself. He didn't have the strength or the desire to face life without Ashleigh. He should have been satisfied with memories.

Postcards. Sometimes Burke receives one, sometimes it is me. We always call and say, She's in San Francisco, or Seattle, or Honolulu. The last was from New Orleans.

There is never a message.

Ashleigh had been gone for months when Burke got the first card from San Francisco—it was of a cable car on Powell Street—he flew up there and spent three days searching for her, going from one tattoo studio to another, showing her picture, describing her.

No one had seen her.

After each postcard, I make a call to the police department of whatever city, get friendly with a homicide cop, ask him to put the word out unofficially, maybe drop by a tattoo parlor or two, even check with vice in case she's gone back to her old profession, fax her photograph.

* * *

Every month, her landlady receives a postal money order for the rent on the house. Burke and I keep an eye on the place. Occasionally, Danny and Burke join me and Elliott and we spend a day cleaning the house. There isn't much to do—dust, vacuum, flush the toilets, run the water in sinks and shower. We keep the place up for her. When she decides to come home, it will be ready.

She is out there somewhere.

Burke and I keep hoping that she'll turn up one day, one night, rather, because she was a woman of the night, a creature at home in the subterranean existence that lives just beneath the surface of any large city, the underground that smolders in another dimension.

I miss her.

Danny and Burke do, too.

FUN AND LOVE!

THE DUMBEST DUMB BLONDE JOKE BOOK   (889, $4.50)
by Joey West
They say that blondes have more fun . . . but we can all have a hoot
with THE DUMBEST DUMB BLONDE JOKE BOOK. Here's a
hilarious collection of hundreds of dumb blonde jokes—including
dumb blonde GUY jokes—that are certain to send you over the
edge!

THE I HATE MADONNA JOKE BOOK   (798, $4.50)
by Joey West
She's Hollywood's most controversial star. Her raunchy reputa-
tion's brought her fame and fortune. Now here is a sensational collection of hilarious material on America's most talked about
MATERIAL GIRL!

LOVE'S LITTLE INSTRUCTION BOOK   (774, $4.99)
by Annie Pigeon
Filled from cover to cover with romantic hints—one for every day
of the year—this delightful book will liven up your life and make
you and your lover smile. Discover these amusing tips for making
your lover happy . . . tips like—ask her mother to dance—have his
car washed—take turns being irrational . . . and many, many
more!

MOM'S LITTLE INSTRUCTION BOOK   (0009, $4.99)
by Annie Pigeon
Mom needs as much help as she can get, what with chaotic sched-
ules, wedding fiascos, Barneymania and all. Now, here comes the
best mother's helper yet. Filled with funny comforting advice for
moms of all ages. What better way to show mother how very much
you love her by giving her a gift guaranteed to make her smile
everyday of the year.

*Available wherever paperbacks are sold, or order direct from the
Publisher. Send cover price plus 50¢ per copy for mailing and han-
dling to Penguin USA, P.O. Box 999, c/o Dept. 17109, Bergen-
field, NJ 07621. Residents of New York and Tennessee must
include sales tax. DO NOT SEND CASH.*